Chautauqua Solstice:

A Goddess Circle Mystery

2nd Edition

A Novel

by

Diane L. Wetzig

Diane L. Wetzig

dianewetzigphd@gmail.com

Table of Contents

Dedication

To my patients who have taught me everything I know.

About the Author

Dr. Diane Wetzig is a Psychologist who has been in practice with adults and teens for many years. She has introduced psychological principles and techniques to patients and clinicians, as well as through her call-in radio show. A writer since childhood, she recently turned to mystery writing at the suggestion of a patient who urged her to "put the information in a novel, doc, then 'I'll be sure to read it." A mother and grandmother to five grandsons, Dr. Wetzig, spends winters in Austin, Texas, and summers in Toronto, Canada.

SECTION I

Chapter 1

"Ugh! Predators are always with us." Georgina shuddered.

He was back. A blue heron poised at the water's edge, prehistoric sentinel eternally waiting for unsuspecting prey to enter his orbit. The heron struck and plucked a struggling fish from the water. He held the thrashing captive aloft briefly before devouring it in one gulp, the death throes of his victim visible all the way down the elongated neck.

Setting the vase of fuchsia gladioli down on the cupola-capped porch, Georgina stepped back to critique it briefly, reaching out to adjust a stem. Satisfied, she drew back the heavy mauve-striped awnings and sank into the shelter of her wicker rocking chair, pulling an afghan around her. She had risen early to watch the faint golden tinge of the eastern sky. The sun began its Sisyphean climb to ignite an early burn off the mists enshrouding the hills on the opposite shore — the harbinger of the sweltering heat of a late June afternoon in western New York State.

Georgina inhaled deeply and exhaled slowly.

"It's going to be a peaceful summer," she promised herself.

Georgina picked up her binoculars to study the heron more closely. Movement at a distance down by the lake caught her attention, and she directed her gaze to the area of the activity. A diminutive Asian woman came into focus. She appeared to be assembling a column out of the stones laid out neatly around her, her movements sure and purposeful. She paused in her work to blow into her cupped hands, warming them against the morning chill. Gathering cups and a thermos, Georgina stepped off the porch and walked down the beaten pathway leading to the water.

"Hello, there," she called out, loud enough to be heard by the slight figure obviously engrossed in her task, yet not so loud as to disturb nearby neighbors.

"Hello yourself."

The woman turned. Early morning light glanced off the icy sheen of onyx hair framing like a helmet, the serene visage of the Asian-American woman.

"I saw you from my porch and wondered whether you'd care for some hot tea?" said Georgina gesturing toward the thermos and cups in her hands. Suddenly shy, Georgina faltered. It wasn't like her to be so forward.

"That would be most welcome." Tawney's eyes glistened as the woman glanced up from her project.

"I am Yan," she said, bowing slightly, hands pressed in a prayer position just below her jawline. She was wearing a heavy silk outfit: an aubergine mandarin jacket with frog fastenings and fisherman pants over serviceable sandals.

"Georgina." She smiled nervously.

She gestured to the figure emerging from the pile of stones, a primitive art form: two granite legs supporting stones of descending size — vaguely robotic. Since arriving at Chautauqua, Yan had scoured the grounds to gather the carefully selected stones — detritus of glaciers strewn like marbles by careless children

"Inukshuk," stated Georgina with a confident nod.

"You're familiar with Inuit art?"

"Yes. First Nations peoples use Inukshuk to mark a spiritual pathway."

"Must be Canadian," Yan mused to herself. Yan lived on the west coast and traveled up to Canada to study aboriginal art, where she picked up the preferred Canadian practice of calling native peoples 'First Nations' and had adopted it herself; she felt it connoted the respect due to this proud culture.

Georgina kneeled to pour Yan a cup of tea, then brushed her hand over the fine close-knit, a beautifully hand-woven blanket spread out by the lake, close to a stand of rushes. "Haida?" she queried, referring to a tribe of Northwestern weavers.

"Right again. You certainly know your subject."

4

"Autodidact, I'm afraid. No formal training. I am a member of the women's committee of the Art Gallery of Ontario, which specializes in First Nations' art. I wanted to be informed about their work. I take my responsibilities on that committee very seriously."

She wrung her hands together and looked out across the lake, seeming to drift off for a moment. "At least I used to," she whispered. Her face contorted as she struggled to subdue a wave of wrenching pain. The effort proved in vain, however, and the spun-sugar gloss of the fragile veneer splintered like the glaze of a caramel apple.

Yan leaned in closer and placed her hand on Georgina's arm. They stayed like that for a heartbeat, then Georgina stepped back, out of reach.

"Forgive me. I didn't mean to alarm you."

Yan dropped her arm to her side, the look of distress on her face mirroring that of Georgina. It wasn't like her to be drawn into such intimacy without knowing the other's personal history. From her years as a psychiatrist, she had learned not to invade someone's personal space without an explicit invitation. It seemed that long-banked embers of maternal fire had been stirred by the shadow of pain transiting the face of the younger woman.

"Oh, it's not you." Georgina had recovered her composure immediately. "My startle reaction seems to have increased lately."

The two women fell silent for a moment: one dark and Asian, the other fair of hair and complexion, betraying a Northern European heritage — foil for one another. By silent agreement, they returned to a lighter, safer conversation.

"The Art Gallery of Ontario, "said Yan. "You must know my friend, Alexandra Romanov Lewis. She is an enthusiastic patron of the arts."

"Of course," replied Georgina absently. "Lovely woman."

She can certainly pull up a 'Wall of Pleasant,'' Yan made a mental note of the polite, almost palpable barrier that had been drawn between them. *I'll bet she's had a lot of practice doing that.*

"Ephemeral art." Yan went on to explain as they turned to admire the Inukshuk.

Georgina shot her a quizzical look.

"Inukshuk is like the Buddhist sand paintings," Yan explained. "Magnificent creations painstakingly built and then swept away upon completion. A reminder that all matter is impermanent."

"Inukshuk reminds me of some primitive forms that I noticed yesterday," Georgina disclosed. "I was walking by the lake and became mesmerized by the alto-cumulous clouds drifting along. They seemed to create images, like ancient First Nations' pictographs."

The color flooded across Georgina's neck and into her cheeks, and she laughed as she became aware that she was returning to a more intimate emotional level of conversation, although she hardly knew this woman.

Darn it. I'm wearing my feelings not only on my sleeve but on my neck and face for all to see.

Yan leaned in, eyes widening, voice neutral.

"Pictographs? Were you able to interpret their meaning?"

"Not really. It reminded me of a group of warriors."Six women and one male — odd."

"Warriors?" Yan probed.

"Yes. Six female warriors and one male," Georgina clarified.

"I like to look at the clouds as well," Yan's voice dropped into a soothing monotone. "Clouds are merely vaporized water — water that has been recycled here for more than four and a half billion years. It feels good to relax and let the cares of the day drift away, lazily watching the clouds, listening to the sounds of the water lapping against the boats," intoned Yan, her voice low and soothing, rhythmic as a lullaby. "You can hear the rush of the waves as they gently wash up on the beach. It's as if the waves are washing the cares of the day away. Relax more and more, deeper and deeper, down and down, heavier and heavier." Yan's breathing had become slow and regular.

Georgina responded dreamily to the sound of Yan's voice; her breathing became slow and regular as she became absorbed in the movement of the clouds as they sailed across the sky. In a few moments, they began to swirl and roil like a dark fog. As she gazed drowsily at the clouds, she could make out figures of Goddesses, the apotheosis of the fearless feminine: strong and upright, confidence emanating from every pore. A series of scenes were projected as the formations, in kaleidoscope motion, continued to change. A seashell-born Amazon emerged from surging waves, energy fanning out like sunbeams before her, wavy hair cascading behind. The Amazon joined several female warriors clad in gray armor, and together they gyrated in ancient combat. As she watched, a taller male warrior appeared, holding something aloft in his outstretched hand. The furry object was squirming, and the warrior taunted the Amazons with it. The Amazons circled the warrior and lunged at him. The male warrior evaporated, leaving two figures crumpled on the ground.

With this final scenario, Georgina stirred. "Peaceful summer. Peaceful summer," she murmured as if to ward off the violence of the scenes. Sinking back into reverie, the clouds began to change once more. As had happened the day before, a series of hieroglyphic-like figures began to etch themselves into the cloud formations, taking the shape of Asian or Sanskrit writing: archaic logograms trying to convey messages, messages that Georgina felt it important she be able to translate.

Willing herself back to present reality, Georgina struggled to shake off the lethargy as she described the pictographs to Yan, omitting the violent scenes that had preceded them.

"Why don't you draw the images here in the sand for me." Yan offered her a stick and then took pictures with her cell phone of the figures that Georgina drew.

"If it's alright with you, I'd like to email these pictures to a friend of mine. 'He's a pictograph expert as well as an ephemeral artist who is lecturing here this week. As a matter of fact, Alexandra is having a dinner party, and he is likely to be there. Why don't you come along so that you can meet him?"

"I'm not sure," Georgina demurred.

"I'd love for you to come, and I'm certain Alex will be delighted to see a fellow Torontonian. There will be some other people there I'd like you to meet as well. I'll drop by your house later on and let you know what time," Yan gestured toward Georgina's house. "That's it over there, isn't it? The painted lady with the rose-striped awning and matching gladioli?"

"Why, yes," said Georgina, taken aback to learn that Yan knew which house was hers. She had surmised that Yan had been aware of her approach, but before she could ask about it, a sudden summer squall sent her scurrying home. As she dodged the puddles and started up the steps, a tall figure materialized from the billowing awnings of the porch. Outstretched hands pressed what felt like a drowned rat into her arms. Georgina thought she made out the words 'I think this belongs to you.' It took her a moment to recognize the sodden, rodent-like animal shivering against her. The dark crimson diamond-encrusted collar — another extravagant gift from her husband to their daughter — identified the creature as 'Princess,' her daughter Elise's beloved teacup poodle.

Georgina squinted through the sheets of rain. The pelting precipitation made it difficult to distinguish the speaker's features.

"What are you doing on my porch?" Her voice was sharper than she had intended. The figure was blocking access to the porch. Georgina was intimidated by the aggressive male energy emanating from the shadows.

"I found this dog on the loose. Someone told me it belonged here."

"Well, I don't appreciate your presumption in coming up onto my porch. In the future, please don't come onto my property uninvited," chided Georgina, growing more alarmed with each second.

A calloused hand emerged from the raincoat and encircled the neck of the bedraggled puppy now snuggled against Georgina's bosom.

"And here I was hoping to make a good impression!" He squeezed the dog's throat once more and started to leave.

"You rarely get a second chance to make a good first impression," Georgina muttered to his retreating back.

At that moment, Princess leaped down to run after the man; shiny nails scratched across the mahogany porch and down the stairs. She jumped against the man's legs, begging to be picked up. The stranger scooped up the poodle, retraced his steps, and handed her back to Georgina. "Better be more careful. You wouldn't want anything to happen to your dog now, would you?"

When Georgina had finally managed to secure the wriggling dog and looked up, all she could see was the receding silhouette of the stranger walking away down the street.

She shuddered.

Chapter 2

Driving through the wrought iron gateway into the serenity of his grandmother's property, Eric Bellamy's mind floated back to the carefree summer days he had spent there as a child. His British Racing Green Jaguar slowly turned around the circular driveway and pulled up in front of the graceful columns at the entrance of the Tudor Estate, a replica of a British country house built on the shores of Lake Chautauqua. Eric unfolded himself from the tan leather driver's seat; he was a tall, athletic young man with wiry ash-blond hair cut short in the fashion of a Greek athlete.

"Mrs. Bellamy is expecting you on the back terrace at tea," stated Mason, the family butler, as he met Eric at the door.

"Thank you, Mason," said Eric, taking note of Mason's solemnity. Mason had been a general factotum for the family for as long as Eric could remember. Now that his slight frame was gently stooped, Mason supervised the other servants on the rigorous housekeeping specifics required by the estate's eponymous chatelaine.

"I'll have your bags taken to the pool house."

Eric stopped to take in his surroundings. Sunlight splashed on perfectly manicured lawns; formal gardens were ablaze in a profusion of color; subtly insulating them from the rest of the Chautauqua Institution was a border of stately maple trees, their lush green foliage fully fleshed; bluestone pathways dotted by welcoming benches sloped down to the lake. Eric parked in the seven-car garage house at the northern edge of the estate and made his way to the guest house. Isolated by the lakefront and kept for his use alone, it featured its own endless lap pool, Jacuzzi, and sauna.

It had been an exhausting year at Harbridge, not just physically — as a member of the rowing team; Eric was required to work out two hours a day on weekdays and five hours on weekends — but mentally and emotionally as well. There had been ugly legal battles. Even though this summer had not been his choice, he had wanted to meet his mates on the Riviera del Sol, "The Boys" had been summoned to the summer residence by their grandmother, she who must be obeyed. Nevertheless, Eric was looking forward to luxuriating in the cocooning comfort of his grandmother's care. He could imagine himself buried in the satiny surrounds of the eight-hundred-count scented linens of Teresa Bellamy's famously appointed household. Wherever grandmother resides, the thread count rises appreciably. Teresa Bellamy, his paternal grandmother, had taken over Eric's upbringing when his grieving mother, Virginia, ultimately succumbed to an alcoholic death two years to the day after his father and sister were killed in a car crash. Those had been dreadful times. Eric could still remember night after night of his mother's screaming lamentation and his feeble attempts to console her. She abdicated the care of her surviving child to her mother-in-law long before her eventual demise. Eric felt sad to realize there were times when he had trouble remembering her face.

***

"Hi, Glammy," shouted Miko as he abandoned his red Lamborghini at the front doorstep and hurried through the mansion, bursting onto the scene in the garden. He picked up his grandmother with his typical enthusiasm, swung her around — all ninety-two pounds of her— and set her gently down.

There must be a portrait in the attic growing older because you get younger and younger each time I see you," said Miko, kissing his grandmother on both cheeks.

"Good to see you again," replied Teresa, holding him at arm's length and smoothing her simple, elegant linen sheath back into its original contours. She was not about to succumb to the blandishments of her second grandson. This time things had gone too far. She knew that as charming as Miko could be, he also had a short fuse. Miko had been relentlessly spoiled by her daughter, Victoria, a socialite who had married a Polish prince in the wedding of the decade. With his mother and her cohorts, every day was a party, and the young Miko was the adored mascot they brought along on their jet-setting escapades. Teresa remembered one summer she spent in the company of Victoria and her girlfriends on the Mediterranean Riviera. They'd arrived at the beach with a cavalcade of paraphernalia: cabanas and umbrellas, coolers full of delicious appetizers: Beluga caviar served with mother-of-pearl spoons, Ceviche Verde, peach and prosciutto crostini, and, Miko's favorite, peanut butter, and caramelized banana choux pastry. Of course, there were nonstop cocktails. Miko was the only child among the adults, and the adults doted on him outrageously.

Mason appeared at the garden gate, approached his mistress, and whispered in her ear. Mrs. Bellamy scowled at her grandson.

"It seems that the Elm Entrance Gate Guard is here to see you."

"Unbelievable. I can't believe anyone would trespass on our property."

Teresa wasn't to be distracted by his tactics.

"Apparently, he is saying that you refused to show him your gate pass and instead sped right past him into the Institution."

Miko swept his arm in a large arc to encompass their surroundings. "He was just being annoyingly officious. He knows who I am. Who we are."

"That attitude is not at all helpful. There is a lot of resistance to showing gate passes, and it is important for us to set a good example."

The Chautauqua Institution is a former Sunday teachers' retreat fronting onto Chautauqua Lake, the thumb of the Finger Lakes, in western New York state. During the nine-week summer season, a lively schedule of lectures and workshops along with daily performances of symphony, opera, and ballet is offered. Visitors and residents at the Institution purchase gate pass to enter the gated grounds. These passes were to be presented and scanned each time one entered or exited the various gates. It was an annoyance to long-time season pass holders like the Bellamies, but it couldn't be avoided. The world-class cultural and artistic presentations to be had at the Institution did not come cheaply.

"Mason," directed Mrs. Bellamy, "Please be so kind as to take Prince Kazmierz's gate pass to the guard so it can be scanned. Also, let him know that I shall be writing the board to commend him for the conscientious attention to his job."

"Yes, madam," answered Mason, who retreated to deal with the irritated official.

"Honestly, let some little peon get in a position of power, and they take delight in trying to one-up you," Miko said.

"You've gotten into enough trouble rebelling against authority figures this year," Teresa stated grimly.

"And all you have to do is to lift your little finger and set these people straight," Miko cajoled.

"I want you to take this summer season to take a deep breath and think about what you might want to do with your life — other than to continue getting into trouble, that is," declared Teresa.

"Of course, Glammy."

Miko, too wondered what he might do this summer. The prospects were not too exciting.

Just like his mother," Teresa sighed, remembering his mother's tumultuous life.

***

Tea was served promptly at 4:00 in the parlor. Wherever Teresa Bellamy was, at 4:00 pm, tea was served. The water at the height of the boil was poured over loose tea leaves — stuffing the leaves into bags diminished the quality — and brewed for precisely four minutes. Mrs. Bellamy poured the tea through a long-handled silver strainer into hand-painted teacups collected from every corner of the globe. On the tea tray, linen, serviettes, and translucent porcelain plates were placed beside a towering three-tiered china platter that held paper-thin sandwiches and pastries. Miko moved to the tea tray and, foregoing the watercress, cucumber, and smoked salmon sandwiches, piled his plate high with petit fours, coconut macaroons, and "Glammy's" famous scones that he smothered with plenty of clotted cream and raspberry preserves from the local farmer's market.

As usual, Miko was holding forth. His scheme this summer was to become an agent for the world-famous Toronto firm that represented major performers. He planned to sign on Chautauqua's most famous entertainer, Jonah Nash, front man for the band 'Herd Mentality' who was rumored to be leaving the band for a solo career.

Teresa smiled at him. Young people today are so hyperactive — always seeking the next stimulation. Inwardly, however, she was concerned about his attitude toward the Harbridge scandal. He seemed to have little remorse.

***

Chester, the son of a former member of Teresa's household staff, arrived at the Bellamy Estate on foot. His mother had been very close to Teresa, indispensable really, and her son had been reared alongside Teresa's grandsons. Eight years ago, however, the woman had left Teresa's employ to return to her hometown to take care of her ailing mother. Thereafter Teresa had received semi-annual letters from her: on Teresa's birthday and at Christmas, primitive letters telling of her mother's health and giving news of her son. Then, two years ago, Teresa received a long letter telling of her son's outstanding achievements and asking if Teresa could find work for him. Teresa had agreed, but she insisted that, at her expense, he first attend college with her two grandsons. Chester, like her grandsons, had proven to be brilliant. He was on the dean's list in pre-med and was well on his way to becoming a gifted surgeon. He was also a talented artist, and Teresa was a patron of his sculpting as a way for him to earn his own independent money. This summer, Chester was staying at the garage apartment, a completely renovated brick structure just up the road from the estate.

"Thank you again for the use of the garage apartment Mrs. Bellamy. It is more that I need," said Chester, kissing her hand. "And the reception you are planning for the opening of my sculpture exhibit is incredibly generous." Chester had shared with Teresa his concern about the conservation of his wildlife sculptures rendered in clay and, therefore, exceedingly fragile. She had responded with the offer of hosting a benefit on his behalf to raise money to retain a foundry to cast the figures into bronze, a very expensive process and one that he had been unable to dream of until her offer. "In fact, I am off now to work on one final piece before the opening," he explained, politely refusing the offer to join them for tea.

"I'll catch up with you later," Chester said to Miko, casually ignoring Eric, who gave him a surly look.

Looks like triangulation going on among those three? Teresa speculated, noting the exchange. Could Eric be jealous of Chester's relationship with Miko? Aloud she declared: "Chester is very caring and conscientious, just like his mother. Typical of her to have done an outstanding job raising her son." She suspected that Chester had excused himself in order to give her an opportunity to speak with her grandsons alone.

"We are avoiding the one subject that we should be discussing," scowled Teresa. "How on earth did you boys get mixed up with that mess at Harbridge?"

"Glammy, you know we had nothing to do with that—we were totally exonerated, cleared of all involvement," blustered Miko, hand to his heart in his best portrayal of innocence.

"And don't think I didn't have to call in a few favors for that." She surveyed them with stern eyes.

"The prosecuting attorney overreached. It became clear that his pursuit of the case was politically motivated." Miko dismissed the subject and turned away.

"The Bar Association saw fit to revoke his license," protested Eric. "Not suspend. Revoke!"

"I know. I know. The District Attorney took on the wrong people, that's for sure. But be assured, at some point, I will want a complete accounting from the two of you. But for now, let's focus on having a good time. There is nowhere like Chautauqua in the summertime." Teresa rang the small silver bell to summon staff to clear the tea service.

"The good times will have to wait. I'm off to check out the gym and get started on training right away," said Eric, rising to leave.

"Give me a break!" groaned Miko.

"Remember, we promised the coach that we would maintain our regular workout schedule this summer. Rowing meets start as soon as we get back."

"Chill, coz. There's plenty of time. Let's catch some rays."

Miko stretched out on the chaise, angling his limbs to get maximum sun. He crooked his arm behind his head and closed his eyes, heaving a contented sigh as Eric hustled down the incline toward the docks.

This restless activity is his way of staying ahead of the darkness. Teresa's heart ached for him. She wouldn't be around forever. She'd like to see him secure in a supportive marriage with children of his own. She worried that it would be a long time coming, if it would happen at all. She remembered when her twins were born, Eric's father and Miko's mother. They had been so close: 'twinning.' Together in the womb and together through their formative years, they shared their own language, could sense each other's thoughts across the miles, and mirrored one another's actions. They were married within months of each other and had their children within weeks of each other; Eric and Miko were almost twins like their parents. When Eric's sister and father —her own son— had been killed, her daughter had railed against her brother's wife. That glass-wristed witch, she should have been the one driving the car. Teresa worried about the darkness that took over Eric. Miko was another story. Miko would be a playboy like his father, the Prince; she was sure of that.

Chapter 3

I'm more centered now that the Inukshuk is in place, sighed Yan. This was a priority upon arriving at Chautauqua or wherever the Goddess Circle was to gather. As she went about her unpacking, Yan decided to establish her meditation space in the small alcove off the living room. She had brought various spiritual touchstones along on her travels, much as pilgrims of old conveyed ornate gilded triptych — moveable altars available for prayer and meditation. Lighting a sandalwood candle, Yan carefully smoothed a hand-embroidered cloth across the cedar cabinet. At the left edge, she placed a miniature 'Buddhist Garden' sand tray bracketed on one side by a tiny garden rake and on the other by a silk-corded pendulum. At the right edge, she carefully laid out her inks and calligraphy brushes. She sat down and stretched out a piece of parchment, selected one of the brushes, and dipped it into the ink. Her hand automatically began the topmost brush stroke that most resembled a rooftop to begin the pictograph representing the concept of mindfulness. Pausing momentarily in her work, she looked up at the statue of Kuan Yin, the Buddhist Goddess of compassion, carefully positioned in the middle of the altar. Her husband had come upon this bronze rendering of the Goddess during a retreat at Green Gulch, a Buddhist spiritual retreat center in Marin County, California, and had purchased it for her as an anniversary present. He explained that the contrast of this gentle Goddess holding dominion over the fierce dragon and powerful ocean waves captured for him the essence of his wife: the heart of steel in a velvet glove.

Yan put her hand to her heart and held close the memory of her husband. It had been three years now since she had finally yielded the family home in Marin and taken up residence across the Golden Gate Bridge in a San Francisco condo. The wondrous view from the windows of her current abode did not make up for the memories cradled in each corner of the now-cavernous Marin house. She traveled widely in response to the never-ending invitations to give presentations on her specialty, Goddess Personality Types. The condo suited her lifestyle now that her husband was gone and her son had moved on to a busy professional life. She thought wistfully of her son; she didn't get to be with him nearly enough, but that was how it was meant to be. If you do your job as a parent well, your children will be strong enough to fly from the nest.

"People make plans, and the Great Mother laughs," Yan frequently told her students. These were not the retirement years of which, eons ago, she and her husband Jonathan had dreamily whispered during the sleepless nights that followed hectic days of demanding residency and busy medical practice. And what an obstacle course medical training had been for women back in the day. Yan's father had been dismissive of her ambitions for medical school: "Why waste years of expensive training on someone who will be at home taking care of children?" he had scoffed. But Yan's undergraduate professors had prevailed, and with a full scholarship and her mother's unyielding support, Yan had been accepted for medical school after applying all across the country and fighting with her male competitors for residency positions. After earning her medical license, she studied further to become a Jungian Psychiatrist, a specialty she felt would provide her with a comprehensive picture of her patients' total condition, both physical and mental. She had met her husband, Jonathan, during residency, and he had been a friend and colleague as well as a lover. She missed him achingly. He had been taken by a brain tumor, the one foe he was unable to defeat. The first step in treatment, the gamma knife, had cut out his brilliance and his personality. After that, Yan was alone to face horrific options. The next logical avenue was chemotherapy. Yan could remember coaxing her frail husband to ingest pills so poisonous that she had to wear rubber gloves to handle them. She raced frantically from city to city, from one world-class hospital to the next, dragging Jonathan to the latest promising clinical trial where world-renowned oncology experts squabbled over the best course of treatment. But as fast as they raced, metastases spread faster. Western medicine had been unable to fix her beloved husband. Yan was seized with the anguish of the twelve ghastly months it had taken Jonathan to finally slip beyond her grasp. Was it worth it to have put him through that cruel process? She would never know. For so many years, Yan and her husband had devoted themselves to the miracle of modern medicine, and, in the end, it had betrayed them. For the year-and-a-half following Jonathan's death, Yan fell into a morass of despair. She questioned the premises on which she had based her life and was disheartened by the ambiguity of the answers she found. Was medicine art or science? It was at this juncture that she realized she'd been shunning her close friends. She had allowed anonymous pseudo-relationships with patients or supervisees, but nothing closer. At that point, her remaining friends had insisted that she accompany them to a retreat center, Wellspring, on the coastline north of Marin established for victims of cancer and their families and friends. They had persuaded her to join the teaching faculty, and she had come to cherish the time spent there. She would arise early in her simple yet comfortably appointed room, step outside to the pounding of the surf a few feet away and stand on the wooden slats of a Japanese-style shower allowing the fresh cold water to wash over her. After a breakfast of steel-cut oats and wheatgrass-infused green tea, she walked the rocky pathways cut through the cypress groves to the cliffs overlooking the ocean, watching the foam-crested breakers rush up on the rocks below, and practice tai chi under a spreading cypress cantilevered above the waves. Mid-morning, she prepared her remarks for that day's group, and afternoons were spent together with retreat participants in one of the octagonal cedar plank buildings scattered around the grounds.

When not reading or teaching, Yan gathered in the community kitchen with like-minded others, refugees of "traditional" healing practices, searching for different answers—not competing for therapies so much as complementary ones. One night, following an evening of great mirth and vegetarian chili, she found herself one of the last two remaining at the kitchen table. Her companion, Ursula, a fellow participant at Wellspring, put down the cup she had been cradling and, gazing deeply into Yan's eyes, shared how concerned she'd been when Yan first came to Wellspring and her delight in the healing she'd observed in her since that time.

"I hope I haven't offended you," said Ursula.

"Not in the least," Yan responded, tears flowing unbidden from deep within her core. She was not offended; she was elated. Preparing for bed, she reveled in the warmth of the bond growing within this band of strong, loving women. Only as her heart began to melt did she become aware of how frozen it had been.

Yan smiled to herself at the memory and turned her mind to the Sarah Chang recording of Tchaikovsky's violin concerto playing on the CD player. Catharine Sobieski, the protégé of her great friend and fellow Goddess, Alexandra Romanov Lewis, would be performing the concerto here at Chautauqua, and Yan wanted to refresh her familiarity with the piece.

Chapter 4

The gunmetal gray Mercedes crunched to a stop in front of a stand of white ash trees bordering the pool area that functioned as a moat, separating the Chautauqua residence of Jonah Nash, front man of the Herd Mentality, from the rest of the Chautauqua Institution. A multi-leveled house sprawled across a lush promontory that jutted out into the lake. Finishing her phone conversation Catharine closed her cell and took the hand proffered by the self-assured Cody McCoy —did he make up that name? — sent by Jonah to escort her to Chautauqua from the nearby airstrip. He was clad in a T-shirt so tight it looked as if it were painted on; his motions revealed deeply cut muscles. His arm accidentally—really? —brushed Catharine's breast as he helped her alight from the car. He continued to hold onto her hand and gaze into her eyes.

"I'm creating a documentary on Jonah and the Herd Mentality, and I would love to capture you -- on film. I will be editing the documentary at my studio," Cody purred, his smile lazy. "Perhaps you can drop by sometime and see my frames."

He's obviously accustomed to picking up Jonah's discards.

"I'll get back to you on that," she replied implacably. "First chance I get." She rescued her hand just as Jonah stepped out of the doorway. His presence radiated powerful charisma despite the understatement of his plain, double-starched cotton shirt and dark jeans. Jonah grabbed Catharine and kissed her with a passion that demonstrated how much he missed her, offering Cody a 'hands-off my woman' message.

Cody pulled open the trunk of the car and lifted out her hand-tooled leather suitcases. Catharine extricated herself from Jonah's embrace to retrieve her violin case from the rear seat of the Mercedes. She had cradled it protectively during the ride from the airport. The case contained a three-hundred-year-old Stradivarius violin on loan to her from her patroness, Alexandra. There were many stories of "Strads" that were stolen or went missing. Not too many years ago, the "Lipinski Stradivarius" had been stolen from the concertmaster of the Milwaukee Symphony, and the world of classical music heaved a collective sigh of relief when it was recovered unharmed. Jonah placed his arm firmly around her waist as Catharine gingerly picked her way along the pathway approaching the house, careful not to damage her Ferragamo shoes. Cody averted his eyes and picked up Catharine's heavy luggage. He carried it upstairs and deposited it in the suite where a man's bathrobe laid out on one side of the king-size bed made it obvious that he and Catharine were sharing the room.

Jonah and Catharine had met the previous March at a benefit during South-by-Southwest in Austin, Texas. Catharine, a world-class violinist, was in town performing as a guest artist for the Austin Symphony while Jonah and Herd Mentality were headlining the famous music festival. Jonah's attraction to Catharine had been immediate. Her flawless white skin, long, abundantly wavy, pale blond hair, and lithe, curvaceous body certainly made her desirable to him, but it was her musical genius that made this relationship so special. It wasn't easy to become a solo artist in the highly competitive world of classical music. It was as difficult as achieving fame in the world of popular music. In the months since their introduction, Catharine and Jonah met as often as their tight schedules allowed. Frequent separations only intensified their relationship. Her biological clock ticking, Catharine was determined to become pregnant and carry on the musical talent embedded in their combined genes; she just hadn't yet found the right moment to broach the subject with Jonah. When Jonah mentioned that he and the band would be spending a couple of weeks at Chautauqua, close to their hometown of Jamestown, NY, Catharine was reminded of her desire. Jonah and Herd Mentality would be at Chautauqua at the same time the Goddess Circle was to convene. She was delighted to agree to his request that she be his hostess at the party where Jonah was planning to make a "big announcement".

Chapter 5

The vibration of the cell phone jarred Yan from her reverie.

"Hi, mom." It was her son, Jack. "So sorry; Susan and I won't be able to come to Chautauqua this season, just too busy; we should have more time to talk next week when this project is finished. Love you." Yan carefully placed the cell phone in the belt holder her son had given her —cell phones were too small and kept getting lost —disappointed to learn that Jack and his wife wouldn't be coming to join her. To her dismay, Yan was not particularly close to her daughter-in-law —you only need one good daughter-in-law, a wise friend had noted —but that wasn't to be. She respected Susan, a successful environmental lawyer and partner to her son both professionally and in life. Yan's own mother had died of congestive heart failure two weeks after her first son was born. There had been no one to advise and support her and her husband, so they had raised Jack with the aid of books. She knew it was easier to theorize than to parent yourself, so she counted herself fortunate that he had turned out as well as he had.

So much had changed since the time when she'd been the only female in her class at medical school. She remembered a joke that Jonathan liked to tell: a boy and his father were in a bad accident. The ambulance brought the boy to the emergency room, but when the surgeon was summoned, the operation couldn't be performed because the surgeon was the boy's parent. But how could this be if his father was in the accident with him? Yan remembered that most people of the time couldn't solve the conundrum. It didn't occur to them that the surgeon could be a woman, the child's mother.

There was so much excitement in those early feminist days: women gathered in consciousness-raising groups and wondered whether the feminist movement had the capacity to sustain an effort that would enable women to have basic human rights. Where there is education, there is progress, she thought; now, over fifty percent of our graduating medical classes are female —women figure they would have to be twice as credentialed to get half as far as a man. Unfortunately, even now, women continue to perform ninety percent of the household duties and often are too exhausted to aspire to corporate Fortune 500 careers. The age of the Superwoman.

But I still miss the days when Jack was young and I had him close to me, she sighed.

Yan knew that she needed to consider passing along the leadership of the Goddess Circle. She felt weighed down after years of carrying the healing traditions and teachings of the group and yearned to hand them over to an acolyte. She planned to address this when the Circle convened here at

Chautauqua; all the members had likely arrived by now. How to proceed, without daughters of her own, to ensure the continuation of practice focused on the old ways rather than on the lightning-quick connectivity of her son's generation and their smartphones. The ways of the Goddess respected boundaries, both physical and intellectual, while her son's generation broadcast private information without shame through various and multiple social networks. Once again, she considered each of the members of the present Goddess Circle to evaluate them as potential leaders. None had evidenced a desire for the role so far, and she could understand their reluctance, although she was disappointed in it. The demands of the job were monumental.

This summer's Circle would take place just after the Solstice, an energetically important time when the earth completed its journey in one direction and came to rest, pausing briefly on its axis, before tilting back, like a metronome, in the opposite direction. As a child, Yan had been mesmerized by stories of unusual happenings at the time the earth stood still: not just tales of eggs standing upright on their base but stories of magic and mischief. She remembered well when her mother and her friends, self-styled crones, gathered down on the beach around huge bonfires to drum and dance as Yan and her friends' fashioned origami boats and launched them aflame into the waves. The women mesmerized the youngsters with the myth of

Amaterasu, an Asian Goddess of the Sun, feted at the summer solstice. Legend held that there was great sibling rivalry between Amaterasu and her brother, Susano. When he caused the death of her companion, Amaterasu was so aggrieved she shut herself away in a cave, causing darkness throughout the land. She only returned to warm the earth when she heard wild music and drumming outside of the cave and ventured out to see who could be holding celebrations in her absence.

So many cultures, at different times and locations, have created a myth of a Goddess, grieving the loss of a loved one, who abandons the earth, thus causing the dark times to fall upon the land, mused Yan, thinking of the parallel Greek myth of Demeter and Persephone. What in that childhood experience prompted me to pursue training as a Jungian psychoanalyst?

Along with her lifelong study of I Ching, Yan used the pendulum, a symbol of the movement of the earth rotating on its axis, to help access her intuition, her inner wisdom. Picking up the tiny rake, she carefully pulled it through the red earth of the miniature Meditation Garden, scratching perfect tracks through the grains of sand. Holding the pendulum over it, she waited for it to swing in the positive or the negative direction in response to her questions. Today's encounter with Georgina was on her mind. She had described cloud formations full of Sturm und Drang:

portents for our Goddess Circle? Georgina seemed unaware of the intuitive power in her possession. The swinging of the pendulum confirmed Yan's initial impression; she decided to introduce Georgina to the Goddess Circle.

Chapter 6

"You adoration addict." Georgina admonished her charge, Princess, a tiny black teacup poodle weighing five pounds soaking wet.

Princess responded with an arrogant gaze followed by a yawn. Georgina had been babysitting her 'grand-dog' during her daughter Elise's absence, and Princess had become a popular fixture in the gift shop of the Art Gallery of Ontario, where Georgina volunteered back home in Toronto. There, Princess would sit decorously with her ankles crossed, receiving the adoration of all; she assumed that deigning to rest on a familiar or unfamiliar lap would be an honor for the recipient. Here in Chautauqua, as in Toronto, it was a trial taking her for a walk. People couldn't resist fussing over her, and so it took an age to finish the trip. And as in Toronto, Princess was in the habit of taking off, presumably continuing her two-month quest to find Elise; the difference being that here in the Institution, Chautauquans who found her would take her to the sheriff's office, who would then return her to Georgina. Georgina had gotten to know the local sheriff quite well.

"Your craving for attention is going to get you into trouble one day," she scolded. "And me as well."

Georgina sighed as she sat beside the now-settled Princess. "You are a lot of trouble," she admonished.

Princess responded by turning over on her side and immediately falling asleep, nostrils twitching with delicate snores. Gently leaving her, she carefully pulled back the curtains, peered outside to assure herself that her unexpected 'visitor' had truly left, and tip-toed into the bedroom. Everything in the bedroom was in perfect order. Georgina was a good girl. A conscientious student of art history, she had graduated from the University of Toronto with the requisite 'Mrs' degree. The beautiful daughter had followed in due time, and her life became centered around Elise's activities. But it hadn't turned out as the fairy tales had promised. Today she found herself alone and empty. For the past six months, she had awakened each morning without purpose and walked through the tasks of the day as if in a daydream. She felt lonely, whether by herself or surrounded by people. Shaking her head as if to dispel the despair, Georgina turned on the water in preparation for her shower, her dependable safe space. She habitually retreated here to be comforted by the calming spray and the delicious scents of body wash and shampoo, and the sting of loofah. But this time, her experience was full of pain; her heart swelled until it threatened to burst. Her mind flashed back to the intervention that had precipitated Elise's anguished departure to be treated for addiction to Ritalin and oxycodone. And at the same time, her marriage had been crumbling. Her husband, Owen, had always worked long hours, was rarely home before ten, and was away on frequent business trips, but he had never humiliated her with his romantic entanglements before. All that had changed. Georgina was out of the shower now, kneading her body with fragrant lotion. The family meetings at Elise's treatment center had exacerbated the long-developing rift between Georgina and her husband. Her husband blamed her because she had failed at the only responsibility he had delegated to her: the supervision of their daughter. Georgina felt a rush of shame at the thought.

She picked up the Chautauqua Daily from the doorstep to peruse the lectures for the week. Last weekend the wooden gavel had rapped to signal the opening of the Chautauqua season: each of the nine weeks of lectures centered around a theme such as education, geology, politics, health, or spirituality. In addition to the informational lectures, Chautauqua showcased symphony, ballet, theater, and opera. 'Disneyland for Intellectuals,' the residents called it. As she read the paper, she noticed that the logogram expert Yan had spoken of would be presenting this week. Perhaps she would talk to him about the hieroglyphics she had seen in the clouds.

At that moment, as if magically summoned, Yan stepped onto Georgina's porch and peered closely at her new friend.

"You seem upset."

"Oh, it's nothing," exclaimed Georgina remembering her recent visitor. "My daughter is due any minute, and I'm hoping everything is perfect for her arrival."

"This seems to be the day for arrivals. The members of my women's group will be gathering today. We meet on a regular basis to learn from one another and practice Goddessence.'

"Goddessence?"

"Yes. We have each adopted the persona of one of the Greek Goddesses with whom we feel most closely aligned. I find these Goddess Archetypes more acceptable than the pathological personality typologies used by today's mental health field, especially with respect to women, in my opinion. The various 'personality disorders' cataloged in the mental health diagnostic systems can be demeaning to women. After examining the elemental essence of each of the Goddess' personalities—the idiosyncrasies, behavioral patterns, strengths, and weaknesses—each of our members has chosen a Goddess archetype with which they most identify and has become the avatar of that Goddess. The Inukshuk I constructed was a spiritual guide for this group,"

"That sounds rather esoteric."

"It's simply a way of being centered and accessing your inner wisdom. Staying fully in the present moment. It's not that complicated, but it takes a bit of practice. Simple, not easy. Like mental weightlifting for the brain. To strengthen our arms, we lift weights. To build mental muscles, we have regular periods of focused concentration. Many spiritual paths use meditation to train the mind, and that is also the royal road of Goddessence. It's about one-point focus. To become adept at this, you concentrate on anything you like: the breath and body are handy as you always have them with you, or you can focus on a candle or an imagined scene, a beach or waterfall; whatever you like."

"I could never do that. My mind is all over the place." Georgina muttered. "Worse lately."

"Then you will be happy to hear that your concentration capacity can be developed. And, as you practice Goddessence, the parasympathetic nervous system, that part of the autonomic nervous system that controls the relaxation response and shuts off the anxiety fight-flight response, becomes strengthened. You will feel less anxious."

"Good to know."

"I didn't mean to get into a lecturing mode. An occupational hazard, I fear."

"That's all right."

"Most of the women in our Goddess Circle are already here or will be gathering shortly for the site consecration. The women of our Circle come from all walks of life. For example, Ursula Andrews, one of our group, represents the Goddess Artemis. She'd be a great one to demonstrate the Goddessence developed capacity for focus.

Ursula is a psychologist who specializes in women's mental health and is the consultant for an Austin TV station. She has traveled everywhere, even going to the middle east on behalf of her network to report on the recent elections from a female perspective. She seeks stories about girls and women and has a knack for communicating in a language that the general public can relate to.

"Well, don't discount the traditional feminine role," Georgina proclaimed tentatively. She had disappeared into the solarium and now returned with a selection of vases. She planned to arrange fresh flowers in anticipation of her daughter's arrival, and there was an abundance of various types arrayed on a nearby table.

"Would you mind if I help?" asked Yan. "Flower arranging is one of my passions. Ikebana is a Japanese tradition, of course, but floral art has been a meditative practice of the Chinese for many centuries."

"Our Circle is devoted to the development of strong, autonomous women," continued Yan as she clipped the ends off the stems and handed them to Georgina, her forehead puckered in concentration.

"I was quite fulfilled acting as a hostess in support of my husband's business empire and staying at home to supervise my daughter, " Georgina professed.

"Those are critical roles that it has become a privilege to fill," affirmed Yan. "Of course, most of our mothers are working outside of the home now."

Yan handed Georgina another flower.

"Exquisite," Yan exclaimed. "Many of the things that are in what is known as the female domain have to do with making our lives more gracious. It is lovely to have fresh flowers."

"I get them daily from the Farmers' market up near the entrance. I can take you there later if you like."

"I'd like that."

The two of them stepped back to scrutinize the final arrangements.

"I like to think of women's lives as having three stages," Yan continued. "In the first stage, as child and student, our various communities, families, and schools identify our potential strengths and provide sustenance for those strengths. In the second stage, we shunt to a sidetrack — by this, I mean in terms of our personal individuation — and assume other-focused roles as wives and mothers, householders, workers, and community activists. Then, in the third stage, we return to the task of nurturing the talents with which we were gifted at birth, but this time we have the responsibility to fulfill our promise."

The two women moved from room to room throughout the house, positioning the flowers; the pink sweetheart roses were for Elise's bedroom.

"Some of us have chosen to assume Circle membership only after maternal responsibilities have waned. You are familiar with Alexandra Lewis. She is married to a newspaper publisher in your city and has been instrumental in the success of his ambitions. But her children are grown and have their own demanding careers, so now she devotes herself to feminist issues through the Circle."

"Of course. She's a member of the board of trustees of the Art Gallery of Ontario, where I am involved; she serves as a board member for the Canadian National Ballet, and you always hear of some benefit that she is chairing. My husband says it's an automatic reflex to hand over a cheque for a couple of thousand dollars every time he sees her; she doesn't even have to ask," Georgina shivered as if a cold wind had swept through; she looked around to discover the source of the chill, and then continued. "Did you know that she is the granddaughter of the Tsar of Russia —the one that was murdered? I remember my mother taking me to see her at some official ceremony when I was a child. I thought she was the most beautiful princess I had ever seen."

"Alex, as you know, is still beautiful. And having the granddaughter of the Romanov Tsars of Russia has been a boon to the Goddess Circle. The Romanov family was introduced to hypnosis by the monk Rasputin. He was able to use hypnosis to control hemophilia from which members of their family suffered and oftentimes died. All the members of the family were trained in hypnosis and self-hypnosis from childhood. Alex is adept at it and has been quite diligent at passing that training along to various members of the Goddess Circle."

At this image, a half-smile of affection tugged at the corners of Yan's mouth.

"We have found that self-hypnosis trains the mind so that you can focus on whatever you choose rather than having a train of thought hijack you. Having that ability allows you to shift the TV channel: to move into the 'witness' position in order to observe your own thoughts and emotions without getting hooked by them." Seeing a look of bewilderment on Georgina's face, Yan patted her hand. "We'll have plenty of opportunities to discuss these practices in greater depth later on."

Chapter 7

As was her custom in the early afternoon, Alexandra Feodorovna Romanov Lewis was seated at an exquisite nineteenth-century Russian writing desk, enjoying the sensation of the movement of her arm as it gracefully looped through the finishing characters of the document laid out before her. The admiring recipients of Alex's missives had often been struck by how similar her handwriting was to calligraphy. She devoted her afternoons to chronicling the history and traditions of the Romanov family—her family. My grandchildren will appreciate the letters I am creating for them, but perhaps not until they are a bit older, she reassured herself. Alex had not yet been born when, during the Russian Revolution, her grandmother, the Grand Duchess Olga, sister to the Tsar, escaped Russia and the fate of her murdered brother and his family and fled to the safety of Britain. Alex had barely entered adolescence, however, when her life veered precipitously from the London social scene, and she moved with her grandmother to an obscure suburb outside of Toronto. In this quiet enclave, her family took up residence on a small farm where Alex attended the local public schools; her anonymity was disturbed only when the front pages of local and national press displayed images of Alex and her grandmother flanked by uniformed Russian military guards. They had been attending an audience with the Queen of England and Prince Phillip aboard their yacht, which had crossed the ocean, navigated the St. Lawrence seaway, and moored in Toronto harbor. Alex chuckled to remember the shocked recognition of her schoolmates as the meeting of royals attained national prominence. It was at that event that she met her future husband, Parker Lewis. With Alex at his side as "managing partner" in every phase of their complex lives, the couple had gone on to expand the business Parker had inherited from his father into a cable and broadcasting giant. At the same time, they became leaders of culture and philanthropy in their cosmopolitan city. Their twin daughters had graduated from prestigious universities and were now working in the family business—from the ground up, Parker liked to emphasize—before ascending to leadership roles. At this point in her life, Alex felt she was free from her maternal duties to pursue her dual passions: the preservation of the memories of the Royal Russian family and the restoration of women to their rightful place of power in the world.

Alex got up from her writing desk and stretched; her trim body reflected her daily exercise regimen. Long slender fingers pushed back the heavy waves of hair that had fallen forward during her writing. One narrow shock of silver hair highlighted the lush black mane that framed a pale white face punctuated by deeply stained, full lips. Black gull-wing eyebrows flew over mysterious slanted eyes. 'Ava Gardner

Eyes,' her many suitors had commented in days gone by, though she wondered how many people remembered her. Alex sighed.

"Cat, do you remember an actress by the name of Ava Gardner?" Alexandra asked the young woman who had just tiptoed into the room.

"No. Should I?" asked Catharine Sobieski. Alex, a patron of the Royal Conservatory of Music, had hosted the beautiful young violinist in her Toronto home several years earlier. Catharine had been one of seven upcoming prodigies invited to participate in a benefit for the Conservatory. Members of the Conservatory board had also brought in a young conductor, Marek Raczkowski, adjudged sufficiently powerful to coordinate this troupe of strong egos; herding cats was his characterization. In the ensuing years, Catharine had been a frequent visitor to the various Lewis residences, befriending Alex and her daughters, becoming like a daughter herself. Of course, Catharine and Marek had powerful and instant chemistry, and Catharine had left to follow him on his nomadic course as guest conductor. The two seemed to have parted ways. Alex may have played a hand in this. A powerful contributor to the Chautauqua Institution, Alex had spent summers at Chautauqua since childhood and was committed to what had become a unique center for education and the arts; she had encouraged members of the Performing Arts Committee to listen to

Catharine's competition videos in order for them to audition her in person. Now Catharine was here to perform as a soloist with the Chautauqua Symphony, not staying with Alex but rather staying as a guest of a famous local rock star. And the Circle had agreed to hold its summer gatherings here every other year. This summer was shaping up perfectly.

Chapter 8

Georgina returned from the kitchen with a chilled bottle of sparkling water, a plate of freshly sliced lime, and silver tongs carried on a tray hand-painted with a scene of the houses along Chautauqua's Lake Drive. "Lime?" she offered.

Yan nodded her assent.

"I suppose the Goddess Circle subscribes to Pagan beliefs," mused Georgina as she poured glasses of refreshing drinks for herself and her guest.

"I think of us more as a gathering of contemporary enlightened women. No orgies or spells," Yan clarified. "We chose to call ourselves a Circle to convey an egalitarian quality. It may be true that some in our Circle eschew the traditional religions, but for others, it can fit within their faith traditions. My sense of it is that our group may have issues with the way the mainstream religions treat women. Certainly, many of them haven't offered women equal opportunity in their power hierarchies — the word hierarchy itself is somewhat patriarchal, don't you think?

Other religions appear so concerned with the potential for sexuality that they keep girls and women captive or constrained: either not able to go out of the house unless accompanied by male relatives or segregated from males in other ways; again, sexuality is a chimera. Beyond sexist considerations, some religions function as longstanding tribal rationales for murder and genocide."

"Well, that seems obvious."

"On the other hand, as a psychoanalyst treating women, I am ambivalent about the sexual behavior of today's young women," continued Yan, lifting her glass and saluting Georgina with it. "I think that recent generations are still in the experimental stage as far as the sexual revolution is concerned. The ones I talk to don't believe their boyfriends will stick around if they don't allow intercourse, and then I worry that they don't value themselves enough to insist upon safe sex in order to protect against STDs or pregnancy. And other extremist religious groups use this to frighten their adherents. I cringe when I hear about terrorists filming our cute teenagers in revealing clothing on spring break and using those videos as propaganda to support the threat that this will happen to their daughters if the satanic Western civilization prevails."

At the mention of the behavior of girls of today, Georgina rose from where she was sitting and moved to a nearby marble-topped stand covered with photographs. She absentmindedly began to run her hand gently across the silver frame of a young woman clothed in a ballet tutu photographed at the apex of a graceful leap.

"That is having been said, the passion of the Goddess Circle has been the plight of girls and women across the globe. One of our members whom I've already mentioned, Dr. Ursula Andrews, does cross-cultural research on the mental and emotional issues of girls. She keeps the members of the Circle, as well as the public, up to date on these issues. She'll be lecturing here at Chautauqua, so you'll get to hear her."

"Does the Goddess Circle always meet here at Chautauqua?"

"Not always. About every other summer. The Goddess Circle is a movable tribute. We gather in different locations, on different occasions, and in each place, we identify powerful sites on which to hold our meetings. Inukshuk, constructed of stones found in the locale, are markers identifying the pathway to the ceremonial site situated on a locus of power at each meeting place."

"How do you determine whether a spot is powerful or not?" queried Georgina.

"There are various ways to identify a vortex — a place where energy is the most powerful. Goddess worship has historically taken place in these sacred places around the globe; it is interesting to note that these sites of Goddess worship are frequently co-opted by later religions Roman temples, Moorish mosques, and Christian churches. Chartres cathedral, for example, was built over an earlier site of Goddess Worship, and there is a tribute to this embedded in the floor: a mosaic depicting the Goddess symbol of the ovaries. There is one of our group who is particularly sensitive to the sacred, and I imagine it is exploring the institution right now to determine the exact site of the Chautauqua Goddess Circle."

***

Ursula Andrews fingered the strand of silver beads around her neck, a complement to her dark blue jeans, cowboy boots, and exquisite hand-woven shawl. Her unruly blond hair was caught back by a silver clip to reveal a set of heavy turquoise and silver earrings dangling beneath her riotous curls. The small, buff-colored cone between her thumb and index finger gave off a subtle whiff of cypress, the fragrant wood harvested from the conifers that thrived in the Hill Country of Texas. Selecting a small white box upon which was artistically scrawled 'Inn of the Anasazi,' Ursula scratched a match into flame and held it upright under the cone. She waited for the incense to ignite until, finally, the match was exhausted. She puckered her lips and blew on the ember, watching it flash and sustain until she was certain it would keep smoldering, releasing the smell of the cypress and restoring for Ursula the sense of home.

Ursula remembered her introduction to the Goddess Circle. She had met Dr. Yan Lin, a member of the academic sisterhood, at Wellspring and had invited her for a semester as scholar-in-residence to lecture at the University of Texas at Austin on 'The History of Goddess Worship'. Dr. Lin had arranged several opportunities for spirited debate — it seemed that any discussion among these passionate women was spirited— held in the comfortable home that a professor away on sabbatical had offered for her use during her residence. As a member of the Circle, Ursula chose Artemis, the Divine Huntress, as her ruling Goddess.

These days Ursula was in great demand as an expert on female mood across the lifespan. She was a consultant to the First Lady of the land, who had identified issues of girls and women as her top priority. In addition to giving presentations, she pursued research and publishing, taught, and supervised a number of promising female post-doctoral psychology fellows. Presently she was in need of a sabbatical. She had just completed teaching her graduate studies this past month and had also conducted a number of workshops across the nation. She was exhausted. Soon she would return to Austin and take off for a month-long retreat, hiking in the mountains and visiting the Native American reservations in the area to learn more about the creation of ceremonial implements, her ardent avocation. Only one more lecture to go here at Chautauqua and, of course, the Goddess Circle. Ursula gazed at the print of a single purple petunia she had brought with her, emblematic of her obsession with the artist Georgia O'Keefe; leaning back into her deeply plush chair, she inhaled the smell of cypress and drifted in her imagination into the Texas Hill Country.

Feeling calm and centered, Ursula left the house and headed to the south side of the institution, past the purple martin houses where inhabitants were busy lining nests for their young. As the member of the Circle with a strong affinity for the Goddess Artemis— Goddess of the moon and of the hunt, patron of the young — she had the most talent for the task of finding a powerful site within the Institution to hold the gathering and so she soon left the house in search of a vortex – a swirling center of energy. She walked along Lake Road, heading to the south side of the Institution, past the purple Martin houses where inhabitants were busy Lining nests for their young. She came upon a road leading up the cliff that overhung the lake. On the side of the lane, a vegetable garden had been dug into the slope of the hill. Nearing the garden, she could make out the yellow-orange of blossoming zucchini, the tender tops of promised carrots, and the lacy fringes of August's Beefsteak tomatoes. A high wire fence stood around the garden.

Another doomed attempt to prevent deer from getting into the garden and eating all the blossoms. Their favorite food. Good luck with that. Ursula shook her head at humankind's continuing efforts to control nature.

The 'Golden Hind', a rich honey-colored stag, was Ursula's Power Animal — a spiritual guide of aboriginal peoples. She had been introduced to the stag while on a distant shamanic journey in the kiva of the Anasazi, carved deep into the elevations of the soft limestone cliffs of Bandolier, New Mexico, a site sacred to the early Native Americans who had inhabited the area since the thirteen-century. Ursula had scaled the sheer cliffs, entered an ancient cave, and climbed down a rawhide ladder into the depths of the ritual space. There, a glowing fire burned hallucinogenic incense, drums and rattles beat a hypnotic rhythm, and a Chief of the nearby Pueblo tribe spelled a vision quest, a Shamanic journey. In a trance, Ursula saw herself racing down the Rio Grande, which was swollen with spring snow melt. She balanced on a wooden log. As the log rounded a bend in the river, there on the boulders, bracing against the vast rushing waters, was the magnificent eighteen-point star. The deer followed the still-dreaming Ursula into the placid pools of an estuary and was welcomed into a relationship: Power Animal and Goddess Avatar.

Crossing the Chautauqua Thunder Bridge, Ursula stopped for a moment to sit on a bench fashioned out of a log sliced cleanly in half. Her glance was drawn to the trunk of a nearby poplar tree that had been cut down to the height of about four feet. Moving over to look at the tree, she saw that the gash across the top of the trunk unmasked the tree's rings. Some were wide in celebration of years of plenty, others narrow, indicating years of drought when the tree had been too stressed to grow. All around her stood poplars of every size and age: some young and spindly, others older and more massive. The tallest of them towered over sixty feet. Like the cypress of her home state, poplars grew in clonal colonies — the root systems of which had been known to extend over one hundred and ten acres in size — and were natural manifestations that validated Ursula's beliefs about the spiritual realm. In clonal colonies, each tree was a shoot originating from the original maternal root, just as in the spiritual realm, each human being was an incarnated expression of the sacred energy of the Sacred Source. This would be the site for the Goddess Circle.

Excited, she stood. She felt the deeply cushioned surface beneath her feet. Following the wood chip path, she came upon a fork in the path. Choosing the spur to the right, she was led downhill toward the meandering brook that had traced a ravine through the panoply of trees. Her descent was aided by steps formed naturally by the roots of the poplars. Walking along the bank of the river, she came upon a fire circle concealed within the forest. Within the clearing was a large fire pit constructed of river stone, surrounded by benches much like the one she had sat upon earlier. This is where the Goddess Circle is to be held. She was certain.

The benches formed an inner and outer ring and were identified by bronze plaques engraved with the names of the Iroquois clans that had populated the area of northwestern New York State: Bear, Heron, Turtle. When she reached the seat of the Deer Clan, Ursula sat and waited expectantly.

Soon she noticed the breeze starting to freshen, rustling the branches above her. The air around her began to snap with electricity. She glimpsed the Golden Stag warily, watching her from the deep green of the nearby grove. The animal slipped into the glen, head with its ornate headdress and neck thrusting with each step. It stood still. Then, as before, the buck turned and looked at Ursula. Time was suspended as their eyes remained fused. An urgent message of impending jeopardy. Ursula's mind sought frantically for more specifics, but the Power Animal vanished as quickly and silently as he had appeared, leaving Ursula bewildered and uneasy. Clearly, the animal had communicated a sense of impending danger. Ursula had no idea what the menace might be.

Chapter 9

Walking through Bestor Plaza, Yan and Georgina passed the front gate of the Institution on their way to the red brick building that housed the farmer's market. The entrance area had been expanded to accommodate the visitor's center. The long, low building was festooned with hanging flower baskets with red geranium, yellow millefleurs, blue lobelia, and vinca vine cascading from dark moss bases.

"I'd love to get some gladioli for our Goddess Circle site consecration tomorrow. I've noticed they are a tradition here at Chautauqua," noted Yan.

They went through the flower sellers that rimmed the market, each exhibiting magnificent arrays of gladioli: reds and yellows, purples, and pinks. Once inside, they were offered a wide variety of food: fresh vegetables in season, herbs, and honey. There they caught up with Alex and Catharine making their purchases at a stall along a side wall featuring lavender in every form, including sweet-smelling pillows, large and small, along with soothing aromatherapy oils. Before Yan could make the introductions, Alex greeted Georgina warmly. They had met previously through their involvement with various cultural and philanthropic committees in Toronto.

Leaving the farmers' market, the women had to detour around the lines of people waiting to purchase entrance tickets that were sold for periods as long as the entire season or for as short a time as an individual evening's performance. More visitors were coming to Chautauqua every year, and on this particular day, the line for tickets stretched out into the parking area; a much younger group than might be typical waited to purchase tickets for that evening's concert

"Isn't it maddening? These people are so boisterous!" Alex, clearly annoyed by the intrusion on her gated community, whipped off her sunglasses and stared haughtily at the T-shirted throngs as if the glare from her eyes could cause them to vanish.

"I trust the security here is tight," Georgina murmured uneasily.

"They're Jonah Nash groupies," explained Catharine. "His band started here in Jamestown, and they often come back to perform. Jonah keeps a house on the grounds. He typically keeps a low profile and tries to maintain some privacy for himself and for his neighbors, but he doesn't seem to have succeeded this time. I imagine that the residents are not too happy with all these crowds. I'll be staying with him."

Yan glanced grimly in Alex's direction. The previous spring, Yan had been traveling in Hungary, and Alex had asked her to check in on Catharine, who was at the Budapest Spring Music Festival in the company of conductor Marek Raczkowski. As Alex had suspected, Catharine was involved in yet another fantasy love relationship. The older women were concerned that Catharine surrendered too much of herself in such "Codependent" liaisons. And now, here she was with Jonah Nash.

Alex waved at a slender man with curly, rather shaggy, dark hair who was over in a corner talking to the owner of one of the bread kiosks. He was wearing a faded green shirt and safari pants rumpled over hiking boots, carrying a knapsack filled with what looked like heavy books. Winding his way through the various stalls, he eventually arrived at their group.

"Looks like you carry your entire library with you," teased Yan reaching up to kiss the man on both cheeks.

"You know I get anxious when I'm separated from my books," came the reply.

"You know everyone here except for Georgina."

Putting his heavy backpack down to rest heavily against his shin, the man picked up Georgina's hand, kissed it, and said. "Surely we have met before."

"Rafi, you need a new pickup line."

"But it's true. I am certain we have been together before," repeated Rafael Betancourt cryptically, turning dancing emerald eyes up to look directly at Georgina.

"You must be mistaken," uttered Georgina, her smile fading. Mystified and somewhat uncomfortable, she folded both hands tightly in front of her and stepped back, glancing questioningly at Yan.

"This is Rafael Betancourt — Rafi. He's the logogram expert I spoke of earlier," explained Yan.

"I hope you will be coming this evening," said Alex.

"Have I ever missed an Alex party if I could help it?"

Rafi and Catharine commenced to regale them with an incident that happened at Alex's Chautauqua house party the previous New Year's Eve. In the winter, Chautauqua transformed into a ski resort. During the day, Alex arranged for her guests to travel in sleighs pulled by Percherons prancing, bells jingling as they pulled the blanketed guests through a snow-shaker winter wonderland, and at night, following a sumptuous meal, the tables were set up for bridge games. Yan knew from personal experience that these high-stakes card games were not for the faint of heart; those points could escalate quickly into thousands of dollars— Alex met with her compatriots all over the world to earn masters' competition points and, of course, to gamble. On this particular winter's eve, there had been so many visiting at Alex's house that Catharine, who arrived late due to a performance commitment, elected to stay at the nearby St. Elmo, an erstwhile Victorian hotel that, along with many of the other hotels on the grounds, had been rehabbed into exclusive condos. As it turned out, the bridge competition had paused only briefly to acknowledge the New Year —

champagne toasts and air kisses all round — then play had resumed immediately. By the time the group had finally broken up, Catharine, far and away from the winner, returned to St. Elmo to find it closed up tight. Exhausted, she returned to Alex's house, crawled under the Christmas tree that remained decorated for the Eastern Orthodox celebration, and fell fast asleep. When Alex rose the following morning, she was greeted by an unexpected present under the tree: her protégé.

"Ladies, I must take my leave. I have to get some work done this afternoon before the party starts," stated Rafi, slinging his backpack up over his shoulder, shifting it a couple of times until it settled comfortably. He sauntered off toward the work shacks up in the northwest corner of the Institution.

Just then, a trio of tall young men carrying large gym bags pushed heedlessly through the stream of humanity before heading off in the direction of the new athletic center located just past the entrance gate.

"That looks like the young man who brought my daughter's dog back."

Yan looked up sharply.

"They must be Teresa Bellamy's grandsons," said Alex. "But I don't know who the third one is. I heard that the boys and perhaps a couple of other members of the Harbridge rowing team were here for the summer training in preparation for a possible Olympic bid."

"Olympics! That's impressive," declared Catharine.

"I don't know about that," asserted Alex, the fine lines around her remarkable eyes deepening. "According to our family newspaper and the national media, the cousins, Eric and Miko, got themselves involved in some nasty business last year, and they didn't get to compete in the 'Head of The Charles Regatta" at Cambridge: an important event leading up to the Olympics."

"Nasty business?" Georgina inquired in a tight voice.

"Seems that the team threw a party where a woman, one of the strippers they had hired, got pretty savagely beaten. There were charges of assault and rape, and the case was dismissed but only after months of sensational headlines. The press had a feeding frenzy. Angelique, one of our fellow Goddesses, was the prosecuting attorney on the case. She'll be surprised to see those two here on the grounds."

"As I remember it, the charges were dismissed because the woman involved was deemed to be not credible as a witness, as so often happens in this type of case. The victim gets retraumatized by the legal process," added Yan.

"Speculation was that Teresa Bellamy walked in with a bag of money and made the trouble go away," explained Alex. "Angel almost lost her law license over the case. As a matter of fact, I think her boss did lose his law license."

"Angel?" queried Georgina.

"Yes. Angelique Beignet, the woman who is the lead facilitator for this Chautauqua Circle, is due to arrive any minute. Angel's the one who was involved in that Harbridge trial in Boston. Now she's just finishing up a murder trial, but she should be here soon."

"Murder. That sounds gruesome."

"Wherever Angel goes, murders happen."

***

Angelique Beignet had fought hard for everything she'd accomplished. Adopted from a New Orleans orphanage by Tulane graduate students who'd named her for the brooding look of her 'Creoles of Color' appearance-the French, Native American, and African American heritage of the original Louisiana settlers-as well as their favorite dessert, she accompanied them as they returned to their home town of Boston. Over the years, Angel's academic prowess and limitless memory earned her full scholarships through the best private, undergraduate, and, ultimately, Harvard Law School.

With the blessing of her adoptive parents, when she was eighteen, Angelique searched for and found her biological family. It was not the idyllic scenario of her childhood fantasy. Her mother was a migrant farm worker who'd given birth to thirteen children by unknown or unidentified male partners. 'Sperm donors,' her brother Rodrigo, the family rebel, called them. When the family did have a roof over their heads, it was frequently shared by others. It was not unusual for the children to have to fight off the aggressive sexual advances of transient male cohabitants. Because of this, she knew Rodrigo, the eldest of her remaining siblings, had developed a "phobia about intimacy" — Angelique couldn't imagine how it could have ended up any other way. Rodrigo had been taken under the wing of a reading coach at a school a group of volunteers had established for the children of itinerant laborers. Though he attended infrequently — when he felt he could leave his younger charges in the care of the next oldest sibling — he sped through all the schoolwork in the primitive school with its makeshift desks and donated textbooks that were ten years out of date had to offer and had won a scholarship to the University of New Mexico in Albuquerque. Angelique had connected her newfound family with social services in the community and brought Rodrigo to live with her in Boston. Various of her colleagues at Harvard provided the theory and perspective to begin to come to grips with the emotional injuries he had sustained in the chaotic underworld of his origins.

Angel's position as Assistant DA offered her a vehicle through which she could best aid those individuals not lucky enough to have been found by powerful rescuers. Not like some others who had been born on third base yet believed they had hit a triple, she mused. But this past year as Assistant District Attorney in the Special Victims Unit had been exhausting. All Public Departments were underfunded; the staff was overcommitted and overwhelmed. In order to successfully prosecute her cases, Angelique spent her free time joining forces with the investigating detectives, helping them collect enough evidence to provide the medical examiner with the relevant information needed to declare deaths due to homicide rather than by unknown cause. Perpetrators soon came to fear the wrath of the avenging angel.

Chapter 10

The earth was uneven beneath his feet as he pounded along the grassy knoll next to the lakeshore, relishing the coil and release of leg muscle. He reveled in the responsiveness of his well-trained athlete's body, lungs pulling in oxygen, heart-pumping fuel throughout his system. From the children's beach, he could hear youngsters newly released from the bonds of school. Many families had already arrived, eager to get there right at the opening of the season. Women in brightly colored bathing suits wriggled pedicured toes in the white sand. Others with bodies honed by expensive personal trainers stood thigh-deep in the water as they supervised nearby children building elaborate sandcastles replete with moats and waterways. One of the children churning through the shallow water just beyond the edge of the beach called out, "Mommy!" in alarm; all chatter ceased, and every woman's head turned until, reassured that all was well, they resumed their conversations.

He knew that the older children were down at the south end attending camp or at the youth club engaged in tennis or sailing lessons. Women and children, fathers absent, came to the Chautauqua Institution, glorying in its long-deserved reputation for safety, bicycles casually left wherever they fell, immune from theft.

These women live in a bubble, sure of their ability to turn men into salivating supplicants, paychecks financing a life of leisure in return for promises of sex and progeny. Someone needs to take these women down a peg or two.

The man's thoughts continued to race as his mind flashed back again and again to each indignity he had suffered at the hands of a woman. There was a time when he and his fellow rowers were celebrating a particularly sweet victory. There were "adult dancers" at the after-meet party. One of the strippers was high. She teetered on stiletto heels, placing one hand on an extended hip. On the other hand, she flipped her hair back in a caricature of the women in the porno flicks she devoured. She had ambitions. She wasn't just going to strip for college punks; she was going to be a star.

"Come to momma, baby," she slurred, holding open the door to the room adjoining the party room.

Losing her battle for balance, she reached out and pressed her hand against the wall, another futile attempt to steady herself.

"Shut up, you disgusting bitch," he growled as he slipped into the bedroom. He began pacing in agitation, running his fingers through his close-cropped hair.

"Come on, baby. Momma loves you." she crooned. Her pancake makeup was melting though the room itself was cool. She wobbled forward and pounced on him, trying to press her body against his. Entwined, they rocketed to the middle of the room in a grotesque embrace until he twisted away and knocked her hand away from his arm. Undeterred, she continued to reach for him and puckered her thickly coated red lips, blowing air kisses in his direction. "Momma loves you. Come to Momma," she repeated.

He erupted. The cords stood out on his neck; the blood beating in his ears and his eyes suffused with the exultancy of power. He began to punch her in the face, over and over, as if to smash the smirking smile. There was a dull, crunching sound as his fist splintered her nose. The stripper fell backward against the bureau, crying out as she landed heavily.

"No! Don't burn my face," screamed the girl, shivering with fear. She lifted her arms, a forlorn attempt to shield herself as the man drew a blow torch from his backpack.

Remembering himself, he ran harder, trying to fight off these dark thoughts, knowing all too well where these fantasies had led in the past.

His brain remained gripped by vague rage as he raced past the Athenaeum, venerable dowager queen of lakeside hotels, with her wraparound porch strewn with wicker rockers and Victorian wooden column, her twin dark mahogany Baroque staircases sweeping up to the porch from the lush lawn bowling greens below; past the replica of the Holy Land extending across the hillock next to the Belltower Point; and turned onto the pathway leading past the boathouses toward North Lake Drive, where the well-groomed lawns gave way to a strip of white sand. It was some time before he sensed the arrival of late afternoon in the coolness of the onshore breeze that failed to stir his wiry dark-blond hair. Only then was he finally able to wrench his mind from past scenes of stimulating torture and focus on a vision of warrior scouts running easily along with this land, spreading alarms to gathered forces. The counselors at the psychiatric ward had encouraged him to distract his mind from the fantasies of warpath bloodletting that obsessed him — scraping scalps off enemies or unsheathing a razor-sharp knife to inflict the agony of 1,000 cuts on prisoners-of-war — and instead to imagine that he was a runner for tribal bands of old and ground himself by concentrating on the sensation of his feet slamming against the earth as he sped through the forests. Since he had left treatment, however, the motivation to redirect his thoughts had grown weaker and weaker. He knew he couldn't stand to be incarcerated again, as had happened after his scaredy-cat girlfriend had overreacted to his boxcutter virtuosity, but lately, the deterrent of that memory didn't seem sufficient to keep his daydreams in check.

Chapter 11

The limousine pulled up in front of the house. Georgina, who had spent the past hour peering anxiously out of the window, rushed out on the porch. She watched as the driver opened the door, and her daughter, Elise, swept gracefully from the limo and glanced up at her waiting mother. A simply styled gloss of sable hair parted to reveal a pale cameo face, broad, intelligent forehead, straight nose, and a cupid's bow lips, highlighted by a dab of gloss.

"Sweetie, how good to have you home." Georgina enveloped her daughter in a fierce hug. She gazed tenderly upon the deep brown eyes edged with a lush fanlike sweep of lashes; pearly skin so translucent it betrayed the pulse of a heartbeat.

"Let's get you settled."

Georgina led the way around the Chautauqua home bequeathed to her by her aunt, her mother's sister, who had raised her after her own mother had died of cancer when Georgina was eight years old. Aunt Aurelia — this name was too difficult for children to say and so she had become affectionately known to all as 'Lola' — had never married and had spent every summer of her later years here at Chautauqua. The living room in which they stood had been designed to her Aunt's taste, the patterns floral and feminine. In front of the floor-to-ceiling windows were a chintz settee and two Queen Anne wing chairs in soft pastel plaids. Table and floor lamps had been strategically placed so that the lighting was soft; Georgina remembered that Aunt Lola disliked overhead lighting, believing it spoiled the atmosphere necessary for the confidential conversation she enjoyed. Watercolors and pastels of the Chautauqua region adorned the walls; one of Georgina's favorites was of a sailing regatta just off the Belltower Point. Positioned at the center of the living room was a wormy chestnut cabinet with paned leaded-glass doors inside of which was displayed a collection of Matryoshka dolls. The nested dolls had been meticulously painted in a costume representative of several of the countries of the world.

"When I see these dolls, I think of the stories you've told me about grandma."

"This is the original set of dolls brought by my grandmother when she sailed across the Atlantic Ocean," said Georgina, pointing to one set of dolls prominently displayed in the center of the cabinet. Surrounding the original set of nested dolls were several more sets, a vast collection purchased in memory of her sister, Georgina's mother, during her aunt's extensive travels.

"My grandmother was expecting to arrive in a country where the streets were strewn with golden nuggets. But it was 1929 when she and her parents came, and the Great Depression that they had hoped to have left behind in Europe was dawning in North America. Those were desperate times. I've often wondered if my mother's death at such a young age was due to those difficult days."

Georgina escorted Elise from the main part of the house into the suite situated on the south side of the house. "I thought the light here would be better for your painting," she said.

The bed-sitting room was decorated in pale mauves and pinks, reminiscent of Elise's rooms in their Toronto home; diaphanous curtains draped the four-poster bed. Elise flung open the French doors that led from her bed-sitting room onto the perennial garden cultivated by her great-aunt Aurelia. The house was shaped in a U, and Elise could see her mother's own suite of rooms across the gardens.

"This is heavenly," whispered Elise as she sunk into the wicker chaise lounge comfortably upholstered in fabric to match the rest of her suite. Georgina perched beside her and put her arm around her shoulder.

"I want to assure you that, whatever is going on between dad and me, we both love you, and Chautauqua is still your home," said Georgina, a slight tremor in her voice.

Georgina could feel Elise's shoulders stiffen beneath her hands a moment before her daughter shifted back out of her embrace, a solemn, almost frozen look on her face.

"Mom, I don't want to talk about you and dad," said Elise, her face ashen. "It's too painful."

At the suggestion of Elise's treatment team, Georgina and her husband, Owen, had visited Elise at her addiction treatment center during 'family week.' There, in the presence of Elise's counselor, they disclosed that the two of them had decided upon a trial separation. Thinking back, Georgina was not convinced this had been the best way to handle a delicate situation, and she was sorry that there had not been an opportunity for more discussion.

"You are absolutely right," said Georgina with a nod. "You need and deserve a loving relationship with each of your parents, even if they can't manage to get along with each other. If anything I say seems designed to alienate you from your father, I want you to object right away."

"I know that at some point, we need to talk more about you and dad separating, but not just now," said Elise sharply. "I'm not ready yet."

"Of course," said Georgina, trying unsuccessfully to plumb the depths of Elise's feelings. "You let me know when it is good for you. I'm aware that you're planning to intern with the fashion photography studios in New York, and I'm just glad that we'll get to spend this time together before you leave." Elise was entering her senior year at college, but she would have some classes to make up before she could graduate.

Georgina got up and went to the delicate feminine desk over by the French windows.

"I know you will love it here, as I did when I was a child." Georgina retrieved the Chautauqua Special Studies pamphlets and brought them over to Elise. "There are several workshops — I know you'll want to go to this writing workshop which starts in about an hour. Other ones are listed here in the Catalogue: there's opera and theater and the symphony, and you already know about the ballet." Georgina stopped, suddenly stricken. Elise's life revolved around the dance company, but the team at the treatment center had cautioned that the competitive atmosphere was a major relapse trigger for Elise's drug addiction. Elise would have to stay away from dance for a long while, a lifetime in the youthful world of ballet.

"It's okay, mom," said Elise, regaining her composure. "I'll just put down my things and go to the workshop right away. I can get settled in later."

"Fair enough. 'Chautauqua Rules' are in order here. That means that we are like roommates: each person decides what they would like to do, and if it is okay for the other person to come along, they can check to see if they are welcome to do so, but no one is obligated to do or agree to anything."

"Strong boundaries were emphasized in treatment; good rules for families everywhere," recited Elise, her tone resolute.

"By the way, where is Princess? I thought she'd be greeting me at the door."

"She's probably where she always is this time of day, on her solar circuit out the back Catching the sun's rays."

Mother and daughter hastened through the house. When they arrived at the rear patio, Princess wasn't there. She was gone.

"Princess tends to wander here. That dog likes me well enough, but I think she goes off looking for you. Just a little while ago, a young man found her and brought her back." Georgina related awkwardly.

"Mother!" Elise sounded alarmed. "Did he say anything? Did he say where he found her? Who was he?"

"No worries. Luckily, Chautauqua is so safe that when Princess gets out, people just pick her up and take her to the sheriff's office," reassured Georgina. "You go off to your workshop, and I'll go over to the Sheriff's office to get her. The sheriff has been most accommodating; often, he'll just bring her back home right away unless he's too busy."

"The Sheriff of Chautauqua is too busy. Really?"

Chapter 12

Elise walked quickly through the grounds to the Alumni Hall, which housed the Center for the Literary Arts, at the far end of the institution across the green from the Hall of Philosophy. The writing workshop scheduled for today was the one activity she was looking forward to. At the treatment center, the clinical staff had suggested daily journaling, and Elise had discovered that she loved it; it gave her something to consume her attention now that she could no longer dance. Standing in front of the graceful building with the curving porch and conversation-inviting wicker furniture arrangements, she hurried up the steps. As she pushed open the screen door, she tripped over the step leading into the hall. She felt strong arms catch her around her ribs. She felt heat emanating from the tall frame of her rescuer's body through the thin fabric of her linen sundress. It pierced her heart like lightning. Half dragging her over to the wicker chair, the man guided her into the deep cushions. The muscles of his thighs bulged as he knelt before her and gently lifted her ankle. The wiry crew-cut of his dark-blond head bowed before her. Once again, the blast of energy from his calloused hands sent a rush up to her legs and into her body. She struggled to keep her composure as he lifted his head. She found herself gazing into bottomless azure pools.

Eric held her for a moment, entranced by the scent of her hair — his mother's favorite perfume, L'Air du Temps? As he lifted his head, Elise found herself drowning in bottomless azure pools.

Elise struggled to free herself … brushing herself off and backing away to establish a safe boundary between them.

"You may have sprained your ankle," said Eric. "Come. Sit over here for a moment, and let's see what's going on."

"Looks like it's swelling. You may have sprained your ankle," said Eric. "Stay here for a moment, and I'll go get you a bag of peas."

"A bag of peas?" scoffed Elise.

"Sure. I always keep frozen vegetables around … not to cook, but to reduce inflammation. And peas are the best. They mold themselves to your body," explained Eric, color rising in his cheeks. "I use them all the time. Twenty minutes on, twenty off."

"I'm fine. I can take care of myself, thank you," said Elise sitting back in her chair. "I'm a dancer. I've had plenty of injuries."

"You're a dancer," said Eric, sounding incredulous. "You had me fooled with that graceful entrance."

"Well, actually, I don't dance, not anymore," murmured Elise looking grim. "But you must be a jock."

"Rowing."

"A rower." Elise shook her head. "And don't tell me you're here for the writing workshop."

"Well, actually," he parroted. "I plan to go into law. As a law clerk, I will need to review legal writings, abstract the relevant facts, and synthesize the information. My writing will have to be excellent to compete for clerkships with some of the more demanding judges."

"Aha, you're a perfectionist," concluded Elise.

"You make a lot of assumptions," said Eric, drawing back to scrutinize Elise more closely.

"Well, I'm interested in writing fiction. I see it as alchemical: transforming the dross of everyday life into gold."

"I've always found fiction writers to be voyeuristic, rather like vampires sucking the life blood of others to animate their pages."

Then there is nothing about me he will find attractive, Elise thought wryly.

Chapter 13

Carrying the box lunch of grilled vegetable salad he'd purchased at the Farmer's Market, Rafael walked to the 'practice shack' at the northwest quadrant of the Institution that had been assigned for his use by the Education and Spirituality Department. Small wooden cabins had been built for the use of artists-in-residence. Rafael had made sure to arrange for a shack as far as possible from the musicians.

He enjoyed working later in the afternoon when others might be preparing for dinner, and the area was deserted. Arriving in front of his cabin, he pushed open the door that had been left slightly ajar and found himself in a very sparse room. A chair and a desk stood by the window, a floor lamp beside them. He'd be making use of the lamp, he thought, since the work of finishing his latest book on hieroglyphics would likely take him far into the night. He was grateful to have this time to concentrate on the book so soon after his archeological group had uncovered new tombs at a dig in Israel containing a significant amount of pottery-bearing inscriptions. Like the Dead Sea Scrolls, he enthused silently. He wanted to process this new information while it was still fresh in his mind.

Paging through the books he gently had dislodged from his backpack, Rafi thought back on his encounter with Alex and the others at the farmers' market. It seemed clear from

Yan's introduction that his hieroglyphics' expertise had been a topic of conversation, and he wondered what that was all about. He was perplexed by his encounter with Georgina. It had felt as if she were an old friend. Could it be that the Hindus had it right after all: had he known Georgina in a previous incarnation? He chuckled to remember her discomfort at his reaction to her. She seemed somewhat taken aback, although she had responded with practiced politeness. Despite her facade of cordiality, he sensed intense pain resting just beneath the surface of her pleasantries and found himself wondering about the source of her pain.

Come on. You promised yourself a hiatus from that worn-out pattern of pursuing enigmatic women who turn out to be ice princesses. He scolded himself back to the task at hand. There are more than enough mysteries to decipher in your work, he resolved once more. It was much less dangerous to deal with material facts than with messy human relationships.

A grating, fingernails-on-the-blackboard squeal punctured his focus. And then it repeated. Annoyed to be interrupted despite his careful planning — it had been more difficult than he imagined to arrange for a work shed that was at some remove from the cacophony of the many musicians who used the shacks for practice— he scraped his chair around to the window and peered out. He guessed that the clatter was coming from across a narrow green space where large iron sheets hung on a heavy wire and could be pulled across to protect the wooden buildings from the raging fires of the kilns. Looking about to see who might be causing the racket, he caught sight of a tall figure screwing what looked like some type of lock to the door of his practice shack. At first, Rafi was puzzled; the cabins were not to be padlocked. Looks like somebody's trust issues aren't even put to rest in this safe enclave, he thought, shaking his head. Then, curiosity somewhat abated, he sternly redirected himself to his work.

Chapter 14

Elise limped slowly through the Institution on her way home from the writing workshop. She was keeping an eye out for Brynn, the young woman who now occupied the position Elise held before she went away: prima ballerina for the Ontario Ballet School, the ballet-in-residence for the summer season at Chautauqua. Brynn had always been jealous of her. One time she came to Elise's home, terribly upset, and accused Elise of telling others that she, Brynn, would never make prima ballerina and would be lucky to dance in the corps de ballet. This, of course, was not true. Elise hoped that they could get along better now that Brynn was the star and Elise was out. Schadenfreude. Elise felt more comfortable out of the spotlight; the nail that stuck out was most likely to get hammered. Mostly she had pursued ballet for her mother. It was one of the very few things that made her smile.

Elise acknowledged passers-by with a 'good afternoon' on her travels — everyone appeared comfortable peering at her wounded ankle as they passed — and saw teenagers laughing as they splashed in the water and jumped off the docks jutting out from shore or set sail from the marina. Out on the water, cigarette boats raced past water skiers, who were forced to hang on for dear life as the wake hit them.

When she arrived at the ballet residence, she saw other dancers, but not Brynn. The housemother pointed to Brynn's room at the back and told her she could wait there. Entering the room, Elise took advantage of the opportunity to visit the bathroom. There, casually strewn on the counter for any observer to see, were the accouterments of a bulimic: laxatives and Kaopectate — for when the anorexia failed, as well as ballerina necessities: various prescription bottles full of Ritalin and Vicodin, instant energy and pain reliever in a bottle. Better living through chemistry. It was not that long ago that Elise herself had been totally ignorant of the lethality of the combination and would have been surprised to hear that such an assortment of pills might appear unusual to the everyday observer. It certainly was not unusual in the world of dance. Elise had been the acclaimed prima ballerina in the ballet school until she had fallen victim to her own perfectionist tendencies. Then, to maintain her energy and her thinness, she gradually upped her use of Ritalin — any fool could memorize the internet list of symptoms for Attention Deficit Disorder and repeat them to a prescribing physician. She also abused her Synthroid, prescribed for low-functioning thyroid, but which also energized her and enhanced weight loss. She had several prescriptions finagled from multiple physicians to manage pain — Vicodin and Oxides had been her favorites — that became her constant companion as she pushed her body to incredible limits. Now

Elise was face-to-face with the evidence that Brynn, too, was using the stimulant and pain medications that had enslaved Elise.

Elise returned to the bedroom just as Brynn arrived, out of breath from a workout. She was a slight young woman with small bones who appeared younger than her nineteen years. Elise was aware that low body fat prevented menstruation; she wondered if Brynn's girlish appearance meant that she did not have regular periods.

When she first arrived, Brynn didn't notice Elise in the far corner of the room. She moved toward the closet, arms gliding gracefully, feet pointed outward in perpetual first position. She opened the closet door and pulled out a rucksack. Suddenly, her head swung around, and she became aware of Elise's presence. She quickly hid the small bottle she had pulled from the sack behind her back.

"What are you doing rummaging through my rooms," she accused as she opened a drawer and deposited the container underneath some clothing.

"I didn't mean to invade your privacy," maintained Elise. "I came looking for you, and the housemother told me to wait in your room."

"These aren't drugs; they're prescriptions that the ballet school doctor has ordered for me," said Brynn, affecting an attitude of studied nonchalance. She put away the rest of the bottles of pills and firmly closed the medicine cabinet.

"You look like you could use some of these pills yourself," she said, gesturing to Elise's damaged ankle.

"I know all about the ballet school doctor," said Elise. "I just got back from treatment for all the 'prescriptions' he gave me, remember?"

"Well, you got addicted. I'm not that weak!" Brynn shot Elise an exasperated look as she threw up the bedcovers and straightened up some of the clothing strewn around the room.

"Everyone is 'that weak'," explained Elise. "When you use these medications long enough, your body grows tolerant to it. Your body will need more and more of the medication to have the same effect. Use more and more medication too often, for too long, and you become addicted. It's a natural process."

"Please, no more lectures," Brynn insisted, covering her ears. "Now that you have decided you don't want to use the medications properly prescribed by physicians, you think everyone needs to get off them. I'm not an addict; I can handle these."

"Why don't you come to a 12 STEP meeting with me?" suggested Elise. "You may be pleasantly surprised. There is an open meeting anyone can attend. You do not have to declare that you're an addict."

"I'll think about it," replied Brynn, her tone exasperated, as she whirled around to confront Elise.

"I truly am glad to be here with you," declared Elise warmly, moving over to hold both of Brynn's hands and look straight into her eyes. "I hear that you have the lead in the ballet. I can't wait to see you."

"Why don't you come to rehearsal at the Amp?" invited Brynn, relieved that someone else had told Elise that she had assumed her role in the dance company. "You'll get to see everyone again."

"I'll think about it." Elise winked, melting the tension that had risen between them. "Just kidding. I'd love to come and see everyone; I've missed them."

Chapter 15

Chester was waiting to meet them as Eric rowed his scull into the marina, followed at a distance by a lackadaisical Miko. Brushing off Chester's offer of help, Eric lifted his small boat out of the water and turned it over on the dock.

"This isn't exactly what the coach had in mind when he told us to practice this summer," Eric called to Miko.

"But I am practicing," replied Miko, exaggerating the laziness of his strokes.

Rowing for a Division I school was no simple task: it required practice as well as daily four-hour workouts throughout the school year. This meant that even throughout the summer off-season, they were to get up at 5:00 am to hit the gym for a rigorous workout schedule. Unlike Eric, Miko often blew off a lot of the practice and workout requirements, especially in the summertime. This past year the Harbridge rowing season had been ruined by the scandal. Not only the Bellamies but the entire team had been at the party where an adult dancer had claimed to be assaulted. The coach had gone ballistic. After that disruption, each of them had vowed that next year they would rule all the way to the Olympics; that was the plan, but everyone had to do their part.

Chester walked to the end of the dock, grabbed the rope attached to Miko's boat, offered him a hand, and then pulled the boat out of the water. He turned it over on the dock and began to secure it, taking a turn around the ring attached to the dock, putting the working end diagonally up and then across the standing part, then another turn, tuck, and slipping it beneath the diagonal so that the finished knot looks like an N.

"Maybe the competition committee of the US National Team would allow you your own personal valet," scoffed Eric.

Chester Albrecht was similar in appearance to the two Bellamy cousins: tall, with the same wiry dark-blond hair and athletic build. His clothes also looked the same — the only way to tell the social status of young people these days was by glancing at their watches and shoes, according to Mrs. Bellamy. She had given Chester a gold Rolex for his academic achievement, and Miko had passed along his handmade Italian leather shoes, cast off after two weeks' wear. But, still, Chester was not a blood relative. He was the son of a servant, Mrs. Bellamy's former housekeeper. His attendance at Harbridge was dependent upon Mrs. Bellamy's largesse as well as upon an academic scholarship: pre-med, which meant that a lot of work had to go into academics, including critical chemistry labs; and he made sure that he was available to do whatever the two Bellamy cousins needed him to do, Miko especially. Miko helped Chester out a lot, not just by giving him shoes and other hand-me-downs.

Miko and Chester had gotten closer. Eric was feeling betrayed; his special relationship with his cousin had been usurped.

Eric figured that Miko's behavior was probably less due to altruism than to ulterior motives: Miko demands significant paybacks. The friendship among the three of them had been more strained since the Harbridge incident. Miko and Chester had reported they were together during the time the assault had occurred, with the result that they each had an alibi. Eric was the odd man out, unprotected, without an alibi during the sexual assault case. Miko was counting on grandmother pulling strings and getting them off as she always did. That is exactly what did happen.

Soon Chester left the two of them to go to the studio on the grounds and put some final touches on his sculptures in preparation for his upcoming one-man show. Mrs. Bellamy had suggested that she sponsor an exhibition for him to raise money for his clay sculptures to be cast into bronze at the Santa Fe, New Mexico, foundry — a process that was too expensive for him even to have imagined. He was not one to miss many such opportunities.

"Hey coz, c'mon, let's go to the Amp," Miko urged, kicking Eric's duffel to one side.

"Cut it out, man. You don't do anything the proper way." Eric picked up his duffel and started to stow it away properly.

"I mean it, dude. Let's go. Herd Mentality is playing at the Amphitheater tonight, and the roadies say Jonah is sure to meet with the guys this afternoon for a sound check. I need to be there to let him know he can count on me to do whatever he needs. I'll close the deal at the party. An offer he can't refuse." Miko bowed with a deep flourish.

"You and your crazy schemes. I have to finish up here," Eric said brusquely.

"Nothing is as important as this. I've been talking to Cody, the guy who is filming a documentary about him and the band." Miko rubbed his fingers together, indicating that some money had changed hands. "I promised to help him get some investors to distribute his movie, and he promised to introduce me to Jonah Nash. According to the word on the street, Jonah is planning to break up the band and go out on his own. I'll bet you a thousand dollars that I can get Jonah to agree to let me manage his solo career."

"You are out of your mind once again. And, as usual, you are nothing but hot air."

"It's as good as a done man. We'll get Glammy to throw one of her benefits and raise money for the documentary guy," Miko stated with a confident nod and continued to elaborate his scheme. 'We'll go meet them this afternoon and then get an invite backstage to the after-show party. I'm the guy who's going to represent him and negotiate his solo deals. Once I sign him, I'll take that contract as my entrée to

EMG — major players, agents for all the biggest stars. That's my ticket to multi-million-dollar talent management.``

"I'm crazy for getting involved in another one of your harebrained schemes."

"You are getting to be a real pain; all work and no play."

"Well, I guess I can break training for one night. A little fun won't hurt," said Eric thinking that this might be an opportunity to restore their earlier closeness.

"Right on, coz. Come watch the master at work." Miko placed his arm around Eric's shoulders. "You know where Jonah's house is here at Chautauqua, down on the south side. It's going to be a blowout party. Lots of great music. Lots of booze and every imaginable mood-altering substance. Lots of sweet babes. It'll be a blast. Totally."

Eric turned to Miko and tried one more time to get him to understand his concerns about Chester.

"I know you and Grandmother think that Chester's cool, but he seems moody and evasive to me. What looks like a reserve to you may be more like narcissistic self-absorption."

"Give the guy a break. He appreciates everything that Glammy has done for him and is just trying to show it."

"Unlike the two of us, I guess."

"If the shoe fits."

"Well, I don't want him doing any favors for me. I don't want to have to owe him anything. My guess is that you are up to your old tricks, getting Chester indebted to you so that you can cash in your chits when you need to."

"Moi? I'm crushed that you would be so cynical, coz," said Miko, playfully putting Eric in a headlock as the two started to scuffle, trying to push each other into the lake. Eric shrugged out of Miko's hold and punched him teasingly on the shoulder; for a moment, they wrestled like overgrown lion cubs. A tiny black poodle, stick in her mouth, skittered up and began jumping up on Eric's legs, eager to play. Eric started to throw the stick for her so that she would immediately fetch it for him to throw again.

"Hey man, let's go" said Miko. "I don't want to miss the sound check."

"Okay," said Eric, throwing the stick one last time.

Laughing, the two of them clattered across the dock and sped off, racing along the edge of the lake and, without breaking stride, running up the hill toward the Amphitheater.

Chapter 16

As usual, the sheriff seemed glad to see her, his office warm and welcoming. Residents would stop by to pass the time and help themselves to ginger snaps, and the herbal tea kept freshly brewed by the ladies of the Institution out of concern for Sheriff Tom Cahill's blood pressure — caffeine was not to be tolerated. Princess, along with other neighborhood dogs, was a frequent visitor there, and home-baked organic dog biscuits were kept in a covered glass jar on the serving table. On this day, however, Princess was not in evidence.

"She's probably followed somebody home, and they haven't gotten around to bringing her in yet," Sheriff Cahill reassured her. "I'll come by and drop her off when she shows up. Will you be around?"

"Either I or Princess' own true love, my daughter Elise, will be there," Georgina said with a sigh. "I am but an inadequate and certainly less desirable caretaker while my daughter is away."

"Well, the Institution is a secure sanctuary." Sheriff Tom was emphatic. "Just the other day, a fella was telling me that when his son carelessly left his bike at the central plaza, he wasn't worried for a minute. He found it the next day just where he left it". It was not unusual for visitors to express their relief at coming upon such an oasis in a world that, for too many, had become dangerous and alien. Sheriff Cahill knew that world too well. For many years before his early retirement, he'd been a member of the FBI Behavioral Analysis Unit. He massaged the back of his neck as he reflected on his years in that culture. Even thinking about it makes my neck stiffen, he thought, kicking back in his recliner and biting into a double chocolate chip cookie, baked fresh less than an hour ago.

On her way back from the sheriff's office, Georgina took a shortcut. She passed tall grasses that had grown up on either side of the dirt passage behind the Gleason boathouse. I'll bet the youngsters have had cookouts down here, Georgina thought as a pungent smell reached her. A fire pit lay ahead of her, and as she approached, she saw smoke rising from it. The pit was about five feet in diameter, ringed by substantial gray bricks stacked two feet high. In the center was a bed of live coals, charred remains of pieces of driftwood, and other detritus that had washed up on the shore.

How irresponsible to leave a fire still smoldering, she thought. Then her eyes widened. For a second, Georgina's mind refused to process the scene before her. Amid the embers was a skeleton-like branch; beside the smoldering branch was what appeared to be a small animal. At first, it looked as if someone had thrown the carcass of a rabbit onto the embers. But the hind legs aren't those of a rabbit,

Georgina thought. She bent forward to get a closer look, and her hand flew to her mouth as she muffled a scream. The rhinestone collar identified the tiny smoldering body as that of Princess. Georgina grabbed the collar, burning her hand without feeling it. She searched for an opening in the trees and raced down the path, not knowing where she was headed except that it was away from that terrible vision.

SECTION II

Chapter 17

Alex arrived at Yan's residence prior to attending the consecration of the Chautauqua Goddess Circle Site to find her in the medicinal herb garden at the side of the house.

"This garden pulses with energy," Alex exclaimed as she and Yan walked along the crushed terra-cotta pathway leading to the garden. "I can feel it as well as smell it."

The garden had been cultivated by the woman, Laura, who had lent Yan her Chautauqua residence for the duration of her stay. Laura was a long-time admirer and a frequent visitor to the Women's Retreat Center, where Yan and the other women taught. The Chautauqua Institution had an active Garden Club whose members had become interested in herbs used for healing and pain management during the Civil War, and Laura was the guiding energy behind the study of those herbs at the Institution. The Club's central garden was behind the Smith-Wilkes Hall and featured many species, but Laura grew additional variants in her home garden. Yan was particularly interested to see what similarities these herbs had with those of the Native Americans of the west coast that she was currently studying. She was aware that the many everyday drugs we take for granted had been identified and put to use hundreds of thousands of years ago.

Alex breathed in the fragrance of the aromatic plants and exhaled deeply. "There is nothing more evocative than scent."

The garden was laid as a circle, the ancient symbol of eternity, with four quadrants separated by pathways. A lavender hedge limned the growing space. Medicinal herbs were grouped together according to the ailments treated: for sedative use, chamomile, valerian, and passion flower; for respiratory issues: hyssop, Catnip, and yarrow; the opium poppy was good as an anesthetic, and wormwood and marigold helped the digestion.

"Do I remember correctly that it was the descendant of an African American slave who helped Chautauquans develop these gardens," said Alex peering at the small labels that identified each plant. I know some of the basics that aspirin comes from the bark of the willow tree, for example." She gestured to the tree at the corner of the enclosure. "And be careful; over there are psychotropics and more dangerous herbs: oleander, nightshade, monkshood, and Datura innoxia.

"For hundreds of years, knowledge of herbal medicine was passed down orally from generation to generation," explained Yan. "Sadly, much knowledge was lost during the dark ages. Female healers were persecuted and murdered as witches. Wisdom regarding herbs and healing was collected from the Greeks, Egyptians, and Romans by these women, but it disappeared when so many of them were burned at stake," Yan remarked in a tight voice, her eyes fixed on something far away. This was among the women's issues topics she was teaching at the invitation of Ursula at the University of Texas. "Some estimated that upward of seven million women—healers of earlier times—had been murdered."

As they moved back to the house, Alex placed her arm around Yan's shoulder, "Luckily, herbal medicine didn't die out in the East. Asian practitioners like you have been able to teach others as well."

"It's true. I am so lucky that my mother and aunts were there to teach me."

"Speaking of the generations, will your son be joining you at Chautauqua this season?"

"No. Jack is happy and busy immersed in his work as photographer, writer, and musician." She paused for a moment, then laughed bitterly. "Isn't it ironic that if we do a good job as a mother, our children feel free to leave us for their own absorbing lives?"

"That is absolutely appropriate." nodded Alex. "But it means that we are left alone."

"Mostly now, I am content being alone," Yan continued as if reading her thoughts. "I had my wonderful husband, poured my love and caretaking into him, and I don't regret those years for a moment. More recently, I am learning to relish my solitude; The regrets I have are about how my husband died; what I put him through because I couldn't bear to lose him."

"I'm certain that, knowing you so well, he knew you wouldn't give him up without a fight."

Silent tears streamed down Yan's face.

"My husband and son never made peace before he died. They were so different. It was hard for my husband to accept that Jack would decide to leave medicine and pursue the life of an artist after everything that went into his training as a physician. It seems he inherited my family's creative genes."

The two women stood silently, together in their grieving of the earlier phases of their lives.

"Tell me what you've been doing," urged Yan, wiping away the tears with her bare hand.?"

"No, you don't. I am not going to let you change the subject that easily. I hear via the grapevine that you are writing a book."

"Yes. I am compiling all the knowledge I have been taught about medicinal herbs and complementary medicine practices. And I understand that Ursula has almost completed her book on the emotional development of women and girls. I'm sure it will include some of the lectures she'll be presenting here."

"It seems to me that the present generation, the post-feminist cohort, believes that there is an equal opportunity," agreed Alex. "Even though women continue to earn only eighty-three cents for every dollar that a man makes, and only two percent of Fortune 500 companies have women in senior management. These are only two of the multitude of issues that we face here in North America; the rest of the world is a whole other challenge."

"I'm certain we'll be discussing it more while we're here. There is so much to be gleaned from our generation. We need a whole new round of consciousness-raising," said Yan, "And new energy. Now that I've entered the Crone stage of life, I'll be looking for someone to take over my leadership role in the Goddess Circle."

"Crone indeed," scoffed Alex.

Chapter 18

At home, Georgina paced back and forth, wringing her hands as she awaited Elise's return. At the sound of her daughter's footsteps on the front porch, she ran to the foyer. "Darling, I have bad news," Georgina said in a tight voice.

"What is it, mother?" Elise appeared preoccupied.

"Come inside and sit down for a moment," suggested Georgina.

"I don't have time," stated Elise. "I just stopped by to pick up something from my room. I have to get going."

"Something has happened to Princess," Georgina blurted out.

"What?"

"She went missing earlier today," explained Georgina. "But I wasn't concerned initially because she often does that."

"And...?"

"When I stopped by at the sheriff's office, Sheriff Cahill, whom I've gotten to know through these frequent searches for Princess, told me that no one had brought her in."

"Mother, please get to the point!"

"I left the sheriff's office and was walking along the lake, hoping to find her, and then I came to the barbecue pit — you know, the one the kids use for their parties, down behind the

Gleason House. As I approached the fire pit, I saw something there that was quite awful. It—it was…Princess."

"What do you mean it was Princess?" gasped Elise.

"I didn't realize it at first," continued Georgina. "As I got closer to the pit, I saw the diamond-studded collar — you know, the one your father got for her." Georgina strung out her account as gently as she was able.

"Are you sure it was Princess?" Elise managed to ask. "Princess can't be the only dog here at Chautauqua with a diamond-studded collar."

"Quite sure, darling," Georgina said miserably. "Of course, I went to get the veterinary tech, and she was able to verify it by her microchip."

"I don't believe it," cried Elise.

Georgina tried to put her arms around her daughter.

"You know, it's quite likely that it was a car accident. You really are not supposed to do much driving here in the Institution," Georgina mused distractedly as if to herself. "I wonder if it was a young person. They may have attempted to cover up the evidence this way in the naïve hope it wouldn't be discovered."

"Mother, I trusted you to take care of Princess," wailed Elise, breaking free of her mother's arms. "I was such a fool. You can't take care of a five-pound dog. You can't take care of your marriage. You can't take care of your family. You can't take care of anything." She ran sobbing from the house, and the front door slammed behind her.

Georgina sank into the chair and put her face in her hands. She was not surprised that Elise had flung the failure of her marriage in her face. Georgina had done the best she could, breaking this terrible news to her daughter. She had not wanted to tell her what the vet tech had told her: Princess' body had been carved up before she had been burned. What kind of person would do that? Wondered Georgina, horrified.

Elise strode across the open green separating Lake Drive from the student residence halls and practice studios. "She's hopeless," she repeated to herself, ruminating about the anguish her relationship with her mother had caused her. "An emotional black hole that sucks up all psychic energy."

Princess had been her truest companion: her emotional support animal. As soon as Elise came in the front door, she would be there to greet her. No matter what was going on in the household, Elise and Princess could go to the park to play with the ball or curl up together in the bedroom as Elise read. She would miss her dreadfully.

During her recent treatment for addiction, Elise had come to see the profound and deleterious effect on her emotional health of the years she spent growing up in her parents' home. For as long as she could remember, her mother had suffered bouts of depression. During those times, her mother would 'get sick,' retreat into her bedroom, and sever contact with the outside world, including her daughter. Sometimes Elise's grandmother would come to help. Once, she and her grandmother had prepared a surprise birthday party for her mother; they had had a wonderful time sending out the invitations and ordering the birthday cake, only to have the deeply depressed Georgina refuse to attend. Even though all the invitees assured her that they understood, Elise had been mortified. But she couldn't express her disappointment and shame because, as her grandmother said, "that would make your mother ill."

In treatment, Elise learned that, under these circumstances, she had become the 'Adult Child.' Instead of a mother sacrificing her needs and feelings to meet those of her child, the process had been reversed; Elise had been required to suppress her own needs and feelings so as not to upset her mother. Elise became the caretaker, the 'good child.' Anything to keep her mother from getting sick.

Elise realized that, from the time she was incredibly young, her father had been absent a lot, losing himself in his business life. She used to wait up, hoping to spend some time with him, listening for his car to pull into the garage, but even when he did come home early, he went directly into his study, pleading, "too much work." She had seen her father in other venues, however — with guests on the few occasions her parents entertained or at other events when her father was in front of colleagues or employees. On these occasions, her father was electric, vibrant energy at full blast. Once, when she was about thirteen, they had held a neighborhood pool party at their home. Her father had been full of fun: delighting the other kids by splashing into the water like a cannonball; hosting the barbecue in his chef's hat and "Defender of the Flame" apron; laughing and joking with the guests as he served up the biggest steaks: "Come on Sylvia, I know you can handle more than that." Later, after the guests left, it was almost as if he imploded. When Elise returned to the pool area to retrieve her favorite sweater, she found him sitting alone in the dark. Dismissing her attempts to keep him company, he sent her off to her room with a gruff, "It's well past your bedtime, young lady." Curled up in the fetal position under her coverlet Elise muffled her sobs in the pillow and wondered whether, in some way, her very presence was so maleficent that it destroyed his vitality. Later, in adolescence, Elise found the magical world of pills that immediately transformed the sting of rejection. Here was the panacea, the perfect antidote for both physical and emotional pain. Ultimately, however, the panacea had enslaved her, taking over her will and her life.

During a family week at the treatment center, the staff supported Elise in sharing her feelings and experiences with first her mother and then her father. She remembered how shocked her parents had been. From their point of view, Elise had had an idyllic childhood: the pampered only child of a well-to-do family. They had given her everything they thought she wanted: the best private schools, piano lessons, ballet lessons, and camps; they had taken her to museums and all the cultural events a world-class city had to offer.

"This is bogus," her father snorted angrily. "Where's the gratitude? I work my butt off to provide the best for my family, and this is what I get in return."

Elise's mother sat silent. She knew how a person could feel totally neglected even though every material need had been met.

Chapter 19

Yan and Alex followed a winding path through the woods and hastened toward the Chautauqua Goddess Circle site. Speckled pebbles scuffed the walkway beneath their feet. They crossed the brook, stepping on rocks laid down by earlier travelers. On the other side of the creek, the path wound through some trees before descending the natural steps shaped by the roots of the surrounding grove of poplars. New leaves, released from their gray velvet winter cradles, swayed gently on branches overhead. Shafts of sunlight slanted through the leafy canopy as the pathway made one final twist. Yan spied the mother trunk of the grove, her bark gray and mottled with charcoal striations limning the smooth areas.

"I can feel the power of this place," uttered Alex. The ground underfoot was coated with wood chips that caught on her hand-embroidered purple silk robe fastened at the waist with a braided belt representing her ruling Goddess, Hera. Hearing voices up ahead, the duo hastened their steps. They rounded a bend and came upon Ursula and Angelique, installing a piece of art to mark the entrance to the sacred space.

Our warrior sisters thought Alex as she watched the physically splendid young women at their work. Ursula was statuesque with the broad shoulders of an archer; sun-golden tendrils cascaded over her forehead and shoulder in a riot of unruly curls. Her tanned legs stretched as she reached up to weld together a rainbow-hued mosaic of found beach glass that formed the eight legs and body of Arachne. The art form was suspended by macramé across the tree branches guarding the Goddess glade. Angelique, equally tall and athletic, wore her black curly hair cropped short. Her muscles rippled under café-au-lait skin that gleamed richly in the dappled shadows of the poplar grove as she put the last touches on the creation and turned to hug the new arrivals.

Within Angelique's welcoming embrace, Yan became aware of the slightness of her own stature. She thought back to the time Angelique had trusted them enough to reveal her story. Working as she did with sex abuse victims, Angelique began to experience long blocked memories of her early childhood years, and she had undergone extensive treatment for Post-Traumatic-Stress Disorder.

Ursula handed Angelique additional glass fragments from her basket.

"The glass used in this sculpture was collected during my early morning meditation walks along the most beautiful beaches of the world," she reminisced. "Each piece reminds me of a special adventure. I brought them as my contribution to the Goddess Circle."

The Goddesses carried objects with them to consecrate their gathering places and altars. "We designed the sculpture as a tribute to Athena, ruling goddess of the Chautauqua Circle," explained Ursula, tossing her hair back out of her eyes. "As you know, the spider represents the woman who boasted that her weaving surpassed that of Athena. For her hubris, Athena transformed her into Arachne, the spider."

"Done," said Ursula, standing back to admire their work. The sunlight streaming through the glass created a twirling kaleidoscope of color.

Their conversation was interrupted by Catharine emerging through the thicket of bushes carrying her flute. She shook the grit from her long skirt, over which was draped a filmy pale blue shawl that floated around her like a cloud.

"A perfect symbol of the Goddess of Wisdom and the Crafts," she said, gesturing to the sparkling spider sculpture now securely in place between the branches of the trees.

Then, bowing first to Angelique, acknowledging her as Athena, the leader of the Chautauqua Circle, the Goddesses walked slowly around the perimeter of the glen in a mindful march: staring at the ground ahead of them and taking care not to make eye contact; concentrating on each movement as they filed slowly by, placing one foot in front of the other—heel first then toe — pausing as the body weight shifted from one foot to the next; sensing each muscle tense and release. As the circling came to a stop, the Goddesses took their seats on the benches surrounding the fire pit.

"Welcome to you all. It is so good to be with you again," Angelique began with enthusiasm. "I can't tell you how glad I am to be here in our Goddess Circle, to move into the goddess persona and shed my skin as district attorney having to deal with all those criminals and murderers. This past spring has been particularly gruesome," Angelique said with disgust and shuddered. "At least here I'm away from psychopathic killers."

The gentle warm wind that had been wafting through the glade shifted, and a blast of icy air rushed into the pastoral scene, chilling the assembled women.

With grim resolve, Angelique lifted her arms and swept away the sudden coolness. Raising her voice, she called on the Great Mother to be with them at this Circle and called for a moment of silence to send energy to suffering women everywhere. A period of Goddessence, and mindful meditation, followed.

As was the custom, after forty-five minutes, Angelique rang the Tibetan bells and announced, "And now Ursula will read from the Chronicles of Goddess History.

"Thank you," Ursula responded. She rose and moved to the front of the group, turned over the heavy cover of the hand-crafted tome placed atop the podium, and began the reading.

Goddess worship began in the distant past. Most scholars believe that human beings evolved between 200,000 and

250,000 years ago. National Geographic researchers who have studied DNA samples tell us that 'Scientific Eve' or 'Mitochondrial Eve' lived in Ethiopia approximately 200,000 years ago — curiously, there is no evidence of a 'Scientific – Y-chromosomal Adam' prior to 60,000 years ago. As early peoples began hunting and gathering, they also sought to understand the spiritual influences on these activities. Their observation that infants were birthed by women — it was many thousands of years before the male contribution to propagation was understood – led them to the conclusion that roots and seeds, as well as animals, derived from female spirits. Thus, began the era of Goddess worship, notable for characteristics of cooperation over competition. Many first-nation cultures, including the Seneca here in Western New York state, still honor the traditions borne of this worship, such as matrilineal inheritance, equality between the sexes, and time as measured by lunar rather than solar calendars. Many artifacts depicting fertility goddesses remain from the period of Goddess worship, including the famous 'Venus von Willendorf,' found in Austria and probably carved 24,000-22,000 BCE — the Upper Paleolithic period. Female adherents of the Great Mother became skilled in the art and science of medicinal herbs and functioned as healers for many thousands of years. However, it is estimated that of the known witch-hunts that occurred between 331 B.C. with the 'Twelve Tables of Roman Law' prohibition against 'evil incantations", through the Catholic Inquisition, and up to the present time, over 7 million female healers have been murdered, many burned at stake as witches. In the 1500s, medical schools originated taking over the role of healing, but only men were allowed to be trained in the schools at that time, and this was true up until about 60 years ago.

"My experience at medical school can attest to that," Yan said grimly.

Chapter 20

Elise was concerned about Brynn and the stress of her new responsibility as a prima ballerina for the Chautauqua Ballet. Her mind drifted back to the support she herself had experienced with the loss of her beloved Princess.

"I can't bear that Princess suffered for even a few seconds before she died. I couldn't sleep last night thinking about some monster setting fire to her." Elise sobbed to her AA sponsor.

Elise and her AA sponsor, Meryl, approached Hurlbert Church, where 12 Step Recovery meetings were held daily. A group of people was standing to one side of the walkway, smoking cigarettes and talking in hushed tones.

"Horrific! But whatever happens, you can't relapse over this," cautioned her sponsor. "There isn't a problem that alcohol and drugs won't make worse."

Meryl was a petite Irish woman who dubbed herself a member of the CIA, Catholic Irish Alcoholic. Meryl's guiding passion was to shepherd young women coming into the program, painstakingly teaching them the skills to remain abstinent and guiding them through the hugely transformative steps of the program.

"You must take care of yourself; get enough sleep."

"I've always had difficulties sleeping, but last night was really awful; I couldn't turn my mind off. But don't worry, I'm not popping benzodiazepines. No more Ativan."

"Good. You know benzos: more and more gets you less and less."

"I'm not that bad," protested Elise.

Meryl shot her a skeptical look. "Remember to add 'yet' when you make statements like that! It's like saying you're just a little bit pregnant."

Sounds of laughter came from the church basement.

"Good to hear the laughter. I'll never forget my first 12 Step meeting. I couldn't figure out why anyone would be laughing. My life was a mess. I was miserable, full of shame," said Elise.

"I couldn't believe it either," agreed Meryl. "Now, I can even laugh at myself sometimes."

Entering the room, they were greeted by two individuals who shook hands and welcomed them. "Roger, Gambling Addict" and "Cindy, Codependent." Meryl and Elise joined five or so women gathered in a circle. There was a young man in his twenties tilted precipitously back in his chair, looking as if he wished he were anywhere else, and a guy in his fifties dressed in khakis, bare feet in topsiders, holding the Big Book of Alcoholics Anonymous open on his lap.

"Looks like the meeting today will focus on the 'Slogans.'" Meryl gestured at a number of signs posted on the walls: 'Easy Does It,' 'Keep It Simple,' 'One Day at a Time,' 'Watch the STRESS..' Meryl took Elise over to five or so women chatting easily and then left to go over to the corner to talk with a woman nervously scanning a long table displaying AA brochures — Meryl made it a point to keep an eye out for newcomers, so they were made to feel comfortable.

"So you're Meryl's new pigeon. How is it going so far?" queried a lithe young woman encased in athleisure wear.

"There's so much to learn. I thought this was a simple program."

"Simple but not easy. Does Meryl have you doing daily meditation on the slogans?" asked the woman.

"You bet."

"She's brutal on all the basics; 'boot camp,' she calls it," the woman volunteered.

"Catharine," said Meryl crossing the room to the two of them. "I see you've met Elise. She's new."

"Lovely to meet you," responded Cat, moving easily to shake Elise's hand. Cat's exquisitely long fingers, absent polish, fluttered from pale blue sleeves and pulled a hand-tooled leather journal from an exquisite Louis Vuitton backpack. A small upturned nose allayed the mercurial intensity of emerald eyes. Palest blonde tendrils flipped up slightly at the shoulders.

"Did I hear you mention Benzos? Panacea for performance anxiety. I used to eat them like popcorn. Couldn't get off them. Then I heard about that singer who became so tolerant of tranquilizers he had to have a general anesthetic just to get some sleep. It ended up killing him."

"Performance anxiety?" Elise's eyebrows rose to a question mark.

"I'm a violinist. I'm playing here at Chautauqua."

"I'm a ballet dancer, or rather a former one." Catharine gazed searchingly at Meryl, but a shoulder shrug was the only response. "I used Ativan to come down after a performance, not before. To use them before you dance would deaden the performance."

"Was it hard for you to quit?" Catharine shivered to remember her own dark time getting off those powerful drugs. She wouldn't wish that on her worst enemy.

"You can say that again. I was in detox for an eternity. The withdrawal from those pills was so nasty." The two women sighed in mutual contrition.

"Welcome. I'm Gary, your alcoholic secretary," a tall, silver-haired man bellowed above the din, attempting to bring the meeting to order. Stragglers were arriving at the last minute and heading over to the long table to get a cup of coffee before they joined the circle.

"Hi, Gary." With an enthusiastic roar, the group came to order. Meryl was the last to hustle to her seat.

"Let's have a moment of silence for the still suffering alcoholic followed by the Serenity Prayer." The group settled into their seats and momentarily fell silent before the commencement of the communal prayer.

God, grant me the serenity,

To accept the things I cannot change,

To change the things I can,

And the wisdom,

To know the difference.

"Amen," intoned Gary. "I'll turn the meeting over to Meryl, our chairperson for today." He turned to smile at the woman next to him.

"Hi. I'm Meryl. I cannot safely drink alcohol."

"Hi, Meryl," came the full-throated response.

"Today, I'd like us to focus on the slogan 'Watch the Stress' as the theme of our discussion. For those who our new, let me explain that we use 'STRESS' as an acronym to refer to factors that make us vulnerable to relapse: 'S' stands for Sleep; 'T' tells us to talk to trusted friends; 'R,' references resolving resentments; 'E,' is for proper eating and exercise; 'S' relates to the need to structure your time, unstructured time with nothing to do is the cause of many a relapse; and the final 'S' encourages self-care, especially to self-soothe using the senses. Let's go around, one-by-one, and talk about how you use this mnemonic in your recovery."

"I guess I'll start," said a well-dressed man in his thirties sitting next to Meryl. "I'll talk about my experience with sleep. I'm Roger, and I'm a gambling addict."

"Hi, Roger."

"Sleep. There were many times when I wouldn't get any sleep at all. I remember standing at the crap tables at the Bellagio seventy-two hours straight. My wife and friends went to bed, but not me. They also went to the pool and the world-class restaurants and the Grand Canyon and the Hoover Dam, but not me. I couldn't tear myself away. Later I learned that the casino owners in Vegas encourage drinking and lack of sleep — the casinos are all lit up so that you don't know whether it's day or night — to impair your thinking and judgment. They want you to lose all your money, and I did, no matter what resolutions I made. The remorse was terrible. When we left for Vegas, my wife would put a hundred-dollar bill under the front seat of the car so that we could get out of the parking lot. Talk about depression. Sleep deprivation in and of itself can create depression and anxiety. Then depression and anxiety exacerbate the sleep problem, and you get into a downward spiral. Today I go to sleep at the same time every night and make sure I'm sleeping well as an important part of my program."

"I go to bed at different hours all the time," exclaimed Elise.

"A variation of even one hour in a sleep schedule will require at least a day to recover. You go through four or five sleep cycles over an eight-hour period. Within each of these cycles is a phase of REM — Rapid Eye Movement — when dreams occur. During REM is when you have 'good' sleep — the recharging kind. Each successive REM phase gets longer; if you get an uninterrupted eight hours of sleep, you will experience the greatest benefit. I pass."

"I can't even imagine sleeping for eight hours straight. I'm much too busy people-pleasing." Laughter burst from the group as they turned their attention to the animated woman sitting to the left of Roger. "Hi everyone, I'm Cindy, a member of Codependents Anonymous."

"Hi, Cindy."

"As a codependent, the second component of 'Watch the Stress,' 'Talking about myself to trusted friends, is a tricky one. I make a great audience. I am exquisitely attuned to the needs of others and habitually deaf to my own. It requires constant effort for me to talk about myself, but I know it's important to learn that others care about what happens in my life and how I feel about it. My sponsor requires me to call her every evening and tell her about my day. At first, I could only manage a couple of minutes, but now I call her and talk for longer. I still have difficulty asking for my needs to be met, but I'm getting better. It's a process. With that, I'll pass."

"Progress, not perfection," chorused the group.

"John, Adult Child of Alcoholics," stated the burly man with salt and pepper hair seated next to Cindy.

"Hi, John."

"I guess I'm supposed to address the 'R,' resolving resentments. Probably I'll be working on resentments for the rest of my life. Both my mother and father were alcoholics. There were nights when they wouldn't come home, and I'd be left in charge of my little sisters. I'd worry that my parents had been in an accident or were dead in some ditch. Then there were the nights that they were home, drunk and screaming at each other. I wanted to get out of there as soon as I could, but I didn't want to abandon my sisters. I carried around a chip on my shoulder. What a waste of time; no one even noticed that I was angry; people and situations taking up space rent-free in my head. These days I take a look at how long I spend ruminating. If I don't have the power to impact the situation, I let it go; turn it over. It takes a lot of work, and I may have to turn it over time and time again, but it helps my recovery. With that, I'll pass."

"I'm Terry, a member of Overeaters Anonymous. Hi everybody."

"Hi, Terry."

"I'll talk about the 'E' of STRESS: eating and exercises: OA has taught me to watch how, what, and when to eat to maintain emotional balance. Eating complex carbohydrates and a little bit of protein every few hours is like slow and steady time-released nutrition that keeps your blood sugar level. On the other hand, when you ingest 'whites' –white sugar, flour, rice, or potato–blood sugar spikes, and the pancreas sends out a flood of insulin to neutralize it, causing your blood sugar to plummet. It sends you on an emotional roller coaster."

"I had to learn a lot about nutrition in my ballet training," said Elise.

"Hmm. Ballet training and proper eating, Is that an oxymoron?"

"Along with nutrition to support emotion, you're required to have a minimum of twenty-five minutes of exercise outside daily. Exposure to sunlight helps modulate your mood. With that, I pass."

"The first 'S,' structure. Gary, again, your alcoholic secretary."

"Hi, Gary."

When I was working, I had the scaffolding of external structure: I arrived at work in the morning and had my entire day planned for me. But the weekends were something else: like falling off the planet into nothingness. I would wake up Saturday morning with the entire day stretching out ahead of me. I felt empty and bored, so I drank all day long. When I retired, it was endless unstructured time. I dove right into the bottle. Word to the wise: retirement is one of the major life transitions that we need to prepare for. I pass."

"And I get to speak to the final 'S'; the fun 'S': using the senses to self-soothe. Hi, I'm Catharine, the relationship addict."

"Hi, Catharine."

"It's great to engage as many of the senses as you can — auditory, olfactory, tactile, visual, taste — to self-soothe. For instance, at bedtime, I turn on my sound machine and play the soothing tones of the rain falling or the surf breaking on the beach. I spray the scent of lavender on my pillowcase and massage my hands and feet with lotion. I like to visualize a pleasing scene, perhaps the beach or an exotic waterfall. This really helps combat the craving for the romance rush."

"I want to thank you all for your comments," stated Meryl. "Allow me to add one more idea to the discussion of stress. We don't like change, but it is the only certain thing. All change, even positive change like an exciting new job, creates stress. When you are evaluating how much stress you are under, be sure to consider both positive and negative changes."

"I'd like to thank Meryl for a lively discussion," said Gary, preparing to bring the meeting to a close. "As is our custom, we'll end with the "Our Father" followed by coffee and fellowship."

"Love addiction," queried Elise. "I haven't heard much about that. My friends say they are turning all problem behaviors into addictions these days." She refused the cream-filled chocolate doughnut Catharine brought over for her but accepted the cup of black coffee. The coffee was strong and bitter. They were standing apart from the group while Meryl conversed with several people clustered around her, eager to share one more penetrating insight. She nodded, signaling that she knew they were waiting for her

"Some believe relationship addiction is the most daunting. Didn't they address this while you were in treatment?"

"Not at all."

"That's surprising. There's a growing consensus that relationship addiction may lie at the heart of all addictions. Think of all the women you know, young and old, who have their noses in romance novels. And men! Having serial affairs is seen as machismo rather than a disorder."

"Someone close to me suffers from that," Elise confessed.

"Really," commented Cat. She allowed a moment of silence, but when Elise refrained from elaborating, she spoke again. "I noticed that you didn't introduce yourself when the secretary asked if there was anyone new making this their first meeting at Chautauqua."

"I'm not too sure yet," explained Elise, the blood rushing to her face. "I'm addicted to prescription medication, but I still take Zoloft to treat depression and anxiety. I get the impression that members of the 12 Step communities don't approve of any psychoactive prescription medication,"

"What gave you that idea?"

"Some guys were condemning 'happy pills' the other day. I assumed they meant psychoactive prescription medication."

"Half of the women in AA are on some form of antidepressant, and the other half should be," stated Catharine, laughing bitterly. "Some individuals on Zoloft or other psychoactive medications say it feels like a 'chemical lobotomy.' They can't experience pain or pleasure to any intensity. And don't even think about having any libido."

Catharine had heard many women complain that romantic difficulties would trigger depression, but when they took antidepressants, they gained weight and lost interest in sex, making the relationships worse and the women even more depressed.

"Don't get the wrong idea. Medication used appropriately to help with painful emotions can help recovery. It's easier to remain abstinent from aspirin if you don't have a headache. It is easier to stay away from addictive drugs if you have less emotional pain," Meryl plunged in. She had concluded her after discussion and rejoined her two sponsees. She didn't agree with the 'old school' AA, thinking that all medications were off-limits.

"I got hooked on Vicodin and Ritalin, and they were prescribed by the dance company's physician," cried Elise. Her distress made it hard to speak. "It made sense to use a painkiller to help me keep dancing when I was injured. In the blinding glare of hindsight, it's not such a good idea. The same with Ritalin. I started using that because I had a mild case of Attention Deficit Disorder, and it helped me focus on overly complicated dance sequences. There were times. I must admit that I used Ritalin to keep my energy up for long dance practices and performances. When you use enough, often enough, for long enough, your body becomes addicted."

"While that might be true, there are certain psychoactive medications just like the medications you would use to treat any other physical condition. These aren't 'happy pills.' If you had hypothyroid, you'd get a prescription for Synthroid — an artificial thyroid chemical. If you don't use this chemical, you will feel fatigued and depressed. It's more like filling up a car with gas," said Meryl, warming to her topic. "If you don't have any gas in the car, it won't run, but a full tank of gas won't make the car run any better than half a tank. Certain psychoactive prescription medications work like that."

Elise described to Meryl what she had found in Brynn's rooms. "She's so reactive. I need to tiptoe around her, like walking on eggshells. Just talking to her about it makes her freak out."

"It may be that the emotionality you see is all on the surface, like a shallow lake with water sloshing around," Meryl encouraged. "The goal of recovery is to be more like the deep ocean: the surface may become turbulent from time to time, but underneath the choppy surface, down in the depths, all is calm and peaceful. That is the serenity that we are promised through working through the steps of this program. Therefore, we call ourselves 'grateful recovering addicts'."

"I wish Brynn were willing to hear this."

Chapter 21

"So good to be gathered once again to look at the individual elements of a balanced mind, body, and soul."

Angelique opened the second part of the Circle meeting. "This past spring, we began with an immersion in the understanding and practice of the Goddessence mental state; in this summer session, we'll focus on managing emotions. Our plans for future meetings include: addressing research on trauma resolution, followed by the theme of 'Designing a Life Worth Living' examining the implications of the positive psychology movement for the Goddess Circle.

"To begin today, Yan will review the basic emotions, and I will follow with a survey of the latest research on thought vis-a-vis emotion management."

Angelique returned to her seat, and Yan advanced to the podium to begin her remarks; She glanced around at the women gathered before her, all well-grounded in the subject she was about to discuss.

"Greetings to you all. I am going to present just the briefest review as I know that you have heard this presentation before on many occasions. First, let me begin by commenting on my version of the 'Triune Brain.' One part of the brain is the realm of emotion, which I will talk about today; a second part is the realm of logic, which Angelique will discuss in a moment; the third part is the one we exercise when we meet in our Circles, Goddessence, the witness or observing ego, the part that provides intuition and wisdom. That having been said, let me underscore that we are all hardwired with the capacity for emotion because it is necessary for human survival. In Paleolithic times, we lived on this planet among multiple life-threatening species. We were frail, puny mammals with few attributes to help us survive. What set us apart was the development of a superior brain."

The Goddesses settled onto their benches, content to sit at the feet of a guru, like professional singers listening to Barbra Streisand launch into one of her standards.

"Mental health professionals focus on six basic emotions: fear, anger, sadness, shame, love, and awe. For our purposes, I will address the four emotions: fear, anger, sadness, and shame — the mnemonic I use is FASS — that humans find uncomfortable and for which they have developed multiple, oftentimes destructive, means of avoiding."

"Sex, drugs, and rock and roll are my favorite ways to avoid an uncomfortable emotion," commented Ursula, shifting her position and stretching lazily.

Yan waited for the polite laughter to subside and then continued. "Emotions are electro-chemically hardwired. Chemicals travel from cell to cell: one cell squirts the chemical across space, a synapse, and the next cell sponges it up. Various chemicals — adrenaline, serotonin, or dopamine, to name but three — are transported from cell to cell and impact the way we feel. Don't forget that we are ninety-eight percent water, and the rest is mainly chemicals."

"Someone once described the human body as 'chemical soup'; the tiniest tweak can alter the composition, just like a chef adding a pinch of cilantro," joked Ursula.

"Well put."

Yan smiled her approval, then shifted the direction of her remarks.

"The subjective experience of emotion develops throughout our lifetime. The first thing the infant is aware of is pain, a hunger pang, for example; on the opposite end, the pleasure of being fed. Everything builds from these basics. The emotions of fear, anger, sadness, shame, love, and awe are variations on these two themes. As we go through life, we encounter situations that trigger pain or pleasure, and our brains create elaborate mythologies, negative and positive, about those experiences. So why did we develop emotions? How are these emotions critical to survival?"

Yan emerged from behind the podium and proceeded from woman to woman, peering intently at each.

"Back in ancient times, when we were alone and vulnerable on the planet surrounded by life-threatening predators, these chemically based emotions could make our bodies stronger and faster. Let's talk first about the emotions of fear and anger. The fictional character 'The Incredible Hulk' is a good example."

Coming now to Ursula, Yan tapped her on the shoulder and motioned for her to demonstrate.

"When aroused, 'The Hulk's muscles pump up, giving him the greatly enhanced strength and speed necessary to combat villains."

Joining in the spirit of the moment, Ursula struck several poses in imitation of a bodybuilder: to the front, to the back; squatting several times to show off the thigh muscles; bending one arm and then the other to accentuate the biceps.

"'The Hulk' is an excellent visual image of what happens to the body under the influence of adrenaline and cortisol. In caveman times, when we wandered into the forest and met up with man-eating tigers, our brains would register a life threat, and adrenaline would course through the body to enable us to run as fast as we were able or, if cornered by the tiger, fight with as much strength as possible."

The Goddesses laughed their appreciation as Ursula took a bow and returned to her seat.

"Sadness is the next uncomfortable emotion. Sadness, thought to be governed by the chemical serotonin, is connected to loss and is important to survival in a couple of ways. If we decided to leave the safety of our village and venture into the woods, say, in search of roots and nuts, we would be like lambs straying from the herd: ripe prey for a predator. For our survival, we are hardwired with serotonin so that when we've been away too long from the people we care about, we feel sad and are prompted to return to our community. Back in the safety of our village, we're less likely to be eaten by the tiger."

"Let me just add that the bonding chemical, oxytocin, partners with the serotonin of sadness to ensure the survival of the species through the rearing of offspring," Ursula interjected. "Bonding begins in utero for incredibly good reasons. If we were to leave our infants unprotected for too long, they would be at risk, but because of the bonding, we miss them and return quickly, thus increasing their safety. There are multiple examples of mothers, human and animal, sacrificing their own lives to protect those of their young."

The audience nodded their agreement on this important principle.

"Shame, the last of the four uncomfortable emotions, is also connected to the chemical adrenaline," said Yan, picking up the theme of the presentation. "Any of you who have had a shame attack probably still remembers it. Within any community, we are taught the rules about how to conduct ourselves. When we don't obey these rules, society punishes us. In ancient times, if our society were to punish us by ostracism— pushing us out of the safe village again, lunch for the tiger."

"Shunning is still practiced in many societies," observed Alex thoughtfully.

"When we were teenagers, it felt like we would die if we weren't included in the popular clique; if we weren't invited to the Saturday night party," added Angel.

"In the Goddess Circle, we practice allowing emotions to cycle through us, like all the great cycles of nature," Ursula elaborated. "Like the tides' response to the moon. Waves brush up on the shore and then wash back out to the sea. So, it is with feelings. As emotions are triggered, they crest and recede, the waves rush up on the shore and then wash back out to sea."

"In my PTSD treatment, I was trained in a Mindful Inquiry practice called "RAIN," explained Angel. "This practice, developed by Vipassana Meditation teacher, Michele McDonald, asks you to R: Recognize an emotion; A: Accept the feeling and allow it to flow unimpeded through us; I: Investigate it; and finally N: Practice Non-Identification or recognize that you are not your feelings and that feeling aren't facts."

"Keep in mind that feelings are distressing but not deadly," Yan reminded them. "Such a chemical surge typically peaks for twelve to fourteen seconds and then begins to ebb."

"That's hard for those of us who are highly sensitive to believe," stated Angel.

"I'm sure," sympathized Yan. "But just imagine that you walk into a room and spot a huge python curled in the corner. Your sympathetic 'fight-flight' system would have an extreme reaction. Then you realize that it's not a python, but simply a rope wound up in a coil. How would that affect you?"

"I'm sure I'd be very relieved."

"And your emotions would return quickly to baseline."

"It's hard to believe my emotions could just come and go in real-life situations."

"Would you be willing to demonstrate?"

Angelique smiled tentatively.

"Okay. Before we begin, do you have your safe place, your emotional sanctuary to which you can return if the emotional intensity exceeds a nine out of ten?"

Angelique nodded in the affirmative.

"That's excellent. Now, allow your mind to travel back to a situation that triggered distress on an intensity level of about seven or eight out of ten."

Angel went back to the moment when she'd been summoned in front of the Bar Association after Teresa Bellamy had registered a complaint about her handling of the Harbridge scandal. She'd barely escaped with her law license intact. "Okay," she signaled. "I'm there."

"As you access the memory, you will have a visceral re-experiencing of the scene. Adrenaline and cortisol will begin to circulate in your body. Don't avoid the emotion or block the sensation in any way. Now, move into Goddess Mind, Goddessence, and begin to count. Notice, as you count, how long it takes for the sensation of adrenaline to crest and then begin to recede."

After a short time, Angelique opened her eyes. "Fourteen seconds," she reported, smiling her delight.

The Goddesses milled around her, each uttering personal words of encouragement, before regaining their seats.

Yan turned, once more addressing the group as they regained their seats; Yan went on with her exposition.

"Thanks for being willing to experiment with us. That takes a lot of courage. Would it be all right with you if I explained emotional reactivity as a learned response, using your personal history as an example?"

Angelique nodded."

"Thanks, that takes a lot of courage," stated Yan, turning to address the group.

"In theory, because of her history, Angel would be at the upper end of the range of reactivity. When trauma is experienced, performers, writers, and composers are individuals who experience heightened emotions and are able, often, to communicate that exquisite sensitivity to the rest of us. Emotions are like the weather, like the clouds that sweep across the sky. They enter our awareness and then are gone," she concluded. "Through the practice of Goddessence, we learn to access the Goddess Mind and watch the feelings pass on through."

Yan waited for the murmuring to subside before she began to introduce the second part of the emotion management presentation.

"And I now call on Angelique, leader of this Chautauqua Circle, to present the rational component of managing emotions: how to identify and challenge thought: the stories our brains concoct about the situations we encounter."

Angelique embraced Yan before she turned to rejoin the group. "We all cherish your wisdom and are grateful that you continue to share your knowledge with us."

"That is a helpful way to introduce the subject of the 'Logic Realm' of emotions: allow me to piggyback on the notion of 'stories our brains concoct.' Indeed, our brains create narratives based on the information we choose to extract from our experiences. Classic example: you're walking down the street, and you say 'hello' to an acquaintance, but they ignore you and keep on going without saying anything to you. What do you think? Typically, a person assumes that the acquaintance is angry and doesn't want to talk to them; snubs them. We search our memories to see what we might have done to offend them,' and I don't know about you, but I usually am able to find something I've done wrong."

There is a buzz of acknowledgment and much head nodding from the assembled group.

"This is what emotional management from the 'Logic Realm' is all about: a situation happens, we make up a story to explain it, the story we make up triggers an emotion, and we act on that emotion. In the example I just mentioned, an acquaintance fails to respond to me; I make up a story that she is angry with me for something I have done, and I become irritated and react angrily toward her. In response, she avoids me because of my anger; and round and round we go — the merry-go-round of ineffective belief systems. It is possible that there are over seven billion stories — that's the number of people alive on the earth — that could have been told about that one incident. What are some other ways to interpret what happened?"

"The acquaintance may not have heard me," ventured Ursula,

"She may have just had terrible news and was mired in thought," suggested Alex.

"Excellent," stated Angelique. "The challenge is to brainstorm many possible alternative stories and choose one that is effective. For example, if we chose to question whether our acquaintance had just had some bad news, we might contact that person to see how they're doing.

If emotion-triggering stories are left unchallenged for a length of time, they can converge and form a 'core belief;' that is, if you feel rejected a lot of the time, you may come to believe that you are unattractive in some way that no one will explain to you, and you may come to act out of that belief. That could turn into a self-fulfilling prophecy whereby you expect that people will reject you before you even get to know whether that is true.

The moral of the story is to find a way to challenge your beliefs and assumptions and to select an effective story.

"Can you expand on what you mean by effective?"

"Well, going back to the story of the acquaintance who ignores you." It's one thing to modify your thinking in order to regulate your emotions by choosing a story that's different from the 'I am a bad person' story. It is also a good idea to check with that person to see if there is a problem between the two of you that you might have an opportunity to address. In that way, you move into problem-solving or being effective by addressing the issue rather than simply altering your thoughts.

"And don't forget, in all things, apply eternal vigilance."

To close the group, Angelique invited all to join in the Goddess Chant:

"We all come from the Goddess
And to Her, we shall return

Like a drop of Rain

Running to the Ocean..."

"Water that always was and always will be, liquid to steam to liquid, circulating eternally for over four billion years," proclaimed Angelique.

The members of the Goddess Circle stood to go, but Yan asked them to stay for a moment.

"I am so delighted that we are meeting more and more frequently. To me, it implies that each of us is getting something essential when we come together. Certainly, mutual support is vital. For many of us, it can be difficult to find a like-minded community to which we can belong, and belonging is a critical need. But equally important is the opportunity to discuss ideas and, through this discussion, gain greater clarity. I call this a 'cognitive realignment.' When we meet, I step out of the regular hustle and bustle and stop for a moment to 'check in,' clarify my values and realign my priorities. But when I leave your company, like everyone else, I get caught up in the busyness of our lives. It can be hard to stay centered."

The group members nodded.

"But for some time now, along with being part of the community, I have longed for more time for solitary reflection. I feel it is the appropriate time in my life for this. Don't worry; I don't intend to become a hermit immediately," Yan reassured them. "I find that I am yearning to mentor one more time."

"You're thinking of retiring? But we depend on you," protested Ursula.

"I'm not going to be leaving the Circle, but I feel it's imperative for me to pass along the wisdom I have gleaned during my time as leader of these Circles. I also think it's important that other women have the experience as leaders as well."

The members of the Circle voiced their concern.

" There'll be plenty of time to process this; I'm not stepping down yet," said Yan. "I also want you to know that I have met a woman who might be a candidate for our Circle."

Yan described her encounter with Georgina and the fact that Georgina had been able to discern figures and scenes in clouds.

"What's so great about that?" scoffed Ursula. "Every kid can do that."

"There is a different quality to her sighting," said Yan. "And there is more about her story that intrigues me. She appears to be a natural Goddess type, perhaps a Demeter; we haven't had the summer goddess in a while. I have invited her to Alex's party. You can meet her and make up your own minds about whether she would be a natural fit for the group.

In the meantime, would it be okay for me to provide her with some superficial information about the Circle?"

Chapter 22

As Eric and Miko neared the amphitheater, they noticed Chester hustling toward them.

"I was wondering how long it would take your 'sycophant shadow' to follow us," griped Eric.

"Knock it off." Miko dug his elbow into Eric's ribs. "Chester may be a little odd, but he's a good guy underneath."

"Well, you're the one who knows his underneath," taunted Eric.

"Hi Chet," Eric said. "I was just telling Miko how unusual it was for him and me to find some time alone. I figured you'd find us sooner or later."

"Please call me Chester."

"Whatever," drawled Eric. The two young men stood nose to nose, holding each other's gaze. As the three stood together, nearly the same height, the similarity among them was startling.

Chester was the first to break eye contact. "I didn't mean to interrupt anything," he said, directing his comment to Miko.

"No problem, man," declared Miko, putting an arm around each of them. "Eric and I are cousins and lifelong buddies, but we're hardly joined at the hip." Miko threw an admonishing look at Eric, who shrugged Miko off and turned away.

Miko glanced at the front of the amphitheater, his attention captivated by the group of ballerinas performing there." Whew!" he whistled. "Look at that!"

"Lighter, softer! You sound like a herd of elephants up there. And you look like one too!" A sinewy older man standing at the edge of the stage hurled a barrage of insults at the dancers. He tapped his cane on the wooden floor and shouted out orders over the music blasting from a nearby boom box.

"Hey! You there!" he yelled, noticing the young men. "You're not allowed in here during rehearsal."

Miko paid little attention to him but continued to approach the stage, totally mesmerized. "So beautiful," he sighed as security guards appeared to escort them to the back of the amphitheater.

Standing at the side of the Amp, Elise watched the interaction between the men and then turned her attention back to the stage as the ballet company finished its practice. A persistent pain squeezed her heart as she remembered all the things that addiction had stolen from her—especially this. And now the loss of Princess. She wasn't ready to talk to anyone about that until she knew they were safe. Too much to bear. It would be at least a year of recovery before she could risk the various relapse triggers embedded within this world. As the rehearsal ended and the ballet master turned to leave, he spotted Elise but brushed past her upon his exit and refused to acknowledge her greeting.

With rehearsal finished, Brynn came over to greet her.

"Wow," said Elise. "What did I ever do to him?"

"You rejected the opportunity to sit at his feet and reflect his brilliance," said Brynn, nodding in the direction of the ballet master.

"Train through shame, twas ever thus," Elise mused aloud. "I wonder if I could still take that."

"Whom the Gods loveth they chasteneth," replied Brynn, looking beautiful in her warm-up pants, a sweatshirt thrown over her shoulders to keep her muscles warm after the strenuous workout. Her heart-shaped face was flushed, and she sponged pearls of perspiration from her forehead. She radiated animal energy.

"Still, that's hard to take, I know," Elise commiserated.

"Are you going to come back to dance with us?" asked Brynn.

"It's hard to say," said Elise. No longer being a part of the world in which she had been an outstanding member was a significant loss. "The competition is so fierce, the push for perfection so great that it might threaten my recovery. I think it would be difficult to stay away from the amphetamines and painkillers that almost killed me. I'll have to see."

The two of them sat down on the steeply raked back rows of the Amp.

"It's no big deal. I'm sure you'd be fine," said Brynn. She bent down and started to fumble in her ballet bag, retrieving a bottle of water and drinking deeply.

"It's very easy to become addicted," insisted Elise, unwilling to be put off by Brynn's minimization of the dangers of these powerful drugs. "When we were younger, it was easier to be as thin as they wanted. But after we hit puberty, you know how those fat cells pop up where they never were before. We used to think that it would be enough just to follow the diet guidelines that Madame gave us, but that didn't work. Then I tried restricting. And when that failed, you remember, the other girls taught us how to throw up. That worked better than following calorie intake; that was the perfect answer to keeping your weight down."

Elise was aware that even as they talked, back at the ballet residence hall, other girls were throwing up or using Kaopectate to purge what they had eaten.

"The downside of bulimia is that you don't have any energy, and you need that to dance. So then you have to trick the docs into giving you amphetamines — I mean 'focus medication.'" she said sarcastically. "I can remember Wendy grilling us on attention deficit disorder symptoms so that we could fool the docs into writing scripts for stimulants. Instant energy: but then I couldn't sleep, and I got into problems with anxiety."

"Boy, I know all about that. First, I had performance anxiety; then, I couldn't sleep, worrying about how the performance anxiety would damage my dancing; not sleeping made the anxiety worse, and so on. It keeps building up. That's when I got Klonopin — to get rid of the anxiety," Brynn agreed.

"I saw all those meds in your bedroom at the residence hall," Elise reminded her.

"How could I forget? Everyone there is using the same drugs. No need to hide them. You know the dance doc gives us everything we want — except for the cocaine, of course. That's the cure-all. Instant thinness and energy — two birds with one stone."

Brynn looked into the distance with that thousand-mile stare. "My mother lives vicariously through me. When you went off to treatment, and I was given the role of a prima ballerina, my mother was in heaven. But then she became really intrusive and tried to control everything I did. Talked to the dance doc to make sure that I got all the pills I would need to be the best dancer around. This is the first time I've been able to get away from her. Master Gregory forbade her from coming to Chautauqua. But now I'm used to using the pills for all the reasons we've talked about. I don't know if I can do what I want to do without them."

"There's an open invitation for you to come to a 12 Step meeting with me. There are a few right here on the grounds."

"Let me think about it," said Brynn.

The three boys had returned to the amphitheater and were strolling down the aisle. Spotting Elise and Brynn, Miko lost no time in coming over to interrupt their conversation and introduce himself and his two companions.

"Eric and I met earlier at the writers' workshop," said Elise.

"Writers' workshop!" chortled Chester.

"Eric's the sensitive one," said Miko.

"Okay, guys. I'm polishing my writing skills for law clerkships," responded Eric. "It doesn't hurt to prep for the future."

"See. He is the sensitive one," joked Miko; then, he became serious. "Do you have any idea what happened?"

"No idea. Some people are saying that teenagers don't have enough to do around here. Maybe there's a drug problem. It seems there's not much here to occupy them, so these kids are meeting down near the lake to get high and do drugs. It could be that they had something to do with Princess's death," explained Elise. "But the burning; that's horrible."

"Elise just got out of treatment for chemical dependency," Brynn declared. "She's our expert on drug abuse."

The trio turned to stare at her.

"That's true," said Elise, blushing to have her anonymity shredded. "It turns out that addiction to prescription medications — stimulants, pain medication, and the like — is very common among high achievers: ballet dancers and athletes. We had a lot of male athletes in treatment as well who got caught on steroids and other performance-enhancing drugs." She looked at the three athletic-looking young men for understanding.

"Well, it is stupid not to realize how destructive these chemicals can be," said Eric. "Not only to the person using them but to those who care about them. Now, you must excuse me." Eric raced out of the Amp and down the hill.

"Don't mind Eric; he's weird sometimes," said Miko. He didn't want Eric's sudden departure to ruin his chances with these young women.

"Was it something I said?" asked Elise.

"We don't talk much about alcohol or prescription pills in front of Eric," Miko explained. "Eric's mother was a severe addict. She started to drink and used every pill she could get her hands on after Eric's father and sister were killed."

"How awful! What happened?"

"Car accident. But it was long ago." Miko was eager to get off this negative subject and on to more exciting things.

"How old was Eric during all this?" Elise probed further.

"He must have been about six years old. Afterward, he came to live with us for a time in England. That's during the brief time that my dear mother was still married to my father, the great Polish Prince Kazimierz."

"Prince?" Brynn had snapped herself out of her self-absorption — practicing hand and arm positions — and turned her attention back to the conversation.

"Why, didn't you know that I am the son of a Prince?" Miko winked.

"You're kidding, right?"

"No kidding. Absolutely." Miko bowed with a flourish, clicked his heels together, and kissed Brynn's hand. "Prince Mikolaj Ladislaus Sigismund Kazimierz at your service. You may call me Miko."

"And so what happened to Eric's mother?" Elise interrupted, refusing to be distracted.

"Oh. She eventually died. Glammy — that's my Grandmother Bellamy — raised both of us. She owns the estate up on the north end. And Chester is my faithful manservant," he said.

"Don't joke like that."

"You know I'm only teasing," said Miko, lightly punching Chester on the shoulder.

"It's not funny," said Chester, clenching and unclenching his fists.

He looks like he should be in uniform, clicking his heels, thought Elise.

"You do look like a manservant when you do that," said Brynn, laughing.

"It is true that my mother was Mrs. Bellamy's housekeeper for many years, but I am a student at Harbridge, the same as Eric and Miko," Chester declared. "And I'm on the Harbridge rowing team, just like Eric and Miko."

"I'm afraid I don't know much about rowing," Elise said lightly, attempting to diffuse the tension. "But I do know about Harbridge. In fact, my father is an alum."

A sudden silence greeted that announcement. Miko and Chester glanced at each other, but neither spoke. Chester muttered something and took off toward the marina. Not one to remain speechless for long, Miko started in a new direction: "Why don't you come along to the Herd Mentality party tonight after their performance at the Amp?"

Brynn and Elise looked at each other, uncertain of how to answer.

"We don't have an invitation," said Elise prissily.

"I'm inviting you."

"Are you sure we'd be welcome?" asked Brynn.

"Sure, I'm sure. You'd be my guests. I expect to be Jonah's manager when he goes solo. I can invite anyone I want."

"We'll think about it," said Elise, as sadness clouded her face. "Right now, I have to go and make arrangements for Princess."

Brynn started to walk along Lake Drive with Miko in close pursuit. Putting his arm around her, he tried to tickle her ribs.

"So skinny. The closer the bone, the sweeter the meat."

Brynn pushed him away, giggling, and sped toward the tall trees that dotted Belltower Point. Miko was in close pursuit. Even in her mock terror Brynn, the consummate ballerina appeared to float on air; her dancer's severe braids had loosened, and her flaxen tresses streamed out behind her. She sought safety behind a tall elm, but Miko caught hold of her, picked her up, and twirled her around in the air. Then, he slid Brynn slowly down the front of his muscular body and held her firmly in his embrace. Brynn squirmed but was unable to escape.

"I could hold you in my arms forever," breathed Miko. He gazed deep into Brynn's liquid brown eyes, their faces barely an inch from each other, lips grazing.

"Well, you'll have to keep chasing me, then." Brynn smiled and, with surprising strength, wriggled free and dashed into the nearby building.

"Oh, I do love a good chase."

Miko ran after her into the building at the end of the pier. Once inside, it was difficult to see in the dark, but he was able to make out her quickened breathing not far away; as his eyes adjusted to the gloom, he spotted her partly hidden behind a column. Moving panther-like across the wooden floor, he caught hold of her wrist and tugged her forward against his hard muscles. He wrapped his arms around her waist, and his hands began to stroke the firm contour of her back, pressing her closer. His mouth found the bare skin of her neck and brushed up to the softness of her lips. With little more than nominal resistance, Brynn melted into his embrace. Her body arched back, releasing the flaxen silk of her hair. She clung to him as his powerful thighs eased them down onto the wooden floor. Her curves molded into his solid angles. Kisses became urgent. Miko's breath became harsher. A groan emanated from somewhere deep inside him. Once again, Brynn wrenched herself from his embrace, putting space between them, and ran out of the clubhouse. She was aware of the rush of blood in her face as she vainly attempted to tame her loosened hair into ballerina braids. Miko raced after her and, standing in the sunlight, cupped her cheek with his hand:

"I want to be close to you," he rasped.

Standing on tiptoe, she reached her lips close to his ear.

"Only when there's an exclusive relationship," she teased, gliding gracefully out of his grasp.

Chapter 23

Georgina went into her room to make sure she had everything she needed. She noticed that the Special Studies Catalog that she had left for her was still lying untouched on her desk. Beside it, and open in full view, was the notebook Elise had generated during her therapy. Georgina put a hand on it and started to page through the journaling and drawings it contained. Her mind turned back to the excruciating intervention they went through in order to get Elise into treatment. She was immediately transported back to a family week at the treatment center, where Elise had shown her the writings she had been working on and the collages she had created in art therapy. The theme of 'mother loss' had been starkly highlighted. It became evident that, as Georgina had become preoccupied with her husband's affairs, she had withdrawn into periods of depression and remained self-absorbed even though Elise clamored to be allowed into her private world. As a result, Elise had become harder on herself and more secretive with the passage of time, believing that if she were more perfect, she would earn her mother's attention. At the treatment center, the counselors had been able to help Elise work through the classic stages of the evolution of the emotional orphan: first, rage at her mother for neglecting the nurturing maternal role, then heart-wrenching grief as she began to understand that she had never received unconditional love; and the final stage, apathy. 'My Mother, the helpless victim' was the main character in her journals. Georgina wept to read the pain and injury the entries revealed.

"I must stop wallowing in self-pity," she admonished herself. Firmly replacing the notebook, she fled out into the garden seeking distraction.

"Hello there," a voice called. It was Yan.

"Come on in," replied Georgina, relieved to be diverted from her thoughts. She put aside her garden shears and approached the gate; both hands held out in greeting. "I'm so glad to see you. I do hope you have time for tea."

Inside the kitchen, everything was in its proper place: an antique glass jar full of ginger snaps, matching glass jars containing tea leaves — each labeled by hand — and an electric kettle, positioned side-by-side on the dark granite countertop.

"Gardens impart so much hope," said Yan, acutely attuned to her companion's distress; they had taken their tea and ginger snaps back out to the patio next to the garden. "Each year, they reawaken with renewed growth and vitality."

"It doesn't look as if my most important relationships can be revived," whispered Georgina softly into her teacup. "My daughter blames me for everything." A tear escaped and rolled down Georgina's cheek, and she delicately dabbed it away with a hand-embroidered percale handkerchief, chanting as if to herself, "Yesterday is history; tomorrow is a mystery; today is a gift. That's why we call it the present."

Yan looked at her with raised eyebrows.

"It's a little saying I picked up at an Al-Anon meeting I attended when I was visiting my daughter at the treatment center."

"That must have been difficult."

"My daughter Elise had to go to treatment for prescription drug addiction this year," confessed Georgina, surprised once again to find herself blurting out private information to this woman who, for all intents and purposes, was a stranger.

"I'm so sorry," Yan commiserated.

"I hadn't realized what was going on," Georgina lamented. "I don't know where my head was. Elise was the most gifted of the ballet dancers in the National Ballet School. I guess she began to rely on the prescription for her Attention Deficit Disorder for the energy she needed for the constant practice. She also abused the pain pills she took to treat the various injuries she sustained."

"It's easy to see how people can get hooked. Many young women involved in dance, swimming, or gymnastics become addicted just that way."

"She also learned from her peers to throw up so she could stay skinny."

"I hear that a lot," acknowledged Yan. "They have 'purge parties' at high school and college: girls get together, binge on pizza or some other food, and encourage each other to throw it up before it is metabolized. They become experts on how long food stays in the stomach before it is digested. They can use laxatives too, although those aren't nearly as effective."

"Sounds like you know a little bit about this."

"More than I ever imagined I would. Unfortunately, being involved in the care of young women has made me supremely aware of the health epidemic associated with distorted body image; the ideal body weight has dropped over thirty pounds since I was a young woman. I know girls who'd been valedictorians of their high school graduation class but dropped out of college by sophomore year due to avitaminosis: their brains are so malnourished they no longer function effectively. It's a tragedy. We may have lost a whole generation of girls to the vicissitudes of self-starvation."

"That's what happened with Elise. When I went to visit her for a family week at the treatment center, she accused me of emotionally neglecting her."

"That sounds hurtful," Yan sympathized, reaching over to squeeze Georgina's hand.

"You started to tell me about a group of women you will be meeting with here," mentioned Georgina, wanting to change the subject.

"Yes, of course. It's a group of women — we call it a Goddess Circle — committed to the practice of Goddessence,' which simply means to train yourself to fully focus on whatever is present at the moment. We come together in order to deepen this practice."

"Why the interest in Goddesses?"

"Some of us were already pretty well-schooled in Goddess history and psychology — it's been a part of Women's Studies for a while now. The ancient Greeks were excellent observers of human behavior, and they created mythological characters, Goddesses and Gods, who exemplified the kinds of individuals they saw all around them. Psychologists borrowed from these stories to create personality typologies based on the Greek Goddesses — and let me tell you, these were far more positive than the pathological ones that other psychology nosologies tend to be. In our Goddess Circle, each member chooses a Goddess persona that best fits with her own personality and commits to becoming an avatar of that Goddess."

"Avatar?"

"An avatar is the physical manifestation of a Goddess or her attributes," explained Yan. "For example, from what you've told me, you might find that you have a lot in common with the Goddess Demeter."

"Demeter. Why?"

"Demeter is the Goddess of Nature and Fertility; in charge of growing crops. The story goes that Demeter's daughter, Persephone, was out picking flowers one day when the earth opened up, and Hades grabbed Persephone and kidnapped her into the underground as his queen. Demeter was devastated. She went from god to god, begging them to help her get her daughter back, but everyone was too absorbed in their own pursuits to come to help her. So Demeter decided to gain their attention by throwing ice over the earth so that nothing could grow — remember, that was her power — and famine was created all across the land. This finally got Zeus' attention, and, together with Demeter, they forced Hades to restore Persephone to her mother. One catch was that if Persephone were to ingest anything, she couldn't go back up to earth. The legend has it that, at the last minute, Persephone ate a pomegranate seed. Because of that, she was required to spend half of her time underground with Hades. And half of her time on earth with her mother. This is how the early Greeks explained the seasons of winter and summer."

"Kidnapped by Hades," said Georgina. "That certainly describes how I feel about my daughter: 'kidnapped' by addiction."

"There are a lot of parallels," agreed Yan. "Back in the day of Eleusinian Mysteries, the attendants would use psychedelics to achieve trance; now we practice Goddessence, a natural path to the same goal."

"You mentioned Goddessence a minute ago."

"It is essential to be able to focus the mind and hold that point of concentration in order to master thought, feeling, and behavior. The predicament is that our brains believe they are problem-solving computers, and so — like the tongue that continues to check a canker sore in your mouth — the brain keeps searching for problems to solve. As you bring your mind to an object of concentration — be it the breath or a yoga movement — the brain is constantly wandering off to chase a thought. The trick is to notice when that happens and, gently but firmly, take it by the elbow and redirect it back to the object of focus. This ability to focus is what Goddessence practice is all about."

"And why is this 'essential'?"

"Well, for example, many people meander through their lives without really participating in that life. Have you ever had a shower, got out and towel yourself dry, and then found that you can't remember whether or not you had shampooed your hair?"

"A lot lately," Georgina laughed ruefully.

"It's a terrible waste to float through the years of a life without truly experiencing it. To have your mind somewhere else."

"In my recent experiences with the Twelve-Step Programs – I attend AL-ANON because of my daughter's issues-I've learned to call that an emotional black-out."

"That's a good word for it," smiled Yan. "And there are other ways to use Goddessence. For example, it is important to be able to redirect the mind in order to rescue it from being kidnapped by an emotion. Let's say you suffered from anxiety and were afraid of heights, and one day, you were driving and coming up to a bridge. Your mind might start flashing a scene where you and the car pitch off the bridge and crash into the chasm below. You would be paralyzed with fear. However, if you were well-practiced in Goddessence, you could redirect your mind to focus on the roadway running straight and sure out in front of you, and you'd be able to continue your journey comfortably across the bridge."

"That sounds too good to be true."

"I heard of a woman once who wanted to go by car from San Francisco to Marin County. She paid to have someone else drive her across the Golden Gate Bridge."

"I can sympathize with that. I can't stand feeling anxious." Georgina winced. "It's awful."

"Actually, an adrenaline surge — the physical sensation of anxiety — only lasts between twelve and fourteen seconds on average. The problem is that the sympathetic nervous system 'highjacks' the brain and gets stuck on a dangerous message: 'run...kill...'. That's helpful when you're faced with a life-threatening situation. Today, however, life-threatening events are few and far between."

Georgina walked over to pour herself another cup of tea, offering some to Yan, who held up her cup for a refill.

"I know that dancers look for an adrenaline high to enhance their performance. They go through a series of jumps to pump themselves up so that they won't be flat when they go on stage," she noted, regaining her seat.

"From what I've seen of the ballet, I'm not surprised." Yan reached over to the tea tray to help herself to another ginger snap. They were delicious.

"For someone with depression, the practice of Goddessence is vital," continued Yan. "In depression, the mind gets tunnel vision and starts to think pessimistically, ruminating on the negative: 'life's difficult, and then you die'; thereby deepening the depression — a self-feeding syndrome."

"I've been depressed all my life," sighed Georgina, slumping back wearily in her chair.

"Depression is your mortal enemy. To combat depression, you must be ready to do whatever it takes and go to any lengths in order to turn the mind over and over and over again. It requires eternal vigilance."

"Maybe I can just become numb. Stop feeling."

"That's like not feeling the wind on your face."

"My husband tells me I'm too thin-skinned."

"Would you be willing to do a little experiment that might help you with that?"

Georgina mutely acquiesced. She wasn't sure she deserved to have her depression relieved, given the agony she had caused her daughter, but perhaps she could still be of help to her if the depression got better. It was worth a try.

"I want you to close your eyes and, with your mind's eye, scan your body," Yan intoned as she began to lead Georgina on an imaginal journey through each part of her body, from her left little toe up to the crown of her head.

"Now, I want you to return to a place in your body where you feel the sensation. Nod when you have identified it."

Yan wanted Georgina to excavate through to the bare awareness of the emotions and symbologist associated with her depression.

Georgina nodded.

"You can speak, but keep your eyes closed. Tell me, wherein your body the sensation is."

"Inside my chest; interior to the sternum."

Excellent, thought Yan, the physical location of the heart.

"And what sensation is there?"

"Heavy. And cold."

Good. The heaviness of the chest was a core characteristic of depression, Yan knew.

"And do you have a sense of what color it might be?"

Yan was guiding Georgina to uncover the specifics of the images buried in her psyche.

"A light metal-gray."

"And describe the shape and size."

"It's spike-shaped, about five inches long, two inches wide, and an inch thick."

"And what does it remind you of?"

Now Yan was looking for the unique images that Georgina unconsciously associated with her experience of grief.

"A sword tip that has broken off."

Yan caught her breath. Georgina had described being stabbed in the heart, the weapon remaining embedded within her. Incredibly powerful.

"And if you wanted to change it in some way, how would you transform it?"

Yan sought an equally powerful symbol to vanquish the depression

"I could change it into a healing crystal," Georgina uttered spontaneously.

"As resilient and brilliant as a diamond," replied Yan. The long journey of healing had begun.

Chapter 24

Catharine moved through Jonah's house carrying her clipboard, checking the food and the bar with the catering crew to ensure everything was ready for the Herd Mentality party that night following their performance at the Amp. She was excited about the fusion menu, which she'd kept secret from Jonah. She'd arranged for a chef to come from Austin — famous for his signature Texas barbecue, according to Ursula — as well as a second chef from Toronto, famous for his preparation of Jonah's favorite sushi. Everything had to be perfect, or Jonah would become enraged. He saw anything involving him as a direct reflection of himself. Cat imagined Jonah as a young boy growing up in nearby Jamestown, New York, watching the activities of the Chautauqua Institution where only the privileged could afford to come — the rich from London and California arriving with their private planes and posh prams. The locals would wait tables, clean toilets, and dream of one day becoming a guest. Now the house Jonah had built on the grounds was not only in the most prominent position, at the opposite end of the Institution from the Bellamy Estate, but was easily the most expensive. As an adolescent, Jonah had been more interested in becoming famous enough to get laid on a regular basis than chords and composition. Now he was into total control and, Cat knew, had plans to ditch the rest of the band in order to go solo. Cat was aware that Jonah subscribed to the 'Marry your Muse' philosophy; he'd been very clear about that. His music was his primary relationship. Also, she knew that when musicians were on tour, what happened on the road stayed on the road. Nonetheless, her biological clock was hammering away, and she wanted to start a family, not necessarily to settle down but certainly to have a child. Like Jonah, she had her own career aspirations. From her standpoint, Jonah was as good a sperm donor candidate as any: talented, intelligent, and not demanding of her time and attention. Some minor changes might be in order, but she was just the woman to engineer them. With that in mind, her thoughts turned to who in the Goddess Circle might be of assistance in this endeavor. Perhaps Alex with her communications contacts?

Cody wandered out to join her by the pool as she was checking the snacks and rearranging the chaise cushions.

"A beautiful woman and a hard-working one as well: a winning combination. Maybe I could give you a massage after all your heavy responsibilities have been taken care of," he said, placing a hand on her shoulder.

"Let me save you some time," snapped Catharine, stepping back from Cody's touch. "I am not interested in 'a little massage' from you or anyone but Jonah."

"Well, keep it in mind." Cody grinned again. "I'll be around." Probably longer than you, he thought to himself.

Catharine flounced angrily back into the house as Jonah stepped through from the front foyer. He was accompanied by his business manager, Nathan.

"Nate, give us a minute?" barked Jonah. "Wait for me in my office." Jonah's office was a dark cave at the back of the house.

Jonah strode over and stood eyeball-to-eyeball with Cody. "You're flying a little close to the sun."

"What do you mean?" asked Cody. Jonah seemed to be working himself into a fury, and Cody was eager that the conversation not flare into a conflict with Jonah.

"You hit on my lady in my house when you're begging me to bless your movie?" Jonah rammed his forefinger into Cody's chest and pressed him backward.

"Hey man, you've got it all wrong. I was just trying to compliment Catharine," said Cody obsequiously, fighting to steady his balance. "And compliment you on your choice of companion."

"Don't try to manipulate me. I want you out of here and now. Get all of your gear out too." Jonah kicked at Cody's camera equipment, and it went clattering across the paving stones toward the door.

"You're blowing this all out of proportion," said Cody, scurrying to rescue his precious apparatus.

"And what's more, I rescind any and all approval for your documentary. There is no film. Period. "

Cody felt sick to his stomach. Most of the docudrama had already been shot, with the preliminary roughs accepted to be included in the Toronto Film Festival–a premier venue for distribution deals — just two months away.

"You'll be receiving a letter from my lawyers forbidding you to use any of the footage you've shot. I will sue you if you show a nanosecond of that film. Now get out of here before I have you thrown out."

Cody packed up his cameras and stumbled from the house. How was he going to explain this to his backers, who were counting on negotiating a distribution contract at the festival?

Nathan was waiting as Jonah entered his office and sat down behind his desk. "I've just heard from my broker that the money I had expected to be transferred to my brokerage account was redirected. What do you know about this?" Jonah's tone was low and menacing; the muscles in his jaw twitched with barely suppressed rage.

"You remember we talked about moving your money to the Caymans and just parking it there to avoid the losses hitting the market recently," Nathan reassured him in a conciliatory tone.

"Yeah, we talked about that over a year ago, but the market has turned around, and I wanted that money put back in!" shouted Jonah, anger escalating. "And what happened with the money from selling all that real estate? Where is that?"

"Six months ago, I told you I was liquidating our real estate holdings in order to avoid similar losses with our commercial real estate. Unfortunately, we took heavy losses in that area."

"So, what happened to whatever money we got from those sales?"

Nathan remained seated in the leather chair as if frozen in place while Jonah got up from behind the desk and began pacing back and forth in front of him. "Again, I am holding cash reserves in our accounts in the Caymans. I think it is a good idea to sit on the sidelines and just wait out this financial insecurity," Nathan explained.

"Jerry Deutsch believes there are opportunities to make a killing now and that our present strategy would be to go long on the strong areas and short on a variety of positions where we can make a lot of money. I didn't authorize you to transfer so much into the Cayman accounts, and I didn't know anything about it. Aren't you a signatory on those accounts?"

"Of course. I need to be a signatory in order to conduct the transactions in your best interests and quickly. I can't always get in touch with you at a moment's notice."

"I'm thinking it's more in your best interests than in mine," said Jonah. "I've given Jerry and his group the go-ahead to review all of my affairs and get back to me with their recommendations."

"This is the first I've heard about this," said Nathan. "Why wasn't I consulted?"

"I preferred that the report be entirely independent."

"It won't be independent if Jerry has his way. Jerry wants the money to be in the market. That's where he makes his commissions: buying and selling stocks."

"Well, we'll know tomorrow."

"Tomorrow? What do you mean?"

"The report will be ready tomorrow. Jerry and his accountants are coming here, and we'll all get together to look at what they've found and strategize for the future. Anyway, I've got to go get to work now." Jonah left the office before Nathan could respond.

Nathan sat frozen for a moment. Then he reached for his cell phone.

Chapter 25

Elise and Brynn hurried through the door of Hurlburt Church and down the dark hallway to the room where the 12-Step meeting had already started. Generic 12-Step meetings were held daily at Chautauqua, and anyone already involved in specific 12-Step Programs was welcome to attend. As they entered the inviting room, they were acknowledged by Elise's sponsor, Meryl, who sat at the head of the circle of approximately twenty people. At her side sat Catharine, the woman Elise had met at the previous meeting she had attended.

"My sponsor said Catharine will be giving the lead today. I'm glad you get to hear a woman lead," whispered Elise as they sat in the last two remaining chairs. "She'll be telling us about how it was, what brought her to the-12 Step Program, and how she follows her recovery program."

"My name is Catharine. I am a grateful recovering psychoactive substance and romance addict."

"Hi Catharine," came the resounding rejoinder.

"I may have been born an addict; I've worked my way through so many addictions." After the Serenity Prayer and a reading of the 12 Steps, Catharine immediately launched into her story.

Catharine was born the sixth of seven children and the second daughter of an intellectual family in Krakow, Poland.

When her sister, older than her by two years, died of pneumonia at the age of six, Catharine's mother fell into a severe depression, escaping death by starvation only through the kind ministries of her spinster sister. Left to her own devices, Catharine had taken to visiting the home of the neighboring Baranski family. A gregarious extended family, the Baranskis loved to get together most weeks for some occasion or other. At these gatherings, every table was Lined with bottles of ice-cold vodka."

"The men took great pride in their ability to hold their liquor, and they would try to outdrink one another," Catharine told the 12 Step meeting. The audience nodded in appreciation. "I did a pretty good job of keeping up with the men," Catharine told the 12 Step meeting, "But often, I would overshoot the mark. The guys would laugh at me when I would get too drunk and pass out, but my friends began to worry."

The Baranski Family's other obsession was music. On the weekends, when chores had been finished, they would gather around the radio and listen to classical music coming from all over Poland. Krakow was a magnificent city renowned for its artistic heritage, so revered for its culture and beauty that during the second world war, Goebbels had ordered it spared by the German military, which had reduced the Polish capital, Warsaw, to rubble. In the evenings, Catharine tagged along with Piotr, the youngest of the

Baranski sons, who played violin with musical groups performing throughout the city. Catharine worshipped Piotr and, in her desire to emulate him, began to play the violin as well. At first, Catharine hung around at the sidelines during practice. Soon, however, Piotr, amused by her prowess, asked her to demonstrate her skills to the other members of the group. They were delighted by her, and at the age of ten, she became a mascot for them. They would invite her up on stage at some moment during the performances to solo for the ever-growing audiences. It wasn't too long before word of her prodigy spread, and various of the city's foremost instructors jostled to offer their services. After that, her life became a symphony of fulfilling the fantasies of others, especially her mother, who urged Catharine to live the life her mother wished she'd had. Catharine was relieved to escape the intrusive designs of others when a scholarship brought her to the music conservatory in Toronto, Canada.

"But the competition was brutal," Catharine explained to the audience. "Competitions are the royal road to a career as a classical musician, but every time I sent in a video to enter a competition, I'd be going head-to-head with the greatest talents in the world. I could wallpaper the room with my rejection letters."

Feeling defeated and discouraged by the vicious world of competition, Catharine would often think fondly of the good times at the liquor-laden Baranski family festivities.

"That's known as the learning phase in the development of an addiction," said Catharine. "I came to know that alcohol could transform my mood and my personality. I was drinking a lot."

She was able to laugh, sing, to dance. It was marvelous. Why wasn't everybody doing this? One night at a party, a joint got passed around, and Catharine discovered an instant relaxant. Worry thoughts turned off, and she became warm and dreamy. The next couple of years were a constant whirl of parties. But the fears returned. Eventually, they became worse. She would awaken after a fitful night to the uncomfortable sensation of anxiety in the pit of her stomach.

"Double Anxiety," explained Catharine, "When the symptoms of withdrawal from alcohol are layered upon the original performance anxiety symptoms. I tried to stay in bed and get more sleep but would soon have to get out of bed and be active to quell that feeling in the pit of my stomach and the racing thoughts in my head."

Catharine hated that. She got to the place where she would dread the fear. Worry about worry. By then, it took two, then three, then four drinks plus increasing amounts of weed to get that effect, to shut off the racing worry thoughts in her head: the 'using' phase.

"And then," continued Catharine, "A helpful dentist prescribed Ativan, at that time thought of as the universal panacea, to help me deal with my phobia about dental treatment. And I began my stint as a kitchen pharmacist. Alcohol plus weed plus benzos: Better living through chemistry."

The audience murmured their understanding.

Catharine was hooked: she had to have the drugs just to function. She awoke in the morning, body in withdrawal. She would arise, throw back two Ativan with a tumbler of vodka and lie in the bathtub with warm water up over her ears. Hydrotherapy: soothed by the sounds of the water moving until her palpitating heart slowed to a steady sinus rhythm. Ultimately Catharine beat substance abuse through the loving intervention arranged by her patron.

"Unfortunately, it didn't end there. I then succumbed to a cross-addiction," stated Catharine. "The most daunting addiction, the natural, endogenous addiction for which the dopamine receptors, the brain's cells involved in cocaine and other substance addictions, are designed. Love addiction is also known as fantasy, love or romance addiction, or sex addiction. This addiction is condoned and encouraged by many societies and promoted through all the consequences: job, career, reputation, and physical harm. I am finally, with the help of the 12 Steps, getting a handle on it, but I promise you, it is hard."

Sitting listening to Catharine's lead, Elise felt herself drifting into reverie, transported back to her own struggles with prescription medications. At the mention of love addiction, her thoughts turned to her meeting with Eric at the writer's center, and the sensations stirred when his body was close to hers; but what a stiff and judgmental jerk he turned out to be.

Catharine was concluding her lead.

"There are two energies within us: like two wolves. One wolf represents addiction, and the other represents recovery. The one we feed is the one that will grow stronger; the one we starve will become weaker. The essence of my recovery: don't give in to the addictive urge —just for today, just for this hour, just for this minute —and the addiction wolf will shrink

"Elise. Elise." Finally, she became aware of someone calling her name. She looked up and saw the circle of faces gazing expectantly at her.

"We're waiting for your comment," said Meryl.

"Forgive me. I must have been wool-gathering. I'm a neophyte with less than ninety days of recovery: one raw nerve. I've just relinquished my only coping mechanisms, prescription medications — self-destructive though they were — and have yet to replace pills with the skills that I'm learning here in these rooms. I apologize to the group." Elise resolved not to allow her thoughts to gravitate to the euphoria promised by daydreams of how it might be with Eric.

"One thing they emphasized in treatment is that cravings are like mosquito bites: you want to scratch the bite, but if you do it, it itches even more: scratching will only make it worse. In the small amount of time I have had in recovery, I have learned that if I just tolerate the itch without scratching, in a little while, it will go away." offered Elise, "Don't scratch the itch! If we just stop and observe those initial urges, those first cravings, they will eventually lose strength."

During the meeting, Brynn had slipped her shoe off and was making patterns on the rug; her pointed toe skimmed out to the front, to the side, and then back to tap one-two-three. Elise recognized a rhythm from the pas de deux of the Sleeping Beauty ballet and surmised that Brynn was rehearsing in her mind the sequence due to be performed at the Amp. Brynn probably didn't listen to much of Catharine's lead. *She was encapsulated in the snow shaker of her own world,* thought Elise.

"And before we bring the meeting to a close with the Lord's Prayer, don't forget," Meryl commented, "Pain is inevitable, but misery is optional: what prevents pain from becoming misery is acceptance. I was taught to allow, not will, myself to progress organically through the five stages of acceptance. First was denial — I don't have a problem; I use prescription medications as my physician prescribes. Then came bargaining: I will only use prescription medications for dance performances so I can control it. Next was anger: why is everybody worried about my using pain medications? It's none of their business. Then grief: using pain medications has caused me a lot of grief; for example, I danced through the pain in my back and may have permanently damaged some discs. And finally, acceptance: I have a mental obsession and a physical allergy to pain medications and am grateful that there is a program of recovery to help me with that. After that came gratitude: because of this situation, I have been forced to grow spiritually."

Brynn was noncommittal after the meeting.

Elise lifted her eyebrows. "Aren't you going to join us for lunch? I'd like you to get to know Meryl a little better."

"I'll take a rain check. I have to be early to warm up for Master Gregory's rehearsal. You remember how he is." With a vague nod, Brynn slung her ballet bag over her shoulder and hurried off toward the Amp.

"Denial is so powerful," sighed Elise, discouraged that Brynn would not lunch with them as she had hoped. "It's not just a river in Egypt."

"Cheer up. She'll be back." Meryl put her arm around Elise's shoulders and gave her an encouraging hug. "Denial functions like the iris of an eye. When a crisis happens —maybe a person gets busted— there is a tiny nanosecond when that person may be open to undistorted information, and you can flood reality through the crack in the wall of denial, like the light streaming through the open iris. Then the portal closes, and information becomes distorted once again: justification, rationalization, and minimization take over. All you can do at that point is wait for the next calamity, another minuscule moment of clarity, and then present another piece of your truth. It can be a long and frustrating process. Sometimes people have to keep banging their heads against that brick wall; keep running into life's lessons until they become willing to turn their lives around. The is no easier or softer way. If left untreated, there are only three possible outcomes for addiction; jail, the insane asylum, or the cemetery."

"I hope that doesn't have to happen to Brynn," muttered Elise.

Chapter 26

On her return from the Goddess Circle, Alex peered into the dining room to check on the progress of the party preparations. The younger set would be attending the Herd Mentality performance at the amphitheater followed by a party hosted by Catharine, while the movers and shakers of the Chautauqua Institution had been summoned to Alex's Chautauqua home for her annual opening weekend dinner party. There, members of the Chautauqua establishment would rub shoulders and exchange ideas with the speakers and luminaries scheduled for the upcoming week's lectures.

"Good afternoon, Your Highness," said her housekeeper, curtseying. Anna stood in attendance, her white long-sleeved shirt and slender dark skirt hemmed just below the knee. Anna was the last of a long line of the family that had attended the Romanov dynasty.

Alex had long ago tired of reminding Anna about using her royal appellation.

"The staff probably gains vicarious glory from their employers' status," Alex had told her children.

"Put on the white gloves before you touch the table linens!" Anna snapped at the crew, unpacking the royal Linens from their crates and arranging the dining tables. She scrutinized the heavy white over white embroidered linens being smoothed over the dining table and the hand-painted porcelain plates and heavy silverware embossed with the crest of the Romanovs, the Russian Royal family. These treasures had been carefully packed in trunks and, along with a magnificent art collection, spirited away from Russia to England prior to the 1918 revolution in anticipation of the later arrival of the aristocratic families

Alex had grown up within the 'White Russian' community that had taken exile in England, where they set about recreating the former extravagant lifestyle that had enraged the Russian proletariat. Beneath massive crystal chandeliers that had been smuggled out of Russia as the Tsar and his family were being murdered, Princes in epauletted splendor escorted magnificently gowned princesses to galas— the Princess Alexandra Aurelia Romanov, the most beautiful of them all.

"I have lived more lives than a cat," Alex mused, shaking her head.

At the memory of the life she had spent with her beloved and revered grandmother, Alex felt tears well up and spill over the lush fringes of her dark eyes. Even as the tears streaked down her porcelain cheeks, she heard her grandmother's displeased voice in her head: 'Never look back. If we ever start to cry, we would never stop.'

"Bring the flowers over here for her highness' approval," instructed Anna to a gardener waiting by the French doors leading to the cutting garden.

Cat slipped from the garden to the dining room of Alex's home.

"How regal she looks," thought Catharine as she caught sight of Alex, lost in concentration, rearranging the jewel-encrusted porcelain Faberge eggs that were kept locked in the dining room hutch.

"Just like the royal family," Alex murmured aloud. "The glittering exterior remains, but the interior has become hollow."

"There's a story there, I'm sure," commented Catharine.

"Oh, I didn't hear you come in." Alex's composure revealed none of the startle response she may have been experiencing. Her hand swept up to clasp the gold filigree barrette that caught her dark heavy tresses at her neck.

"How did your afternoon go?" she asked.

"Oh, fine," responded Cat.

"All set for tonight?" she asked, thinking that Cat had been busy all afternoon preparing for her party...

"Mostly, I think."

"Mostly?" Alex turned her full concentration on Cat. "Now you're sounding like my daughters when they were adolescents 'What did you do? ... Nothing...Where did you go? Nowhere. Who did you see? No one. Did you have a good time? Mostly.'"

"Maybe you're right," said Cat and laughed. "But I'm abiding by Chautauqua rules. We do what we want, and if we want anyone to accompany us or if we want to talk about it, we do. Otherwise, we aren't required to."

"You catch on fast," observed Alex.

"I'm a quick learner. Most of the arrangements for the Herd Mentality party are in order, and I thought I'd drop by to see if I could give you a hand."

"No need," said Alex. "I'm quite content just puttering around in 'entertainment trance.'"

"As you wish," said Cat, leaving Alex puzzling over this encounter. Her puzzlement was short-lived, however, as her thoughts turned toward the arrival of her husband, Parker, who was flying in for this evening's party.

Chapter 27

The gym was at the western edge of the Institution, close to the access road. The facility itself was high-tech, modern —every newest gadget in place —built to meet the needs of the younger, entitled crowd obsessed with total fitness. Eric and Miko entered the workout area and passed numerous young people on treadmills and step machines, each absorbed by the motivational music piped into their ears via iPods.

"Hey, they were sweet chicks we ran into at the Amp," Miko said. Miko moved into a light stretching program as Eric picked up some free weights. "Maybe this summer won't have to be so boring after all; that ballerina is one sweet girl."

"Oh, here we go again," muttered Eric. "I didn't think a small-town girl would be to your taste."

"Did you see her move? So graceful. Light as air."

"Do we have to watch you go through another infatuation? How many girls has it been so far? They are all 'the most beautiful.'"

"This one is different."

"You say that about each one. You go through love interests the way I go through vitamin water."

"I got the feeling that Brynn was really into me," Miko went on rapturously.

"You think every girl is really into you."

"Jealous much? How about Elise? She's another beauty."

"Right now, I'm only interested in studying for LSATs and getting into a good law school," said Eric, slamming the weights down perilously close to Miko's foot as he got up to leave.

"Don't sweat it. Glammy can get us anywhere that we want to go. Hey man, where are you off to?" yelled Miko.

"Have to go and check on the rowing schedule. Can't remember when the first race is tomorrow."

"Don't forget we're going to the Mentality party tonight," Miko reminded him. This was what was most important to Miko, not rowing. "I'll see you back at the house."

Eric left without answering, almost bumping into Chester.

"Where are you going, man? Have to stay in top shape for August training camp, you know."

"Got things to do," said Eric. "Miko is in the weight room. You have him all to yourself. But you're going to have to listen to another ongoing love fest."

"What do you mean?"

"He's in love. Again."

"Really, who is it this time?"

"You'll find out," said Eric. "One of these times, Miko might really get hooked on one of these girls. You never know."

Chapter 28

Georgina gazed around the high ceilings ablaze from the light of an exquisite cut-glass chandelier dominating the center of the elaborate decor. The walls of the room were covered with burgundy silk damask, and dark bronze tassels held back the heavy brocade draperies. Monogrammed white linens and heavy silver were impeccably arranged on the heavy ornate Russian Empire dining table. She spotted her hostess graciously greeting the streams of arriving guests resplendent in evening wear, each more distinguished and powerful than the one before.

Yan had dismissed her protests that she had not personally been invited, stating that their hostess Alex would welcome a fellow Torontonian. "Toronto is a big city but a small world. I can't imagine that you and Alex haven't met in some venue or other."

She was right, of course. Georgina had met Alex on several occasions. As usual with such encounters, Georgina wondered, with a hint of shame, what Alex might know about Owen's womanizing. It had always been important to maintain appearances, for her daughter as much as for herself, but she feared she might not be able to keep the latest events under wraps for long.

On their arrival, Yan made sure Georgina was introduced to many people and pointed out others whom Georgina might like to meet. On the far side of the room Chas Dawes, governor of Virginia, was gesticulating broadly, threatening to spray those standing around him with the red wine held in his glass. On the sofa by a large gilt-framed mirror, writer-in-residence, Jeffrey Canto, spoke intensely to his seating partner, Maria Cameron, Director of Education for the Chautauqua Institution. Finding herself stranded between several lively conversations, with a heavy heart Georgina escaped into the coolness of the garden. The meticulously tended garden had been tempting her throughout the excellent dinner, and on more than one occasion, she had found herself gazing wistfully toward the French doors leading to the outside. Here, edged by gray stone-sculpted ledges, perennial beds were dotted by brilliantly vibrant annuals that glowed richly in the gloaming.

"I'm so ignorant." Georgina thought about the earlier situation at the dinner table in which two men on either side of her kept a conversation going around and over her as if she were invisible. Her husband was always berating her for not keeping up with current events, even if only to be able to make small talk on social occasions. Georgina had explained to him that she was reluctant to accompany him to dinner parties because she stumbled over intellectual conversations.

"If you read anything other than the arts section of the paper, you would be more informed," he had replied brusquely.

Afterward, Georgina had diligently read the Toronto Globe and Mail and the Toronto Star and had spent several hours each week memorizing the Sunday New York Times, but the stories never seemed to hold her interest or stay in memory very long. This evening's party had been particularly difficult. On top of her usual insecurity about keeping up with dinner party conversation, thoughts of her daughter and poor Princess invaded her mind. She had had a momentary respite in chatting with Alex's assistant, who was vigilantly overseeing the progress of the party. Anna described how Alex had brought with her to the Chautauqua social season certain Canadian foods and beverages, favorites such as "butter tarts," and the richly brewed coffee Georgina was now enjoying. "President's Choice," she remembered. Anna told about crossing the Canadian-U.S. border at the Peace Bridge, her van loaded with the specialties. When asked by the border guards if they had anything to declare, Anna sighed regretfully 'twenty-seven cans of coffee' and settled in to wait for the thorough search since coffee was a favored medium of drug smugglers.

"An interesting anecdote," thought Georgina. "Probably rehearsed for just this type of situation: having to entertain a socially inept guest."

But Georgina couldn't dwell on her failure for long. The garden was too magical. Tiny lights wove throughout the branches of the bushes that Lined the flower beds. The light seemed to sparkle in response to the blinking of fireflies among the leaves. The background sound of the dinner party chatter going on inside faded as she drifted past Victorian settees positioned in discreet areas throughout the garden and headed towards a conversational grouping at its farthest corner. Alex's garden backed onto a common space where strolling couples could be heard whispering to each other.

"This furniture seems casually scattered," said a voice from the gloaming, "but whatever Alex does, there's a lot of forethought that goes into such a placement. Don't you agree?"

A slender forty-something man materialized from a trio of silver ash nestled at the corner border.

"Won't you join me?" he patted the ruby velveteen cushion next to him.

Georgina's heart slowed from its startle response as she sat down.

"Everyone calls me Rafi. I won your heart earlier at the Farmer's Market. Remember?"

"Yes, I remember," murmured Georgina. "I thought I would step out and catch a breath of fresh air."

"And I'm out here to catch my breath from the nonstop small talk. I hate it," he confessed.

"Are you here at Chautauqua to give a lecture?"

"Workshop," he replied. "I get to pester people for one week, not just one hour. I work with hieroglyphics."

"Oh," Georgina said. "Yan has told me about you. I am to talk to you about the hieroglyphics I seem to see in cloud formations."

"In cloud formations?"

"It sounds odd, I know. But the other day, I was walking along Lake Drive early in the morning, and as I was watching the sun rise over the hills, my attention was caught by the clouds. I sat down on one of the benches by the water and kept looking at them, and as I watched, various scenarios and hieroglyphics seemed to appear. Yan made me draw them for her in the sand down by the beach."

"Could you draw them for me?" asked Rafael.

"Yan took pictures of the figures I drew for her in the sand. I can show you those if you are sure you can spare the time."

"Oh, I am quite sure." His gaze was penetrating.

"I think everybody who is anybody is here tonight," said Georgina, standing up from the seat and glancing at the garden doors leading back to the party. Fighting the intensity of his gaze.

"This is Alex at her best," he agreed. "There will probably be enough money raised tonight to cover the whole Chautauqua season next year. And I am delighted that my group is to receive some of that money. Like most researchers, we depend on the kindness of strangers in order to fund our work. I carry my beggar's cup to all the social events thrown by the legendary Chautauqua hostesses, Alex and Teresa Bellamy."

"Are you referring to Teresa Bellamy, the woman that owns the Bellamy Estate?"

"Yes, down at the end of Lake Drive. Have you been there?"

"No, but I think that I may have encountered one of her grandsons."

Chapter 29

A crush of people was dancing to the latest Herd Mentality album piped through the two hundred-thousand-dollar sound system Jonah had recently installed. People were everywhere. Catharine recognized many of them as regular attendees of parties past. There were the usual suspects, agents, and other business types in expensive 'country casual' sipping long island iced tea as they worked the room. There were singers and musicians in their more colorful, even bizarre, get-ups. Cat recognized Rufus, a tall, dark-haired fellow whose dreamy looks and intense masked ambition, according to Jonah. Rufus had been the lead guitarist for Jonah's band and Savannah the singer back at the start, but the two had left in pursuit of their own phenomenally successful careers. Cat had been surprised that Jonah, hearing that Savannah was in the area visiting her parents, had invited her and her now-husband, Rufus. She knew that Savannah and Jonah had been an item for some time before the lead guitarist had convinced her to leave. Let bygones be bygones, he had said. The band has survived the departure of its main members before, Cat said to herself, thinking of Jonah's own plan to leave the group. Walkouts were as common with bands as with hairdressing salons.

And there were the ubiquitous young women, beautiful of faces and fabulous of figures. Groupies thought Cat contemptuously. Their self-esteem depended on being attached to famous people. "And the girls' outfits get skimpier every year," she commented to no one in particular.

Many of the young men and women swayed close together, barely moving to the music. Cat noticed the grandson of Teresa Bellamy, a Polish prince she heard, dancing with a beautiful young woman from the Chautauqua ballet troupe. You can always tell a ballerina by her carriage, she noted. In another corner, girls were dancing in a group, bunched together, bodies in frenzied motion, arms waving over their heads. Many of them were clearly high, eyes vacant and mouths slack. The catering crew moved among the dancers carrying trays of drinks. Bowls of cocaine were out in plain sight on many of the tables. The air was heavy with the smell of pot.

I could get a contact high just standing here, thought Catharine. She wanted a clear head as she was fasting and preparing for the Goddess Circle rituals that would be ongoing over the next couple of days. She saw Leni sprawled in the corner, surrounded by young women, each more beautiful than the next. She knew that part of most young men's dream to be a rock star involved having easy access to young women who would do anything to be invited into back rooms at concerts and parties, strictly for the purpose of having sex with a star or with someone connected, however remotely, to a star. She felt this was more to be pitied than scorned, but she knew that Jonah, who was surprisingly ascetic for a musician, didn't approve of Leni's excesses and thought his practices threatened the band.

"Savannah will be singing in a couple of minutes," announced Leni, abandoning his harem to mount the stage. Jonah's musician friends often came to his parties, and he always made sure they had a stage to perform on. There was a stampede as everyone rushed outside to watch the former lead singer for the Herd Mentality

Savannah was reaching the explosive peak of her performance when Elise noticed Brynn exiting from the back of the audience. She followed her to the bathroom and sat down to wait for her outside. Brynn came out.

"You can't keep doing this, you know," Elise said quietly.

"Oh my God!" gasped Brynn turning, her hand flying unbidden to her mouth, "You scared the living daylights out of me."

"If only that were true. We need to talk."

"Why so gloomy?" Brynn deflected.

Brynn had the same thousand-mile stare as the dancers in the nearby room, probably high from something she had taken in the bathroom; Elise was uncertain whether anything she had to say would get through to her.

"It takes one to spot one," said Elise. "I know addict behavior when I see it. I'm worried about you."

"Worried about me?" said Brynn. "Everyone is worried about you."

"No one knows better than me about scoping out the nearest bathroom," said Elise. "Listen, I know how tough it is to keep up your pace: constantly in pain, constantly exhausted, and constantly worried that you won't be good enough and will be replaced by the next upcoming ballerina."

"Just because you couldn't cut it and were replaced doesn't mean the rest of us are like that."

Elise expected this response. As the 'identified patient,' she was the one who had disclosed her behavior; others could just point at her as an overreactive convert and pretend they weren't similarly impaired. She had role-played such encounters in therapy.

"Brynn, there are only three ends to the life you are leading: jail, the insane asylum, or the cemetery. And I am too fond of you to stand idly by while you destroy yourself."

"You don't know what you're talking about. I'm in control of the cocaine. I just use it to have fun occasionally. You might need 12 Step meetings, but they're not for me. They're just cults for weak people." Brynn walked past her back to the party

Elise wondered whether she'd sounded like that, knowing immediately the answer was yes.

Susannah continued to wow the crowd from the stage, but Jonah had left the show and was back in his studio fooling around with a new composition on the keyboard and enjoying the Cuban cigar Cody had brought him from Canada.

"That doesn't have the 'Herd Mentality' sound," charged Leni, helping himself to a cigar from the humidor on Jonah's desk. He lit up and inhaled with gusto.

"Hey man, you're welcome," said Jonah. "What gets you away from the chicks to come in here?"

"Wanted to see what you were up to," said Leni cryptically.

"I'm up to getting away from the noise and the crowd and coming back to what made me in the first place: composing."

"What made you?" An edge crept into Leni's voice.

Jonah's silence was deafening as he turned from the keyboard to look directly at Leni.

"Word on the street is that you are going to dump us and go out on your own," said Leni. "You're dumping us just like Savannah dumped you."

"I've made no secret of the fact that being on the road all the time in front of thousands of screaming kids is getting old for me," said Jonah.

"You say that every time you get interested in a chick."

"I miss having time to really get into my music," said Jonah, ignoring Leni's remark.

"What do you mean? We are into our music. Whatever we compose, I do the lyrics, and you make the music."

"I need a change. I'd like to have time alone to think about what music I might make on my own, try out different sounds."

"What does that mean for the rest of us?"

"You're always talking about starting your own band. Maybe it's time," said Jonah.

"Are you just going to kick us to the curb after all these years?" Leni was yelling now. "I could have had my own band or gone out with other bands so many times, but I didn't because of my loyalty to you."

"Don't blame me for the decisions you've made," said Jonah. "I never promised to spend the rest of my life with this band. I've made no secret of the fact that I was more interested in composing than in performing."

"You. Composing! There you go again," scoffed Leni. "We've always worked together on new material. You can't tell who did what."

"You don't understand," said Jonah. "I am truly happiest when I am by myself with my music. It's always been like that."

"This is unbelievable. I'm not going to allow you to break up the guys. I'm not going to allow you to go on alone riding on the fame of the Herd Mentality."

"I am the Herd Mentality," retorted Jonah.

"We'll see about that." Leni slammed the door on his way out

Leni almost bumped into Catharine on his way out. Jonah saw her and shook his head. "There's something about that guy who brings out my inner fascist."

"You promised you'd come upstairs with me." Cat came up behind Jonah and put her arms around him. "They're all stoned; they won't miss us."

"You go on up. I have one more thing I have to do."

As Catharine left to go up to the bedroom, Jonah hastened along the path back to the party, eager to get back to Cat.

Everybody wants a piece of me; he thought as a young man grabbed him by the arm.

"Hey, Jonah. We finally have our moment alone to talk."

Jonah stood frozen and stared down at Miko's hand on his arm, but Miko refused to take his hand away.

"And you are...?" Jonah queried.

"I am Miko, Prince Mikjal Kazmierz. Various important people who know you have sent emails to offer introductions and let you know that I would be here tonight so that we could discuss your plans to go solo."

"I don't know who you are," declared Jonah. "I don't know what you mean by my going solo, and I don't have time for the likes of you." Jonah freed himself and started to walk away.

Miko grabbed his arm again. "Hold on a minute. I have endless contacts and limitless resources and will do a terrific job as your new manager. I am prepared to offer you my exclusive services. I am prepared to devote all of my time and attention to you."

"I don't know who you think you are, but I'm telling you, for your own good, let go of my arm before I call my bodyguards to throw you out."

Miko dropped his arm and took a step back. "I'm telling you," repeated Miko. "This is a once-in-a-lifetime opportunity. I am offering you my exclusive services. I am prepared to devote all of my time and attention to your career."

"What makes you think I need you? You are a nobody. You are no one. You have nothing I need," sneered Jonah. Alerted by the tone in his boss's voice, Jonah's bodyguard suddenly stepped out of the shadows.

"Get this guy out of here, "ordered Jonah, "and don't ever allow him near me again."

The bodyguard twisted Miko's arm behind his back and propelled him through the crowds and, in front of the now curious onlookers, jettisoned him out the front door onto the lawn.

"You have no idea who you are dealing with!" Miko picked himself up and dusted off the front of his pant legs.

Brynn was preparing to leave the party in order to meet curfew at the ballet dorm. Miko had dismissed her invitation to leave with her, claiming that he had "business to conduct with his new client." She wandered through groups of people chatting, using drugs, making out. At one point, she thought she'd sighted Miko on the side of the house; she called out, but the shadowy figure melted into the darkness. Brynn shrugged and continued on her way home, eager to get back. The last thing she wanted was to be suspended from the program for the upcoming performance, her debut as prima ballerina now that Elise had stepped down. She knew that prominent patrons of the ballet would be in attendance. And perhaps Miko as well? Perhaps he'd be impressed enough to pursue a deeper commitment.

Chapter 30

Alex watched the gravitational pull of her husband, Parker, the energy rising in the group around him as one after another tried to get his attention. "Parker is better-looking this evening in his dinner jacket than on the day we met. Some men just become more attractive and more distinguished as they age," she whispered to herself. "And too often, women become invisible as they grow older." Alex was aware that, on occasion, Parker became involved with other women, but she was confident that these women were merely distractions, like playing blackjack or sailing; these pastimes didn't interfere with their family, their business, or the interests important to them. For example, sustaining the Chautauqua Institution was important to Alex, and so Parker flew into the local airport, his private pilot sitting right chair, and arrived just an hour before the party in order to support her philanthropy. They had made the best of the scant time they had had in private: they had a great sex life, no matter what else was going on, they always had that — and Alex was feeling warm and contented as together they greeted their guests.

As Yan and the other goddesses left the party and sauntered out to the garden, Yan caught sight of Georgina and Rafael and led the other women over to meet them.

"Georgina, let me introduce Angelique Beignet and Ursula Andrews. I see Rafi has captured you."

Rafael greeted the others and addressed Ursula in particular. "It is a great honor to meet you. I'm looking forward to your presentation."

Ursula had led many studies on the socialization of women and girls. Her earlier studies had focused on girls in U.S. schools and how they were brainwashed by subtle forces to restrain their opinions in favor of winning popularity among their peers and others. "I know a lot of women have been interested in my research and lectures, but it's nice to have a man be enthusiastic about my work," Ursula said. "As a matter of fact, I'm trying to find a publisher who is interested enough in the global issues of women and girls to support my next book on the impact of microfinancing — the feedback I've had is that my niche audience is too small. Maybe if I were to title it 'Microfinancing in the bedroom,' I'd get more male attention."

Rafael chuckled. "I've been to many underdeveloped areas of the globe through my work, areas where women are second-class citizens if citizens at all. The micro-financing of women's cottage industry supports the status of women, and when the status of women is supported, health care and education increase and conflicts decrease."

"A man who appreciates the importance of women can be very sexy," stated Ursula with a wink. "In this post-feminist world, there remain gains to be made; today's superwoman is working so hard that she does not have residual resources to look up from her hectic schedule. The fact remains that only a tiny percentage of industrial and political leaders are female, and women still earn seventy-nine cents against the male dollar earned. And this even though in many areas women represent seventy percent of the financial heads of households and another large percentage are contributing heftily to their family finances."

"Well," Georgina blurted out, "I am concerned about the trend that has sixty percent of our mothers of pre-school age children 'finding themselves' by earning a paycheck working at a cash register in some 'big box' store. Our children are not getting the proper care and direction in the home, and this is affecting their school performance. The schoolrooms are out of control."

The conversation came to an abrupt halt, and Georgina felt the blood rushing to her face as she caught Angelique glancing over at Ursula and rolling her eyes. Yan moved protectively to Georgina's side, glaring sternly at the other women.

"I certainly agree that while more and more mothers of school-aged children are working outside of the home, the childcare situation has not improved to the same degree; in fact, it may have gotten worse than it was when I was a young working mother," interjected Yan, attempting to dissipate the sudden tension.

"Tomorrow is a working day for me," uttered Rafael, tactfully bowing out of the discussion. "I must get my beauty sleep."

"Perhaps we should all get back in. Alex will be wondering where we are," said Angelique.

"I'm just going to sit out here a bit longer," said Ursula. "I'll be in shortly."

The breeze whistled through the tops of the surrounding trees; all around her, the leaves rustled. Ursula sat on a settee at the edge of the garden and allowed herself to fall into the comfortable lethargy that preceded Goddessence:' the deep trance that she would use to access the power of the Goddess Artemis. Remaining motionless, she awaited the arrival of her power animal, wondering from what direction the deer would emerge. The scent of burning seemed to saturate the air, and figures materialized out of wisps of smoke and floated, one by one, to the ground in front of her. One of the figures was clad in a deep cherry red woolen robe that had a brilliant blue heron emblazoned on the back. Her thick black hair, parted in braids, framed her diamond-struck cheekbones. She rose slowly and addressed Ursula in a commanding voice:

"We are the Clan Mothers, leaders of the six nations of the Iroquois Confederacy, the names of which are carved into the benches of the sacred fire pit. Our desire is to live in peace; however, as 'Keepers of the Western Gate,' we sorrowfully gather in this place to decide whether to send our brave warrior-sons into battle to protect our way of life. As women and mothers, we make that decision with aching hearts. The women of the Iroquois are respected and revered; men neither rape nor abuse us. We are respected. We come to you tonight with a message of danger. Our spirits have been disturbed by the spirit of violence here at Chautauqua — a place sacred to us. This night the one with red hair will be raped; another will die by fire. This savagery must be stopped."

With these final words, the figures before her dissipated. Ursula emerged from her reverie to the sound of twigs snapping nearby and the presence of her power animal, The Golden Hind, at her side. In the distance, she could hear the eerie shriek of fire alarms. Behind the black profile of the house, the glare of red sheared the southern skies.

Inside, dessert was being served in Alex's dining room: Crème Brule with a curl of chocolate, raspberries, and blackberries strewn tastefully on top. Yan and Georgina joined the group of violinists from the music school that had been playing softly throughout the party. One of the violinists, noting Catharine's absence, began telling about the "Strad fiddle" that had recently sold for over four million dollars

"Boy, my husband may not necessarily be impressed by the music itself, but he certainly would be impressed with those figures," remarked Georgina.

"So, nothing's changed since he and I were in the same fraternity at college," said Parker coming over to greet Georgina with a kiss on the cheek. "Where is Owen anyway? Is he here with you at Chautauqua?"

"Unfortunately, the business has kept him in Toronto this summer," said Georgina, color rising to her face.

Just then, the door slammed open. Ursula burst into the room shouting, "Fire! Big fire down at the south end of the Institution!"

The party swept from the front rooms onto the lawn. People strained to watch the huge blaze, which was sending showers of sparks onto the roofs of the vulnerable historic frame houses of the Institution. From the west end could be heard the oversized bell of the firehouse clanging the alarm. Frightened whispers of "tinderbox" and "the ecoterrorists again" swept through the frightened throng as they began to move en masse toward the Herd Mentality house at the south end.

Chapter 31

"Lazy, languor, languid," crooned Catharine, enjoying the sensation of the words rolling off her tongue. She could feel lassitude radiate steadily across her limbs as she glided farther away from the sounds of Savannah's performance and up the staircase. Not everyone outside was watching the performance, however, and her exit was noted by more than one person. Raul, one of the roadies, noticed a slim shadow move stealthily away from the crowd toward the stairs. He thought to mention it to Jonah, but glancing around, he was unable to find him. Soon his attention was drawn back to the stage, and this strange sighting was soon forgotten in the mind-numbing ecstasy of the pulsing rhythms.

Upon entering her suite, Catharine slid out of her deep pink clinging gown, the sheath for which she had momentarily forsaken her signature short-short skirt and cowboy boots. Her subtle curves were those of a woman at the peak of her beauty. Naked, she moved onto the balcony overlooking the playing fields, sensing the coolness of the evening breeze in the quickening of her nipples, and scanned the darkened skies above the lake for the first glimpse of the crescent that would herald the moon phase of the Goddess Circle. For the past two nights, the skies had been black, and she was hoping that this night she would be able to discern the first etchings of the new moon. But had it been just two nights that the sky remained black? She wasn't as sure as she would have liked. Her memory felt blurry. Wasn't it last night that she was finally able to identify the nimbus of an approaching moon? The dreaminess of trance beckoned, but she shook her head in order to complete her assigned task. She took in a deep breath of the pure and cleansing air. She picked up a girdle of seashells and clasped it about her bare waist. Her ruling Goddess, Aphrodite, had woven such a girdle to render powerless all males who caught sight of it. Her mind was now truly fuzzy. She wanted to be present for what she knew was to come, but she kept being lured into her interior world, where it was warm and dreamy. Did she remember putting down her glass of water momentarily? She knew that once you put down your drink, it was no longer yours. Anyone could slip a drug into an unattended drink: GHB, the date-rape drug, had been common on university campuses, and Cat was more than familiar with its usage by predators. She moved about the bedroom suite and touched familiar objects, naming each one aloud. She picked up her favorite lotion brought with her in anticipation of this night and inhaled its intoxicating fragrance deeply. She emptied some of it onto her palm and rubbed it into her skin, luxuriating in her body's arousal. Finally, she fell back onto the silken sheets and gave herself over to the dreamlike state. She floated off into the goddess fields of Beltane: sweet grasses growing all around her and garlands of daisies in her hair. A slight shift in atmosphere confirmed the anticipated arrival of potent male energy into the room. Flashes of vibrating color penetrated the opaque veil of shuttered eyelids. She remained still, breath shallow as a bunny sensing an approaching predator. Yet, she was not alarmed. She felt a whispering of the sheets. Muscular arms encircled her. Hands transmitted desire to her breasts and lower. Primeval surf sounded in her ear. Above the roaring of ancient waves, she was aware of Yan's voice circling in her mind. Words that whispered of Beltane, the summer solstice rite of the great queen and the great king mating anonymously to create the next powerful leader. The building heat of her lover's body burned across the bedclothes. Her own being ignited in the eternal flame of creation.

Startled awake by the sounds of sirens and screams, Catharine staggered down the stairs as she continued to fight against the fog in her mind. She reeled out the front door and attempted to fight against the fog in her mind. She could just make out the glowing pile of metal and recognize it as Jonah's car when strong arms wrestled her to safety behind a tree. Hungry flames reached the gas tank, and an explosion spewed sparks that merged with the star-strewn sky.

SECTION III

Chapter 32

"How quaint. Early Chautauqua Ladies' Guild?"

Angelique gazed pointedly around the sheriff's office. She had arranged an appointment to check on the investigation into the death of Catharine's lover, Jonah Nash. Country-lace curtains adorned the windows, and the comfy sofa and nearby chairs were covered in chintz and arranged in a cozy semi-circle that invited visitors to sit and stay a while. Angelique noticed the coffee cart featured a single-serving coffee maker and an array of Wolfgang Puck Rodeo Drive coffee pods, along with an assortment of sweeteners and flavored creamers. An array of coffee mugs completed the setting. It was a far cry from the paper cups and day-old bitter coffee dregs that she was accustomed to at her District Attorney's office.

"Ms. Angelique Beignet, I presume." Sheriff Tom Cahill paused briefly in his perusal of The Chautauqua Daily. The newspaper typically featured the special events of each day at the Institution, but on this day, the death of the area's number one celebrity was splashed in bold headlines across the front page. The sheriff scowled as he read the coverage. He knew his job rested on maintaining the impression that Chautauqua remained a safe retreat for the many residents who escaped here from crime-infested cities.

"Do you always leave your office open?" challenged Angelique with a barely suppressed surprise.

"Haven't you heard? Chautauqua is among the safest places in the country," replied Tom brusquely, holding up the front page of the newspaper to show his visitor. The pupils of his eyes dilated, and his jaw clenched. He was definitely not in a good mood.

"And what can I do for you on this busiest of all days?" Sheriff Cahill's burnished Georgyo Brutini tasseled loafers kicked up onto the mahogany desk, and his lengthy muscular frame tilted back in an ergonomic dark green leather swivel chair

"I was hoping we could talk about my helping out with the interviews of those present during the time of the murder," Angelique said.

"So far, there is no evidence to suggest murder."

"You can't possibly be considering this an accidental death." Angelique was shocked.

Sheriff Cahill stood and drew himself up to his full height; his jeans retained their knife-sharp crease, and his shirt had clearly been double-starched.

"It could be that Jonah Nash had enough drugs in his system to anesthetize a horse and he just passed out with one of his fancy Cuban cigars still lit."

"You're kidding, right?"

"May I remind you, Ms. Beignet: this is not your precinct, this is not your jurisdiction, and this is not your case." The sheriff's expression was unyielding.

This is going well, thought Angelique. "Nonetheless, I have extensive experience,"

"You seem to know who I am, so I'm sure you're aware of my reputation as an expert on profiling and micro-expression. I am trained to note how a person's physiology shifts as their emotional state changes. When a person's eyes widen, the mouth opens, or eyebrows arch, for example, this reflects the interior experience of that individual. For example, it's obvious that you're not having a good day." She left unsaid her suspicions that the Sheriff had no such experience, assuming he'd spent his years in the safe confines of Chautauqua.

"Ah yes," he responded, ignoring her last remark. "You blink more rapidly when you're stressed, purse your lips when irritated, raise your eyebrows when angry, and lower them when afraid. They teach stuff like that at college now, do they?"

"You've studied micro-expression?"

"I spent years with the FBI Profilers Unit, and, more importantly, I've been involved in enough poker games in my lifetime to be somewhat of an expert on my own on what gamblers call 'tells.' I, in turn, can tell by your posture that you have nothing but contempt for what I've just told you and believe that understanding body language can only be learned by sitting in some college classroom."

Angelique regarded the sheriff and then, in an exaggerated pantomime, softened her posture and dropped her arms, which had been crossed in front of her chest, to her side.

Sheriff Cahill chuckled. "Oh, did I say that out loud?"

"It may be that women spend a lot of years at college because we have to be twice as credentialed to get half as far, especially in law enforcement. There's a lot to be learned about the physiology of the body," Angelique reiterated.

"Hmm. You don't say. I wonder if that works on our hardened criminal types," Sheriff Cahill scratched his head and innocently looked up at the ceiling.

"I'm hardly an idiot. Sheriff. I realize that although the research shows that people scratch their noses when they lie-lying causes an adrenaline rush that causes capillaries, including the ones in your nose, to expand, creating an itch-it doesn't work with sociopaths because they have very low adrenaline release." Angelique was annoyed that he continued to toy with her.

"My apologies. Truth be told, I might need your help," said the sheriff thinking back on the headlines of the paper he had just put down. If it turned out that the death wasn't an accident, if it turned out that there was a murderer at the Institution, the pressure to solve the cases and restore confidence would be intense. "There's only me on the case, and I am expecting the press to arrive en masse any minute. Can we call a truce?"

"Truce it is. Now, what have you found out so far? Not that this is a homicide."

Chapter 33

Ursula and Angelique hurried along the tree-fringed red brick walk on the east side of Bestor Plaza but soon found their path blocked by a line of people, some standing and chatting, others seated in folding chairs reading the morning papers.

"Merciful heavens," exclaimed Cat, weaving among the people on the walkway.

"What's going on?" Angelique's eyebrows lifted.

"With all the chaos, I almost forgot. Catharine is the guest violinist for the concert this afternoon. They give away a number of tickets for the performance. These people are probably waiting for them. They mustn't have heard what happened."

They finally arrived in front of a quaint, beautiful residence. Last night, in confusion following Jonah's death, the Goddesses had spirited a dazed Catharine from Jonah's house to 'The Dollhouse,' a residence right on Bestor Plaza offered to Yan by a grateful patient. There they had hoped to keep Catharine buffered from the circus that was bound to occur in response to the death of her famous boyfriend. The Dollhouse itself was tiny but of perfect proportion. The exterior was painted bubblegum pink, while the Victorian gingerbread fretwork adorning the porch and second-floor balcony was in contrasting white lacquer. Ursula and

Angelique opened the gate into a small formal garden enclosed in an ornate white wrought iron fence and framed-in boxwood. As they mounted the porch with its white wicker furniture arranged just so, the leaded glass front door opened immediately, and Yan, who was standing guard.

"Shh," cautioned Yan, lifting a finger to her lips, "Catharine finally fell asleep just as morning was breaking.".

"I hope she can rest for a few hours before she has to return to the chaos. How is she doing?" asked Ursula.

Yan squinted as her eyes adjusted to the light of day after being in a darkened room with Cat. "She is terribly upset, naturally. I gave her some valerian tea, and she finally fell asleep close to dawn."

"I went to see Sheriff Cahill, "reported Angelique, sounding discouraged.

"What did he have to tell you?" asked Yan.

"It doesn't sound as if he is ready to call this a homicide. He's going to wait for the results of the autopsy." Angelique was sick and tired of the way law enforcement and medical examiners went about their business. By the time they were ready to declare a homicide, a lot of vital evidence had been destroyed or had evaporated. People only retained uncontaminated memories of events for a short time.

"Of course, it's a homicide," exclaimed Ursula. "First, the dog. Now Jonah. There is a murderer running scot-free around the grounds."

"I'm sure the powers that be here at the Institution do not want the public to think this is a dangerous place. At least he has cordoned off the house as a potential crime scene," said Angelique. "That might salvage some of the evidence. Also, he has interviewed some of those who were present. I was hoping I could be involved in the questioning while the information was still fresh and uncontaminated in the witnesses' minds. You know that when you change the things you're looking at, the things you are looking at change. I worry now that a lot of what witnesses observed might be lost with time and intervening information."

"Do you think the sheriff would let you be involved in the interviews?" asked Yan.

"Somehow, I didn't get the sense from our conversation that he was enthusiastic about my involvement. At least, that is what his body language told me. What he actually said was that he would welcome any help if this turns out to be a murder investigation."

"That's a real disappointment. I wonder if Alex would get a chance to hypnotize the witnesses and retrieve information that way."

"That would be an enormous help, but I can't imagine the sheriff allowing that." scoffed Angelique walking to the edge of the porch and staring off into the distance as if seeking divine intervention. "Confessions elicited under hypnosis are still inadmissible in court."

"What if we Goddesses used our gifts to help out with the investigation?" offered Ursula. "Not that this is a homicide," she added with a smile.

"What are you suggesting?" queried Angelique, turning now with genuine interest on her face. Maybe the Great Goddess had heard her plea.

"As you know, we each have a way of accessing information that may not be readily apparent to others," Ursula replied. "I know, Yan, that you gain a lot of insight using your pendulum."

"Of course," said Yan. "I consult the pendulum, and I Ching about many things. There are four billion bits of information in any situation. In each moment, it's too subtle for the conscious mind to discern but gets stored in the unconscious. My unconscious communication through the vibrations of my fingers guiding the pendulum swing. In this way, I can access the millions of bits of information that reside in my unconscious-making the unconscious conscious-rather than just the small percentage of information that is available to the conscious portion of my mind — like the iceberg that has the tip showing and the mass beneath the surface of the water."

"That is exactly how micro-expression investigation works. A person's face and body unconsciously respond to questions and situations in ways that a trained observer can identify," said Angelique. "They talk about "Known-

Unknown Quadrants." In one quadrant, there are known knowns, things you know you know; in another, there are known unknowns, things you know you don't know; then there are unknown unknowns, things you don't know you don't know; and the final quadrant involves things you don't know you know, this is the quadrant that is accessed through our various practices. As you said, Yan, we make the unconscious conscious."

"I know the other Goddesses have illumination practices that would be helpful in this investigation as well," said Ursula, her eyes gleaming with excitement. "For example, I communicate with my power animal as well as the Anasazi, the old ones, from whom I get a lot of insight. Angel, I know you utilize Voodoo as well as body language. Alex works with hypnosis and tarot cards. Perhaps we can prevail upon them to help as well."

"Good idea," said Yan. "We can get together and go over the ways we can assist in this investigation." A moment passed as each mulled over the implications of using the Goddesses' powers to help solve the deaths. Yan sat down on the white wicker rocking chair and carefully folded her hands in her lap before continuing. "And there is something else I wanted to talk to you about. Georgina."

"Please don't ask us to do this!" groaned Ursula loudly, putting her hands over her ears.

"To do what?" asked Yan, eyes wide, all innocence.

"To invite Georgina to join the Circle," asserted Angelique, sounding disgusted.

"Please keep your voice down," said Yan, getting up and rushing to check that the front door was properly closed, concerned about waking Catharine.

"What's your objection?" Yan turned to Angelique, unable to keep from sounding irritated.

"My objection is Georgina herself," exclaimed Ursula, now pacing the small parlor. "She's antifeminist; a throwback to the fifties; practically June Cleaver. I'll bet she has an apron collection. Did you hear what she said at Alex's party?"

"She said that women should stay at home, barefoot and pregnant in the kitchen," said Angelique. She had succeeded in lowering her voice, but her whispers expressed indignation.

"She said women were abandoning their children in favor of working the local cash register," added Ursula in a harsh whisper.

"And that society in general and schools, in particular, were breaking down because of the emancipation of women," said Angelique.

Yan sighed. "That's not exactly what she said." She raised her hands to her temples and started massaging the trigger points as if to dispel a headache. "Georgina is concerned, and rightly so, that we are not doing enough to have adequate and affordable childcare for most families."

"Georgina is a throwback to Paleolithic days when women were denied the right to choose to do anything other than household work," argued Angelique, clearly exasperated.

"It's still that way now; in most parts of the world today, women are not allowed to work, even if they are widowed, and their family no longer has an income. Women and their families starve unless they can beg enough for subsistence," Ursula chimed in.

"That's right," continued Angelique. "And that continues around the world. In India, over forty-four million women are segregated into orphanage-like widows' residences when their husbands die. There are nine-year-olds in these places which had been married to eighty-year-old men who perish soon after the marriage."

"Many places in the Middle East, women who went to work were sent 'night letters' telling them something horrible would happen to them or their families if they persisted in working. Some of the women were murdered; their loved ones were killed if they didn't quit their jobs and stay home. Their fate stood as a warning to any other woman who would dare to work," added Ursula.

"Well, that is certainly not the way it is here, thank goodness," responded Yan. "Women may choose to stay at home or to go to work. Men may choose to farm as was their traditional role in the days of old, or they may choose to have a career. It's the same for both sexes. The feminist philosophy I espouse believes that choice is the operative word here."

"I don't know. It just seems like Georgina's point-of-view is anathema to the true spirit of feminism," grumbled Ursula.

"Let's bring Alexis in on this decision as well," suggested Angelique.

"Of course," said Yan. "But know that Georgina has my imprimatur. She is able to discern messages in cloud formations. My take is that she is a Goddess Demeter. I'll bet she is able to do fire meditation as well."

A sharp knock interrupted their discussion. Angelique opened the door to find Sheriff Cahill standing there.

"I'd like to speak to Ms. Sobieski," he said, looking around at the gathered women. "Privately."

"I'm not sure that's a good idea, Sheriff," Angelique said. "She's been through a lot and has just fallen asleep."

"Are you speaking as her lawyer?"

"No. I'm not sure that she needs a lawyer, but I do wish to be present. Catharine is drowsy as well as in shock — it's possible that she may have been drugged — and so it would be a good idea for me to be there in case she needs support, stated Angelique in a carefully neutral tone calibrated to diffuse the tension."

"I think it would be helpful to interview her as soon as possible as I am sure she has information crucial to the investigation of Jonah's death — not that it's been declared a homicide," declared the Sheriff.

"Let me go up and see if she's in any shape to talk to you," said Yan, disappearing up the steep flight of stairs.

Yan gently pushed open the door to Catharine's bedroom. The heavy draperies had been drawn across the windows, blocking the bright morning sun. Rousing reluctantly, Cat pulled a hand-painted silk wrap protectively around her shoulders and carefully descended the stairs leaning heavily on Yan's support.

"I'm sorry for your loss, Ms. Sobieski," said Sheriff Cahill. 'I appreciate you agreeing to see me. I know how difficult this must be. However, I'd like you to tell me what happened while it's still fresh in your mind."

"Are you going to find out who killed Jonah?" Catharine was now weeping silently.

"Well," responded the Sheriff, "we are not sure that foul play was involved."

Angelique groaned. "Did I do that out loud?" she queried demurely.

"May we speak in private?" growled the Sheriff, clearly irritated.

"These are my trusted friends on whose support I depend. I would prefer that they stay," replied Cat.

"I have no legal right to require your friends to leave," acknowledged Sheriff Cahill, clearly displeased.

"What do you remember about last night?" he began.

"Nothing," uttered Catharine, squinting as if the light was hurting her eyes. "Everything is blank."

"I need you to try; it's very important we talk this through while your memory is fresh."

"I think my drink was drugged. I passed out. I remember nothing from the time I left the party to go upstairs. I did not see Jonah after that. At least, not that I can remember." Catharine began to sway in her seat.

"Sheriff, I would prefer that we postpone this interview for another day. Catharine really needs to go back to bed." Angelique's tone was resolute.

The Sheriff had no recourse but to accede to her request. He bowed to the ladies, and Angelique saw him out the door and then returned to confront Catharine.

"That was some performance, Missy," said Angelique.

"I don't know what you mean." Cat appeared subdued, head down, her copper-blond textured hair tumbling over her shoulders, one hand clutching her robe around her, the other smoothing the fabric over her thighs as if to soothe herself...

"It's all over your face that you are concealing something. Sheriff Cahill is no fool. He's a lifelong poker player and can tell when you are being deceptive as easily as I can. And at this moment, I can tell there's something you're not saying."

There was a moment of silence with Cat visibly struggling with emotions. She took a deep breath, and tears streamed down her cheeks.

"I'm not entirely sure what happened. It's as if it were a dream. I was expecting Jonah to meet me in the bedroom so that we could have some intimacy —time together is always a challenge, and we have to steal it when we can." Catharine lifted her head, shoulders back, lips tightening up with anger as the victim's rage began to course through her. "He said he had some business to tidy up before he joined me, but he didn't think it would take too long. I went up to my suite to wait for him, but when I got there, I started to feel woozy."

Catharine got up from her chair and began to pace, fingertips pressed against her temples. The other women started to breathe rhythmically in unison, palms up, transmitting calming vibrations into the room to help quiet her agitation.

"I sat for a moment, hoping my head would clear, but it only became cloudier. Earlier in the evening, I had set down my drink. I wonder if something was put in it to make me lose consciousness." Cat spoke in a low, urgent tone.

"Once you leave your drink unattended, it's no longer your drink," stated Angelique.

"Thanks for the tip," Cat said sarcastically.

"I'm sorry. Go on, please." Angelique went over to try and pat Catharine's hand, but Cat brushed right by, too disturbed to respond.

"That's when it really gets foggy. I got into bed and may have fallen asleep. Someone came into bed with me, but somehow it seemed like a dream, a pretty erotic dream. The next thing I know, there are sirens and fire alarms. Somehow I got myself out of bed, and by the time I got downstairs, Jonah's car was up in flames with him in it." Catharine put her face in her hands and started to sob.

Yan helped her back into the chair and stroked her hair, talking calmly. "Catharine, I know this is difficult, but you need to know if there was actually someone in that bed. You need to know if something happened. I could examine you, or we could take you to the medical center."

"No need, Yan. I know someone came into bed with me. It wasn't Jonah. Jonah was already dead."

"I assume you mean you found physical evidence of rape," stated Yan matter-of-factly.

Catharine's grim countenance tightened further.

Chapter 34

"I don't think I need distraction techniques. I've been abstinent from mood-altering substances for a while," said Elise. She and Meryl had picked up salads and were carrying their trays to the back deck of the Refectory to eat lunch while they reviewed some of the recovery skills Meryl felt it important for her sponsee to learn. They set down their trays, and Meryl patted Elise on the shoulder condescendingly.

"There is nothing sicker than a sick addict, and nothing 'weller' than a 'well' addict, my sponsor used to say."

"Are you implying I'm a little overconfident?"

"Perhaps a little," chuckled Meryl. "Even after years of recovery, you'll still run into cues —triggers— for your addiction. Let me tell you a story that brings that home very well. One day I was walking to a meeting with Burt —the big rough guy at the meeting who hadn't had a drink in over a year —when I happened to pop the top of the Diet Coke can I was carrying. Burt said that the 'popping' sound triggered an overwhelming craving for beer for him. Cravings continue well into recovery. Every time you engage in an addictive action, the brain associates the power of relief and pleasure with whatever was present at that time. If there's a blue placemat under my cheesecake when I eat it, that placemat, or even the color blue, can become a cue for craving cheesecake."

Meryl took a bite of her salad: marinated brussels sprouts and leeks, sprinkled with chopped walnuts, over a bed of arugula. "Delicious!" She pressed her fingertips to her lips for a kiss and tossed it into the air.

"I understand. I studied Pavlovian conditioning in my Psych 101 class: every time the dog was fed, they rang a bell; soon, when you rang a bell, the dog would salivate even though there wasn't any food there. You're saying that if there had been a pink towel in the bathroom where I purged after binging, the color pink would become a trigger, and thereafter each time I saw the color pink, I would want to binge and purge."

"That's the gist of it. You can imagine how your whole world can become contaminated with multiple triggers because you binge and purge in different places and at various times."

Elise sat like a fixture, not eating, her eyes downcast, then mumbled:

"I used to restrict my intake of food all day long and then binge. After not eating all day, I couldn't control myself, like someone who wanders in the desert for a long time and then comes upon a water hole and can't stop drinking. I starved myself all day, and then I binged in the evening. But then I couldn't stand the fullness in my stomach, so I'd purge. At the treatment center, we'd have to stay together after the sensation so that we'd stop each other from going to the bathroom to throw up."

"Good spotting. You can see a lot when the fog of addiction lifts?"

Meryl reached over and cupped Elise's chin in her hand, gently lifting her head until she was looking directly into her eyes.

"Don't be disappointed if you have the urge to binge and purge now and again. It happens to everyone. It can take ninety days to change a deeply entrenched habit and carve new behavior pathways in your brain. That's why distraction techniques are so important. The idea is to let the craving move through you, but then put a period at the end of that and start to utilize a distraction technique. Okay?"

"Okay."

"So, let's talk about how you experience a craving."

Elise nodded mutely, grateful that Meryl hadn't given up on her. "How do I do that?"

"You want to be able to move into the observer position and just be aware of what happens."

"What do you mean by observer position? This language is all new to me." Elise shrugged her shoulders helplessly. She had a look of despair on her face, certain that she would never be able to do half the things Meryl was asking of her.

"Do you want to try it? A picture's worth a thousand words."

Looking around, Elise realized that the other diners had vacated the porch and that she and Meryl were the last ones there.

"Okay. I'm willing to do whatever it takes," said Elise grudgingly.

"That's the spirit. Go ahead and relax. Focus on your breathing."

Elise's face became slack, her breathing audible.

"Now go back to a time when you were craving Vicodin. You can just sense the euphoria that will happen."

Elise's head nodded to indicate that she was there in her imagination.

"See if you can determine where in your body the physical sensation of craving starts."

Head bobs. —maybe a stop sign or a raised hand."

"Got it. A big red stop sign."

"Okay. You can open your eyes now."

"How was that."

"That was great. So far. Now, what do I do to distract my brain?"

Meryl reached into her ubiquitous satchel and pulled out a felt-tipped pen and a stack of 3" X 5" cards.

"Each person has to create their own 'DISTRACTS' program. Let's create one for you. I'll tell you the skill, you let me know within that Category what might work for you, and then we'll write it here on this 3" X 5" card. Ready."

Elise assented.

"The letters in the acronym "DISTRACTS' stand for different strategies. For example, the first letter 'D' stands for 'Distance,' by which we mean that when you are overwhelmed by an emotional event, 'move your muscles' and get away from the immediate environment; leave the room or the situation that is connected with the emotional trigger."

"You mean a change of scenery like getting out of the house and going to the park or somewhere?"

"Exactly. Or, for problems you can't control, you can write them on a slip of paper and put them in a God's box or spirit pouch.

"Got it."

The two continued to work on Elise's individually tailored program, stopping only now and again to go into the Refectory and refresh their iced tea. At the end of an hour or so, they had completed what appeared to be a workable "DISTRACTS" program for her and printed it out on a 3" X 5" card:

D = Distance. Move her muscles and get out of the house.

I = Imagination: Imagine herself at the beach watching a sunset.

S = Shift emotions by singing 'I am Woman, Hear Me Roar.'

T = Thought challenge. Replace remorse by validating effort for recovery.

R = Relaxation: Yoga and bubble bath.

A = Activities: Go for a walk.

C = Contribute. Call on someone you know is suffering.

T = Turn over problems you can't control. Write it out on a piece of paper and put it in a Spirit Pouch.

S = Soothe through the senses. Smell: aromatherapy; Vision: watch a sunset; Hearing: listen to beautiful music; Tactile: massage lotion into your body; Taste: chocolate.

"I sure hope this works," Elise remembered Catharine's lead about cross-addiction. How when you get one addiction into remission, another will pop up to take its place. She realized that Eric had been on her mind a lot. Maybe it was true that, as Catharine had stated, relationship addiction was the source of all the others.

"It works if you work it," assured Meryl. "Make up a number of 3" X 5" cards and place them everywhere."

"I'll paste one on the bathroom mirror and put a couple in my pockets," promised Elise. "Now, the first distraction technique I choose is to get some ice cream."

Chapter 35

As she neared her destination, Georgina encountered a wall of people, mostly women, streaming toward the two o'clock lecture. The benches within the Hall of Philosophy were already filled, and attendees spilled out onto the green lawns surrounding the Greek Revival enclosure, now dotted like a pointillist painting with colorful lawn chairs. Shading her eyes with her hand, she scanned the area on either side of the brick path leading to the site. She noted that many of the women present had arrived in pairs, the younger women helping the older ones set up their chairs in a bag. She spotted a familiar figure seated on a blanket to the far right of the audience. Georgina picked her way through the assembled chairs and blankets and arrived at Rafael's side.

"A lot of mothers and daughters," she winced, thinking of Elise.

Rafael glanced at her sympathetically and indicated a space beside him. He had set up under a tree and was leaning against its trunk, his head down, focused on a needlepoint canvas: a bright and cheery scene of Belltower Point.

"Mindfulness practice?" Georgina nodded to his handwork as she unpacked the blanket she had stashed in her bag and nestled comfortably at his side.

"Right. Back in the day, my dissertation advisor taught me how to train my mind to one point focus. Little by little,

I expanded the time my mind would stay focused on one thing, starting at three minutes and then ten minutes, finally to an hour or more. In the end, I was able to trust that my mind would stay in one-point concentration for longer and longer, but I still have to maintain the practice; needlepoint helps."

"Yan has talked to me about Goddessence.' Sounds something like your 'Mindfulness.'"

"Similar concepts appear in different wisdom traditions, and some form of centering practice seems to appear in most spiritual paths. Others may call it contemplative prayer or meditation. I do a form of mindful physical practice, Tai Chi, down at the Belltower Point in the early morning. I see a member of your Goddess Circle doing yoga down there at the same time. Speaking of the Goddess Circle, Yan mentioned that I should talk to you about translating some cuneiforms that you had?"

"They're nothing really. She shouldn't have mentioned anything. Oh. Here comes one of their members now. We must be ready to start."

A loud murmur began to rise from the assembly as Ursula, and another woman walked through the crowded benches and mounted the dais, which was crowded with an array of chairs, a draped piano, and a podium.

"We are fortunate to have with us today a woman of the highest distinction," the stocky woman with short salt and pepper hair whom Georgina recognized as the Director of Religious Education announced into the microphone. The enthusiastic audience fell silent as she rapped the gavel. "Dr. Ursula Andrews is a pioneer in the field of research on women and girls; in particular, she was ahead of her time in studying the development of girls' personalities and social voices through the first two decades of life. She later wrote about this experience in her book Women's Global Status: 101. Dr. Andrews continues her research and writing from her home base in Santa Fe, New Mexico, and we are honored to have her here with us today. By the way, Dr. Andrews will be signing books following the lecture at the Author's Alcove beside the Chautauqua Bookstore."

The audience was well-grounded in her topic. A number of students from SUNY Buffalo had traveled to Chautauqua today to hear the renowned Dr. Andrews discuss what was old and new in the realm of women's issues. There were many topics they were ready to present in the question and answer segment as Ursula brought her prepared remarks to a conclusion.

"Throughout our lives, but most especially in the tween-adolescent phase, we are continually painting an internal portrait of ourselves. When girls are eight years of age, they are the Queens of the playground. They have an energy and self-confidence that trumpets out loud. However, between the ages of nine and fifteen, we begin a major transition. Our internal portrait becomes impacted more by our peers than by anything else. We become focused on belonging to the group. If we are rejected and ostracized by the 'mean girl' group, we can be devastated. This happens more than you know."

There was a rustling in the crowd as neighbors turned to neighbors, sixties, something grandmothers looking to twenties something mothers, and nodded acknowledgment of the truth of this observation no matter the generation.

"We can emerge from this dangerous passage with a vastly altered internal portrait. Along with the "mean girl" passage, we are also entering the romantic partnership phase. Here, the relationships we experience with romantic partners color our self-portrait, and that also has the potential to be destructive. If there isn't a safe wise adult person with whom we are willing to reveal our broken interiors, we are left to try to repair ourselves—like fixing a broken bone on our own. Often, when that happens, the bone heals but is disfigured. Ideally, there is at least one knowledgeable adult to whom we can disclose our most shameful images and have those images modified, like going to an orthopedic physician to have the bone set. This is the power of women coming together in community to be there for each other."

The audience erupted in applause and cheers, and it took a few moments and a determined rapping of the gavel for the audience to quiet down for the question and answer period.

"Those who would like to ask a question of Dr. Andrews are invited to line up at the microphone on the west side of the hall," announced the moderator.

The regular Chautauqua lecture attendees were aware of this tradition, and so they had already Lined up for their opportunity while the neophytes hurried over for their turn. The first to pose a question was an impeccably groomed woman dressed in white sharkskin pants and a St. John's top; her hair pulled back in a smooth chignon. "Back in the sixties, we fought hard for women's rights. Recent events have made me wonder whether the 'post-feminist' generation understands the monumental changes that were forged. What do you make of the fact that we are among the few industrialized nations who haven't yet managed to elect a woman as head of government?"

A round of applause greeted the question. Hillary Clinton had been both a visitor and lecturer at Chautauqua —the Clintons had held a Renaissance Weekend there —and many presents had worked hard for her candidacy.

"Our present-day culture avoids this subject, even actively represses the subject. It is rare that I hear this issue debated directly," commented Ursula. "If I were a conspiracy theorist, I might begin to wonder how the power of the press has been complicit in demonizing our female candidates. When every other disempowered group is able to coalesce around one of their own in order to get them into places of power, 51% of voters, the majority of voters, can't elect a female President of the United States. We need a whole new round of consciousness-raising, just like in the sixties."

The last question came from one of the visiting college students, a young woman in her early twenties, black pedicure peeking from platform sandals, low-slung yoga pants revealing a tattoo homage to Pearl Jam. The audience parted to allow the visitors access to the microphone.

"You allude to the impact of romantic relationships on the internal female self-portrait. Could you speak to the impact of the sexual revolution on the esteem of young women of today's generation?"

"Romantic relationships present a separate problem. Certainly, the sexual revolution has freed girls and women from the worry of pregnancy, but it also renders them vulnerable to STDs and weakens the powerful bonding that monogamous sex provides, escalating single-mother births. Still, I loathe what is being done in the name of protecting our girls' chastity: kept prisoners in our own homes, allowed in public only when totally shrouded by body tents, having our clitoris scraped out with rusty knives. It's a dialectic!"

Chants of 'institutionalized misogyny' and '130 million mutilated' were shouted from diverse locations in the audience, then quickly shushed by others.

"Contrast the way we treat girls and women to the way they are treated in the rest of the world. Each approach has pros and cons. In this part of the world, we don't lock our daughters away to keep them safe. That means that we have to watch as they try out various life adventures, both good and bad; it's like when our daughters are young, and they take their first ride around the block on a two-wheeler, we see them fall and scrape their elbows. It's painful. The world into that we allow our children to venture is a dangerous one; we choose to let them go because the only other option we have is to shackle them inside the house until we become demented or die don't have to undergo the pain of watching them take risks and get hurt. It's hard to watch, but the alternative is unacceptable to me."

"That's all the time we have for questions." The Director of Education was bringing the gathering to a close. "I'd like to thank Dr. Ursula Andrews again for her compelling remarks and the audience for their informed questions. I urge you to attack the global problems of girls and women: female babies being left out to die from exposure; girls being sold as sex slaves; Afghani women getting 'night letters' telling them they and their families will be harmed if they work; forty-four million widows in India, girls, and women, being relegated to orphanage-like institutions; and other injustices too numerous to mention. We need to hold hands across the nation and around the globe, young and old, and combine our resources to free our sisters. Thank you all."

***

Georgina and Rafi packed up their belongings and came over to stand and wait their turn to speak to Ursula after her presentation. Ursula came over, eager to tell them what she had learned regarding the Seneca women who had originally consecrated the site where the Goddess Circle was being held.

"Up to your old tricks, I see," teased Rafi. "Talking to ghosts."

The Iroquois League of five nations—Cayuga, Mohawk, Oneida, Onondaga, and Seneca—was, in fact, a matriarchy. Women were leaders not just of the spiritual and social life of the community but of the economic and political institutions as well. Under the confederacy, women nominated the candidates for chief, and if the chief disappointed them, they arranged for his removal. All inheritance was based on matrilineal inheritance: women-owned all property and the property was passed to her female heirs. In marital areas, women choose their husbands, and the husband enters the house and world of his wife's family. If the husband disappointed an Iroquois woman, she would divorce him with a verbal dismissal, and he would have to leave.

The crush of admirers finally parted to allow Ursula to join them. "Our historic Goddess cultures, as well as many of the aboriginal cultures, including the First Nations Peoples of the west coast and Alaska, have matrilineal traditions," she added before she and Ursula left to attend a Goddess Circle.

Sauntering into the Refectory following the lecture, Rafael reviewed the various ice cream flavors exhibited in the cooler. "Yum, can't wait to get into that ice cream; I think I'll have a double just to give the finger to death. And I will not be dissuaded by a few righteous words about the layering of plaque on my arteries, thank you very much," he teased, a bright smile reflecting his delight.

"I'm not your mother," said Georgina, aware that she was probably a decade older than her companion.

"I'm well aware of that," replied Rafael, his glance raking her from head to toe. His eyes were heat-seeking hers.

Blushing, Georgina led him to the antique bronze cash register, where they purchased two chips for double servings of ice cream each and then joined a long queue for the ice cream counter.

Waiting in Line, Georgina returned to the subject of Goddessence. Rafael had encountered wide-ranging applications of the trance state during his international travels and had met shamans who, in his opinion, were deemed spiritual leaders purely on the basis of their capacity for trance. What Buddhist monks call mindfulness can be either internal or external. With internal focus, you sit and watch your thought stream or monitor changing physical sensations. Shamans might imagine vision quests and power animals. A time when everything in your life feels connected. With external focus, you can beam your attention on objects outside of yourself. It may be that athletes are great due to their ability to 'hit the zone' and perceive events almost as if there were in slow motion. Some of the great baseball hitters are said to see the ninety-mile-an-hour pitch come at them so slowly that they can see the stitching on the ball; the ball seems to just hover in the air waiting to be hit."

Finally, first in line at the ice cream counter, Georgina perused the unique homemade flavors —salted caramel, red velvet cake, moose tracks —as Rafi sized up the strength of the servers: "I need someone who works out," he explained as he urged the muscular young man to "dig deep" into the ice cream vats and come up with a double-dip cake cone that ended up looking like the Sagrada de Familia, Gaudi's endlessly constructed Barcelona Cathedral. Navigating their way through the crunch, they came to an empty bench on the green and sat down to enjoy their confections. Georgina fell silent. A moment passed, then two more.

"A penny for your thoughts."

Georgina's eyes had clouded over. "These killings make me very sad. When my daughter was young, I remember my aunt and mother talking about how great it was that they were never concerned about her safety while we were in Chautauqua's bubble: like a Mayberry snow shaker. Yesterday one of the speakers was telling a story about how wonderful it was that when his son had left his bike down by the beach, not only had it not been stolen, not only had it not been stripped, but it had been turned in to the lost and found. Now it's as if all that sense of safety has been swept away. I feel as if all the locks in the world can't keep my daughter secure anymore when there is a killer among us."

Chapter 36

"One, two, now pirouette and lift higher and lighter." Meister Gregory banged out the cadence with his ever-present cane. They have been practicing for what seemed like forever. The ballet was to be performed in two days, and the ballet Meister was becoming more and more demanding. Brynn could feel the heat rising through her body as, once again, her partner lifted her in the classic pas de deux of 'Swan Lake.' She couldn't wait to cool off. Finally finished, she came out to join Elise and acknowledge compliments from the large number of bystanders who had gathered at the Amp to watch the dancers rehearse.

"The verbal abuse continues," she noted. She knew how frustrated Elise had been by Meister Gregory's constant fault-finding. She bent down gracefully and pulled various woolen items from the ballet bag she had dropped at Elise's feet: a scarf which she twirled around her neck and leg sleeves which she pulled on to keep her muscles warm...

"It looks as if you and Miko are getting along very well," ventured Elise casually.

"Isn't he wonderful?" Brynn's face glowed with happiness. Patting beads of perspiration from her face, she glanced sideways at Elise. "What do you think of Eric?"

Elise shrugged her shoulders and tried to summon up a smile. "I don't think about him. I find him arrogant and judgmental."

"Well, Miko has a lot to say about Eric. Like that, he is chronically ambivalent and pathologically indecisive. Miko is the very opposite of Eric; fire then aim, that's Miko. He may not do the right thing, but at least he does something. He says that only the most confident women with lots of star power women hit on Eric."

Elise felt a wave of fear and pain wash through her. She was sick to death of womanizing men. She had spent years watching her mother attempt to put on a brave front in the face of her father's infidelities. Elise herself had spent some time as an intern at her father's company and had personally observed her father's behavior with the young and beautiful women working —his harem, she'd dubbed them. Disgusting.

"Eric and I are acquaintances, that's all. I see him in my writing workshop, but that's it, and that's enough."

Brynn considered her a moment before she commented. "He's pretty hot. And supremely eligible. It would be fun if you dated him. The four of us could go out together."

"I'm not allowed to enter a romantic relationship until I've been in recovery for a year."

"You're kidding, right?" Brynn looked at Elise, astonishment written all over her face. Brynn knew very little about the recovery movement culture but what she was hearing now wasn't very appealing.

"I wouldn't kid about a thing like that." Elise reiterated grimly. "And don't forget what Miko said about what happened to Eric's parents. He won't have anything to do with an addict."

"You're no addict," snorted Brynn dismissively, hands on her hips. "Anyway, are you coming to the party on the Chautauqua Belle tonight? Yes or no?"

"Don't know for sure. But what about you. I can't imagine that you'll be allowed to stay out late?"

"Of course, ogre Gregory has us under curfew," Brynn wrinkled her nose. " But I'm going to sneak out. There's no way I'm going to leave Miko alone with all those other girls. It's more important to be at his side than to get my beauty sleep."

"Brynn, I hope you're not thinking of giving in to pressure and having sex with Miko. You and he have just met."

"He's wealthy royalty. Both he and Eric can have any woman they want. Miko's not someone who would put up with a non-sexual relationship; he'd just go and find someone else who would give it to him. I'm so excited— he's stopping by to pick me up. He wants to show me around his family estate before I have to drop in at the Ballet office and get call information for tomorrow."

Elise knew how important these things were to her. Brynn had been a 'scholarship' student at the ballet school: code for too poor to afford the tuition. Surrounded by other girls with their McMansions and exotic vacations, she had often voiced her sense of inadequacy.

Turning, Elise could make out the figure of Miko lounging at the back of the amphitheater. He waved indolently and beckoned them to join him.

"Why don't we meet at the north courts and play some tennis later this afternoon, say around 4:00?" Said Elise as she hurried to keep up with Brynn as she sped up the raked aisle to be with Miko.

"Hope to see you at the party on the Chautauqua Belle later," said Miko on their approach. He put his arm possessively around Brynn's shoulders.

"Not sure," responded Elise. She was not as easily swayed by Miko's swagger as was Brynn.

"You young ladies are missing a lot of fun because you have to get your beauty sleep. I wouldn't have thought you'd want to leave me unprotected from all those other young beauties," he teased.

Elise rolled her eyes at Brynn, who seemed completely dazzled.

Meister Gregory passed by on his way out of the Amp and called, "Don't forget your curfew, young lady, or there will be another Swan Queen dancing quite soon!"

"I won't forget," Brynn promised, winking covertly at Elise.

"I was just stopping by to talk to Brynn for a moment." Elise stretched out her arms, palm up, trying to explain to the ballet Meister. He turned his back on her and stomped away without a word.

Miko readjusted the shawl around Brynn's neck and shoulders, cupping her chin in his hand. "We have to take good care of our prima ballerina," he said, gazing into her eyes. Sexual tension sparking between the two of them.

Was she batting her eyelashes? Elise wondered disgustedly as she made her goodbyes, saying that she had to go to the library to look up something for writing class.

"Let's take a walk," Miko nuzzled Brynn's neck.

"Good. I need to cool off."

"That's not exactly what I had in mind," said Miko.

The two of them meandered off, side by side, arms around each other, following the pathway behind the Amphitheater that led down the incline. At the bottom were parked several huge 'Bluebirds': the elaborately outfitted buses used to carry the sound and other equipment when the Herd Mentality was on tour. The buses were airbrushed with magnificent designs celebrating the famous group.

"Gosh, I never thought about how much equipment the Herd Mentality has carted around on their road trips. I wonder what's going to happen to the band and their equipment and everything after what's happened to Jonah," remarked Brynn.

"Lots has been left hanging in limbo," said Miko, testing the handle of one of the doors until it swung open before them. "Let's take a peek inside and find out how these famous bands travel."

"We can't. What if someone sees us and calls the sheriff? I'm sure he is investigating everyone," hesitated Brynn, glancing around to see if anyone was watching them.

"He sure is. He stopped by really early this morning and tried to get Mason to wake me up, but Glammy made short work of him." Miko said absently.

"Who are you talking about?" Brynn asked curiously.

"Glammy is my grandmother—and a force to be contended with. I've called her Glammy since I was little. When she would get dressed in the evening to go out to a ball, my nanny would take me in to kiss her goodnight after I was ready for bed. My nanny taught me to say they looked 'glamorous,' but I wasn't able to say that and said 'Glammy' instead. It's been what I have called her ever since. Mason is our butler." explained Miko.

"But what about your mother?" asked Brynn, stroking his arm.

"Oh, she's one of the beautiful people: always gallivanting around the globe chasing the next, most exciting pleasure." For a moment, Miko looked intense, but he brightened momentarily. "But you are the beautiful and glamorous one that I am interested in now, and this RV is quite the romantic setting."

Stepping up into the interior, they gazed around. Muted mauve bucket seats of hand-tooled leather were arranged so that groups of musicians could play together during their long bus tours around the nation.

"And look at this," said Miko as he pulled aside a curtain towards the back of the bus. He grinned. "A built-in boudoir."

He gently nibbled Brynn's ear, and she swooned gracefully in an imitation of the ballet pas de deux, though this was a more ancient dance than the one she had just rehearsed. Miko's hands framed her face as her eyelashes fluttered and her eyes gazed achingly into his; a moan escaped as his lips parted hers and his tongue urgently explored the wetness within.

"Wait. What if someone comes?" she said with a shake of her head.

"You will always be safe with me." He bent once more to brush her lips and breathe in the sweetness of her essence as the two sank into the luxury awaiting them.

***

Chester was loading cartons of liquor onto the Chautauqua Belle as Brynn and Miko emerged from the tour bus and sauntered down to the docks.

"I wonder what there will be for us to drink after the first hour of the party," joked Miko, appraising the mountain of boxes waiting to be taken onto the boat.

Chester opened another box and slipped a small bag into Miko's breast pocket. "Don't worry; there'll be every possible supply on board."

As the two are talking, Brynn sets her hair to rights, capturing the slippery, silken strands and pressing them firmly into her ballerina bun. Any makeup she'd had on had been worn from her face, and in the harsh daylight, a weeping cold sore was prominent on the side of her mouth.

Miko stared at her in disgust. "What's that?" he growled.

"What?" she cried, reaching her hand to her mouth.

"That thing on your mouth?" Miko replied tightly.

"Oh. It's just a cold sore. I got it this morning." said Brynn apologetically.

Miko glared at her.

"You'd better run along now. I'm kinda' busy. Have to give Chester a hand." he said dismissively.

Chester glanced at him in surprise.

"Will I see you later at the party?" Brynn was taken aback by Miko's abrupt tone and posture.

Miko looked at Chester, who picked up another carton and carried it up onto the dock of the boat.

"I'm sure Meister Gregory won't let you come. The boat won't be back until way after your curfew. Maybe some other time."

Without a backward glance, Miko raced up the steps to the deck, leaving the bewildered Brynn to wander alone up the incline toward the ballet residence.

"Herpes! And she didn't give me a heads-up." spat Miko.

"That's what you get. A girl in every port," Chester groused.

"That's no girl," said Miko, shuddering in revulsion. "That's a skank."

Chapter 37

The Goddesses reconvened at the Mabel Powers Fire Pit in response to a call for an emergency meeting. Each woman selected a bench appropriate for her chosen Goddess from those that encircled the glade. From the vantage point of her Deer Clan seat, Ursula could check the shadowy edges of the glade for a sign of her power animal, the Golden Hind. The forest remained still. Ursula lit the waist-high pyramid of timber laid in anticipation of today's Circle and threw into the flames fragrant stems of salvia taken from the woven pouch dangling from her belt. When the herb began to smolder, she cupped waves of smoke and inhaled deeply, allowing the hallucinogenic fumes to enter her lungs and transport her to an altered state of consciousness. The Goddesses processed to the fire and, one by one, allowed their faces to hover slightly above and to the side of the flames, taking in deep breaths of the fragrant salvia. When everyone had filed back to their seats in quiet meditation, Angelique carefully positioned herself at the center of the Circle before she spoke.

"I have asked that we gather in a special session to talk about the evil lurking in our precious sanctuary."

Sunlight penetrated the curtains of leaves surrounding the clearing as Angelique glanced around at the circle of powerful and perceptive women now observing her closely. She had certainly won their attention.

"We may never be able to determine whether Jonah's death was an accident or murder. At least the Sheriff did go ahead and interview the people at the party rather than wait until later after their recollections were lost. Everyone submitted to an interview in order to be allowed to leave the compound. I would have liked to be present for the questioning so that I could study their body language, but the sheriff didn't think I needed to be there. It appears he fancies himself a body language expert by virtue of the time he has spent playing poker."

An angry buzz ran through the group, with the odd 'boo' and 'hiss' coming from Ursula. She had stopped looking for her power animal and was now focused on what Angelique was saying to the group.

"I know about the physiological reaction," she said. "Breathing becomes shallower to bring more energy into our body through increased oxygen intake; the heart speeds up to pump the oxygen fuel throughout the body; hands feel cold as blood vessels drop deep within the body so that we will not bleed to death if we are injured; beads of sweat moisten the palms to enable our hands to slide out from a dangerous grasp. The body magically transforms under the influence of adrenaline —the fight-flight system."

"Like the 'Incredible Hulk,'" chuckled Alex.

Yan spoke from her perch on the Beer Clan bench. "In Paleolithic times, when we shared the forests with predatory animals, adrenaline let us run as fast as possible away from tigers or, if cornered by one, fight with optimum strength. There are stories of women picking up a car to release a trapped child. With adrenaline, all functions that support fight and flight are activated, and anything not involved is deactivated."

"The downside of the fight-flight system is that our thinking ability is hijacked and becomes centered on 'run' or 'attack.'" stated Ursula. She continued to tend the fire and fan smoke from the salvia towards the group.

Angelique considered her comment, then spoke again. "There's a downside to the body language approach as well. Micro-expression analyzes data such as the raising of eyebrows or dilation of the pupil of the eye. This occurs when adrenaline and cortisol race through the body. Unfortunately, a sociopath has a lower level of adrenaline and therefore demonstrates little physical reactivity. What this means is that if the Sheriff depends on information from body language to solve the murder, it won't be of much help. He won't be able to detect a sociopath that way."

"Are you saying that sociopaths can cheat, steal, and murder without being bothered by the uncomfortable body sensations of adrenaline that other human beings come to understand as the conscience!" Alex appeared incredulous.

"That's right. They have a very low adrenaline response and therefore wouldn't manifest the telltale signs of guilt that a micro-expression, or body language, an expert would detect," Angelique affirmed. "No conscience and therefore few biological symptoms of guilt."

"In other words, they don't have a 'Jiminy Cricket,'" observed Alex. "I think I've met a number of them in the corporate world." She pressed her fingertips to her temples as if to derail a headache.

"That's for sure. Sociopaths have no empathy for other human beings; humans are merely pawns manipulated to meet their needs. They become 'sensation seekers' Some of them become serial killers. Without the readily available sensation of adrenaline, he has trouble feeling 'alive.' He'll go to extreme lengths in order to experience adrenaline. In order to feel alive, the psychopath requires a hit of adrenaline, and this is his grotesque way of achieving that. That is what we may be dealing with here."

Catharine was playing distractedly with the hem of her robe, doing her best to manage the strong emotions streaming through her, so impacted by the death of her lover as to be a mere silhouette of her former self. Her grief was compounded by her having lost trust in the world in general. If this could happen at Chautauqua, there was no safe place anywhere. She shuddered and pulled her shawl more tightly around herself as if she had felt a sudden chill, prompting

Yan to move over to pat her back, sending healing energy through the palm of her hand

Brushing a tear from her cheek, Catharine emerged from the depth of her grief enough to join in the discussion:

"You keep saying 'he.' Couldn't it be a woman? What about Savannah?"

"It would be more likely to be a woman if we were dealing with a single killing. But if we take the death of Princess into consideration, it's more likely that we're looking for a serial killer," added Ursula somberly. "According to the statistics, a serial killer is a hundred times more likely to be male than female —something to do with oxytocin; the bonding chemical women produce in order to protect and provide for our offspring ameliorates the aggression. There are some notorious cases involving women, but they are quite rare. Aileen Wuornos is one female serial killer who was convicted of killing six or seven men down in Florida in the late '80s."

"I agree. It's hardly a coincidence that Jonah's death followed soon after Georgina discovered her daughter's dog, Princess, burned up in the fire pit," reasoned Ursula. "You could argue that there is a murderer here at Chautauqua and that the dog was the initial kill —it's possible that the dog could have been killed as an accident or in a moment of rage —that triggered a taste for blood. Angelique, you know better than anyone that if we are dealing with a psychopath, one's too many, and a thousand aren't enough: once he gets the taste of the power of life or death, he's bound to escalate and keep on killing until he is stopped. Killing provides the ability to gain control, dominance, and power. It allows one to feel better about himself and, like all addictions, killing is progressive: the thirst for blood escalates with each murder."

"As my particular area of expertise, body language, may not help uncover the murderer, I'd like to propose that we take advantage of the unique intuitive powers each of you possesses for this investigation," said Angelique.

"It sounds as if the sheriff has brushed off your offer to be involved in the case. No doubt, his attitude regarding the intuitive powers of each of us gathered here would be equally condescending. Many people look at intuition as science fiction rather than a natural human ability that can be enhanced with practice."

Angelique's brow furrowed as she recounted her conclusions based on the information derived from the sheriff's interviews with those present at Jonah's party.

"The Sheriff can utilize the information we produce if he wishes or totally disregards it. But that he would do at his peril. There were a number of people who had both motive and opportunity to kill Jonah Nash. First, there's Cody, the guy who was shooting a film about the band. Apparently, Jonah rescinded his approval for the documentary that was due to be screened at the Toronto International Film Festival this fall. Second, he had accused his manager of embezzlement. Third, he told a fellow band member that he would be dumping the band to go solo. Then there's Savannah and her husband. Jonah had been suing to block her from using the music they had co-written," Angelique reported. "We're waiting on blood tests to tell us what happened; we did find bottles of oxycontin in his bathroom, along with whatever recreational drugs were available at the party —probably anything you could ask for. We're theorizing that Jonah may have been drugged or already dead when his body burned up in the fire — there's nobody to find out if there had been a struggle."

Garbed in the regalia of the Goddess Athena, Angelique ranged in a semi-circle around the fire, carefully stepping over the protruding roots of the poplars surrounding the glen, pausing now and then to silently acknowledge the sacred trees. She stopped at each of the Goddesses in turn as she roamed, checking for any need for clarification of the information. Their full understanding would be of critical importance to their investigation.

"The dog tags were never found. Perhaps the killer took them with him. Psychopaths like to take trophies and use them to re-imagine their killings. For a while, those fantasies are enough, but then they have to get into their killing rituals once again in order to achieve a level of satisfaction."

"Perhaps the dog was the killer's first experience with extinguishing life. If so, this is a progressive problem, and he will need to have greater and greater stimulation in order to become aroused. Soon he will begin to fantasize about the next victim. He'll watch and begin to stalk the person he has picked out, daydreaming about how the next murder will occur. Another factor to consider is that the first two killings involved fire. It may be that the killer is fixated on fire and needs it for the rituals he has created. If that's the case, the next planned killing would involve fire as well. If, however, the progression of his disorder has twisted, more personal contact might be required. I've worked on a number of murder cases when this was true, most recently a serial rapist who also strangled his victims because that act offered more intimate contact."

"Something else to keep in mind is that the serial killers typically 'peak' in their middle to the late twenties," Angelique pointed out.

"So, we're looking for a male, in his twenties, with a history of sociopathic behaviors. And what are they again?" asked Alex.

"The sociopathic triad is often identified in childhood: bed wetting, cruelty to animals, and fire-starting," stated Angelique, rising to stoke the fire once more. "Profilers joke that if a person comes into your office, sets fire to a dog, and urinates to put the fire out, you are face to face with a sociopath."

"Just curious. Are you born with it, like the legendary 'bad seed,' or is it something that is learned?" asked Alex, thinking of some of the bizarre behaviors her friends' young adult children had exhibited.

"The debate continues. Certainly, brain damage, especially damage to the frontal lobe, has been identified in serial killers; it amplifies emotionality, impairs judgment, and reduces impulse control."

Yan gave Ursula's shoulders a final squeeze and retook her position on the bench of the Bear Clan. Ursula remained alone on her chosen bench, her arms folded tightly across her chest.

"Certainly, lack of empathy has been identified as a major contributor to evil," added Yan. "When circumstances interfere with a child's bonding, as could happen when the child is orphaned or provided inconsistent foster care, an 'attachment disorder' can occur that dramatically reduces the individual's capacity for empathy. Such persons perceive other humans as objects, pawns to be manipulated for their satisfaction."

"In other instances, 'failure to thrive' syndrome occurs," noted Angelique. "An infant is born with an understanding that unless she has the primary caregiver's complete devotion, she will surely die. These infants may not be physically neglected— they may be kept dry and given nourishment —yet they will turn their heads to the wall and perish.

"Or there could be a third outcome," said Angelique. "As an abandoned child, I coped by over-functioning, a CoDependent: being the perfect provider of service to others in order never to be abandoned again."

Angelique remembered how she had been discovered in a New Orleans orphanage when her adoptive parents were graduate students at Tulane University. They had fallen in love with this tiny baby whose appearance reflected the 'Creoles of Color' heritage —French, Native American, and African American —of the descendants of original French settlers of Louisiana. The family later relocated to Boston, where Angelique overperformed so that her academic prowess and limitless memory resulted in her being offered full scholarships through the best private and undergraduate schools, finally graduating from Harbridge Law School in the top ten percent of her class. Before them now, tall and athletic, with a runner's elongated muscles, she appeared to be in motion even while standing still. She had selected Athena as her ruling Goddess because of her logical, strategic approach to things. According to mythology, Athena had sprung into life fully clad in armor from the forehead of Zeus, and that is how Angelique pictured her own birth. She was passionate about stopping crimes committed against children, and this past year her job as Assistant District Attorney in the child abuse unit had been an exhausting one. All public departments were underfunded and understaffed, and as a result, everyone was overcommitted and overwhelmed. In order to bring perpetrators to justice, she joined forces with the investigating detectives to collect enough evidence to first provide the medical examiner with enough information to declare a homicide rather than death from unknown causes, and second, to successfully prosecute her cases.

"So, have we arrived at a consensus?" she asked

"You're asking us to use our intuitive powers to provide information in a murder case." Yan clarified.

"Absolutely. Any logical approach would simply duplicate what the Sheriff is able to do. Our strengths would complement his efforts."

"I could check in with my power animal; the Golden Hind tends to show up right where we are now," suggested Ursula. She hadn't told everyone about the Clan Mothers' appearance yet. She felt it a sign of respect to check with these forerunners of the women's liberation movement to obtain their permission before revealing their presence.

"I could investigate with my astrology," said Catharine.

"Isn't it true that, given the nature of your relationship with Jonah, you would expect a good deal of distortion?" Alex inquired.

"Astrology is not like your Tarot card reading," snapped Catharine, momentarily roused from her dysphoria. "The positioning of the planets is concrete and unequivocal. They have been studied for millennia." Catharine had long been a student of astrology as the progressions in music were not unlike those exemplified in mathematically based pursuits such as Astrology.

Alex bit back a terse retort out of respect for Cat's grief and promised herself to spread out her Tarot cards later in the day. The Devil would be the perfect Major Arcana significator card to represent the perpetrator.

"Perhaps you could hypnotize Georgina to see if you can retrieve any additional information about the dog's death," Yan suggested to Alex. Frayed nerves were understandable; however, they were rarely helpful. "She might know something that might supply further data that she is unaware of in her conscious state. Pyromaniacs love to watch the burning they have initiated, and he may have been lurking nearby, watching to see what would happen when Princess was discovered."

The Goddess Circle dispersed, each of the Goddesses leaving to apply their special intuitive practices as requested by Angelique. Ursula was emotionally drained from her lecture and the subsequent Goddess Circle. The prospect that a serial killer lurked among them was terrifying. How were they to discern if and when he would strike again? Who might be his victim? She felt wrung-out, like a dishrag. Despite her exhaustion, Ursula walked slowly to the Goddess Circle Site to prepare it for the next day's gathering; in reality, she was eager to catch up with her Power Animal, who had been lurking in the shadows just beyond the Circle. Leaving the immediate confines of the Fire Pit glade, Ursula picked her way along the riverbed, disturbing a cloud of bats in her haste. The dark flying creatures, emblematic of the Chautauqua Institution, squealed above her, hunting mosquitoes. Just a short distance along the side of the creek, Ursula caught sight of the Golden Hind, prancing as if awaiting her arrival with impatience. As she caught up with her, the doe began to paw the earth and snort as if frustrated by her inability to immediately press Ursula into action. *What is it?* Ursula attempted to communicate her lack of comprehension. A sound to her left alerted Ursula to the appearance of the Clan Mothers materializing from mist drifting along the surface of the water. Ursula waited as the Clan Mothers conferred with the Golden Hind. They then turned, and Ursula was able to discern from their communication that a young woman was in immediate danger. Danger? Can you be more specific? Unfortunately, they responded that there seemed to be some powerful force blocking further information. Something had to be done to combat the obstruction. As long as the barrier remained, the main intuitive pathways used by each of the Goddesses would be impeded. It was imperative that this problem be addressed as Death was once again haunting the grounds of the Institution.

***

Back in her dining room, Alex unlocked her Tarot cards from their gilded gold miniature chest. She slid them from their silken envelope, hand-painted with a depiction of The High Priestess. Next, she lit a scented candle and put on her favorite meditative music, allowing herself to release all the toxins from the recent past and drop into Goddessence. Picking up the Tarot cards, she chose as the significator card, The Devil as Querent — his inverted Pentagon denoting black magic and evil — to represent the unknown energy associated with the recent deaths. Alex began to meditate on the cards, ritually passing them through her hands, shuffling them over and over until she felt satisfied that this was the mix ordained for the reading. Cutting the cards three times from right to left, Alexis next reconstituted them into one deck. Then she began laying out the cards across the luxurious mahogany of her dining table. One by one, she dealt the cards from the deck in the ancient ritual of a Celtic Cross Spread.

1. General Atmosphere: Emperor (Reversed)

2. Opposing Energy: High Priestess

3. Heart of the Matter: The Alchemist

4. Recent Influence: 5 of the wands

5. Possible Future Event: 9 of Pentacles

6. Expected Future Event: Moon

7. Fears: 8 swords

8. Family Opinion: Star

9. Hopes: King of Swords

10. Final Outcome: 10 of Swords.

The first position of the spread provides the general atmosphere surrounding the issue in question. Alexis turned over the Emperor's card reversed: a control freak out of control. In the second position, which reflected forces in opposition to the first card, The High Priestess was revealed, suggesting that intuition could be helpful in solving the mystery. The third position card at the base of the Celtic Cross Spread describes the basis of the matter. Alexis turned over the Alchemist: an archetypal figure capable of willing hidden agenda into being. The 5 of Wands in the fourth position described how the Querent had been recently involved in an intense conflict, perhaps a lawsuit. The 9 of Pentacles appearing in the fifth position offered the hope that a peaceful and bountiful lady could salve the Querent's internal turmoil. The Moon in the sixth position, however, suggests it is more likely that the Querent would harbor apprehensions of secret enemies plotting against him. Indeed his fear of betrayal is highlighted by the 8 of Swords in the 7th position in the spread. Except for Family hopes of insight (Star in the eighth position), the remaining cards were

Swords replete with themes of stress, hostility, and in the end, more death.

"I wonder how this will unfold," Alex murmured to herself.

***

Once in the safety of her Chautauqua residence, Yan went over to the hearth and took from the black pottery bowl placed on the mantle a cone of pinon incense. Pinon was like her, resilient, growing high up on the mountain where less sturdy trees perished. It was harvested by aboriginal peoples and then compressed into this small cylindrical object between her fingers. From her satchel, she drew a white book of matches with the name "Melina" scrawled in black. This is the al fresco restaurant where she liked to while away a summer's afternoon: to feel the golden softness of sunlight slanting through the trees, the shadows of leaves dappling the cobblestone patio, to watch the shifting light painting Mount Tamalpais with the colors of the sunset. Setting fire to the incense, she pursed gently to blow on the embers. She stared into the glow as she watched the smoke spiral upward, shaping soft curls. She slipped into Goddessence and began to visualize a sole menacing figure igniting a torch and blowing on the flames, just as she had done with the incense cone. A sacrifice to the Gods? She strained to make out more detail, but the harder she tried, the quicker the image faded. Allowing herself time to sink into a deeply meditative state,

Yan selected three figurines: one canine, one female, and one hooded, from among the number arrayed on the shelving surrounding the Buddhist sand tray garden. She then unwrapped the pewter pendulum and allowed it to dangle from her fingertips, her elbow resting on the burnished rosewood desktop. The pendulum continued to swing in circles, not forming a decisive 'yes' or 'no' pattern. Suddenly, a hologram appeared at the very center of the sand tray; within it was a tiny figure that Yan recognized as that of her mother, now deceased these many years, repeating: "Help her. Help her. Help her." The figure slowly faded, leaving Yan with an empty hollow in her heart as she was reminded of her own battle to leave her mother's protection."

Chapter 38

"How awful. I'm still shaking from everything that has happened. Did I tell you about the angry young man who brought Princess to the house the other day? So menacing!" said Georgina, reaching to comfort Elise." I'm positive he had something to do with the horrible thing that happened to her."

"Mother, for God's sake, you are such a Cassandra. All you seem to care about is what rocks your small, contained world." cried Elise, turning to avoid Georgina's embrace. "I can't bear thinking of the suffering that Princess endured."

"Well, I care about you, and I'm trying to support your recovery. I don't want you to get upset."

"You've tried to manage my entire life. You can't control me. I feel like you have a plastic bag over my head. You treat me as if I were still a child. I'm not. I'm my own person."

Elise slammed out the door.

"I can't do anything right." moaned Georgina as Yan arrived and joined her on the porch.

"Adult children's behavior as they begin to fly from the nest can be very chaotic: hurtful and harmful," stated Yan in response to Georgina's obvious distress. "A myth from my own philosophical tradition portrays Buddha in his youth as a prince: Prince Siddhartha. Prince Siddhartha's father, the

King, did his best to protect him from worry or harm; provided him with every extravagance. But one day, events aligned to catapult Prince Siddhartha from the palace enclosure into the outside world. There he saw illness, old age, and death. Siddhartha was devastated. How could anyone be happy, he wondered, given that this fate awaited us all. Siddhartha left the palace and his family and started upon his quest for answers."

"How does this apply to Elise?" muttered Georgina bitterly.

"Elise is leaving the protected palace of childhood," explained Yan. "She is becoming aware of the world of adulthood with all its victories and vicissitudes. She is experiencing crises that you and I have come to know simply as life. She is a highly sensitive person, and the everyday trauma she experiences have triggered her to escape through extreme activities such as ballet as well as pharmaceuticals. You are powerless over her path".

Yan came to Georgina's side and gently took her hand,

"Children do fly the nest. It is happening all around us, and yet we mothers remain in denial about its inevitability." Yan drew back to peer closely at how Georgina was receiving this counsel. "Once we have thoroughly grieved the passing of the mothering phase of our lives, to begin to move from a place of quiet desperation to a place of quiet dignity and to begin to design a life well-lived."

Georgina sighed. "I can't even imagine what that looks like. I have built my life around creating a life for others, living vicariously through them."

"It is difficult but not impossible to let our children follow their own path." Yan continued now she had determined that Georgina was interested in what she was imparting. "It seems, despite our expectations, that there is no fairy Godmother that comes to play social secretary for us. At this time in our lives, we women look forward to creating our own full, satisfying lives and move from a victim to victor. There's often a natural pairing between vampires and victims, and you may find that you have been paired up with vampire types —people who suck up all the oxygen in the room— specifically because you appear passive and submissive. As you develop assertiveness and independence, it may be that you will be abandoned by those who are presently in your sphere; however, in time, you will be a more 'natural fit' for those seeking mutuality and reciprocity."

"I get sick to my stomach to think she is leaving to go out on her own," said Georgina shakily.

"Before you are the task of tolerating the body of pain endured by mothers through the ages: inner physical sensations and the thoughts and images lodged in your brain that are associated with abandonment. The task is to ride the wave of grief. You will find that it crests and recedes, then crests and recedes again, and then one day, you will emerge at the other side. The challenge is to allow the grieving rather than avoiding or fighting it. It, too, shall pass. So tell me, as you think about life without Elise in it every day, where in your body do you feel a sensation? Explore it; label it; change it; distract."

"Just as we did before?" Georgina clarified.

"Exactly. The mindful approach to emotions enables you to move to Goddessence, the witness position, and objectively observe the unfolding of the physical and mental phenomena we call feelings."

Yan moved over to the sand tray and began to trace lines deeper and deeper into the sand to demonstrate how neuroplasticity worked.

"Throughout our lives, tracts were laid down during each thing we experience as brain cells connect to one another over and over again and, like the Rio Grande River running over rock for centuries, eventually become The Grand Canyon of brain ruts. This is the old fear of learning that we're working to combat. In order to develop different brain responses such as the 'spot and distract' approach —we have to create a 'ceroplastic bypass'; i.e., scratch different tracks in the brain that reflect the more efficient processes, and continue to practice these until they are deep pathways in the brain. We also use meditative practices such as Goddessence that strengthen the parasympathetic nervous system that runs counter to the programmed fight-flight response of the sympathetic nervous system. We in the Goddess Circle meet several times a year to enhance these practices."

Yan fell silent as Georgina set down her cup of coffee and began to move about in an effort to shake off her despair. It was important that she hears some of what Yan had to say, and yet it was a difficult time to assimilate these esoteric principles given the high degree of crisis presently in her life.

"I want to assist in the Circle's efforts to find the killers, but I don't know what help I can be. Earlier I tried to work on Goddessence; down by the water's edge, I completed a muscle-by-muscle relaxation of my body and attempted to narrow my focus, just as you had shown me, but as I looked towards the sunset, the clouds began to roil again. What looked to me like a paddleboat chugged through the rosy hues, streaking the colors of the sky, shocked me out of my meditation."

Before Yan could ask Georgina for more information about her vision, there was a knock at the door. She opened the door to find Rafael on the porch.

"Just dropping by to show various translations of the shapes Georgina had drawn from memory," he explained.

Yan departed, pleading for work she had promised to do to aid in the investigation.

Rafi spread the papers that he had been working on out on the table in front of them, explaining that there were a couple of logogram systems that might apply to the characters drawn by Georgina.

"You mean there is any number of ways this could be interpreted? How will we ever figure it out?"

"Perhaps the Goddesses can conjure up a Rosetta stone: a key that repeats the same instructions in three different languages and that, therefore, provides an interpretive tool. These seem to me most like Chinese logograms. Thousand years ago, the Chinese developed a writing system of communication based on characters that represent syllables rather than sounds, as our writing systems do now. The oldest inscriptions were records of divinations prepared for Royal Chinese —divinations coming now to you. They were called Bone Script because archeologists found them on bones or turtle shells."

As Georgina turned, she found her breast touching Rafi's chest. Somehow his arms were around her, and without conscious thought, she melted right into him. She was aware of spreading warmth and deep longing that culminated in a low moan emanating unheralded from deep within her chest. A small, isolated part of her brain directed her to separate herself from him, to back away somehow, but her body refused to obey. She raised her face from where it was snuggled into the sweet spot on Rafi's chest —the thin covering over his heart just below where his shoulder met his collarbone, a spot seemingly created just for her —and gazed directly into his smoldering eyes. Their mouths came longingly together, hungry as if from a great fast. At the sound of the front door scraping open, they sprang apart. Chests heaving, hearts pounding.

"Mother!" screamed Elise. "What are you thinking?"

Elise rushed through the room, through the hallway, and into her suite. She slammed her door.

"I'm so sorry. Looks like this will cause problems between you and your daughter," said Rafi, looking at Georgina, who was obviously shaken.

"Things have not been going well between us," whispered Georgina.

"It's pretty common for children, even adult children, to continue to hope that their parents will get back together. Are you sure about this?" murmured Raphael kissing the inside of her wrist.

"Absolutely certain."

Chapter 39

Meister Gregory entered the residence, moved to the front of the common room, and waited for those assembled to fall quiet. Tomorrow would be their first performance as the resident ballet company, and it was important that they do their utmost to make it a success. He read from the notes he had prepared during the afternoon's dress rehearsal, with specific and lengthy references to the pas de deux performed by Brynn and her partner.

Do hurry up! Brynn groaned inwardly. The ballet Meister just liked to hear the sound of his own voice. Finally, he dismissed them with the reminder to get a good night's sleep. Everyone was to be in bed, lights out, at ten. Brynn bid her fellows good night and sped to her room as quickly as polite convention would allow. She was frantic that Miko had seemed so dismissive and wondered whether, now that they had been intimate, she had become less tantalizing to him. She knew that some men were only interested in the hunt. Once they achieved their goal, they lost interest. Slinking from the residence, she hastened through the square and raced down the incline, heading to the dock below. Disturbed that Miko had dismissed her in such a cavalier fashion, she was determined to show up at the party tonight on the Chautauqua Belle. She would be so beautiful that Miko couldn't fail to continue to find her more attractive than anyone else there. In the bushes a short distance from the boat, Brynn put down her practice knapsack and extracted a figure-hugging emerald silk sheath, knowing it complimented her green eyes and fair hair. Shaking out the party dress, she quickly slipped it over her head and hurried onto the dock just in time to leap aboard the departing Chautauqua Belle. As she moved carefully along the polished deck, she was reassured by the knowledge that she had Ativan in her bag. She had been relieved to access a new drug pusher when she arrived at the Institution. Finding a contact was always a challenge in a new location, and she had been concerned that it would be especially true here in a gated community established by Sunday School teachers. But happily, that had not been the case, and now, in this highly agitated state, she needed a calming substance to soothe her raw nerves. Hidden in a handy washroom accessible from the main deck, she popped two Ativan and waited, elbows propped on the sink, head drooping until the effects of the drugs washed through her body, and a warm 'high' filled her. Then, shoulders back, head held high, once more the consummate ballerina, she strutted from the small room.

In the dim light of the stars that, free from the light pollution of cities, shone brightly in the black ink sky, she could discern the outline of the lifeboats suspended above her. Off in the distance, from the direction of the bow of the boat, she could sense the pounding rhythms of the band and the muffled cacophony of excited voices. Once again, she blinked away insecurity and ventured a smile as she imagined Miko's delight at her surprised appearance. He wouldn't be expecting her. He knew that if she missed curfew, she would be forbidden to dance in tomorrow's performance. But that risk hadn't deterred her. She knew there was any number of beautiful young women who would be throwing themselves at him, and he was the type to love the one he was with. Earlier this evening, distraught at what she perceived as Miko's sudden coolness to her, Brynn told Elise of her plan to break curfew and sneak out of the residence to attend the party. Elise had counseled her not to Angelique after Miko but to play the game and wait for him to pursue her. But Brynn was too impatient to be strategic. Miko offered everything she had ever wanted, even more than she'd dared dream of. She wasn't about to risk losing him to some other predatory female, not for an uncertain future as a ballet dancer. Injuries were too frequent. Ballet directors are too fickle. You couldn't put all your eggs in that basket.

Hearing the heavy door scrape open behind her, Brynn stumbled onto the deck. The mist had rendered the deck slippery and treacherous. She lurched against the railing, aware of the cold metal against her ribs and the cold wind pressing against her face. She turned to see a dark shadow approach with a predator's patience. She felt a sudden urge to flee. It occurred to her that if she went overboard, no one would even know she was gone.

Chapter 40

Yoga mat slung over her shoulder in a batik sleeve, Ursula walked to Bell Tower Point in the early morning darkness. She paused to gaze to the east, sensing the oppressive late June heat intensifying just over the horizon with the lurking sun. The air was sodden and still even this early in the morning. A number of sailboats moored just offshore were barely visible through the graying mists —sails furled awaiting the early morning regatta. Except for lanyards clanking in the faintest breeze, all was quiet. Fishermen slipped rowing skiffs off to the icy chill of deeper water. Ursula stretched out her mat on the small sandy space made sacred by the Inukshuk.

As the sun peeked above the towering heights across the waters, she lifted her hands in prayer mudra from the heart chakra to just above the crown chakra, arching back before swanning into a forward bend in the ancient early dawn yoga ritual of Surya Namaskara —salute to the sun. She was but one member of the wave of figures around the globe making a tribute to the eternally rising sun. She had faith that with this ancient practice, as each worshiper breathed in the pain of the planet and exhaled peace, the universe was positively impacted: a butterfly effect, the smallest movement rippling across the entire planet. Ursula focused on the sensation of warmth spreading down her hamstrings as she stretched through the opening postures of Surya Namaskara. The muscles of the small of her back engaged as she sprung into downward dog and then swooped through into upward dog; moisture beading on her upper lip just as the sun continued its climb and rose above the hills across the lake. Then, completing her worship, she stood for a moment, pressing her hands together in namaste.

Moving out of prayerful trance, she became aware of something nagging at her unconscious. As she wandered to the water's edge and waded through the tall grasses and lilies edging the shoreline, she thought to herself how terrible it was that youngsters were congregating at night to drink and drug at the Bell Tower Point, leaving detritus. *Youngsters needed something more to do in the evenings,* she thought as she picked up empty beer cans. She spotted one of the plastic bottles bobbing a couple of feet offshore. Wading out to retrieve it, her gaze was transfixed by the luxurious dark silk that rose and fell with the faint ripples from a passing motor launch. As she parted the water lilies and gingerly waded into the water, some aspect of her mind registered the rich yellow silk fanning out and framing the slender, delicate body bobbing face-down in the water. Arms that the day before had graced the stage of the Amphitheater now floated in a graceful arabesque. Splashing her way back to shore, Ursula paused once more to solemnize the moment with palms pressed together at her chest in namaste —a moment of prayer to honor this vibrant young energy too quickly snuffed out. Then she tiptoed over to find her cell phone and call Angelique.

SECTION IV

Chapter 41

A nerve-shattering ring woke Georgina from a deep sleep. It took her a moment to identify it as the telephone. She threw back the down quilt protecting her from the cool Chautauqua nights and finally located the house landline in the farthest corner of the study, picking up the receiver on the thirteenth ring.

"What the hell is going on up there?" demanded the disembodied voice. It was Owen.

"I suppose you're referring to the deaths."

"The Chautauqua serial murders," sputtered Owen. "It's all over the news."

"They still haven't decided whether it was murder," mumbled Georgina, still half-asleep. Her husband intimidated her even from a distance.

"Oh sure, not at Chautauqua," Owen scoffed. "Not in the bubble."

"I'm not surprised the press is sensationalizing everything. Jonah Nash —the frontman for 'Herd Mentality,' a rather famous rock band that keeps a house here at the Institution— was incinerated when his car went up in flames. For now, the sheriff has called it an accidental death."

"Accidental!"

"Jonah was known to be addicted to any number of drugs, and so it is possible he overdosed, and his lit cigar dropped from his fingers and set the car on fire."

"And, pray tell, how is he rationalizing Brynn's death? We've known her since she was eight years old. Elise has to be beside herself!"

Georgina found herself falling into the seat beside the telephone. The breath left her body. She felt dizzy. "What are you saying about Brynn?"

"It's all over the news. Two deaths in as many days. They're talking about a serial killer. Brynn's body was found early this morning down by the Bell Tower Point. Someone found her floating near the edge of the shore. Someone who had gone there early to do yoga, no less. Yoga! Figures."

"Do they know what happened?" Her lips began to quiver, and her eyes filled with tears.

"They are doing an autopsy and tox screen to determine the cause of death, but the media is reporting that she was known to be on several pain killers and stimulant drugs."

"How awful for her family." It felt like she was being hit by a pile of falling rocks. She rubbed tears from her cheeks and took a deep breath.

"Is everyone up there on drugs? You took our daughter there in a very fragile state. She was supposed to spend the summer with you to continue her rest." As usual, Owen was on the offensive. Georgina was seized with a wave of powerful anger that flashed between her shoulder blades.

"You mean her recovery from addiction," she corrected.

He just doesn't get it despite the family week at the treatment center. What a powerful denial system he's wrapped himself in.

"Whatever."

"Elise is the canary in the coal mine: a symptom of our toxic relationship," she protested.

"You promised me that Chautauqua was the safest place in the world. Now there have been two deaths. How is she doing with all of this?" He spoke bitterly.

"Of course, even before this happened, Elise was tremendously upset by the death of Princess and by the way that she died. Elise mentioned she'd left you a message letting you know that Princess had been found burned up in a fireplace down by the boat house. "Georgina's mouth contorted with pain. "I'm surprised we haven't heard from you before now. "

"I've been out of contact. Away on business," he replied in a frustrated tone.

"Of course, business," Georgina said stiffly. Darn, I try so hard not to get hooked, and yet here I go again, sounding like a bitter fishwife.

There was a long pause at the other end of the telephone. Finally, Owen spoke. "Is Elise available?"

"She hasn't woken up yet. I would prefer she hears the news from me." Said Georgina firmly.

There was a lengthy silence. He was accustomed to Georgina obeying him when he spoke. He finally spoke:

"Let her know I need to talk with her. You can be sure that the place is going to be crawling with news people, and they will probably want to talk to Elise. I want to talk with her before that happens." There was a click at the other end of the phone.

Georgina tiptoed down the hallway and gently knocked on the door to Elise's bedroom, not wanting to startle her from her dreams.

"Come in," invited a voice clear of any vestiges of sleep. As Georgina entered the room, she saw Elise at her desk, writing in her journal over in the window seating area that she had so lovingly arranged for her daughter.

"Mother, I just love this room. It's beautiful and comfortable as well. I am quite at home here since my arrival." Elise rose and came to give her mother a hug. "Thank you."

Could it have only been a couple of days since she got here? So much has happened since then.

Elise peered intently at her mother's face. "What is it?"

Georgina grimaced as she was reminded once again that her daughter's antennae measured every nuance of her mother's emotional shifting.

"I've just had a telephone call from your father," Georgina said as calmly as she was able, watching for her daughter's reaction.

Elise sighed and rolled her eyes.

"He has called with some very tragic news." Georgina continued grimly.

"I'll bet. People certainly seem to relish sensational events. I'm sure that the murder of Jonah Nash has made headlines everywhere." Elise frowned.

"That is to be sure, but it is not just Jonah's death that's in the news," Georgina replied gravely.

"You can't mean Princess made the news." Said Elise, mystified.

"Why don't we sit down?" there was no mistaking the seriousness in her tone.

Georgina led Elise back to the seating area that just a moment ago had seemed so inviting. Elise sat down opposite her, a quizzical look on her face.

"A body has been found down by Belltower Point."

"A body?"

"I'm afraid it's Brynn." Elise blanched. She was in shock; for a moment, she couldn't think of anything to say.

"But I just saw her yesterday afternoon," she uttered in disbelief.

"I'm afraid it is true. She was found early this morning. I'm so sorry."

"What happened?" The tears had begun to stream down Elise's face as the reality of her mother's words began to register in her mind.

"That's all the information I have." Georgina was powerless to save her daughter from this pain.

Elise stood and began to pace back and forth, wringing her hands, and shaking her head in distress and confusion. Georgina found herself rising and reaching out, but Elise put up her hands, unwilling to be comforted.

"What can we do?" she cried. "It's as if some part of the energy field has been violently disturbed."

"The best thing we can do is try to be of some comfort to one another through this terrible time" Georgina took a few steps to get closer to her daughter. "It might get worse. There will be a lot of chaos. I'm afraid we can probably expect an onslaught of media."

"How hateful. Just when the world should stop and mourn Brynn," said Brynn indignantly.

"I'm concerned, and I'm sure your father is concerned that along with this tragic loss, you might be questioned in connection with an investigation because of your close relationship with Brynn," said Georgina anxiously.

The two of them came together, and Elise finally allowed her mother to take her into her arms. She began to sob.

"I have to go to the ballet residence," said Elise distractedly as she finally stepped back from her mother's embrace and picked up the tissue Georgina had ready for her, gently patting the tears from her cheeks.

"Your father has asked for you to call him," said Georgina hesitantly.

"My father is the least of my worries."

***

As Elise approached the ballet residence, she saw that news of Brynn's death had already arrived. Dancers were gathered whispering together in twos and threes: on the lawn, on the porch of the ballet residence, and in the common area. Nodding to a couple of the dancers that she knew as she moved through the ante area and came to the closed door of the office of Ballet Meister.

"Enter," was the terse response to her knock. Elise opened the door to find Meister Gregory seated at his desk. A model of the dance stage replica opened before him on the desk.

"I came to tell you about Brynn, but it seems that the news has already arrived. I am so sorry," said Elise, wringing her hands.

"I can't imagine that you care about how it affects the ballet company or me," he said stiffly.

"That's not true. I care deeply for everyone here. And I am devastated about Brynn, who was my dear friend as well as colleague," said Elise with a sigh.

"That's hard to believe, given your defection. First, you abandon me, and now Brynn. I have to redo everything," he said bitterly.

"I didn't 'defect' from the ballet. I had to save my life. I was doing my best to achieve the highest excellence as a dancer, and in trying to please everyone else, I almost destroyed myself," said Elise defensively.

Gregory gestured toward the door." That's the flimsiest excuse I've ever heard for just giving up. Now leave me to my work. I have to redo everything now. You can close the door behind you,"

Gregory immediately became absorbed in the virtual choreography before him.

Elise didn't even bother holding back her tears as she hurried through the dancers scattered around the grounds.

Chapter 42

Angelique pushed her way through the crowd of murmuring onlookers. She spotted Ursula over near the water's edge, talking to Sheriff Cahill. An ambulance idling on the roadway nearby and various uniformed figures crouching purposefully among the trees dotting Belltower Point provided a reminder of the solemnity of death. Gaily striped sails skimming the glassy surface of the lake afforded an ironic contrast to the grisly scene unfolding behind the garish yellow crime-scene tape.

"How awful," exclaimed Angelique, hugging Ursula.

"Ms. Beignet," acknowledged Sheriff Cahill, tipping the golf visor that disclosed the pastime from which he had been rudely yanked.

Angelique stifled her sarcasm and focused instead on her dear friend, whose beautiful face was streaked with silent tears.

"What a tragedy," Ursula repeated.

"What happened here?" Angelique peered at Sheriff Cahill as she maintained Ursula in a secure embrace.

"It's still too early to tell."

Angelique stifled an inward groan.

"The information we have so far is that there was a party of young people on board the Chautauqua Belle last night.

So far, no one who attended that party has reported noticing anything amiss. Apparently, the young man with whom Brynn has been seen, Miko, was at that party, but we haven't yet talked to him. As a matter of fact, we haven't found anyone who was aware that Brynn was aboard the boat —for that matter, we are not even certain that she was there; it's just speculation— however, she was found this morning floating up close to the shore by Dr. Ursula Andrews, whom you obviously know."

"What happens now?"

"It's important I interview Miko as soon as possible."

"Good luck with that."

***

Sheriff Cahill steered his van carefully between the red brick columns through the wrought iron entrance gates of the Bellamy Estate and drove around the circular driveway. He parked the vehicle out of the way, under the junipers just off the northern arc. Reluctant to disturb the peace of this serene oasis, he shut the door of the van as quietly as he could and strode up the wide flagstone front steps. He waited for a few moments after he rang the bell at the side of the immense hand-carved wooden doors and was about to ring the bell a second time when he heard steady steps inside. The door was opened just a fraction by a medium-height muscular man in his late sixties wearing a three-piece suit, face glowering.

"Yes?" The greeting sounded like a challenge. The servant had positioned his body to prevent any view of the interior.

"I am here to speak with Miko. I am Tom Cahill, the sheriff here at the Institution."

"I am afraid Prince Kazimierz is not available."

"When might he be available?"

"I really couldn't tell."

"And what is your name?"

"I am Mr. Mason, Mrs. Bellamy's assistant."

"Well, is Mrs. Bellamy available?"

"I will go and see. Wait here." The door shut firmly.

Not knowing for how long he would be kept waiting, Sheriff Cahill strolled around the impeccable gardens at the front of the property. Colorful annuals lining the border of the driveway were backed by larger green bushes. In late June, the rhododendrons were still blooming —Chautauqua tended to be a cool micro -climate —and a series of bushes that would provide a continuing succession of blooms through the entire summer season framed the verdant lawns.

What God could have done with a little money, he grumbled to himself as he looked around at the elaborately staged exhibition of landscape architecture.

After an undetermined length of time, the front door opened again. Mr. Mason was back with a response.

"Mrs. Bellamy will see you on the terrace. You may follow the bluestone pathway to the left of the house, and it will lead you around to her."

"Am I allowed to go there unescorted?"

"She is waiting there for you."

The sheriff followed the path to the back terrace of the mansion, keeping close attention to anything out of the ordinary. There was nothing of interest other than gardens and grounds that were so immaculate that you could see the exactly measured rake tracks freshly scratched into the ground.

"Good morning Sheriff Cahill. Won't you join me for tea?" Teresa Bellamy was positioned on her grand terrace that overlooked the lake, the flowers, and the trees of the back garden as a lush backdrop.

As perfect a staging as any Broadway production.

"I do think that tea is such a delightful ritual, don't you, Sheriff? This is my own blend of tea leaves —chamomile, mint, lemongrass, with a hint of orange, blueberry, and passionflower leaves along with rosehips."

Ah. Obstruction by a wall of pleasantry. So this is how the grand lady is going to play it. Two can play that game. The sheriff was aware that Mrs. Bellamy had destroyed the career of the previous law enforcement officer who had threatened her grandsons. She would not hesitate to do the same to him.

"And please do call me Tom. I am fascinated that the ancient tea ritual has so many similarities among the numerous cultures. When I was an officer in Japan, I became an admirer of their tea ceremony."

They fell silent as Teresa Bellamy avoided pursuing that thread of conversation and instead moved quietly and unhurriedly through her formalities. She picked up the hand-painted porcelain teacups one by one, placed the silver strainer on top of the delicate cup, and carefully poured the steaming tea through the strainer.

"Here's to protocol."

"This tea is delicious. And I thank you for your hospitality. Unfortunately, I have some sad business to attend to. I don't know if you have heard that there has been a second unexpected death." Sheriff Cahill scrutinized the composed mask that was secured firmly across the face of his hostess. All expression was wiped away

"How unfortunate," came the ambiguous response.

"Yes. Unhappily, the body of a young girl was discovered this morning floating in the rushes just off Bell Tower Point."

"Do we know the identity of this young lady?"

"The body has been identified as that of Brynn Robinson. She is the prima ballerina with our residence ballet company. I understand that she was a friend of your grandson, Miko Kazimierz."

"A friend of my grandson, Prince Mikolaj? Really? I don't believe I know her."

"It is imperative that I speak with Miko as soon as possible. We need to find out everything we can about what happened."

"I'm certain I speak for all members of my family when I assure you that we support your efforts to maintain the safety of this Institution. But you understand that I must first contact our lawyer. He is adamant that I have his consultation in these matters."

And there it is. The impenetrable curtain.

"Of course, when do you suppose you might confer with your lawyer? Time is of the essence if we are to find the circumstances of the death of this poor girl."

"First chance I get. He's a very busy man."

Sheriff Cahill paused for a moment and turned to look at Teresa Bellamy, but her face and body were perfectly still.

***

"That went well," sighed Sheriff Cahill, returning to his office and slamming his empty report down on the desk.

"That good, huh? Imagine my surprise," teased Angelique, who had been helping herself to coffee and pastries as she waited for him in the office. She knew all too well how non-disclosing the Bellamies could be.

"Mrs. Bellamy is a Master of stonewalling. She won't let me question her grandson Miko —excuse me, Prince Mikolaj —without the express consent of her lawyer. According to the Chautauqua grapevine —which is usually pretty accurate— Miko has been pursuing our beautiful ballerina, and she might have been with him at a party that he held on the Chautauqua Belle last night just before she died."

The sheriff helped himself to the largest Danish on the hospitality table. He then sank into his chair, eyes unfocused, eating in silence.

"Well, it's a concern if the Bellamies stall and too much time elapse after Brynn's body was found. The first forty-eight hours are critical. After that, important evidence deteriorates," said Angelique.

"Tell me about it. Oh, and by the way, you can forget about reading Teresa Bellamy's expressions. Her face is a kabuki mask."

"That's for sure. Years of self-restraint accented by the modern miracle of Botox. Cosmetic surgery is surely messing with micro-expression science these days —all those facial muscles paralyzed by botulism toxin. Doesn't help our investigations much."

"How do you know Mrs. Bellamy?"

Angelique shielded her own face, getting up to help herself to another cup of coffee provided so thoughtfully by the Chautauqua Ladies Guild.

"Spill it. And don't pretend you don't know what I mean."

"Well, let's say I was peripherally involved in a case in Boston involving her grandsons."

"Let's hear it." The sheriff cursed himself for not paying attention to Angelique's uncharacteristic reticence before.

"You may already be aware of the case. Two years ago this past spring, a young woman, an adult dancer, was beaten almost to death at a party thrown by the rowing team at Harbridge."

"Yeah. Everyone involved in law enforcement heard about what happened to the district attorney in that case. What's the dope?"

"There were two female 'adult dancers' at the party. They were performing off and on, and when they weren't 'dancing,' there was probably another kind of entertainment going on. We know for sure there was a lot of drinking and drugging by the guests as well as by the strippers. One of them, Sheri, was in the bedroom with someone she later identified as one of the Bellamy grandsons. She doesn't know what set him off, but according to her report, he beat her to a pulp and set fire to her hair. Luckily, she had her cell phone with her and managed to hit 911—I guess the working girls have that on speed dial —but by the time the police got there, she was a mess: her eyes all blackened, her jaw and nose were broken."

"Was the grandson charged?"

"Well, that was one of the problems. You know, those grandsons really look alike, and so Sheri, the victim, kept changing her story: first, she said it was Eric, and then she thought it was Miko. It didn't help that she had a long rap sheet for possession, prostitution, and child endangerment."

"Child endangerment?"

"Don't ask. It turned into a big fiasco. The District Attorney, my boss, went ahead with the prosecution despite these gaping holes, and, as you probably know, he made a big deal of the case in the news media."

"Up for reelection, was he?" the sheriff nodded knowingly.

"That was the speculation. At least, that's what the Bellamies and their team of lawyers convinced everyone was going on."

"Do I remember that he withheld evidence as well?"

"You got it. It turned out that the DNA of several men was recovered from Sheri, none of it that of the Bellamies. The District Attorney neglected to inform the defense of this. By the time they got through with him, he had resigned; the State Bar Association had disbarred him, and the Bellamies successfully sued for over $30 million."

"At the time, I remember reading a lot about that."

"Well, I'm just giving you fair warning. That is what can happen when you try to go up against the Bellamies."

The sheriff acknowledged this with a rueful nod.

"I'd really like to go with you when you go back to the Bellamies. A second pair of eyes and ears might be able to pick up something you might miss while you're interacting with them."

"But you were on the team that bungled the case last time."

"I consider it "lessons learned," a rehearsal for success. The Bellamy grandsons are involved; they deserve to be punished just like anybody else."

"We don't know if these cases are murder, much less whether the Bellamies were involved now or at Harbridge. And I don't know if that's such a great idea given your association with the Harbridge case. They might refuse to talk to me at all if you're there."

"On the other hand, the shock of seeing me might knock them off their game. Despite all the inappropriateness and illegality that was involved in our side of the Harbridge case, I am convinced that there was truth in what the stripper had to say about the savage attack. I saw her just after the incident, and she was terrified. Her face was a bloody mess. I'm certain one of those Bellamy grandsons is a sadistic sociopath, and I would like to be involved when he's brought to justice."

"Oh, great. A vendetta."

The phone ring tone —Beethoven's 5th — penetrated the silence following Angelique's plea. The sheriff spoke tersely:

"We'll be right there." The sheriff sprung to his feet and started for the door. Pausing briefly, he held the door open.

"After you, Ms. Beignet. You might as well just call me Tom."

***

As he pressed the doorbell to the massive, carved wooden front door of the Bellamy Estate, Sheriff Tom Cahill took in a deep breath.

"I'm sure Ms. Bellamy's haughty behavior intimidates some —and I'm also sure she knows how effective that can be —but you can't let her arrogance interfere with the investigation and the safety of the residents and visitors here at Chautauqua," Angelique said briskly.

Though there was no sound audible from within, the door swung open to reveal Mr. Mason, still in his pinstripe three-piece, manner half a degree less icy.

"Sheriff. Do come in. Mrs. Bellamy is expecting you. She is in the sunroom. Good morning, Ms. Beignet."

The sheriff glanced quickly at Angelique. Apparently, her involvement in the Boston incident had been more memorable than she had let on.

"Thank you, Mr. Mason. It seems you already know my associate, Ms. Angelique Beignet."

"Yes indeed. Follow me, please." Mason's voice betrayed little emotion.

Mason led them down the hall and through a doorway to the bookcase-lined study, where they were ushered into the presence of Teresa Bellamy and a man in an impeccably tailored business suit.

He sure got here in a hurry. Apparently, he's not too busy to miss a call from his powerful client. That suit has to be six grand if it's a penny, clearly at the beck and call of Mrs. Bellamy, who obviously pays dearly to have him immediately on hand.

The lawyer, who introduced himself as Jonathan Roberts, immediately took charge of the meeting, shook hands all around, and gestured toward two chairs near paned French doors. Angelique chose the high-backed leather wing chair with the window at her back where she would be out of the direct gaze of either Teresa or Mr. Roberts, and the light from the window would be shining in their faces.

"Mrs. Bellamy has been filling me in on the recent tragedies. I understand there have been two deaths here at the Chautauqua Institution," stated Mr. Roberts.

"That's correct," replied the sheriff. "The leader of a rock band, The Herd Mentality, was discovered dead in his vehicle, and then this morning the body of a young woman found floating just offshore of the Institution."

"I can understand how distressing this must be for all the residents here as well as for you, Sheriff, but what does this have to do with Mrs. Bellamy and her grandsons?" The lawyer sounded only mildly inquisitive.

"We are interviewing anybody who might have some information pertinent to the case," offered the Sheriff.

"I am still not clear about how interviewing the Bellamies could shed light on this." the lawyer shrugged.

"Mrs. Bellamy's grandson, Prince Mikolaj Kazmierz, had been seen frequently with the dead girl." The Sheriff frowned at Angelique's interjection.

"I see. Please enlighten me. Has the coroner declared either of these deaths a murder?" queried the lawyer innocently.

"Not yet. Autopsies are being performed, but it may be several days, even weeks, before all the test results are in. We need to talk to anyone with any information before people's memories become dim." the Sheriff pointed out.

"I can understand your need, Sheriff. However, my need is to protect my clients."

Angelique spoke. "Mr. Marshall, Mrs. Bellamy, there are pieces of evidence that people don't even know they possess until they are questioned in a systematic way. It is important to the families and loved ones of those who have died that all information be obtained that will assist the investigation."

Mr. Marshall took a long moment to shift in his chair. He turned to Angelique with an icy glare. "Ms. Beignet, you know better than anybody that Mrs. Bellamy and her family have suffered greatly at the hands of over-reaching investigators and politically ambitious prosecutors. We are adamant that that should not happen again. It is unfortunate for the loved ones of those who have died that that avenue of investigation is closed because of the earlier unethical behavior of those in charge. Our position is unshakeable. Good day."

At that moment, Mason appeared to lead them back out to the front entrance.

***

"Dear Jonathan, I am getting too old for this," commented Teresa Bellamy, sitting down wearily after Angelique and the sheriff had left.

"Nonsense. You have more energy than people half your age." Mr. Roberts reassured.

"The thought of having all that garbage resurfacing and the Bellamy name dragged through the mud is almost more than I can bear." Teresa's shoulders sagged at what her family might have to endure once again.

The lawyer nodded. "It's a shame our legal system allows people to be sensationalized with impunity."

"The scandal was on the front page of the national newspapers for what seemed like an eternity, and the retractions when they came were buried on the way back on the ninth pages, of course."

"A terrible time."

"You know when Reid was killed, and Alicia descended into drug-induced madness, there seemed to be no option except to take over the care and raising of Eric."

"And you've done an outstanding job. No one could have done better."

Abandonment issues are not logical. Eric has been scarred by the deaths of his parents and sisters. Emotionally he could believe that it was his responsibility in some way- that he was "not enough" for them to stay alive.

Teresa Bellamy had been in the midst of her own grieving when she assumed care of Eric. Since that time, she had found a special bond with mothers who had lost children. There would be a special connection with mothers who had suffered. And she could identify them; something in the eyes. They would touch each other and ask the inevitable questions. How did it happen? How did they die? Surprisingly, mothers who had been with their children when they died were often grateful for that experience. "I brought them into the world, and I was there when they passed," were words Teresa had heard more than once.

"And as for Miko, he is exhausting." The smile on Teresa's face belied her complaint and instead disclosed the fondness she had for her daughter's son.

"And where is the Prince?"

"Probably still sleeping. My guess is that Miko will wake around noon and that Eric is already up in the guest house studying for his LSAT."

There was a polite knock as the study doors opened, and Chester entered.

"Mrs. Bellamy. Mr. Mason – it is good to see you. I trust your arrival is not because of some difficulty?"

He bowed slightly from the waist and turned slightly as he greeted the lawyer.

"Ah, Chester," the lawyer said. "So good to see you again." During the Harbridge investigations, Chester had been an invaluable support, keeping the grandsons preoccupied and distracted so that their anxiety and frustration didn't cause further damage. "I wish I could assure you that the matter is pleasant, but there is a possibility that there may be some uncomfortable moments awaiting us in the next few days."

"Please let me know if I may be of any assistance," said Chester. Turning to Mrs. Bellamy, he said, "I was looking for Miko. I thought he might be in here with you."

"You might check his suite. It's a little early for him yet."

"It's time for his workout; if you will excuse me, I'll go fetch him now."

"What a polite young man," exclaimed Jonathan. "I really came to rely on him during the Harbridge debacle."

"Very much like his mother," explained Teresa. "As you know, his mother was a beloved and invaluable member of our household staff for many years. She was devoted to us all. She knew what needed to be done and would have it looked after before I even thought about it. But she had to leave just as Chester was approaching adolescence; her own mother became very ill, and she had to go and look after her. I still miss her to this day."

Chapter 43

Back at the office, Sheriff Cahill leaned back in his swivel chair and propped his feet up on the cherry wood desk. "It seems our hands are tied. We don't even have a determination by the coroner that either of these deaths was murder. "

"What's your opinion of the coroner?" Angelique asked.

"What makes you ask?" queried Tom.

"I know how understaffed we were in Boston. It got so that I was doing the detectives' jobs so that we could gather enough evidence to suggest murder. And then I would have to prod the Medical Examiner as well. It got to be too much after a while."

"Sounds frustrating."

"It was. Especially when murders don't look like murders. I was looking forward to a break during my time here at Chautauqua."

"Well, I repeat, we still don't know if we are dealing with murder."

"I realize that taken by themselves, none of the incidents have evidence of foul play. Not one but two deaths of young, healthy people. Hard to believe it's a coincidence. How would it be if I went ahead and talked with persons of interest, especially people who were at the Herd Mentality party and on the Chautauqua Belle that evening? Unofficially, of course. I believe people really want to help and are looking for a conduit through which to talk about what's going on. They might have seen something and not realize the significance of what they saw or heard."

"Alright. But only if they'll agree to it. Officially we are stymied unless the coroner comes through with a determination of homicide. Until then, we have run into a brick wall and not just with the Bellamies."

"There's something else I'd like to talk to you about. I'd like to talk to the members of the Goddess Circle gathered here and access their Goddess Powers to aid in this investigation."

"Goddess powers." The sheriff was leaning forward now, hands-on-hips, contempt spread across his face

"I know it sounds New Agey, Tom. But there is science behind this. For example, let's say we were investigating a murder. We'd collect the tapes from any security cameras that were around. We'd also secure any photos or videos of what happened when the fire department arrived from the media and any other photographers that were around. You never know. These pictures might reveal someone who stands out from among the curious onlookers —it's typical for the murderer to return to the scene of the crime in order to participate in the investigation. Now, when we bring in a group of people to look at these pictures, probably a seasoned veteran would be better able to identify a guilty person than a raw recruit. They've just had so much more experience. What we mean by experience is that they have been involved in similar situations and similar scenes over and over again, many times. The veteran has seen hundreds of crime scenes; has viewed the reaction of criminals hundreds of times, and so is able to pick out the person who would most likely be the perpetrator from among the crowd of spectators."

"Agreed."

"What is happening, actually, is that the veterans are unconsciously connecting thousands of dots —like TV pixels —from that emerges an internal composite that is then matched against the faces and figures of the assembled bystanders. This is done in a nanosecond, without the veteran even being aware of it."

"Unconsciously."

"Exactly. The mind is like an iceberg. What we believe we know —what is actually in the conscious mind —is only the tip of the iceberg. The conscious mind contains seven plus or minus two bits of information —five to nine chunks. Massive amounts of data, some argue that most of what we have seen, heard and sensed throughout our lifetime, is stored in the unconscious; that part of the iceberg that remains under the water."

"So, what does that have to do with 'Goddess Powers'?"

"This group of women is that they have trained themselves to have an awareness of the many pieces of information that are available at any one given moment. The women of this circle have practiced being totally present to these auditory, visual, tactile, olfactory, and gustatory stimuli. Like a high definition camera, they register an extremely detailed 'snapshot' that they can then access for our investigation."

"But if this is done unconsciously, how then are we able to get into this information?"

"The women of the Goddess Circle use various methods to enter an altered state of consciousness and review the information at any time, and then they can provide it to us."

"Like the Oracle at Delphi?"

"Do you really want to know?"

"Actually, yes. If— and I'm only saying if—I decide to get involved with you and this Goddess Circle, I might as well know what I'm getting myself into."

"Okay. You know Alex Lewis, of course, the grandniece of Tsar Nicholas, who was murdered in Russia in 1918."

The sheriff nodded.

"Alex is one of the members of the Goddess Circle. She uses the tarot cards to access the information that has been stored in the unconscious mind through her acute perception."

"Tarot cards." He uttered disgustedly, slapping his forehead with his hand.

"Sheriff, keep an open mind. Tarot cards depict ancient universal symbols interpreted in the same way by people wherever and whenever they have lived all over the globe

"Give me a break," he groaned.

"And the illustrious Alexandra Romonov Lewis is also an expert hypnotist. Alex's ancestors, Tsar Nicholas and his family, had a history of hemophilia when members of her family suffered cuts and wounds where the blood would just gush from their bodies, and there was no known way to stem the blood flow. Many of the Tsar's family died because of this."

"Yes, I've read about that."

"Well, Tsar Nicholas' son and heir to the Russian throne was born a hemophiliac. His wife, the mother of his son's, despaired of keeping him alive. She heard of a monk, Rasputin, who was probably a hypnotist. When the son suffered an injury, Rasputin would put him into a hypnotic state and suggest that the blood vessels contract and stem the flow of blood so that his life would be spared. You can imagine how grateful the mother was."

"Indeed, I can."

"Not surprisingly, Rasputin was embraced within the royal family where he performed hypnosis on many members of the family and trained some of them on hypnosis and self-hypnosis. Alex's grandmother, the Grand Duchess Olga, became skilled in hypnosis, and she trained Alex. And the other women's Goddess Powers?"

"Dr. Yan Lin, an Asian physician from the West Coast, utilizes the I Ching —an ancient book of divination that employs the throwing of three coins —and the pendulum. Dr. Ursula Andrews, noted psychologist and author, will enter a Shamanic Journey to access the state of an alternate reality."

"Tell me, does Dr. Andrews throw mind-altering herbs on the fire to enhance this process?"

Angelique did her best to ignore his sarcasm.

"Catharine accesses information through astronomy and astrology. When you questioned her, you may have noticed the telescope that she keeps with her wherever she goes. At Jonah's home, there was a very powerful one that Jonah kept just for Catharine's purposes."

From the time Catharine was young, she was captivated by the night sky in Krakow. She found the stars and their constellations fascinating from a sheer historical perspective. Her young mind was entranced by stories of billions of universes. Later in life, after her initiation into the trance deepening practices of the Goddess Circle, planetary alignments became objects of concentration for her.

"I do remember the telescope. It seemed out of character for Jonah."

"And, as you know, I use micro expression and certain Voodoo practices from New Orleans.

"I know about the micro-expression, but Voodoo?" scoffed the Sheriff. "Any other 'members' of the 'Goddess Circle?"

"Not as of right now. There may be someone else in the wings. It is too soon to tell."

"As you explain it, it makes logical sense. I have worked with a number of forensic hypnotists who hypnotize witnesses in order to get at the information they possess but aren't aware of. I know that we aren't talking about a magical mystery but about the science of accessing information already collected. But I am not sure that the general public is ready to consider this type of evidence."

"We would only use this unconsciously accessed virtual information to guide the actual investigation. We'd have to collect concrete evidence admissible in the courtroom. We are dealing with at least two deaths. If you include the death of 'Princess,' the Winslow dog, it may suggest a serial killer whose blood rage is escalating. We can't afford to ignore this possibility."

"I can't make up my mind until I hear from the ME. But I don't want to be caught unprepared if that is indeed the case."

"If it's okay with you, I'll talk to the members of the 'Goddess Circle. We've got nothing to lose."

"Only the remaining shreds of my reputation."

Chapter 44

"Is anyone home?" came a voice from the front of the house.

Georgina awakened groggily; she'd slept for what felt like days. "Rafael."

They had talked about getting together to do more work on the symbolism from Georgina's cloud formation readings. Georgina checked the mirror quickly, splashed cold water on her face, and tucked a wisp of hair behind her ear. Willing her body to move through the living room, Georgina forced a smile, opened the front door, and stepped out onto the porch, finding Rafael peering at her from a chintz-covered wicker rocker.

"Are you alright?"

Georgina considered her response before she spoke.

"I'm not sure. All the tragedy in the past couple of days has taken the starch right out of me. Brynn was a dear friend of my daughter's, they danced together since childhood, and we've known her for many years.

"You must be just devastated."

"I don't think I can do any work today. I'm sorry."

"Perfectly understandable. But I insist that a walk to the plaza will do you good. Nothing like a big dish of ice cream to lift your spirits. You do know that stressed spelled backward is desserts, right? And let's forgo any lectures about the plaque that the cream will layer on our arteries."

Rafi crooked his arm and held it out for Georgina to hold as he guided her down the steps.

"I appreciate what you're doing, but I'm not very good company right now."

"I won't take no for an answer. You don't have to talk; let me do the talking, and you can just come along for the walk. It'll make the gloom more endurable."

Not having the strength to resist, Georgina allowed herself to be led along the road, past the Athenaeum—Chautauqua's Victorian hotel —and up the hill leading to the plaza. As they moseyed past the impeccably maintained houses, Rafael entertained her with commentary on the various artists and writers who would be presenting at the Institution in the upcoming days. The only allusion he made to the catastrophes was a comment about a spate of recent fires that had been set in "gas guzzlers" in nearby Erie —presumably by the same eco-terrorists who were alleged to have been implicated in the Institution fires.

"Speaking of which, there's another target for the eco-terrorists."

Rafi pointed at a gleaming white Escalade dominating the visitor's center at the entrance gate.

Chapter 45

It had been late morning by the time Owen drove through the entrance gates of the Chautauqua Institution. Billowing clouds provided texture to the radiant vista. He normally enjoyed the drive to Chautauqua, the verdant energy of a newly arrived summer. Chautauqua Lake was one of the finger-shaped lakes created over twelve thousand years ago as giant glaciers scratched deep furrows in the landscape, abandoning the mile-high mountain of ice to melt. Owen had spent wonderful hours casting his winter-prepared lures to tempt the wily muskellunge that teemed in the pure waters of the winter runoff.

On this trip, however, Owen found himself preoccupied with worries about his daughter. Elise's struggles were his fault; he knew it. If not for his absence from and betrayal of the family, she would have been happy and healthy. Yet, he'd been raised to believe that a man's rightful path was to provide financially for his family. Now, however, these received beliefs have been challenged. He had learned a lot from watching the younger men whom he had mentored in business. The first few times he had interviewed the new graduates from the much-ballyhooed business schools— Wharton, University of Toronto—the men as well as the women were as interested in the family values of his company as they were in work itself. Most of his own time and energy had been devoted to his business. And yes, there were dalliances as well. This last one, with the Director of Marketing of his corporation, had gotten out of hand and become conspicuous. Something Owen regretted, both due to the fact that it had hurt his wife but also that he had lost the respect of his peers and subordinates. Further, when he had tried to break it off, Kim became shrill and demanding; she'd threatened to destroy Owen's company. The threat to his business brought Owen to his senses. Owen had offered her a significant bonus and had found her a position with one of his friends. Still, Georgina had been deeply hurt, and he hoped he could make it right. But that was for later on. Right now, he was frightened for his daughter and for the danger lurking at Chautauqua that had culminated in the suspicious death of her friend. Pulling into one of two parking spaces allocated to his friend's Chautauqua house, he walked up onto the porch and opened the front door, commenting grimly to himself: "Still not locking up houses in Chautauqua, that's about to change." There was a sobering sense of the loss of simpler times, soon to become much more complicated with the violent intrusion of death.

Things had not been simple in his life. Owen grew up in a brutally chaotic family. By the age of eleven, he was disarming his alcoholic father, who, in a drunken rage, threatened to shoot Owen's mother and two younger sisters. One Christmas Eve, he had been deputized to go down to the local bar and bring his father home. His father had come stumbling home, but the screaming confrontation that followed ended with his mother and three younger sisters cowering in the basement as Owen wheedled the loaded shotgun from his father's flailing grip. The numbness developed to enable him to function in his dysfunctional family served him well when, at eighteen, he left home the only way he knew how: he joined the military. When psychologists assessed his steely nerves, high intelligence, and lightning-fast physical reflexes, they sent him to train as a sniper. In this capacity, he became their most effective killer. Every day, at dawn and as night settled in, he would go out with his spotter, and by the time they returned to base camp, his spotter would post his 'kill' score; inevitably, the highest of all the scores posted. Upon discharge, he returned to Toronto, completed his college education, and quickly latched on to the burgeoning 'healthy living' movement, building a highly profitable water-bottling company. Now that many of his goals had been met, he found himself without the riveting distractions necessary to keep powerful tectonic plates under control. Vivid flashbacks began to wash up in an unstoppable tsunami: bloodied images of human heads shattered like exploding pumpkins and nightmares of women and children lying in the grotesque arabesque of death. The only activities that were effective palliatives for the symptoms of his post-traumatic stress disorder were illicit affairs, a not-unknown pastime of the predators of today. This pursuit might keep the nightmares at bay; however, it was threatening to destroy his family, the most important thing to Owen.

From her vantage point on the refectory porch Georgina caught sight of Owen walking along the brick walk on the other side of Bestor Plaza, a caramel cashmere sweater draped casually across his broad shoulders. Jeans brandishing a knife-sharp press topped his butter-soft Berluti loafers. He was a handsome, confident man with the look of a leader about him. She knew too well how the length of the muscles of his tall, lanky frame camouflaged the sinewy strength underlying his smooth tanned skin. Short graying waves framed the sharp planes of Owen's high cheekbones. She watched as he frequently stopped to chat with various Chautauquans lounging on the park benches. He would be sampling the local emotional barometer concerning the recent deaths, Georgina knew. Her husband did little that wasn't calculated.

People continue to be drawn to him, just as I was. When Georgina was with Owen, people often asked, "Is he somebody?"

"No. He's nobody," Georgina had replied at first. Later, however, she began having fun when this happened and, much to Owen's dismay, fabricated stories in response: "He's a senator...a judge...a famous actor, but he prefers to have his privacy respected," she would caution, holding a single finger up to pursed lips. Once, right here at Chautauqua, she and Owen had been strolling along the lakeshore when a gentleman, out walking with his family, spotted Owen and started jumping up and down in excitement. "I saw you at Bayreuth. I saw you three times in Bayreuth," the elderly man cheered, hands gesturing wildly. Owen soon settled him down and returned him to his embarrassed family.

"What was he talking about?" he'd asked, and Georgina explained with a smile, "He mistook you for a famous conductor from the Wagnerian festival in Bayreuth, Germany." At this memory, a smile played unbidden across her lips, and she was snapped out of her reverie by Rafi's touch on her arm.

"A penny for your thoughts?" Rafael asked. Georgina was startled from her reverie.

"Oh, it's nothing. Let's go back to my house and get some work done on my infamous cloud symbols."

Georgina led the way around the back of the refectory and down the hill from the plaza to her lake house, hoping to avoid being spotted by Owen. Once back at the house, Rafael rushed straight away to spread his research texts and papers out on top of the desk. He turned and rubbed his hands together excitedly, eager to get to work on the symbols that Georgina had divined in the clouds. "So you say that you and

Yan took pictures of the pictographs that you carved in the sand soon after your sighting of them in the clouds. Let's have a look at those for a start."

Nonplussed by Owen's appearance, Georgina didn't feel up to the task of concentrating at that moment. "That's right. But just now, I developed a splitting headache. I hope you will forgive me. I'll have to take some aspirin and lie down for a bit. Perhaps we can get back to this later."

"Of course,' Rafi reassured. He was concerned that he had overwhelmed her with his enthusiasm. "Take care of yourself, and I'll check with you later to see how you are doing."

"I'll be just fine…I hope," she whispered as Rafael let himself out of the house, closing the door softly behind him. She knew that Rafael was attracted to her; she remembered the tension between them. But Georgina felt that her issues with trust would hamper any development of a relationship. She wondered whether she was frozen because she hadn't gotten over the twenty-five years of codependence with her husband or whether she was paralyzed by the terror of having to risk feeling again. A sharp rap on the door interrupted her musings. Thinking Rafi had forgotten something, she slowly swung the door open to reveal her husband's suave, smiling face.

"Your visitor didn't stay very long," drawled Owen.

She opened her mouth and shut it, flinching under the steady gaze of her husband's crystalline blue eyes. "What are you doing here?" She pushed past him and out onto the porch. "I thought we had an agreement not to pop in on one another during our separation."

"You couldn't expect me to stay away with all this chaos going on, could you?" Owen's handsome face was knotted up with tension. Georgina could tell that he was already in a foul mood.

"No good crisis should be wasted. Isn't that what you always say?" She tried to maintain a neutral tone.

"Could you make this not about you and me, just this once? My main concern is Elise." His voice had gotten louder. His nostrils flared.

"Now you're concerned about the effect of things on Elise?"

"What's that supposed to mean?"

Georgina chewed her lip; she knew that nothing infuriated him more than sarcasm.

"It means that it wasn't just me that you betrayed. Elise suffered because you were never there for her or for me." She made her point, but she didn't know what good it would do. Anything she could say at this point would be useless.

"Here we go again. It doesn't do any good to point fingers now. We were both at fault. Elise was always so tender and vulnerable. We both let her down."

"How can you say that?" Despite her best intentions, she was starting to cry. "I devoted my entire life to her. I did my best to keep our family together even with all your infidelities. You have no idea what a betrayal it is to learn that your husband is unfaithful. Nights when you were late, I would imagine that you were with other women. When our friends asked about you, I wouldn't know whether they'd slept with you or not. I suspected everyone."

Irritation consumed him now. "Is it any surprise that I turned to other women? At least they showed me some affection."

Georgina was thrown off balance by the cruelty of his words. "I did my best. It became harder and harder when Elise hit her teens; there was no way I could manage her alone. We needed you, and you weren't there." She turned away to hide the tears streaming down her face.

"Georgy," he groaned. "We've been over this a thousand times. I was working hard to give you everything you wanted."

"What we wanted was you, and you were off chasing other women when your daughter was into drugs and threatening to kill herself. Those were drugs her doctors had prescribed; they're the professionals."

"Oh sure, doctors prescribed painkillers and stimulants —just what Elise needed. You never came to the doctor's appointments with me, although I begged you. You'd breeze in from a "business" meeting to minimize and dismiss my feelings."

Owen lashed back. "You overreacted and smothered her. She had to rebel just to breathe; you had the plastic bag tied so tightly around her." He had been building to this moment over many difficult years.

Her hand went to her heart, and she hugged herself more tightly.

"Sure, I became hypervigilant about her moods," she countered. "If she became more talkative, I became frantic; if she talked less, I became frantic. If she slept all the time, I became frantic. If she didn't sleep, I became frantic. I was making decisions for her safety all by myself, wondering if I was doing the right thing. Making the decision to take her to rehab in Tennessee was one of the hardest things I have ever done. And do you remember what she said when she confronted you at the family week in her rehab? She told you that you hadn't earned the right to act as her father. That whenever you attempted to control her, it would only trigger her "little rebel," and she became more self-destructive, even suicidal at times. Really, that's the only way she could finally get your attention."

Owen just stared at her, face white with fury. He didn't need another lecture on how much he'd failed his family.

"Did you think those ballet lessons, only the best, were cheap? That addiction rehabilitation Elise underwent cost a fortune, and I was glad I was able to afford it."

Georgina took a deep breath as a current of pain ran through her and settled in her heart. "We never had a chance. We were never on the same page about what to do for our daughter. And I was willing to go along with the marriage to keep the family intact. Willing to try to tolerate your multiple indiscretions. But when Kim called me and told me she was pregnant, that 'is when everything changed."

"I'm sorry you found out that way." He had enough insight to realize how devastating that must have been for his wife.

"Are you? Do you know that I am unable to continue this mock marriage when you got another woman pregnant? One of your 'work wives' —only the latest in a long line of office girlfriends. I'm only surprised that she was the first one to figure out that getting pregnant was the way to hook you."

His face softened, and he ran his hand through his hair. "Georgy, I am truly sorry. I should have been the one to tell you" He wanted to put his arms around her and console her as he had done so many times before, but he knew that this time he couldn't alleviate her suffering.

He cleared his throat. "Does Elise know?"

"I didn't tell her. That is something that, finally, you will have to discuss with her yourself. And I recommend that you do it soon so that she doesn't receive a phone call as I did. Now please leave."

Georgina mustered what was left of her pride, padded back into the house, and closed the door. Owen's head and shoulders drooped as he left the porch and stepped into the bright sunshine of a glorious Chautauqua day.

Chapter 46

The walkers chattered excitedly as they moved along in an unending wave toward Linnea Hall, a modern half-circular structure with impeccable acoustics recently constructed on the western section of the Institution. Because her protégé, Catharine Sobieski, was the principal soloist in this afternoon's concert, Alex didn't want to miss the show, despite the message from Angelique calling for an emergency meeting of the Goddess Circle. Just ahead of her on the walkway, Alex caught sight of Yan anxiously looking around for her.

"How are you bearing up?" Alex studied her dear friend's face.

"About as well as can be expected. These are hard times. Such negative energy is poisoning our atmosphere."

"I, too, sense a powerful energy working against us, "Alex nodded in affirmation. "I'm having a devil of a time —forgive the pun— getting an unambiguous message from my Tarot cards. Usually, there's more clarity than this. Something evil is blocking my intuitive vibrations."

"By the way, did Angelique reach you? She's trying to get us all together for some 'emergency.'"

"I did get a message from her. We'll get to her right after the concert."

Volunteers handed them copies of the afternoon's program notes extolling the wonders of this afternoon's performance, Beethoven's 6th symphony, conducted by Marek Raczkowski. The music hall buzzed with energy and enthusiasm; warm applause greeted the principals gathered from every corner of the world. Catharine rose to play the violin solo; ethereal in her thin black sheath, her only ornament was a single fuchsia gardenia holding back the fair silken tresses threatening to cascade over the "Strad" she held lovingly to her milky white throat. The symbiotic relationship between performer and conductor was apparent immediately: Catharine responding, pliable as a willow, to Marek's direction. And yet even as she bent to the will of the conductor, Cat's musical genius effortlessly transcended the enormous technical demands of the taxing material, textures clear as the mercurial fast-slow-fast movements unfolded. The evocative tonalities of the work were magnified under her insinuating ministrations, and the incandescent soarings of the symphony were sumptuously celebrated. With the audience rising ecstatically to celebrate the marvelous solo, Mar tenderly took the hand of his star performer and kissed the top and then the palm, holding it for a fraction of a beat too long before bringing her forward to present her to her audience.

"I should have known," groaned Alex. "I was worried she'd be too upset to perform today, but her romance addiction appears to have papered over that wound. She's immediately back with Marek. So soon. We'll have to postpone Angelique's meeting. We have to talk to Catharine right away."

"Do you think we should risk delaying getting together with Angelique?"

"It's unfortunate, but it can't be helped. Catharine is having a love addiction relapse. We probably should have expected she'd try to assuage the pain of Jonah's loss with another relationship."

The two of them joined the throngs exiting the concert hall and streaming over to the post-performance reception to be held at the Lewis-Wilkes Hall.

"You're probably right," agreed Yan. "I was thinking about when she fell for the second-chair violinist in Vancouver? What a disaster —almost as bad as her seduction of that conductor visiting from Tokyo with his family. She manages to ruin every opportunity she gets with romance. It's stimulating at the moment —that dopamine high is fun for six months or so. Then you have to move on to the next relationship to get another infatuation rush, like a monkey grabbing at a shiny new object. Over the long haul, it's a losing game."

The usher flashed a smile, remarking, "Lovely concert," and closed the carved wooden doors securely behind them.

"She has a brilliant future except for this romance addiction. I can't believe she became involved with Marek so soon. You need to feel it to heal it. Escaping into this addiction rather than grieving Jonah's death will allow the unprocessed negative energy of the trauma to shape her behavior outside of her conscious control," noted Alex. "And, he's married. Not available. After Marek resigned from the symphony when the new conductor found out she'd had an affair with his predecessor, Catharine was fired... 'Bad for morale.' When we talked about the dangers of her infatuations and how they were interfering with her career and personal development, she seemed to agree, but it looks as if things are right back where they were."

The two women walked vigorously past the Children's School, then turned right along the side street lined with multi-generational residences until the large houses gave way to the open space of Bestor Plaza.

"I threatened to withdraw my support as her patron over the Toronto incident, and I may have to do that again," continued Alex. "That situation was very embarrassing for me. I considered interfering, but Parker didn't think it prudent given the circumstances. Losing that position must have given her an excuse to follow Marek wherever in the world he is conducting. She's probably planning to follow him to Santa Fe for opera season in August. You know she's staying at my house now."

"Oh, dear. I was going to talk to you about having Catharine meet with Georgina and explain sex and love addiction to her. This may not be the best time for that to happen. Especially as it appears, she has not yet overcome this addiction for herself."

Yan recalled that Cat's response to their earlier intervention had been suffused with existential terror. She alternately raged and cajoled, petrified that getting rid of her love addiction would destroy the internal representation of romance on which she felt her very life depended: her fantasy relationship with Marek, an internal entwining through which her fragile self-esteem was buttressed like a fragile tendril upon a trellis.

The women remained adamant. This pseudo-relationship drained the resources she required to pursue a real-life relationship. The first step, they insisted, was to become aware that romance addiction was a problem. Take a look at the harmful consequences: how it interfered with her personal life, her career, and even her health. Also, look at the 'Payoff': what benefits romance holds for you. Examine the pros and cons. If it's more trouble than it's worth, then create an action plan for overcoming that habit. If not, you can take your misery back at any time.

At the after-performance reception, Cat twirled her champagne flute and watched the energy rise in the group of admirers surrounding Marek. He was a frequent guest conductor at Chautauqua and at the multiple venues from which Chautauqua summer residents arrived for the season —Austin, Palm Beach, San Francisco— and beloved by subscribers to these orchestras. She was also thinking of the "intervention" engineered during their Toronto residency. Yan Lin had flown in from San Francisco to explain the psychological and physiological underpinnings of the relationship disorder. According to Yan's explanation, love addiction was based on a child's experience of being either suffocated by the primary caregiver —required to abandon her own independent strivings— or, at the opposite end of the spectrum, injured in that relationship, abused, or neglect. The child came to believe that intimacy is incredibly painful. Despite this, there is the belief that unless our desirability is reflected by the mirror of the admiring reactions of others, we will be alone and vulnerable in a dangerous and indifferent universe. Outcome: ambivalence.

"Be careful," Yan had admonished. "Poets have written of the power of love since the dawn of time. These days romance is brainwashed via a virtual industry of mythologizing: romance novels, television, movies; you name it; all extolling the magic of love. Heaven helps us all."

Much of what they had to say had been on the mark, reflected Catharine. She wandered over to the corner of the room to sit unobserved and watch Marek, dynamic and charismatic, expounding on his music theories —gray hair flowing away from his high forehead and touching the top of his snow-white collar. Cat had been trailing along behind him for the past two years, ever since their departure from the Toronto symphony. They had performed in Manhattan and London in the spring, and she hoped they would be going to Santa Fe for the opera season later in the summer. Since the Goddess' intervention, however, her doubts about the wisdom of continuing to follow him had grown. He was married and not about to leave his wife. In order to be at his beck and call, her own career and personal aspirations had had to be tabled —more like encased in a Sarcophagus. She was also aware that this was a pattern of hers. Before Marek, she had been involved with other unavailable men: one was a violinist who had the reputation of seducing female members of the orchestras where he played. That affair ended in heartbreak when he began preparing for an audition for a first chair position at the London Philharmonic. When Catharine had pleaded for him to forgo practicing in order to spend more time with her, he had dropped her in a New York minute, rejecting her as 'too needy.'

There were others, but the one that nearly ended her career was her affair with Marek. She had been the Associate Concertmaster for the Toronto Symphony under him. However, when he left and a new conductor was installed, the new conductor hastened to get rid of his predecessor's detritus. To do this without inciting Cat's supporters, he created a position, 'First Associate Concertmaster,' who was ranked between Cat and the main concertmaster—in effect demoting her. Cat was forced to resign in protest.

Cat realized that her life as a violinist, while deeply satisfying, was also interfering with her ultimate goals. At thirty-one years of age, she found herself wondering whether she would ever realize her dream of becoming a wife and mother. That aspiration had died with Jonah. Previously, her personal life had had to take a back seat to her talent, and though her outstanding performance brought with it the worship of anonymous audiences, when the applause died down, she collapsed into abandonment depression —a chasm of nonexistence. The only panacea was to pursue further applause or begin a new romance: a never-ending cycle of disaster.

"I see Marek is basking in the glow of his worshipful fans," observed Alex after they had wound their way through the excited throngs offering their congratulations on a magnificent performance.

"As always," said Cat ruefully. "Don't think that I haven't considered what the two of you had to say back in the springtime. Actually, I have been giving it a lot of thought lately."

"We only want the best for you."

"So far, I haven't been at the stage of motivation where I am prepared to act on your advice.'

"How can we help?"

"Just listening to me, I suppose. I've been seduced by the stimulation of infatuation —it hits the dopamine brain receptors just like cocaine— but I'm no longer in total denial of the negative aspects of this pattern of relationship addiction. That places me in the second stage of behavior change, contemplation. Right?"

Their hostess was a round, apple-cheeked woman with bobbed strawberry blond hair who encouraged them to sample the buffet Catered by her special chef, Michael, whom she had brought with her from her hometown of Pittsburgh. "Michael's one of the iron chefs, you know," she told them. The three of them obeyed, eager to escape the flutterings of the hostess and resume their conversation.

"Sure, it's exciting to find a new love, but I am pretty sure love addiction has more negatives than positives for me at this time of my life," stated Catharine. She sipped from a glass of Perrier scooped off the tray of a passing waiter.

"But so far, that hasn't worked for me. I'm at the point where I have achieved what I wanted to achieve as an artist, and now I want to have the experience of being a wife and mother —or at least that of being a mother if the marriage thing doesn't work out."

The three of them continued to move smoothly through the buffet line. Their progress frequently halted as numerous patrons stopped to congratulate Catharine on her superb performance.

"Change is hard but inevitable," said Yan. "Old habits run deep. From a physical point of view, habits are hardwired into us —they come in handy so that we don't have to relearn how to walk every day; the ability to walk has been 'learned' or deeply etched into our cellular system. On the other hand, when you want to change a habit that has been around for a while, you are going up against a well-entrenched system."

"It sounds impossible," said Catharine, nibbling a strawberry from the cranberry cut-glass bowl on the sideboard.

"Difficult; not impossible. Deeply drawn neurochemical pathways undergird habitual behaviors. Like the Grand Canyon."

Yan picked up the butter knife and began to run the tip of the knife lightly across the smooth surface of a gelatin mold, and then traced over and over the original Line so that the knife began to push deeper and deeper, eventually slashing a large gash down to the platter below.

"The Colorado River made a scratch on the surface of the earth millennia ago, and over time, water running over rock carved the deep chasm that we know today as the Grand Canyon. That is the way our neurochemical system works. When we perform a behavior, brain cell A connects electrochemically with brain cell B, and then to Cell C and so on until a physiological 'Grand Canyon' is created between the neurons."

She gently laid the knife on the side of the buffet table.

"This is how a habit is carved into the neurons. In order to change that habit, you have to repeat a different behavior over and over many times until it forms a 'bypass' neural pathway for the new way of behaving. It can take a while."

"Cat," said Alex. "We'd like to talk to you about someone who might benefit from your experience and strength. I know you usually wait around until Marek is ready to pay attention to you, but this time why don't you leave with us."

Nodding her assent, Catharine put down her plate and glass and left the room with the two women without stopping to say goodbye to Marek. "Give him a chance to miss me."

On the way to Georgina's, Alex began to fill them in on what her husband had told her about Georgina's husband, Owen Winslow, the night of their party.

"In a world of players, he's a mega player," Parker had asserted as they lolled together in bed after lovemaking. "He's had multiple serial affairs. He's the first guy I would call a sex addict." The two of them loved to discuss their various guests after the end of the party. Parker had come to depend on Alex's penetrating judgment of people and frequently invited various prospective associates to their get-together just to get her to take on them. Alex knew that although Toronto was a cosmopolitan megalopolis of over five million, it was truly a small town in so far as the business-philanthropic community was concerned.

"Owen is opening up a new water bottling plant, and he was looking for some fresh money for capital expenditures recently. A new twist on 'hiking the Appalachian Trail,'" he scoffed. "Several guys, including myself, have refused to invest with him because consensus is that one of these days, he is going to be involved in a scandal, and there'll be a costly divorce. No one wants to get caught up in that mess."

"You really think that would happen? Georgina doesn't seem the type to make a fuss."

"Maybe she wouldn't, but some lawyer could get a hold of her and take Owen for all he's worth, along with anyone else who is foolish enough to do business with him."

"So that's why you're a devoted husband. Being a philanderer is bad for business."

"You keep me too exhausted to fool around," teased Parker as he nuzzled her neck.

"Is his business going to be okay?" She eluded his grasp, rose from the bed, and slipped on her diaphanous Lingerie —the partially concealed body was so much more alluring than the fully naked one.

"Owen is skating on thin ice, and it's starting to crack all around him." Parker slid out from his side of the bed as well and headed to the shower. Alex gazed lovingly at the back of his long, muscular body, still trim and fit. After all their years together, she still found him utterly desirable.

"What are you saying?" probed Alex, eager to pick up as much information as she could before Parker entered the busy mental world of his business affairs. He would be soon unavailable to her, intensely immersed in whatever was to be 'gamed' next. She sighed deeply, fully satisfied with the profound intimacy they had just shared.

"Just rumors for now. I'll let you know if it comes to anything. By the way, I hear that Owen has brought in a young guy who seems to be pretty sharp. Maybe he's the succession plan: the hope for the future. I understand that the daughter is not at all interested —unlike our children, for that I am eternally grateful."

"And this is relevant to me, how?" queried Catharine, bringing Alex sharply back to the present.

"We'd like you to talk to Georgina about the ravages of Codependency and relationship addiction."

Chapter 47

Elise walked across the lush rolling lawns toward the Athenaeum. She was about to begin to ascend the sweeping staircase leading to the large porch when she caught sight of her father leaning over the balustrades. Her pace slowed as he caught sight of her and waved. She dreaded these audiences. They rarely went well. On the porch overlooking the lake, the tables had been set with spotless table Linens and heavy silverware. The maître d' guided them to a table and solicited their drink orders.

"Just water for both, with lemon," ordered Owen. "And we'll both have the trout almondine — freshly caught this morning, I assume."

"Absolutely, Mr. Winslow, an excellent choice," enthused the maitre d' as he sped away to place their order, herding servers in his wake. Owen opened the conversation by expressing his condolences regarding Brynn and gently inquiring into how his daughter was doing with her death.

"Of course, I am desolate. I'm trying to keep myself distracted by assisting the sheriff by writing down everything I can remember about the events surrounding Brynn's death."

"Elise, I forbid it. I don't want you to get involved in this in any way. Whoever gets mixed up in this investigation is going to be tied up in it for a very long time."

"You can't order me around as if I were still a child. I intend to work with the case to offer any information that I might have. You don't know what you know; that might be an important clue —that's what Yan said."

"That's it exactly." Owen shook his head impatiently. "If we are dealing with a serial killer, as I believe it is a possibility, and it becomes known that your information that would reveal his identity, you might become a target as well. And who is this Yan anyway?"

"She's a friend of mother's. Mother has become involved with a group of interesting women here at the Institution. I'm quite impressed."

"Oh, your mother and her friends."

Elise stared silently at her father as the waiters served the magnificently presented entree: golden almond walleye pulled from the lake this morning on a bed of couscous with mango-fennel salsa and pine nuts accompanied by local grilled asparagus.

At that moment, their meal was interrupted by the arrival of a young man: Hayden Guilford, the son of friends of the Winslows and a childhood idol of Elise's whom she had not seen since he left to go to Eton for high school. She knew he'd returned from the UK to attend university state-side and had been working in her father's business for a while now —apparently anointed as the heir apparent. After shaking Owen's hand, Hayden moved around the table to kiss Elise on the cheek and, stepping back, murmured admiringly, "I remember you as a meddlesome tweenager —a tag-along— you are hardly that now."

"I'm glad you're here, Hayden," said Owen. "I'm concerned about Elise and her mother with all this killing going on. I would appreciate it if you would keep an eye on them for me."

"If it's okay with you, Elise," offered Hayden.

"I'm quite experienced at taking care of myself," retorted Elise. "But if it will stop my father from hovering over me, I guess it's all right. I can't speak for my mother."

"I would consider it an honor then. And now I will leave you two to resume your conversation." Hayden stood. "Again, so good to see you."

He declined Owen's invitation to join them, explaining that he had just come from the golf course where he had been entertaining some important customers. He gestured toward a nearby group that waved in acknowledgment. Owen agreed to drop by their table and talk with the group following his lunch with Elise.

Elise gave her father a 'So what was that all about?' eyebrow arch, but Owen just composed his face into an innocent mask as the waiter cleared the table and brought them coffee.

"There's another matter I'd like to talk to you about," resumed Owen. "You are probably aware that your mother and I have not had the best marriage for a long time."

"That's an understatement."

"Your mother is a wonderful woman, but we are just two people who should never have gotten married. I am, however, eternally grateful we were together because we had you. I will never regret our marriage because of that."

Elise sat awaiting the 'but.'

"But, now it is time for your mother and me to go our separate ways and move on with our lives."

"It was my impression that you already did that a long time ago."

Owen glanced sharply at her. "A lovely lady has come into my life and made me very happy."

"I thought 'lovely ladies' were a constant part of your life," she groused.

Owen continued, "You may remember her from the time you interned at our office your junior spring semester, Kim Campbell; she was the Marketing Director."

"The blond with the décolleté? She made sure no one could forget her. Remember when I interned at your office? Didn't you know what that would do to me? Didn't it occur to you that I'd be exposed to your multiple affairs? My God, Sally, the receptionist showed me the bracelet you bought her; Priscilla would wink when she referred to 'working late.' Your extracurricular activities were the source of constant gossip at the office. How could you have rubbed all that in my face?" Elise's voice had risen.

"Keep your voice down," shushed Owen, looking over to the table where Hayden was entertaining their customers.

"If you've got it, you can spot it," muttered Elise.

"What did you say?"

"When I was in treatment, I had to do a genogram to see where I might have inherited an addictive personality. It didn't take much awareness to peg you as a workaholic and sex addict. That had to be where my risk for addiction originated."

"That is a matter that we can discuss at another time. What I wanted to tell you today is that Kim is pregnant with my child."

"WHAT!"

"The baby is due in a few months. You are going to have a baby brother."

"This can't be happening. You were never there for me. You were never interested in being a father to me. You didn't pay attention to my small triumphs, never attended any parent-teacher conferences, never took me on any camping trips for Indian Princesses as the other fathers did, never came to any of my ballet recitals."

"Please, Elise. You know I don't care for ballet. Your mother attended for the two of us."

"Maybe now that you're going to have the son you've always wanted, you won't even notice that your daughter has left your life."

After Elise ran, crying, from the balcony of the Athenaeum, the maître d' came over to see if everything was alright. Owen assured him that it was, gave him a massive tip, and arranged to send a bottle of wine over to Hayden's table. Then he sauntered over to meet the clients he was entertaining and talk business, something he understood, unlike his daughter.

Chapter 48

Eric caught up with Chester and Miko in the weight room. The rowing team at Harbridge worked out assiduously: two hours a day during the week and four hours on the weekends. This training needed to be kept up during the summer as the rowing season started immediately upon their return in the fall. Chester was on his knees, pressing down on Miko's feet as Miko did his crunches.

"Hey Miko, I heard the sheriff was at the estate wanting to question you about Brynn's death," said Eric.

"Oh yeah. Don't sweat it. Glammy scared them off," grunted Miko between crunches.

"I'm worried. I don't want to go through the level of scrutiny and notoriety that we had at Harbridge. That was extremely upsetting."

"I thought it was amusing. That district attorney certainly got his wrist slapped. Lost his license, I believe," observed Miko wryly. "That should be fair warning to the sheriff and his cohorts here."

"I don't see it as a laughing matter," said Eric. "It totally disrupted an entire season of study and rowing. The scandal smeared the Bellamy name. It seems to me that scandals are featured on the front page of the newspapers while retractions are buried in the back pages. Wherever I've gone since then, people somehow get around to mentioning it."

"Any publicity is good publicity," quipped Miko.

"Maybe you think so, but it doesn't endear me to the kinds of people I want to impress. And Glammy was mortified. All you care about are women and how you're going to seduce them. I may forgive you, but I will never get over what the hell we went through because of your messing with you and your adult dancers. And now this. One is understandable. Two is more than suspicious. Now we're involved in another case of a woman who is not only injured but dead."

"I can't help that," said Miko. "Sure, I found her attractive at first, and we may have fooled around a little, but that's all it was; nothing serious. Those dancers are nothing but a headache. All eating disorders and addictions. Drama queens!"

"As disrespectful as ever, I see. That poor girl is dead. I'd think you'd have some compassion for her," said Eric, walking to the cardio side of the gym. "I'm going to hit the elliptical and then do my strength training."

"I guess I'm a little surprised that you dumped her," commented Chester as he massaged Miko's back and shoulders. "You really seemed into her."

"Too many fish in the sea. Besides, I found out what a skank she truly was— STDs. I blew her off. Let her know in no uncertain terms that I wanted nothing more to do with her." Miko shuddered.

"I've seen how these women throw themselves at you. But what a goody-two-shoes. Eric's the good one, never getting into trouble, always on the dean's list. And you're the troublemaker. Must drive you nuts."

"On the other hand, the girls really seem to go for the bad boys." Miko sighed contentedly as he gave into the marvelous sensations of the massage.

Eric completed a strenuous sequence of cardio and strength training during the time Miko was getting a rub down. "Let's get going," he said, toweling himself off as he returned to their side of the gym. "We're supposed to meet up with Elise. Remember? She promised us a picnic dinner if we could help her with something."

"So it seems like you think at least one ballet dance is worth getting to know," noted Eric.

***

Before picking up the picnic from the maître d', Elise attempted to reach the sheriff but was unsuccessful. When the answering service announced his absence, she left a message letting him know that she was reviewing her memory of the events leading up to Brynn's death. She hung up and picked up the legal pad before her on the desk. She had always found it easier to write her journals in longhand, even though she had been plugged into the computer since childhood. At that moment, her cat, Mrs. Quigley, stirred from the sun spot she had occupied before moving on to the next sunspot when, upon observing Elise at work at her desk, she approached the desk and, measuring twice with an up and down nod of her head, leaped expertly and gently as a butterfly, to sit on the papers positioned in front of Elise and offer her back to be scratched.

"Oh, Mrs. Quigley," crooned Elise. "Thank goodness I still have you."

She nuzzled her face into the cat's fur, soothed by contact with this independent but momentarily available creature. Mrs. Quigley soon moved again to take up a position on the far side of the desk where the sun's rays were fast approaching. Sighing, Elise turned back to her task and began to chronicle her recollections of the brief time since she arrived at Chautauqua and met up with Brynn again. She and Brynn had been fast friends and furious competitors since the day they met many years ago at the auditions for the dance school of the National Ballet of Canada. Elise remembered that spare, cold, and uninviting ballet audition room as if it were yesterday. 'Spindly fillies, ' Ballet Master Gregory had called them.

Elise moved around the bedroom her mother had gently draped in pastel pinks and greens and picked up a delicately fashioned musical jewelry case displaying a twirling ballerina. As she wound up the music box to hear Tchaikovsky's Nutcracker Suite, her mind traveled back to the times when she and Brynn performed in the corps de ballet for the sumptuous Christmas Eve Scene of the National Ballet's rendition of this classical ballet. Elise's mother had given the music boxes to each of the girls following their performance. It seemed impossible that Brynn lay dead now. Such vital energy is gone. Such talent was wasted. The staff at the treatment center had helped her develop her own unique ritual, which she performed now prior to beginning a period of automatic writing through intensive journaling. She donned a beloved comfortable shirt of her favorite color, mauve; slid on her hand-made pendant earrings; chose an incense wand from among the selection in the desk drawer, and lit it, cupping the scented smoke with her hand and inhaling deeply. She then returned to sit at the hand-painted desk positioned for the best light under the paned window overlooking the garden. She began to journal about being with Brynn at the amphitheater ballet rehearsal. She remembered Meister Gregory's gruff rebuff. She wrote more about meeting the Bellamy boys — was there anything in those meetings that could be tied to Brynn's death. She went over the times when she introduced Brynn to her sponsor and took her to a meeting. Then there was the party at the Herd Mentality house and Jonah's death. As she revisited these scenes, she was aware of information attempting to bubble through the barrier into her conscious mind, but it hadn't been able to percolate to the surface yet.

At long last, Elise gave up trying to force any more information through —it obviously wasn't yet ready to be revealed. She felt that somehow the Bellamy boys were connected to Brynn's death, though she wasn't sure how. She was hoping that time spent with them at the picnic would jog a piece of unconscious memory. Before she left the house, she tried the sheriff one more time. The phone rang until the answering machine clicked on, broadcasting Elise's disembodied voice to the visitor waiting alone in the sheriff's office.

Heading down the steep hill leading from the plaza to lakeside, Owen caught sight of two young men tossing a Frisbee back and forth on the green space next to the lawn bowling courts in front of the Athenaeum. An early evening breeze off the lake offered welcome relief from the heat of the day. The duo glided effortlessly across the verdant surface, oblivious to the strength and beauty of their bodies in motion: leaping to retrieve the missile and then crouching in the classic stance of the ancient Greek discus thrower; quads coiled and released as arms carved a powerful arc and propelled the plastic discus through the awaiting air. Owen harkened back to the days when his body responded as did theirs; he still had a body memory of how that felt, strong muscles flowing powerfully under flexible skin. Though still extremely fit —Owen never missed his daily cardio and strengthening routine no matter how urgent the crisis —he was acutely aware that he was approaching his fiftieth birthday and about to become a new father. I'll be close to seventy by the time this baby graduates from high school, he groaned to himself.

As Owen stood partially shielded from sight by the thick hedges watching the two young men, he was surprised to note the arrival of his daughter Elise carrying a rather large picnic basket. The two abruptly ceased their game and hastened over to help her spread the picnic under gracious old trees that shaded the edges of the lawn. It appeared that the young men had been awaiting her arrival and, like puppies, had merely been releasing an overabundance of energy until that time.

A picnic fit for a princess, prepared by the Athenaeum, and no doubt billed to my account. Elise is not as independent as she thinks she is.

Intrigued, he slid along the edges of the green, as close to the picnic party as he dared, in order to eavesdrop on their conversation. Clearly, Elise had not mentioned this picnic dinner when they had met for their early dinner: what, he wondered, why the need for secrecy?

The young men eagerly consumed the luscious meal Elise had spread before them —Owen was vindicated in his suspicion that the picnic had been prepared at the Athenaeum. He overheard them offering their condolences regarding Brynn. They then reminisced about the brief but enjoyable time they had all spent together since meeting up at Chautauqua. After this avenue of discussion had been exhausted — she must have picked up a thing or two about timing and persuasion from me, he thought— Elise casually turned the topic to the sheriff's investigation. After discussing their theories for a while, she asked them if they would be willing to assist her in dredging up any and all information that could be of help in finding the killer.

"Killer! People keep talking as if there had been killings. We understood that both Jonah and Brynn were accidental deaths —tragic to be sure— but accidental nonetheless."

One of the young men was standing now, towering over Elise. Owen resisted the urge to rush in between them. Owen felt the hackles on the back of his neck settle down as Elise rose to stand beside the agitated young man and placed her hand on his arm.

"You're probably right," she said. "But just in case that turns out not to be true, I would like to review the information we do have before the memory fades and valuable details are lost. I am willing to be the scribe, and I would like to meet with each of you individually and go over everything that had to do with Brynn."

Owen left as surreptitiously as he had arrived. He called Hayden immediately and hastened over to his condo to enlist his help in heading off what he considered to be a dangerous route that his daughter seemed intent upon pursuing.

"How nice to see Elise again. What a lovely young woman she is! You neglected to tell me how beautiful she has become."

"She's beautiful like her mother, but unlike her mother, she is very willful, I'm afraid. She went against my advice. I specifically told her that I didn't want her involved in the investigation of these deaths. If there is foul play involved, I'm concerned for her safety."

"I just happened to be there," Owen went on. "Walking down for an evening jog along the lakeshore, and there were two young men throwing a Frisbee, waiting for Elise, who showed up with a picnic."

"So these young men whom she met with, what did they look like?"

"They were about my height, over six feet, and athletic. Their upper torsos and legs were well developed, and they seemed to run effortlessly for quite a while."

"Sounds like the Bellamy boys. They're here to spend the summer with their grandmother, Teresa Bellamy. She owns the big estate at the north end of the Institution."

"Sure, I know who she is."

"Well, she has commanded her grandsons to be here for the summer due to a scandal they were involved in at Harbridge."

"You don't mean the guys who were charged with rape and assault of that adult dancer?"

"The very ones."

"I know the charges were dismissed, something to do with overreaching on the part of the District Attorney."

"While that's true, however, often where there's smoke, there's fire."

"I couldn't agree more, and I don't want my daughter immolated in flames. I want you to dig into this and find out everything there is to know about the Bellamy boys and about the investigation. Call in our internal security and get everyone you can in on it."

"You can trust me with this, boss. I have a personal stake in keeping your daughter safe."

Chapter 49

Comfortably ensconced at Alex's home, Yan asked the Goddesses to help her piece together what they knew about Owen and Georgina. She seemed to be codependent: someone who exists only through her reflection in the eyes of others, in her case, her husband or daughter. If validated by them, she exists; if not, she's apt to slip into an abandonment depression, hollow and achingly empty. She wanted to help Georgina free herself from the emotional bonds of the relationship and move forward as her own woman—with or without her husband— and, perhaps, become a member of the Goddess Circle.

"When a codependent drowns, someone else's life flashes before their eyes," Catharine said drily.

"When I've met Owen, I have the feeling that he might be an 'everyday sociopath': the type that feels dead and bored without some intriguing game going on," said Alex. "Gets his "fix" through power; uses the business world as his playground. It seems that Owen was rarely at home, but when there, he was emotionally abusive and controlling. He sees Georgina as merely an extension of him —his trophy wife. He insisted she was perfectly put together at all times. It was easy to see what must have happened to Georgina —water on rock— her self-confidence eroding until she didn't think she could function without her husband."

"Sex addicts dehumanize and exploit people, just like sociopaths; Owen fits the profile. If it walks like a duck and talks like a duck, it's probably a duck," Catharine pronounced.

"That sounds somewhat pathological. It could be an Attention Deficit Disorder: a person who feels okay when totally absorbed in something, like business or sports, but feels restless, irritable, and discontent when they're not," mused Ursula. "They seek 'unitive' experiences, where you lose the sense of time and place."

"Or music," commented Catharine. "In music, we talk about being in the zone. Being really good in hot water; nothing focuses the mind like danger, and some people are always creating chaos in order to feel complete

"In therapy, we encourage people to be 'choiceful.' Build awareness up front if you're the kind of person who gets addicted to an activity and is uncomfortable without it; at least you can choose before you decide to put yourself in that position. When awareness is not developed, you can become kidnapped by your activities."

"Well, whatever the origin of Owen's behavior, it's been very destructive to Georgina," said Yan. "Do you think it's worth trying to drag this 'fifties' June Cleaver' kicking and screaming into the twenty-first century?" Catharine waved a dismissive hand.

"Georgina is worth saving. Underneath that detritus beats the heart of a woman of valor. I can sense it," said Yan firmly, folding her arms.

The Goddesses glanced at each other. Yan had not been this adamant in a long time. Alex shrugged and led the others through the door and out along Lake Drive.

***

After they had declined Georgina's offer of tea and ginger snaps, an awkward silence descended. Catharine cast about for a way to break the tension. She wanted to establish rapport with Georgina to ease the discussion of codependency and relationship addiction. It was important for Georgina to understand that they had come to alleviate her suffering, not to humiliate her. Her opportunity came when Ursula spied the magnificent collection of Matryoshka dolls —wooden dolls of decreasing size placed one inside the other— displayed in the breakfront that dominated the living room.

"These are magnificent," she extolled. "In all my travels, I have never seen such an extraordinary collection. These dolls must come from every part of the world."

"Wherever she traveled, my mother would bring back a set for me. Every time I look at them, I'm reminded of her," Georgina smiled wistfully.

There were a number of finely crafted stacking dolls in the collection: an elaborately painted set from Russia featured dolls in traditional peasant dress; a second depicted Japanese geisha holding a fan and wearing a dark red kimono; one set featured a girl in an Indonesian batik robe; another carved in a caricature of Margaret Thatcher, former Prime Minister of Britain; and even a set shaped like kittens. Georgina opened the glass doors of the display and brought out the Matryoshka painted as 'Klara,' the girl in the 'Nutcracker' ballet. She unstacked the set, placing each wooden doll of decreasing size side by side on the coffee table."

"If I'm not mistaken, the Matryoshka tradition began in Russian," stated Georgina, looking up at Alex.

"Matryoshka represents the Russian peasants who murdered my relatives, Tsar Nicholas and his wife Alexandra," Alex spoke haughtily; and, turning her back on display, went as far away as possible to the other side of the room; face set in granite; clearly separating herself physically and psychologically from the conversation. "My grandmother survived the revolution but never recovered from it. She said that we must never cry; if we were to start, we would never stop."

This is no time for a royal sulk, Catharine fumed inwardly. Mostly she enjoyed Alex; she was normally a thoughtful and highly entertaining companion. However, when provoked, as she was now by the reminder of her painful history, she could be quite the diva. Shooting Alex a warning glance, Catharine once again turned to Georgina. "Reminds me of codependence: layers and layers of masks piled one on top of the other," she segued smoothly.

"Codependence?" Georgina, seizing on the opportunity to change the subject and diffuse the tension, turned questioningly to Catharine.

Peace at any cost; a truly codependent stance, noted Catharine. She went on to explain further. "Codependents try to figure out what someone else wants them to be so they can construct that mask and win the attention and affection they crave."

"I'm confused. I was taught that caring about others is important, don't you agree?" Georgina said, cocking her head to one side.

"That's true. However, it can become a problem when it goes too far. For example, some people believe that if a certain individual isn't paying attention to them, it's because they are unlovable; rather than that the other person has other things on their plate —they take it personally."

"Codependence is a survival strategy," Yan explained. "Infants need to know their primary caretakers will sacrifice their own lives in order to save the child's —they intuit this instinctively; to be born with the knowledge that if they are not loved enough, they will perish. Babies may be given food and shelter, but they will themselves die if they don't get enough of the right kind of human contact: failure-to-thrive syndrome. Luckily, when a baby is born, a mother is born, and maternal instincts are awakened. The maternal lion will attack a much stronger predator and risk her own life in order to save her cubs."

At this point, Alex, bored with her self-imposed isolation, elected to reenter the conversation. "Of course, it's dangerous! For instance, becoming as actively self-destructive as you seem to have." Holding one of the doll sets aloft, she pronounced, "Sarcophagus. Beautifully painted coffins for the living dead."

Georgina hurried to Alex's side and firmly extricated the 'Klara' doll set from her grip. Alex flounced back to her seat, and Georgina stood alone in the center of the room, tight-lipped, her face pale. Yan came to stand beside Georgina in solidarity.

"And there must be some reason that you all have come here today," ventured Georgina, suddenly wary. "We've come to talk about addiction and those harmfully involved with an addict," said Ursula, wanting to return to the subject at hand.

"The addict needs a hostage, and codependents are natural partners," explained Catharine. "The addict's primary relationship is with the addiction. He is enslaved by it. He devotes all resources to maintaining his lines of supply. He is enslaved by the addiction, and so he takes a hostage: a partner who is prepared to distort reality and sacrifice her own sanity and suspend disbelief in order to accept the world according to the addict — a match made in hell. Like a 'failure to thrive' infant, the codependent will ascertain what her partner wants of her; abandon her authentic self; rigorously 'cut off' undesirable characteristics; and construct the 'ideal self' masks that present the characteristics of her partner, the addict, has indicated he wants.

"Your husband is a particularly loathsome type of addict —a sex addict," blurted Alex.

Georgina's face and neck stained scarlet; she had no idea her shameful secret had been outed.

"Because of the years you've spent with him, you have become codependent," Yan stated gently.

"In short, the codependent partner of an addict will adjust and readjust until she is maladjusted," stated Catharine.

"Like your Matryoshka dolls, as each layer is removed, the casing beneath it reveals yet another painted layer, and then another, until you reach the center and there is no there there," said Alex.

Georgina pressed the palms of her hands over her ears, attempting to wall out the painful information. Part of her knew what they said was true. Yan gathered her in her arms and began to stroke her hair, crooning: "It will be alright. It's going to be alright."

"Can I ever get over this? But how can I wipe out all that brainwashing? It's become a part of who I am now?" wailed Georgina. Her voice was hoarse, revealing the desolation of betrayal.

"Absolutely, you can. Your true nature, like a precious diamond, cannot be defaced. But we have to dig it out from years of detritus." Yan's voice was firm.

"But how?" Georgina drew in a shaky breath and made a robust effort to pull herself together.

"Paradoxically, the way to silence the past is to give it voice. Face it to erase it."

"Are you implying I'm supposed to think about those things on purpose?" Georgina felt a frisson of fear. "I couldn't possibly. I would rather die than talk about those painful memories."

"Shall we get comfortable first?" suggested Yan, steering them to the inviting conversation area at one side of the living room, where Georgina sank into the settee and cradled her head in her hands. The others sat tight-lipped. "Let's all take a deep breath," said Yan, glancing around at the grim-faced group. "Would you take some tea if I made some?" This time there was unanimous and effusive acceptance.

Yan left them, went through to the kitchen, and put on the electric kettle, pausing at the sink to allow her emotions to settle down and gazing around at Georgina's well-stocked kitchen. From the shelves, she selected a white and pomegranate tea whose label promised "peace and harmony" and carefully poured the boiling water over the leaves. She mindfully arranged ginger snaps on a floral porcelain dish and placed everything she needed on a tray. Several minutes had elapsed before she returned with her refreshments and gestured for Ursula to begin.

Ursula began to explain prolonged exposure —the evidence-based treatment for post-traumatic stress disorder —which involved revisiting scenes of trauma and sticking with them long enough to become desensitized.

"That sounds counterintuitive. I've been attempting to avoid any reminder of the painful memory," Georgina sipped her tea and inhaled the comforting aroma of pomegranate.

"It's pretty common to try and avoid present pain and seek immediate pleasure, but that doesn't work in the long run. We want to avoid avoiding. Addiction is fueled by the need to avoid suffering. You must feel it to heal it."

"But it's horrifying," said Georgina, putting down her cup.

"The fear that reprocessing these situations will destroy you is chimerical —like the mythological fire-breathing monster with a lion's head, a goat's body, and a serpent's tail. FEAR is: False Evidence Appearing Real."

"Avoiding those painful memories is all I have been attempting to do." Georgina shook her head ruefully.

Ursula finished chewing her ginger snap before she spoke again. "Think of what happens when you are cooking broccoli. If you stand in the middle of the kitchen while it is cooking, you initially become overwhelmed by the smell; however, after a while, you actually cannot prevent yourself from becoming so used to it that you aren't able to smell it at all."

"I remember that a major challenge that the astronauts faced during their space travel was not the travel itself, but the body odor of unwashed bodies together all that time. They couldn't get out of their space suits to get themselves bathed. However, it turned out that it didn't take long for them to get desensitized to the scent of one another; they couldn't smell it at all," said Ursula. She had visited the Space Center in Florida when she was there for the opening of one of her pieces of installation art and was amused by this interesting piece of trivia.

"I think about those humiliating encounters all the time; my problem is that I can't stop thinking about them. I can't get them out of my mind," she said defensively, her eyes drifting around. "These feelings are distressing but not dangerous. The experience is different when you are in control. If you and I were standing talking, and a flock of birds suddenly flew right in front of us; we'd be startled; our fight-flight adrenaline system would get triggered. That would be uncomfortable. Instead, imagine taking a cage full of pigeons out to the front lawn and releasing them. We'd be ready and in control, and our adrenaline reaction will be lessened. Gradually, we'd get so used to it that it wouldn't bother us at all. That's how exposure works."

"I'm worried that I'll get stuck ruminating about these scenes over and over again." Her voice had a flat tone.

"You just want to visit the memories, not move in to live with them. Then use Goddessence. Switch the TV channel to something else. The trick is to turn the mind to something else again and again. We can create a menu of things for you to think about that your brain enjoys. That will make it easier. Okay?" Georgina nodded, unable to deny her need for healing.

Yan lit a candle and suggested that Georgina sink back into the sofa, becoming more and more relaxed. In unison, the women began triangle breath: inhale counting to three; exhale counting to three; hold to three. The sound of Juliann's breathing gradually became deeper and more rhythmic. It soon became obvious, from the flickering of her eyelids, that she saw images in her mind; that memories were surfacing. Ursula silently picked up a pen and the pad of paper Yan had left for her on the end table and nodded that she was ready to transcribe.

"What's happening?" asked Yan softly.

"I'm arriving at Owen's Christmas company party. I'm alone. Owen is already there. As I enter the room, it seems everyone falls silent. People are gathered here and there in groups, talking and socializing, but when I walk in, everything stops. I see Owen in a corner talking to some people, and when he notices me, he leaves them to come over to greet me. As he is walking, I see an attractive young woman among those in the group he's just leaving. There is something about her that just strikes right at my heart. For the rest of the evening, I am hyper-aware of her every move, and I am noticing that people seem to be looking at her and then back at me. Somehow or other, I manage to get through the evening and am able to leave after a short while. I realize that my husband is involved in yet another affair. This time with his PR Director, Kim Campbell."

"What is happening now?" It was critical that she not lead the imaginal journey but allow Georgina to go in her own direction.

"It's a month later, early in the new year. Owen comes into the living room. He goes over to the bar, fixes himself a scotch, and tells me that we have to talk. I try to put off the conversation, reminding him that we're due for dinner at the neighbors. He insists. Now he's saying that he can't live without her."

"How are you feeling?"

"I am beginning to feel numb. My head feels dizzy. I can feel my heart pounding in my throat, and the back of my neck is beginning to stiffen."

"On a scale of 1 to 10, how distressed are you?"

"Ten."

"Go on."

"Owen is telling me how sorry he is. He's saying that he thought this affair would be like all the others. That it would run its course and die a natural death. But that's not what's happening."

"How are you feeling now on a scale of 1 to 10?"

"Eight."

"What happens now?"

"He just leaves the room." Georgina crumpled and started to sob.

"Come back into the present, and let's talk about what happened," guided Yan, "Drifting back through time and space; back to Chautauqua; back to this room' back to this chair. As I count from 1 to five, feel the energy come back through the soles of your feet; on the count of 2, bring the energy into the trunk of your body: heartbeat quickening; on the count of 3, energy runs down your arms, fingers flexing and stretching; on the count of 4 energy up the back of your neck, brain focused and attentive; on the count of 5 all the way up, eyes open; back to regular time and activity.

Georgina had stood up and was pacing back and forth, wringing her hands. Yan and the other women breathed with her in the calming triangle exercise they had practiced earlier.

"Not like the other ones," said Georgina bitterly after a moment. "I know about those other women. But I always believed that he would always come back to me and our life together would go on."

Catharine finished transcribing the narrative and presented it to Georgina. With Yan and Catharine on either arm, the women moved out to the back of the house. There, positioned in the middle of her Aunt's garden, was a large abalone shell provided for this purpose from Ursula's collection. Ursula took the handwritten transcript of the exposure and slowly tore it into strips, placing the strips into the shell. Yan then handed her a box of matches, and Georgina struck and lit the strips of paper that held the history of her painful relationship with her husband. Together they watched this recounting go up in flames

Yan turned to Georgina and ceremonially welcomed her into "the sisterhood of the Goddess Group And your new life as the avatar of Demeter."

"I'm grateful that this initiation process is over," Georgina said wearily.

"Oh! It's only just begun," laughed Catharine. "You'll be coming with us to the August retreat in Santa Fe. That's where we all continue the process of desensitizing the painful scenes of our history. It's an ongoing process."

"Your new life as the avatar of Demeter has only just begun," said Yan.

Chapter 50

Elise was stirred from her reverie by the sound of a fly buzzing against the nearby window. The facilitator had given them an in-class assignment: select a scene between themselves and a parent and write about it for fifteen minutes. *I'm sure this will be difficult for Eric,* she worried as she considered the stories she'd heard. She turned to see if she could catch his eye and was alarmed to find his chair empty. Sensing all was not well, she gathered her things as unobtrusively as possible and quickly and quietly tiptoed out of the room, exiting the side door into the bright sunlight of the warm summer day.

There was no sight of Eric. Some instinct guided Elise across the plaza, down the hill, and toward the sports fields at the south end of the Institution. As she came over the rise above the fields, she spotted him sitting alone, chin on his arm, gazing out over the lake. She called his name softly. As she came closer, he lifted his head; his face contorted by desperately holding back the tears; his shoulders convulsing with unuttered grief. Wordlessly, Elise sat down beside him and held out her arms. As he gave himself over to her waiting arms, harsh, labored keening emanated from his very core. Elise held him close, stroking the back of his head, whispering, "It's alright," over and over. They stayed like that for what seemed like an eternity until the sobs subsided.

At long last, Eric gently extricated himself from her arms and began to pull himself together.

"I don't know what came over me." He wiped off his tear-streaked face with the palms of his hands.

"It sounds like years and years of unexpressed grief." Elise pressed an embroidered handkerchief into his hands.

"I certainly wasn't expecting this," he groaned ruefully. "I signed up for this workshop expecting to improve my skills for writing some exceedingly dry legal briefs and found myself in over my head."

"Perhaps in over your heart is more like it." She tried her best to smile and squeezed his hand. "Do you want to talk about it?"

"I don't know where to start." Eric looked at her in dismay.

"Start wherever you like."

"There seems too much yet not a lot to say." Looking back over the lake, he began. "My memories are very vague. Hard to piece together. I was about six years old, and my sister would have been three. I was in school when it happened. My grandmother came to pick me up. I didn't learn all the details until much later. My mother and father were taking my sister to an interview for a new school where they were thinking of sending her. It was raining that day. Father was driving. They came to an intersection, and they had the green light, but another car coming along at the same time didn't stop for the red light —a drunk driver— and plowed into the driver's side of the car, killing both my father and my sister. They had to use the jaws of life to extricate them. My mother was trapped in the car for a long time and watched them die."

"How awful." The color drained from Elise's face.

"My mother never recovered from that day. Things were never the same again. She began to drink more and more after that; she wandered in and out of treatment but wasn't able to stay sober for long. While my mother was in treatment, I would stay with my grandmother. Soon that became my home. I saw my mother less and less, and then one day, my grandmother came to tell me that she had committed suicide. End of story."

"I'm so sorry."

The brave face Eric had managed briefly morphed to sorrow.

"Why wasn't I enough? Why wasn't I enough for my mother to want to live?" Eric looked away and held his breath, trying to choke off another spell of tears.

Taking his hand on her lap, Elise stroked it gently. They sat together in silence and watched the regatta unfolding out on the lake against a magnificent backdrop of rolling hills and azure cloud-streaked sky.

"I need to move now," said Eric after a while. Getting up, he reached for her hand and carefully pulled her to her feet. Gripping her shoulders, he looked deeply into her eyes.

"Thanks for being here with me."

"I'm happy that I was," said Elise, returning his gaze before she brushed off her clothing and leaned over to pick up her belongings.

"May I walk you somewhere?" He offered her his arm.

"Well, I hope you won't laugh. My mother and her friends are getting together this afternoon. One of the women, Alexandra Lewis —I'm sure you know who she is— is a hypnotist. Her family has used hypnosis to stem hemophilia and for other things since the days of Rasputin. She's going to hypnotize a couple of the women. They may possess important information but be unaware of it if that makes sense."

"Those royals are a strange bunch." Eric shook his head and smiled slightly.

"It's good to see you smile." Elise looked up and briefly, touched his cheek before she went on. "Anyway, they're going to attempt it. I'm going to transcribe everything that happens. I'm compiling all the information I can gather to give to the sheriff to assist with his investigation. It seems the least I can do for my friend."

Elise paused, sick inside at the memory of her friend.

"My only problem is that the sheriff may not be able to read it. No one can understand my unique style of shorthand; I can barely decipher it myself." She grimaced at the thought.

"Listen, why don't you use my computer at the guesthouse? It's somewhat messy as there haven't been any guests, and Mason hasn't had the cleaning crew there for a while, but it's quiet, and you'll be able to get your work done." It suddenly occurred to him that this would solve more than one issue.

"Oh, I couldn't. Wouldn't your grandmother object?" Elise protested

"Actually, I think she would be rather pleased." Teresa Bellamy was quite vocal about his avoidance of commitment; she worried his family's tragedy had caused him to fear intimacy: the limitless emptiness from his mother's abandonment; the chasm of despair that came with rejection. "Why don't you come to the reception grandmother will be hosting this evening for the 4th of July celebration? I can show you around then."

"If you're sure it won't be too much of a bother…."

"I look forward to it."

As they sauntered in the direction of the plaza, Eric felt a smile tugging at the edges of his mouth. The heaviness in his heart was lighter for the first time in years.

Chapter 51

Yan stayed behind after the others left; she couldn't help but notice that Georgina had been very quiet since the exposure experience. Yan glanced over, sensing her dark mood.

"I've been thinking about the impact on Elise of my relationship with Owen. Owen was unfaithful to me throughout our entire marriage. When I first stumbled upon one of Owen's infidelities, I fell into a deep depression. I just wanted to curl up and die. Of course, the situation only became progressively worse."

Georgina sighed and dropped her head; her voice was becoming almost inaudible.

"There were many occasions when I spent long periods of time locked in my bedroom, barely able to function. It took a dreadful toll on Elise. She has every right to be angry with me; left on her own without a parent; her mother locked in her room, depressed; a father off chasing women."

Her voice was by now just a fraction above a whisper.

"Inevitably, Owen would tire of his latest "love" and beg me to forgive him; I would, but trust became frayed: I vacillated: alternating between being suspicious or detached. I decided to remain with him for the sake of Elise, but in light of what happened, I may have made a mistake."

Yan paused, choosing her words carefully. "It's hard to know which is the better choice: too good to leave and too bad to stay. But now, you can make amends to Elise. Show her, through your own example, that you can overcome depression. Depression is a choice. This amends can be more powerful than anything else you can do."

"What makes you so sure?" Georgina was hungry for a few crumbs of hope.

"Depression is a progressive, self-feeding syndrome that impacts far too many of our women. The very characteristics of depression——negativism, loss of pleasure, energy, and motivation— actually deepen the depression. When you don't want to do anything except lie in a dark bedroom with the covers up and the blinds down, relationships deteriorate. Then you get even more depressed. No shock there."

Yan watched as she absorbed the information.

"You're right. It's very seductive. It felt as if depression was sitting on my shoulder, whispering in my ear: "go somewhere quiet where no one will ask you for anything." That's all I ever wanted to do, just go to my room and be alone, not have to talk to anybody who expects me to plaster on a happy face and chit-chat." She shook her head in amazement at how she had behaved.

"I understand, but the problem is that that very behavior strengthens the depression. Think about it. Depression is your mortal enemy. It's damaged your relationship with your daughter and robbed you of so much of your life. You must fight depression with all your might and main."

"But nobody tells you how you're supposed to do that." moaned Georgina. "It's like nobody gave me the Instruction Manual for Life."

"The antidote for depression is to do the exact opposite of what it tells you to do: move your muscles, get out and talk to anybody. Do the things that you found interesting and pleasurable before the depression struck."

"Easy to say but hard to do."

"Absolutely. Simple; not easy. But I promise you it works. Inch by inch, you emerge from the depths of sadness back into the light."

Georgina slumped down, plagued with guilt.

"Why didn't I know this? I didn't know I could choose whether or not to be depressed. My life has been one failure after another."

Yan leaned forward in her seat, fighting her maternal instincts. She wanted to go to her new friend and smooth away her self-loathing, but she also felt it was important for Georgina to learn to self-soothe.

"It is too bad. Most people don't see depression as a choice. And then there's the downside of recovering from depression or addiction; you experience profound remorse when you realize how much has been lost. There is no benefit from looking back, however; you must vigilantly turn your mind from such musings and redirect your thinking to what can you do to make things better today; what is the next right thing."

"Eternal vigilance, right?" Georgina lifted her chin and gazed steadily at Yan.

"Right." She responded lightly.

"Elise knows nothing about this. I'm sure my disrespect for Owen was difficult for Elise to understand, but she's her father's little girl, and I didn't and didn't want to interfere with that. My issues with her father have nothing to do with her. I want her to feel that she has a loving and caring father who would do anything for her. Girls need their fathers."

Yan was all too familiar with the ravages caused by serial infidelity. The damage was brutal and often passed from generation to generation. It wasn't unusual for women to come to her private practice complaining of a lack of intimacy in their relationships. Often, in cases of this sort, she would advise patients that they had three choices: stay miserable —hated that—; change themselves by individuating and creating a full life of their own; or divorce. Of late, it seemed, more of her patients were involved with sex addicts. Maybe it's just me, she conjectured; but she didn't think so.

"It's hard to protect our children from learning the truth about their parents. Elise is probably aware of more than you know. She is a very intuitive young woman."

Yan narrowed her eyes and cautiously appraised her friend.

"It's a boundary violation for a mother to tell her daughter the grisly details of her parent's marriage." Georgina declared. "Elise inherited my highly sensitive, reactive emotional system, but she is just beginning to acquire the tools to deal with it. I don't want her recovery to be jeopardized now after all she's been through."

She swallowed hard. Her jaw muscles were beginning to ache.

"I agree with you about healthy boundaries," stated Yan. "But each of us, mothers and daughters, has to learn to deal with hurtful emotions. We must each follow our own path of healing; this situation may be the agent of her realization."

Yan's eyes narrowed, and she carefully appraised her new friend's response to this advice. If they were to make progress, it was important that Georgina trust her.

"I have to believe you. The guidance you've given me so far has been solid."

"I'm glad you find it so. Truly, our job is to be present in our daughter's journey: to share our experience and offer hope along the way, not to remove obstacles. It is through dealing with these obstacles— like practicing hurdles for a cross country race —that our daughters acquire emotional resilience. When we interfere with that process, our daughters become emotionally incapacitated."

As they prepared to leave the Goddess site, Yan took one last look around. She and Georgina shoveled more sand over the fire to ensure it was safely out. Together they began to wend their way up the wood chip pathway and under the sheltering grove, up onto Thunder bridge.

"The daily amends you make to your daughter is the training you are submitting to here and now. The emotional roller coaster you were on as you reacted to your husband's behavior has ruptured the bond between you and her daughter. The way you make daily amends to your daughter is by working to make yourself emotionally and spiritually fit. All you can do is all you can do, but you must do all you can do. You are powerless over how your daughter reacts, but you are required to do the work."

The two stopped and looked down over the river, watching the rushing water skip over the rocks, then flow along down past the sacred site.

"I am willing to go to any lengths and to do whatever it takes to become more emotionally grounded," promised Georgina grimly. "I can't go back to the way things were."

Chapter 52

A meeting with the sheriff yielded little – the sheriff was reluctant to spread gossip and further complicate the delicate situation – so Hayden decided to go to the library and find for himself the information regarding the charges the adult dancer had brought against the Bellamy boys in the notorious Harbridge case. The library, an impressive red brick building with wide cement steps, was positioned on the south side of Bestor Plaza. Only recently had the library been pulled into the twenty-first century with the installation of a computerized catalog; the librarians were loath to change and were more comfortable with the card catalog. As he entered, Hayden checked the worn orange two-by-three-inch library card he had possessed since he first came to Chautauqua; he knew it would still be honored as entrée to the contents of the Chautauqua library. The circulation desk was on his right, piled high with newly returned books to be shelved; on his left were about twenty Chautauquans, young and old, seated at long, distressed-oak tables, reading international newspapers held straight on wooden dowels. Passing a central counter laden with brochures displaying the various activities at Chautauqua, he took the circular marble stairs leading to the second-floor reference section. There he was greeted by the reference librarian who had known him since he was first reading. Hayden had been coming to stay at his grandparents' summer home – he was third generation Chautauquan, a more common event than one might imagine – and had attended children's programming since the age of three. Eager to enrich his education beyond the excellent pedagogy provided by his boys' private school, his grandparents enrolled him in the academic, musical, and sports camps and summoned numerous tutors to attend to him during his visits. Hayden had gone on to major in business at the University of Toronto, ultimately earning an MBA from the London School of Economics. A background including international experience was of great value to Owen's global ambitions, and he had welcomed Hayden as a trusted and indispensable lieutenant.

Despite the expert and enthusiastic assistance of the librarian, the vast contents of the library revealed little more than he already knew. What was chronicled by more recent news reports was that the adult dancer at the center of the charges continued to be mired in trouble and controversy. There were reports that, in the recent past, she had been accused of assaulting her live-in boyfriend for two weeks, and her children had been taken from her by social services. Hayden could see that, because of her behavior, she would make a poor prosecution witness, the reason the case against the Bellamy boys had been abandoned. That did not mean, he knew, that she had not actually been assaulted and raped at Harbridge. But because the sole witness was not credible, it would be difficult to win a jury verdict in court. Momentarily stymied, Hayden elected to go back to his condo to shower and change before he decided what next to do.

Elise has certainly become an ineffably lovely young woman. Not the awkward young colt he remembered from before.

Hayden had heard rumors that Elise was involved with drugs and had been sent away for treatment, but her appearance belied the gossip. She appeared refreshed and radiant when he saw her with Owen on the Athenaeum porch. Owen had not been silent in his desire for Hayden to follow in his footsteps, nor had he been subtle about his desire for Hayden and Elise to 'get to know each other better.' Owen was notorious for dismissing others' opinions of his decisions, but Hayden wasn't yet in a position to do that. Though in the past, his dating preferences leaned more to show-stopping, long-legged cover girls, he had found Elise quite acceptable. He wanted to be assured that there wouldn't be strong opposition to his taking over the company from some unknown future son-in-law with his own ambitions. Shaking his head now and shifting his thinking back to the matter at hand, Hayden exited the library, turned to the right, and started walking to his condo.

On the lawn in front of the Athenaeum, early evening croquet matches had begun in the gloaming of the spreading sunset. Players were formally attired in their cream-on-white outfits: white belts, shoes, and caps for the gentlemen, bonnets for the ladies. Hayden could make out muffled murmurs, deferring to one another as they struck gaily striped balls with their mallets. Scorekeeping was overseen by a referee who discreetly slid cardboard oblongs along a wooden stand at the edge of the green. Onto this quiet pastel scene emerged three young men, a trio of dark princes in the guise of sleek athletes. Each over six feet tall with short-cropped springy hair, their loping gait effortlessly eating up the manicured length and breadth of the lawns.

Hayden was certain he was looking at the grandsons of the matriarch of Chautauqua. But who was the third runner? One of the trio slowed down and looked straight at him as they swept past, then hurried to catch up with the others. Hayden, meanwhile, had snapped a number of photos with his iPhone, which he immediately emailed to the security chief of Winslow Industries. He wanted to get as much information as possible as quickly as possible.

Back at the condo, Hayden called the head of security to confirm that the photos had been received and asked him to dig around with his sources. He was to send along any information he could uncover, including background data, family history, all available documents concerning school disciplinary incidents, and investigation of rape and battery charges for both of the Bellamy boys and — "Oh yeah; include the third, as yet unidentified, male as well."

SECTION V
Chapter 53

Morning fog rolled in off the lake and heavy-laden skies drizzled on the brightly colored activewear of the crowd gathered in front of the Sports Club. The clanging of the nearby sailboat riggings provided percussion for the cacophony of the runners milling around as they awaited the start of the annual July 4th run. Angelique found herself shepherded by the army of red, white, and blue garbed volunteers into the area designated for her age class. One of the volunteers, a wiry sixty-something woman with sun-damaged skin and wash and wear grey hair sporting a red and white striped sun visor with blue and white stars curving one of the sides, pinned a race number to the back of her Wickaway T-shirt featuring a four-color artist's rendering of Bell Tower Point.

"I'd be running myself except that I had a knee replacement six weeks ago," explained the woman who was moving exceedingly well without a cane or other visible support. "I've participated in every run for the last forty years."

Angelique had been duly impressed by the Chautauquan's level of commitment to exercise and had no difficulty believing the woman's claim. The walkways, bike paths, tennis courts, and baseball diamonds were constantly filled with people walking, biking, or playing sports at all hours of the day and night. It seemed everyone there was fit and only getting fitter.

"I haven't had my quatro shot coffee brewed with Red Bull this morning," quipped Angelique, momentarily annoyed by the nonstop healthy lifestyle of the Chautauquans. She was rewarded by a disapproving gaze of her assistant.

Oh my, Angelique thought. She doesn't understand me any more than I understand the droves of earnest new law school graduates arriving at the prosecuting attorney's offices, the latest touch screen electronics clutched lovingly in their hands.

As she remembered the latest class of young lawyers, her attention was captured by the trio of gods breaking through the morning mist and breezing in to join the crowd, which had gone silent at their arrival. Even up close, it was difficult at first to distinguish among the three —each a couple of inches over six feet, dark ash blond wiry hair cropped close to the skull in gladiator-style, smooth tanned skin drawn tightly over cheekbones chiseled so sharply they could cut glass. The camaraderie of the three was evident in their incessant jostling —the energy of superbly conditioned athletes charged the air like ozone following an afternoon thunderstorm. Miko came up from behind Eric and tried to startle him, but Eric demonstrated no outward response.

"What's up? You must be distracted. I can't even get a rise out of you."

"My mind just isn't into competing today." Eric was focusing on his pre-running stretching routine.

"You're always into competing." Miko also began to stretch, although his efforts were somewhat superficial. As usual, he was busy checking out the lovely female bodies in their skimpy running apparel.

"I've been thinking over the spectacle at Harbridge and all the chaos that has been happening here at Chautauqua. What a year! Elise has asked us to spend some time going over these events to see if there is anything we can add. As a matter of fact, she tells me the Goddess Group her mother is involved with plans to meet later today in order to use hypnosis to enhance their memory; perhaps they can dredge up more information to help with the case. Elise is recording all of it and putting together a report to give to the authorities."

"Do you really believe in that stuff? Hypnosis sounds dumb to me. I didn't think information from hypnosis was allowed in court," ventured Chester.

"There might be something to it; who knows," said Eric, shrugging. "But you're right: information extracted under hypnosis is not admissible in court. But it might help the investigation."

"Bunch of batty women if you ask me," declared Miko.

Hearing the word 'hypnosis,' Angelique moved closer to the young men. "My gosh. If it isn't the Harbridge rowers," she gulped, remembering the chagrin of her colleagues at what they considered obstruction by very powerful figures in Boston.

Sidling up next to them, she kneeled as if to tie a shoelace and attempted to eavesdrop on their conversation. Before she could overhear anything, however, she was ushered back to the area designated for her age class by an overzealous volunteer, lips clamped firmly together, attempting to get everyone into place for the start of the race. Before she had another opportunity to listen in on them, the trio sped off.

It appears they're paying attention to what our Goddess Group is doing. I wonder what they intend to do about it?

Chapter 54

Owen was squeezed between two ladies who were examining the tchotchkes in the display case of the Chautauqua bookstore, a low brick building on the northeast corner of Bestor Plaza where he and the rest of Chautauqua had rushed to secure copies of the Sunday New York before they were sold out. Owen knew the bookstore carried an array of unique greeting cards and was not surprised to spot Elise smiling to herself as she perused the contents of the card carousel. He edged up quietly behind her and tapped her on the shoulder.

She gasped, dropping a couple of the cards she had selected. "Dad, you startled me!" she said, leaning over to rescue them.

"Sorry," he said, quickly squatting down to help. "I was hoping to talk to you. It should only take a couple of minutes."

"Alright," she agreed reluctantly and, carefully replacing the cards she had been considering, followed him through the bookstore, past the shelves prominently featuring the various authors who lectured there, past the umbrella stand that held umbrellas for the use of residents who might be caught unprepared by an unexpected shower, up the steps and, opening the glass-paned double doors, out into the sunshine.

"Where can we sit and chat undisturbed for a while?" he said, looking around.

"I thought you said, 'a couple of minutes'." She was used to his manipulative ways.

Grinning slyly, Owen took her arm and guided her around the boxwood hedges at the perimeter of the plaza that created privacy barriers and enclosed sets of benches arranged in conversation areas in an alfresco living room. Owen gestured for Elise to sit on one of the benches and then settled himself on the bench facing her.

"I just want you to know how sorry I am about everything that's happened. I wouldn't for the world have hurt you and your mother. I hope you can find it in your heart to forgive me." Owen molded his face into a solemn mask, blue eyes clouding over.

Elise regarded him silently for several seconds. It was difficult to gauge the level of her father's sincerity. She had observed him, like a consummate actor, feign genuineness on any number of occasions. Pausing to weigh the probability of her words having the power to impact her father in any way, she plowed forward. She had nothing to lose.

"While I was away at treatment, I had lots of opportunities to review the history of our lives together. One of my assignments was to take a look at my life decade by decade." The troubled look on her face deepened.

"Well, there are only two of those, thank goodness," he grinned, attempting to dispel the seriousness of the situation.

"Dad, I need you to listen to me," Elise was becoming exasperated with his tactics. She wanted to stamp her foot like a two-year-old, but she stopped herself.

"I'm sorry. Go on." Owen sat back and restored his expression to one of penitence.

"So, I took the two decades of my life and plotted the significant emotional events."

"Significant events, meaning...?" He squirmed uncomfortably in his seat. Looking at him, Elise wondered whether it was worth her while to explain.

"All those times when you were unavailable to me, not only physically but emotionally. It is easy to identify the times when you were not there in person: when you would be working late or away on a business trip. Emotional absence is more difficult to understand."

"Emotional absence!" he groaned, looking around as if for support.

"That's right. My counselor had to guide me through this. For instance, I remember a time when I attended a party with you and mom; I saw you laughing and joking with everyone; very much having a good time. Later, however, at home with us, you became quiet and retreated into yourself: an all-powerful, charismatic man reduced to an imploded shell, a caldera. I began to believe that this dramatic change in you —this diminution of your energy— was because I was such a disappointment to you. That's when I began to be a perfectionist. I thought that if I were more —fill in the blank— you would pay attention to me."

"Elise, you couldn't be more wrong." he contended fiercely.

"Let me finish. It is important that you hear me out." Elise's composure began to crumble; her lower lip trembled as she fought for control. "That's when I became obsessed with ballet and everything that came with the territory: using medications to dance through pain, using amphetamines for energy and weight loss. First I used those pills, and then they used me: paradoxically, I lost the control I was using them to gain."

Despite her best efforts, she was weeping. Seeing Owen glance around to see if others were noticing, her voice grew more subdued. "Through therapy, I came to see your behavior more clearly. It wasn't because I was so boring. It was because you were obsessed with the admiration of multitudes of people, even people you didn't know: the adulation of the anonymous audience. Mom and I weren't nearly enough to fill the monumental vacuum that is within you. And do you remember when I came to intern at your office; again to make you notice me? I got to meet all your work wives! It was a disaster."

"Sweetheart, I didn't mean to hurt you. I love you. I can still see you now as you were then, so tiny and helpless." Owen held his arms out, pleading his cause.

"Your own narcissism blinds you to the effect this has had on me." Elise could feel her hands shaking; rage percolated through her despair.

"I have devoted myself to my business all for you. Right now, however, everything I have built and accomplished is at risk. I know you aren't interested in business, but I am presently working on a recapitalization project, and Hayden Young is a crucial part of this. As you know, he comes from a well-respected Toronto family; he finished his MBA in the UK. In the next few years, the success of all of my efforts is going to rest on whether he commits himself to the company and me or not. I really wish that you would get to know him better."

"So this is the real reason that we are having this conversation," said Elise, standing up from the bench, her voice rising in anger. "Come on, dad, how twelfth Century: marrying off your daughter to ensure the viability of your organizations, just like the Borgias? Like always, dad, you're working to ensure your own interests, not to heal the breach of the relationship with me."

"You're not looking at things clearly. I want to tell you some things I have discovered about the Bellamies; I saw the picnic you had for them down at the park. I've started an investigation into their activities, especially as they relate to Brynn's death. I forbid you to have anything more to do with them."

She crossed the narrow space between them and stood before him, hands on hips. "I won't listen to any more of your interference. You are to stop this right now. Do you hear me? Ruining a person's reputation is like releasing down feathers from high up in the Bell Tower. You can never recapture them all and stuff them back into the pillow sack."

"Believe me; their reputations were ruined long before I came along." His tone was stern. A flicker of unease fell across Elise's face.

"Stop right now, or I will never speak to you again. Do you understand?" she said through gritted teeth. "

Elise turned on her heel and walked out of their makeshift meeting space, anxious to get as far away from him as possible, leaving Owen totally mystified.

Chapter 55

Ursula walked up the brick walkway that divided a small patch of green grass framed by deeper green fern fronds and led to the art gallery, a white frame building constructed in 1893, according to the pewter plaque on the column to the right of the door. At nearly six feet tall, her height usually drew attention, and tonight was no different. This evening she had pulled her springy blond hair into a tight chignon at the back of her neck. She looked resplendent in a gold ensemble: a satin man's style blouse, open two buttons at the neck, and a slender riding skirt also fashioned of golden satin. Her belt was faux snakeskin, as were her boots, and four faux snakeskin bracelets rose up to her left forearm. As she squeezed her way through the overflow of people talking and laughing on the front porch, Ursula noticed one of the serving staff circulating among the guests offering champagne and canapés. Ursula had known that the young sculptor being featured at this gala was a protégé of Teresa Bellamy, and so she was eager to view the work of this unknown talent. Looks well-attended, she thought, aware that many at Chautauqua were eager to retain Mrs. Bellamy's favor.

Inside the gallery, the Chautauqua movers and shakers had gathered. Ursula, who had attended many such parties, noted that this was a different group from those who had attended Alex's party, where wit and stimulating discussion were the tickets to gain entree to the evening. This was more the monied crowd than the intelligentsia. The purpose of the event, according to Alex, was to raise money to enable this talented young artist to have the clay figures on display cast in bronze at the Santa Fe foundry. Picking up her champagne flute, Ursula pushed her way through the crowded art gallery towards Catharine, a beautiful quasi-widow in body-sculpting black, with no adornment except for the pale curls that cascaded down her shoulders. She was off in the corner talking to one of the Bellamy boys. As Ursula drew nearer, she heard them discussing this year's Toronto film festival to be held the week following Labor Day.

"Catharine, how wonderful to find you here," said Ursula. "How are you feeling?"

"As well as can be expected. Have you met Prince Mikolaj Kazmierz?"

Catharine gestured toward the young man at her side in an exquisite European-tailored dinner jacket; he was taller than Ursula by a couple of inches.

"Of course, I know who the Prince is." That dinner jacket cost six thousand dollars if it cost a penny. It's amazing that these young people looked so impeccable at night while by day, the only way to tell their degree of wealth was through their watches and their shoes.

"Please call me Miko." The young man bent to kiss Ursula's hand. "Everyone knows the esteemed intellectual, Dr. Ursula Andrews. I had the pleasure of attending the opening of your lecture in Boston and am most interested to hear your comment on this exhibit. The artist is a close friend; we have known each other since childhood."

"Miko and I were just discussing the documentary about Jonah and the Herd Mentality. I understand that Cody McCoy is going to go ahead and enter it in the Toronto International Film Festival this fall. Miko had been talking to Jonah about representing him, but of course, that was just before he died."

Ursula fell silent.

"I didn't know that they were going to go ahead with the documentary. Where will Cody be doing the editing?" asked Miko.

"Jonah had set up editing facilities right here at Chautauqua, in the Bluebirds parked down by the lake. I'll drop by later to see if I can lend a hand. I see the documentary as a tribute to Jonah. It would be a shame to let it molder unattended on some editing room floor."

"Do you know if Alex will be attending the film festival?" Ursula asked Catharine.

"I'm not sure," she answered. "Typically, Alex retreats to her home north of Toronto to escape the mobs in the city at that time. It seems that a lot of business is conducted at that particular festival, and so many people in the film industry choose to attend. But talk to her about it. I'm sure she would be there to support you if you ask. She has always been eager to have us visit her. Maybe we can hold a Goddess Circle up at her residence. It should be lovely that time of yea

Miko noticed Cody McCoy on the opposite side of the room, and he and Catharine excused themselves to go over to him and continue the conversation.

"Ms. Andrews," a disembodied voice spoke at her elbow. Another of the three musketeers. No wonder people mistake them for each other, thought Ursula as she turned and found herself eye-to-eye with a tall, slant-cheeked man as sleekly outfitted as Miko.

"I am so honored that someone of your stature has come to my opening. I am a great fan," he stated.

Ursula found various thoughts speeding through her brain. Is he trying to seduce me into sponsoring him? She was aware of how dependent struggling young artists were on patronage in order to bring their creations into being. The foundry was so costly. But surely, if Teresa Bellamy were throwing this reception for him, that part was taken care of. So what else could it be?

"She's beautiful," ventured Ursula.

They were standing in front of the clay rendition of a panther, muscles prominent under a sleek coat, cubs at her side.

"The female is the predator among the panther clan," Chester said.

"Are you suggesting that this is true of all species?" Ursula couldn't imagine what about this young man stirred her competitive inquiry.

"Females are much more capable of destruction than are males. Males only destroy the external. Females crave the viscera."

Ursula was taken aback by the vehemence of this announcement. "I'm impressed by your understanding of the anatomy. That's usually an area of great difficulty for both two-and three-dimensional artists." She was startled to observe Chester smooth his countenance and instantaneously transform from angry scowl to effusive charm.

"I agree," said Chester as he shifted again and withdrew into a thousand-mile stare. "When I was a child, I spent a good deal of time out of doors roaming the nearby ravines, where I caught squirrels and raccoons and brought them back to my house. There was a stainless-steel room set up in the basement of our house where hunters would bring their game back for dismembering. That's where I brought my own catch: small rabbits, squirrels, and raccoons, and carefully dissected them until I became familiar with anatomy. Later, I was able to obtain a job as a taxidermist assistant so that I would have access to more cadavers." Chester caught himself and shifted back to the present. "But what a gruesome discussion for a beautiful evening and a beautiful lady. Once again, I am honored that you took the time to attend my humble presentation. Please enjoy the exhibit."

Chester melted back into the crowd.

Chapter 56

"Where is he? It's very important."

It was Thompson, Owen's security chief, on the Line.

"I don't know where he is, but you can give me the information, and I'll be sure he gets it," promised Hayden.

"I'm sure Owen will want me to give this information directly to him." Thompson pushed back. "It's about the guys he asked me to look into. You know, the Bellamy boys."

Hayden chewed his bottom lip in frustration.

"Well, if you recall, I was the one whom he asked to call you in the first place."

"I remember. Still, this information is only for the boss. If he wants you to know about it, he'll have to tell you himself."

"So what do you want me to do? I don't know where he is." Hayden's voice revealed his growing irritation.

"Tell you what. I am sending this information directly to his Blackberry. You go find him and let him know that he can access it there, and he can give it to you if he wants to. But it's important he get this right away. Have him call me when he has the info. I can clarify anything he needs then."

Hayden hung up and left the condo to go and look for Owen. Outside everyone was laughing and shouting, busy with July 4th activities. Hayden hurried through the impromptu family picnic sites, sidestepping abandoned bicycles and wagons, and headed for the plaza.

Somehow or other, I don't think the boss will be doing much celebrating after he gets this.

Chapter 57

Ursula's front door was open. Alex and Yan closed it behind them and walked to the front room, gently calling out to their friend. In the front room, they saw that Elise was all set to transcribe the proceedings: a Parson's table nestled behind the tan leather sofa; a chair upholstered in Navajo weavings matching the scattered throw pillows afforded her an unobstructed view of the session. Ursula's Goddess shawl, soft and luxurious, was draped across the couch, awaiting her presence. Soft chanting emanated from the CD player enclosed within the bookcases, and the scent of pinon wafted through the room. Ursula arrived from various parts of the house, and they joined hands for a moment of silence.

Yan began by reminding everyone that hypnosis was an altered state of awareness during which Ursula's brain would be highly focused. The expectation was that additional information would be gleaned to assist the investigation.

"Our best guess is that she picked up a lot of information —four billion bits of data may be contained in any one event— the morning she discovered Brynn's body. This was picked up by her senses —eyes, ears, nose— but remains in the unconscious part of the mind and hadn't yet percolated to the surface. Ursula had agreed to hypnosis in order to see if it could be retrieved."

Ursula made herself comfortable on the sofa and nodded to affirm that she was ready to begin. Alex covered her with the cloudlike shawl and watched as she closed her eyes. The first phase was for relaxation. Then, when she was sure that Ursula felt secure, she would move to the induction phase and have Ursula revisit Belltower Point and the scene of the discovery in her imagination. The other two fell silent as Alex, in a calm, rhythmic tone, led Ursula deeper and deeper:

"As you gaze around, you see a way to descend to go down deeper; it might be a stairway; it might be a little incline; look around and find the way to go deeper, and now going down deeper and deeper; level by level; as I count backward from five to one; five – allowing yourself to go deeper now with each muscle of your body totally relaxed; four – still deeper; breathing slow and rhythmic' three – you are approaching deeper levels of relaxation that will be merging into hypnosis; two – almost there now, almost entering the deepest level of hypnosis; and one – now at the level of hypnosis and yet continuing to go deeper and deeper with each breath that you take and with each word that I speak.

And now, gaze around you, and you will notice that you are on the Belltower Point; it is early morning, and you can feel yourself gliding through yoga movements. Nod one time when you feel you have completed the sun salutation and are standing in the final mountain pose."

Ursula's head was still momentarily and then slowly nodded once.

"Good. Now gaze around and tell us what is happening now."

"I am standing in namaste," Ursula began haltingly, alluding to the standing prayer posture that begins and ends the yoga sequence. "Something, I don't know what makes me decide to go over to the water's edge." She stopped.

Just keep breathing deeply and rhythmically, deeper now.

"I see debris around, you know, from the kid's partying there the night before. I'm picking up bottles and cans and placing them in a pile." She was almost whispering now, and Elise had to lean closer over the couch to hear what she was saying.

"I think I see a plastic bottle floating just off the water's edge. I'm pushing the lily stems apart and wading out for it." Ursula started to weep silently.

"It's okay. You are safe and secure. Safe and secure."

"It can see strands of silk waving in the water. It looks like silk, but I can't quite make out what it is. I am wading closer now, and my hand brushes an arm." Ursula's sobs became audible as she reexperienced the recovery scene; Alex continued to croon in soothing murmurs.

"I am trying to rescue her; I am trying to pull her to shore. She is so tiny, but her body is so heavy. I turn her body over, and her hair sinks back into the water; I am dragging her up onto the shore. I'm trying to make her comfortable." The terror in Ursula's voice is palpable as she gives herself over to sobbing.

Elise wanted to hug her, to comfort her, but Alex held up a restraining hand. Elise gestured that she would like to ask Ursula a question, and Alex acquiesced with a nod.

Another voice is asking you to join in now; Elise has a question for you. Raise your right index finger if this is acceptable.

Ursula's right index finger trembled slightly, then lifted.

Just allow yourself to rest deeply as you will hear Elise's voice begin now.

Ursula, I have a question. As you turn Brynn over, her hair falls away from her face. Are you able to see a necklace around her neck? Lift your right index finger if the answer is yes."

All waited patiently for the right index finger to rise. It remained still.

"Ursula, it's Alex again. Allow yourself to see the entire scene from beginning to end, take your time, and see if, at any time during the recovery of Brynn's body, you notice a necklace or anything that looks like a necklace. Lift your right index finger if the answer is yes."

Once more, the group around Ursula watched intently to see any movement in her finger. Once again, the finger was still. Alex continued:

It's now time for you to return. And so, travel back and back through time and space; back to this house; back to this room; back to this couch. The energy moves up your spine and into your brain, mind focused and alert; and finally, on the count of five, eyes open, back to regular time and activity.

Ursula roused and opened her eyes. "Why were you asking about a necklace?"

"I'm trying to determine whether the speculation about a serial killer is reasonable," explained Elise. "Angelique told us these murderers like to collect trophies from their kills so that they can spend time with them; handle them and relive these experiences as they touch their trophies."

"Are you suggesting that the death of Brynn may have been committed by the same person who set fire to Jonah's SUV?" challenged Alex.

"Well, Angelique says that the act of killing allows the sociopath to feel alive, but soon the sociopath needs greater and greater risks and atrocities to achieve that same thrill. Don't forget my dog, Princess. Her diamond collar was found among the ashes, but her dog tags are missing. Brynn's necklace is missing. Brynn always wore that necklace —even over the opposition of ballet master Gregory who didn't think it appropriate for performance— but it hasn't turned up among her effects. The killer may have first tasted blood by killing Princess and then escalated to Jonah and finally to Brynn. It's not beyond the realm of possibility."

"There's a chance that we are dealing with a serial murderer," said Alex. "But I'm not convinced that it is more than the faintest possibility."

Several minutes of speculation could draw no further conclusions. The group checked in with Ursula to make sure that she was fully back in consciousness and then prepared to take their leave.

"Don't forget we're all invited to the Bellamy estate to watch the fireworks tonight," Yan reminded them. "It has the best view of the entire Institution."

"Oh yes, the Bellamies," sighed Alex. "Such a tragic family. Teresa's son and granddaughter were killed in a car accident many years ago. After that, the mother became 'emotionally fragile' —a euphemism for being an alcoholic. She had a number of 'nervous breakdowns.' Teresa put her in an institution up in Lenox many times, but she ultimately committed suicide. Poor sad thing. Left a young son, Eric, of course. Teresa stepped in to oversee his upbringing and sent him to the best private boys' schools. Then last year, he got mixed up in that Harbridge scandal —something to do with a stripper at a frat party? Teresa has had a lot to contend with."

"Eric has offered me the use of his guest house to compile the information that I'm preparing for the sheriff. I told him I would stop by later, so I guess I'll see you there." When Elise had gathered up her writing implements and exited, a look of concern passed among the three women. Alex voiced their worries:

"If Elise has feelings for Eric, I'm worried that they won't be reciprocated, not because Elise isn't a wonderfully desirable young woman, but rather because of Eric's family's tragic history with addiction. And there's her father's desire to have her get together with Hayden. The successor he has identified for his business. Sometimes I think that young people and their infatuations are like elephants in a three-ring-circus, each chasing the other in an endless circle: Hayden pursuing Elise, pursuing Eric, and so forth ad nauseum."

Chapter 58

Ursula carefully raked the soft sand around the fire pit, etching precise rows into the ground. She remained in a trancelike state following the hypnosis experience. Around her, the silver-gray bark of the poplars reflected the radiance of the late-dying summer sun. Ursula felt she could already sense the now-diminishing light, strongest a few days ago at the summer solstice and weakening day by day until the winter solstice when it would be reborn once again. The Goddesses would gather to watch tonight's fireworks display, and then there would be one final ritual gathering of the Circle before they departed the Institution tomorrow morning. She dug a deep pit near the riverbed where they would bury the ashes from the final burning of the Chautauqua Circle and scattered fragrant flower petals to purify the barren fire pit. The site was almost ready to be restored to its ghostly inhabitants. Ursula paused to await the reappearance of the Clan Mothers. Soon the scintillating hologram of the Seneca Clan Mother could be discerned near the edge of the clearing. But she was not standing still. She was hacking at something with her tomahawk. Over and over again, the tomahawk sliced through the strands of a cocoon-like object woven from what looked like grapevines. The sarcophagus finally split open, revealing the desiccated carcass of a newborn fawn that had been dismembered and reassembled before being bundled into its organic coffin. Ursula knelt before the meticulously preserved creature. Certain now, Ursula's eyes probed the lengthening shadows at the sheltering edge of the aspen grove, finally coming to rest on the grieving visage of her beloved power animal, the Golden Hind. Her baby had been surgically dissected. Ursula tenderly rewrapped her tiny precious cargo. The doe insistently nudged Ursula and, breaking into a trot, led the way back along the pine-strewn path. Away from Thunder Bridge. Towards the north end. Towards the Bellamy Estate. Towards the killer.

***

"There's been an awful lot to take in." protested Angelique.

She gently rocked back and forth on the front porch swing, taking a moment to collect her thoughts before she got ready to attend Teresa Bellamy's July 4th party. The sheriff had allowed her to accompany him on many of the interviews; she had access to the evidence that had been collected regarding the killings, and she had the intuitive input of the Goddess Circle to take into consideration. Leaning her head back on the comfortable cushions, she allowed her own unconscious to bubble up information that might be of help. Lying there, drifting in and out of a light doze, her eyes spotted a spider patiently lurking at the margins of a web spun some time before. Arachne, the spider, was closely associated with the Goddess Athena, to whom Angelique gave allegiance. Greek mythology held that a woman, widely known as a gifted weaver, challenged Athena, the Goddess of crafts and herself a weaver, to a contest. When the mortal woman was proclaimed the winner of the weaving contest, Athena was so enraged that she turned her into a spider, forever weaving her webs. Arachne.

Three holes had been torn into the fabric of the perfect trap the spider had fashioned just above Angelique's head; gashes rent as hapless flies struggled against being snared and eaten. The spider's vigilance indicated that she was patiently awaiting a fourth victim that she was certain would appear.

Angelique sat up, cracking her neck uncomfortably. Four victims. Four victims. We've had three: Princess, Jonah, and Brynn. Now there is to be a fourth? Somewhere with cobwebs? Where in the fastidious households of Chautauqua would there be cobwebs?"

Chapter 59

An onshore breeze stirred the leaves of the sheltering maples as Mason repositioned the last serving spoon on the red, white, and blue buffet in preparation for this evening's celebration of the nation's Independence Day; around the courtyard were a number of tables covered in white linen cloth. Red, white, and blue flower arrangements sprouted little star-spangled-banner flags. Sunset inflamed the western sky with mauves and purples, rose and bronze, a brief brilliant blaze to herald the advent of darkness.

When nighttime spilled its ink across the lake, the northern shore would explode with pyrotechnic splendor: starbursts, chrysanthemums, and rockets bursting with every color of the palette. On Chautauqua Lake, the longstanding tradition was to insert flares at the water's edge around the entire perimeter of the lake, and, when nocturnal gloom was blackest, the flares would be ignited in order, one after the other, across Belltower Point, across the Bellamy estate, finally closing the circle where it first began.

Eric found his grandmother with Mason, reviewing the readiness of the party prior to the arrival of the guests.

"Perfection as usual." He kissed his grandmother's still-smooth cheek.

"Appreciative as always," said Teresa, glowing as she patted the cheek of the young man she'd cared for since childhood.

"Glammy, before the others arrive, I'd like to talk to you about something. One of the participants in my writing workshop needs a quiet place to work. I was wondering about her using the guesthouse."

"Her?"

"Yes, Glammy, Elise Winslow; I believe you know her mother, Georgina."

"Of course. She'll be attending the party tonight."

Georgina was indeed known to her, as was the addiction history of her daughter. Teresa was surprised her grandson had struck up what seemed to be a close relationship with Elise, given his attitude towards alcoholism.

"Whomever you wish to invite is welcome, of course. This is your home."

"But, Madam, not the guesthouse," exclaimed Mason. "As we have been doing so much entertaining in the main house and no guests due until next week, I haven't arranged to have the cleaning crew in the guesthouse."

"Not now, Mason," retorted Mrs.Bellamy. "Tonight's guests are arriving."

The first guests to arrive were the President of the Institution and his wife; Marek Raczkowski, the conductor of the Chautauqua Symphony, and his guest artist, Catharine Sobieski; Owen Winslow and Hayden Young, along with a crunch of neighbors and luminaries. They all came into the garden at once. Sheriff Cahill was looking not-at-all official in a cream summer jacket. A clique of women Teresa frequently saw together arrived. Elise's mother, Georgina, was not among them this evening. Angelique —Teresa had a very icy relationship with her since the events at Harbridge and was certain she hadn't invited her— breezed in and hurried over to talk to the sheriff. The tinkle of glasses and the sound of laughter wafted through the garden. The party was in full swing when at last, Elise appeared, writing tote on her shoulder; she spotted Eric off to one side talking to Chester.

"Glad you're here. I know you'll enjoy the fireworks; we have the best view of the whole institution from right here," said Eric.

"I'm sure that's true, but right now, I'm eager to get to work. Remember I mentioned that we were going to hold a hypnosis session? Alex put Ursula in a trance to see if we could recover any information to help with the murder investigation, and it was quite successful. I want to make sure I get everything transcribed while it's still fresh in my mind."

"Murder?" sneered Chester.

"A group of my mother's friends thinks the people dying here have all been killed by a serial murderer. I'm pulling together all the information we've gathered to see if some sense can be made of it."

"And I have offered her use of the computer in the guesthouse to put this all together," said Eric.

Chester stood as if stunned, staring at the backs of the couple as they strolled over in the direction of the guesthouse. Eric led Elise through the rooms and into the study that looked out over the lake.

"What a breathtaking view," exclaimed Elise.

"You may be distracted by the fireworks set to go off as soon as it is dark enough."

"I don't know. I'll probably be so immersed in the report that nothing will take my attention away."

"I won't distract you anymore then. Before I leave, let me show you where the supplies are kept in case you need them, and let me take you through all the bells and whistles on this computer." As Eric was completing his run-through, Mason arrived with a tray carrying snacks and a pitcher of punch, blanching at the untended state of the room.

"I didn't want to be a nuisance for Mrs. Bellamy," Elise demurred.

"Mrs. Bellamy insists that Mr. Eric's guests are treated to the best we have to offer," Mason insisted.

"You'll learn sooner or later that it's easier to go along with my grandmother's wishes," advised Eric. He and Mason retreated from the guesthouse and rejoined the party, by now in high gear, leaving Elise alone to work.

Chapter 60

Georgina and Rafael were strolling leisurely along Lake Drive. Earlier that day, Rafi had paused to take in the All-American scene when he arrived at Bestor Plaza. The sun shone brightly on crowds of people dressed in red, white, and blue in honor of July 4th, Independence Day. The fences of the century-old houses facing the square were festooned with bunting of stars and stripes; from every doorway, flags flapped in the breeze. Tents had sprouted on the north side of the square offering hot dogs and hamburgers; volunteers with red, white, and blue strands of beads around their necks were setting up tables and chairs for the afternoon barbecue. As usual, the water fountain in the center of the plaza had attracted numerous squealing children, making wishes as they threw in their pennies. On one side of the plaza, a grandmother and her granddaughter stepped off ten paces and carefully placed small stars and stripes flags in regular intervals along the sidewalk. On the other side, fathers were helping their young children weave streamers of red, white, and blue through the spokes of their bicycles. Three youngsters were completing the serious business of decorating their bikes for the upcoming parade, carefully winding sparkling strands of red, white, and blue around the handlebars and through the spokes of their wheels. Finally satisfied —or bored— they climbed aboard their bikes and entered the parade as the silver-haired conductor, dressed in a uniform from the turn of the century, raised his baton. The band struck up, and the trumpets blared to the delight of onlookers.

Rafael hurried past the array of families that, with their picnic blankets and folding chairs, overflowed the plaza. The atmosphere was more subdued inside the bookstore, but the vibrating energy managed to seep along the bookshelves as Rafael sought out the manager and arranged to use the quieter authors' alcove at the south end of the building. The library, his usual place of research, was closed for the national holiday. With his knapsack unloaded and glasses, paper and pen spread across the sturdy oak desk, he was quickly immersed in the sprawl of books and papers depicting ancient scripts and caricatures promising to elucidate the pictographs drawn for him by Georgina. Georgina was blocked by a group of tanned adolescents Lined up outside the Refectory joking and jostling as they awaited their serving of the deeply rich and creamy ice cream dug out of the freezer by their peers. She sighed; she was late for her meeting with Rafael,

"Looks like you worked on that upper arm strength over the winter," joked one young man as he reached for a double scoop serving the size of the Empire State Building. Happy chatter and laughter abounded on this glorious summer day. A little girl about four years old, strawberry blond ringlets bouncing, shrieked in delight as her older brothers chased her around the tree. Racing away from them, the child bumped into Georgina and fell backward, crying. More frightened than hurt, though, Georgina as she kneeled to comfort her. Quieted now, the little girl proudly displayed fingernails polished in red, white, and blue to her admiring rescuer.

"Where is your family?" asked Georgina.

Squirming from her grasp, the girl raced off to rejoin her brothers. Georgina felt as if she had been sucker-punched; for a few moments, she had difficulty breathing. Will I ever be rid of this fantasy? She groaned as she swept down the bookstore steps and entered the doors, waiting for her eyes to adjust to the dim light before she looked around for Rafael.

"Are you okay?" he inquired, scrutinizing her face.

"It's nothing. Let's get to work on those scribbles."

"It's just frustrating that we can't uncover any information from the hieroglyphics to help with the investigation," confessed Georgina.

"What investigation?"

"Oh. I guess I didn't tell you. The Goddesses are convinced that the killings of Jonah and Brynn are related. They think there is a serial killer here at Chautauqua."

"No," said Rafael, raising his eyebrows. "You neglected to mention that."

"I don't know if I agree, but there certainly seems to be something going on. Brynn's poor family. Jonah. And our Princess. It just seems unbelievable that this is just all coincidence."

"I hope you can put it out of your mind and enjoy the party tonight. You need to recharge. You've been working hard studying the meanings of these logograms. It's taken me my entire professional life to become a recognized expert in this field, and you have become well versed in it in a short time."

As Georgina focused on deepening her breath and looked out over the lake, the descending sun-splashed golden rose across the heavens with its dying flush; the evening zephyr blew staccato waves along purple ridges. Lighter clouds floated lazily over the horizon. Georgina found herself becoming engrossed in the cloud formations. The sunset caught fire. The rose background of the sky flared into an aggressive orange; yellow fanged spikes lacerated the billowing gray of the clouds. Georgina became aware of a powerful sense of danger. As before, dark-gray clouds morphed into figures, a powerful shape emerging from the paler background holding a small wriggling animal aloft —an animal that, upon reflection, looked like Elise's dog Princess. This time, however, Georgina intuited that what was represented here was not Princess but Elise herself. She stood mesmerized as the clouds conflated with smoke, the waves with actual flames, and darker gray clouds morphed into frantic profiles of humans racing to escape the conflagration.

With a scream, Georgina raced in the direction of the Bellamy estate; Rafael closed at her heels.

Chapter 61

Swinging around in the butter-soft leather swivel chair, Elise was grateful that Eric had offered her the use of his office. But the puzzle was proving difficult to piece together; her brain was feeling a little fuzzy. Some of the pieces seemed to fit at first but then had to be put aside; other pieces were put in their place. Taking a moment to clear her head, she looked around. The den where she worked was separated from the spacious bedroom by a pair of antique beveled-glass French doors. On the opposite side of the bedroom, another pair of French doors opened onto a sheltered patio overlooking the lake. The terrace, with its cushioned chaise lounges, looked particularly inviting. It was a comfortable and gracious space.

It was certainly easier to organize the information with a computer than with a regular typewriter — she had grown up touch-typing, and so she could think and type at the same time and didn't have to write things out in long-hand in order to allow herself access to the right side of the brain — the creative half. And the service was awesome, she thought. It wasn't every day you had a butler present a beautifully arranged tray to "keep up your strength," as Mason had put it. A pitcher of iced lemonade, and several scrumptious wraps: chicken salad with cranberries and tarragon mayonnaise, one of her favorites, had already induced her to eat more than she would normally. As a matter of fact, right now, she felt very sleepy. Carb coma, she thought. She gave herself permission to take a break from her writing and sink back in the chair.

She soon drifted into a deep sleep and so was unaware of the dark presence that entered the room. The figure crept over to the desk and leaned across Elise to scroll through the report still visible on the computer. It was clear from what was on the screen that Elise had made considerable headway, more than she realized. She'd been able to fit together both the hard evidence and the intuitive insights of the Goddesses. The wary eyes could determine that the several patterns clearly emerging in the report held the possibility of revealing how the killings had been carried out as well as the identity of the murderer.

The figure straightened up and sidled through the French doors leading to the patio; turned up the flame on the Weber grill built into the fieldstone walls surrounding the portico; and set fire to the cushions of the porch furniture. Sparks jumped across space, igniting a river of flames that engulfed the diaphanous curtains draping the French doors. Confident that the conflagration had spread to the interior of the guesthouse, the presence slipped out quietly into the night. Elise stirred slightly, the acrid smell of smoke penetrating her unconscious. A part of her could feel the adrenaline attempting to course through her body, triggered by an overwhelming sense of life-threatening danger, but her limbs didn't respond. Struggling against the inertness of her body, she was only able to utter a weak cry of 'help' immediately swallowed by the sound of the waves crashing just outside.

Moving over to the water's edge, Eric joined Miko to watch the spectacular pyrotechnics now exploding across the lake. In the pause between starbursts, Miko looked him over and observed, "I don't know where your mind is these days, old buddy."

"I guess I've been upset about all the killings here, haven't you?"

"Sure, I guess, but it has nothing to do with us."

"Well, it's been quite a year given the incident at Harbridge and now this."

"That Harbridge incident was nothing. Just a hysterical female and some people trying to capitalize on the situation."

"Look, Miko, I see it differently. I was not at all happy with all the chaos last year. It's important for you to understand that that's the last time I'm going to cover for you. I'm not going to do it anymore, so don't count on me. I'm giving you fair warning."

"What do you mean, cover for me? I didn't have anything to do with that girl. And I sure don't have anything to do with whatever's going on here."

"That girl sure described someone who looks either like you or me; remember, the description fits either one of us. And I know it wasn't me, so it has to be you."

"It wasn't me. You can take that to the bank. Wait, are you saying you believe I raped and battered that skank at Harbridge?"

"Well, didn't you? We all know what a short fuse you have. She obviously said or did something that set you off."

"You are way off-base. She made that whole thing up. When I left her, she was perfectly all right. The whole thing was about publicity for her and then for the district attorney's political agenda."

"If that's what you say."

"That is absolutely what I say."

"She was so certain that one of us was the attacker, she picked me out of the line-up. I knew it wasn't me. I assumed it was you."

"Who else might it have been who also is confused for one of us?"

They stared each other down, nose-to-nose, but then Miko's gaze was captured by something over Eric's shoulder. "Eric, look at that."

The line of red flares erected along the water's edge, beginning at the property line and extending over to the guesthouse, flickered eerily with a peculiar brightness.

Ursula ran up to the two of them standing by the lake, "Chester …Chester …" she uttered.

"What are you saying," gasped Eric.

"Where's Elise," screamed Georgina, who raced in, all out of breath.

"A message in the cloud formations warned Georgina of danger to Elise from fire," explained Rafi.

"Elise! Elise is in the guesthouse!" Eric shouted as the two of them stared in terror at the guesthouse just as sparks began to shoot up into the air heightening the pyrotechnic brilliance. Fingers of flame belched from the windows. As the blaze grew, smoke spiraled up, and the roof began to buckle. Heart pounding, Eric sped towards the guesthouse, crossing the distance at record speed. He tore open the door, not heeding the scorching heat of the handle, and ran into the fire, unsure where to search for Elise but hoping against all hope that she would still be where he left her in the den. A wall of intense heat roared up before him, gusts coming at him in waves. Clouds of smoke. His eyes smarted from the pungent chemical fumes exuding from the burning upholstery. Eric wiped away the tears streaming from his eyes and crouched low, trying to stay under the smoke. as he doggedly tried to get to Elise. A beam fell in front of him, sending up a shower of sparks as he rushed through the foyer into the interior rooms. Finally, there she was, in the den, slumped in his chair, surrounded by piles of still glowing embers, smoke seeping steadily into the atmosphere. He reached her. She saw him but was barely able to lift her head, tears tracking down her soot-blackened face.

As he started toward her, he was hit from the side by an intense, powerful tackle. Knocked back on the floor, he thrust up his arm to ward off a murderous blow that grazed the side of his head. Twisting away, he stood up from his crouch and landed a kick right in his opponent's solar plexus, stunning him momentarily. Eric raced once more over to Elise and, in one sweeping motion, folded her up in his arms. Just as a third and then a fourth figure entered the room and pinned the hooded attacker firmly to the ground.

Shielding Elise's limp body, he crashed through the double French doors into the fresh night air of the terrace just as the guesthouse erupted into a towering inferno behind them, emerging with her in his arms to a crowd of anguished onlookers. Georgina rushed to their side, terrified moans emanating from her throat

"She's safe. She's alright," gasped Eric, gulping for air.

Several figures whose identities came into sharper focus as they approached through the darkness: Sheriff Cahill and Miko leading between them a defiant and struggling Chester, wrists shackled by handcuff, followed closely by Angelique, who had rescued the computer and its evidence and was carefully carrying it out of the guesthouse as the burning roof collapsed.

Chapter 62

Everyone was too adrenalized to sleep. Mason and his staff continued to serve drinks and snacks to all gathered in the various rooms of the Bellamy estate, sharing information and speculation. Sheriff Cahill had handcuffed Chester and pushed him into the back of his official vehicle. He had contacted the state police in nearby Jamestown, and they'd arrived within fifteen minutes to take the suspect over to the Chautauqua County Jail. The sheriff and Angelique had accompanied them to fill in background information and complete the booking it was close to midnight before they got back to the Institution.

Everyone began talking at once. The sheriff, though clearly exhausted, took charge and ordered everyone to be quiet. "Chester has confessed," he said.

The room erupted, and the Sheriff shushed them again.

"What did he say?" Teresa called out.

"It seems we are dealing with a series of murders," the sheriff said.

"See, I knew it." Angelique pumped her fist, then winced as the others glared at her disapprovingly. "I've been carrying that one for a long time," she explained.

"But here, as at Harbridge, neither Eric nor myself were the culprits," injected Miko.

"Chester admitted to all the killings. He believes he was doing it for you." The Sheriff turned to look at Miko. "That's how he justified it in his mind."

"Me? What was that all about?"

"For example, he felt that Jonah debased you and threatened to destroy your future as an agent, and so he murdered him and made it look like it was an accidental fire and smoke inhalation that had killed him. He put tetrodotoxin, puffer fish poison, in the sushi that he ate just before he went to the car. It can't be detected if the body is burned up, as, unfortunately, it was with Jonah Nash."

"Oh my God. And Brynn."

"He said Brynn had exposed you to herpes."

"And so, she had to be murdered as well," whispered Elise sorrowfully from her seat in the corner with Eric and Georgina. Her body ached, and she was feeling lightheaded; "I'm afraid so. Miko told us that Chester once said that herpes-infected people should be exiled to an island, like lepers on Molokai, to keep them from contaminating the rest of us," the sheriff concurred. "We had known that Brynn was injecting oxycontin in order to manage pain, so we weren't overly suspicious when we saw tracks from intravenous needles in her arms. What we later found out was that Brynn was injecting herself between her toes and up under the eyelids in order to hide this practice; the tracks on her arms weren't from her regular intravenous use. Chester told us he promised her heroin —she felt heroin would be more accessible as you don't have to keep going to doctors and making up symptoms in order to get more. However, rather than providing a manageable dose of heroin, he overdosed her with fentanyl that he helped her inject intravenously."

"He's crazy," uttered Miko.

"Not in a not-guilty-by-reason-of-insanity' way, though.; We once had a 'sociopathic' cat. At night, she would stalk and catch her prey, then climb up a tree, enter through the window, and throw whatever she'd caught into the bathtub; then, she would watch the animal scurry around all night, terrified and unable to climb the slippery sides to escape. At dawn, the cat would finally eviscerate and leave it for dead, and then come to get me as if to offer this trophy to me," said Angelique.

"I hate to sound ghoulish, but I'll be very interested in the psychiatric testimony at trial," Ursula said.

"But why me?" asked Elise. "What was my connection with Miko?"

"It wasn't your connection with Miko. Chester found out that you were close to discovering him, so you had to be dealt with as well," explained the sheriff.

"Chester heard that Elise was compiling all the available information and intending to see what picture emerged and to take that to the sheriff, so he spiked the drink that Mason was preparing to take to you. His intention was to render you unconscious and then create another "accidental" fire at the guest house," added Angelique. "Fire, along with bedwetting and cruelty to animals, is the sociopathic triad. Each of the murders, except Brynn, involved fire. I imagine that Chester's plan to drag her to his workshop kiln was interrupted somehow."

Rafi rubbed his grim face as he remembered the time his focus was interrupted by the scraping of doors in the workshop area. "I must have scared him off when I yelled at him at the studios that day," he volunteered.

"Elise, I appreciate your courage in getting all the information together. But I know that everyone has a piece of the puzzle; now, we need to put the pieces together. I still don't have a clear picture of where this case began," said the sheriff.

"I'm guessing it started back at Harbridge with the alleged assault on the stripper that we had at our team party," said Miko.

"You may be right," Angelique joined in. "At the prosecutor's office, we were all pretty certain that the adult dancer had been attacked and raped, but she was not a credible witness, and so we couldn't pursue the case."

"Not only was she a poor witness, but the District Attorney clearly overstepped his duty in so many ways," admonished Teresa.

"And was punished soundly for it. The man lost his position and his license to practice," Angelique said.

"Much deserved," Teresa added.

"But in the Boston DA's office, we were sure that a crime had been committed, even if we didn't have a sufficiently credible victim statement to prosecute," Angelique continued. "And so the unanswered question; who was the perpetrator, and would he lash out again?"

"I happen to agree. There was much about the woman's testimony that was believable. She was so certain about what happened and so clear on the description of the perpetrator that part of me believed that there might be something to her story. Given that I knew it wasn't me, I was wondering whether maybe Miko had been involved in some way," Eric said.

"Thanks for the vote of confidence," retorted Miko.

"I feel responsible," Teresa said, shaking her head. "Chester was the son of the housekeeper who had been with me for years. I trusted her implicitly. I was terribly upset, although I certainly understood when she had to leave my service and go to take care of her ailing mother."

"It turns out that that wasn't the reason she left," interrupted Owen. "I have had my security chief do some investigation to see if we could discover anything to help with the Chautauqua deaths, and he has unearthed some rather startling information."

With that, Owen introduced the security chief, who took out his notepad and began to talk in a strong monotone.

"It began earlier than at Harbridge. I tracked Chester's mother down in a nursing home in the town where she and Chester had been living. She suffers from dementia now, but she chronicled everything in a journal left in the safekeeping of her caregiver in case anything should happen to her or to the Bellamies. It turns out that she didn't leave Mrs. Bellamy's service to care for an ailing mother. Her mother was already deceased."

"I can't believe Mrs. Albrecht would be deceitful; I trusted her completely," said Teresa, shaking her head in confusion.

"She lied to protect you. They left because Chester was becoming such a problem. Chester would hunt and dissect animals from the woods and ravines nearby. Soon that didn't satisfy him. He began to kill the neighbor's animals and bully the neighborhood kids. His mother even brought him kittens to strangle or mutilate in a naive attempt to satisfy him in order to spare Teresa's grandsons, with whom he played. Then, when he was twelve years old, he was annoyed with one of the helpers who irritated him by chatting incessantly, and Chester took a baseball bat and beat him senseless. At this point, his mother realized that she had to get him away from Mrs. Bellamy and her grandsons, so she made up the story about an ailing mother. In reality, she moved to a small town in Ohio, Zanesville, where she got a job in the school cafeteria. Chester attended school in that town, and his teachers were impressed by his obvious intelligence and especially his artistic talent. But he also left behind quite a record of delinquency. In one instance, he developed a romantic fantasy about another young male student who was caught bringing a box cutter to school. He later told mental health workers that he fantasized about cutting this guy open 'to see what was inside.' Following that incident, he was kept in a mental institution for a couple of days but was ultimately released; the clinicians concluded that he was demonstrating harmless delusions. From the record, it looks like there had been opportunities to identify Chester as a danger, but he managed to elude the law."

"But what of the letter I received from Mrs. Albrecht?" asked Teresa. "She praised Chester's artistic and academic prowess and asked me to sponsor him at Harbridge, which, because of my regard for her, I was happy to be able to do."

"That letter, along with transcripts, were totally fabricated by Chester," answered the sheriff. "We are dealing with a young man of high intelligence, that's for sure."

"And a young man full of psychopathic rage," added Ursula. "Even if he were under the care of mental health professionals at one time, there is no cure for psychopathy. We know that because of either constitutional or environmental factors, the psychopath possesses a brain that is nonresponsive to the calming effects of serotonin. Animal torture and dissection are not unusual in these cases. Psychopaths have no empathy for others, but some of them have been known to have a ferocious commitment to one person. In this case, that person is Miko. He may have seen him as his protector; he may have had a homoerotic passion for Miko that superseded his lack of empathy."

Owen offered more of his security chief's findings. "It turns out Mrs. Albrecht has covered up for Chester all his life. From infancy, he was never able to warm up to physical affection. She said hugging him was like hugging a Cat. Chester's body would go all stiff, and he would push you away. He was destructive and often smashed things. His mother would find things hidden away in his room: things that she was familiar with from Mrs. Bellamy's house that he had stolen. She would find animal carcasses, mostly roadkill, which he kept in the downstairs refrigerator. He was fascinated by fire, and his mother was forever putting out fires that he had started. In school, teachers had assessed him as brilliant but with a vague learning disability; however, he had great talent in art, and so his artistic side had been fostered. Through his wildlife sculpting, he had hit upon a credible way to dissect animals. At Harbridge, he was in pre-med with the goal of becoming a surgeon...became a drug supplier, notably GHBs, to all guys who wanted to date rape girls...Hard to believe as he was so charming and ingratiating to most outsiders, though not with his mother."

"Our Goddess Circle has long suspected a killer who would exhibit the sociopathic triad; bed wetting, fire starting, and cruelty to animals. One joke used among forensic psychologists is that if a patient walks into your office, sets a cat on fire, and urinates to put it out, you're probably looking at a sociopath," Ursula offered with a small smile. They don't have a Jiminy Cricket; they don't experience fear or shame the way that others do. Also, they can be incredibly charming, like Ted Bundy. They study how others express emotion and practice acting the part until they are really very convincing."

"It seems that Chester was a projective, a Rorschach for everyone," said Ursula. "To Mrs. Bellamy, he was the helpful, responsible son of her devoted housekeeper; to Miko, the tag-a-long who would do anything for him; for Eric, the obsequious sycophant; to his professors, a dedicated student; to his art teachers, a talented prodigy. Chester, like many sociopaths, figured out what people wanted him to be and became it."

"And what about Princess?" Elise asked, her voice low and bitter.

"I 'm sorry to report that Princess was probably one of Chester's victims as well," said Rafael.

The group turned to look at him.

"I was working at my studio translating the cloud shapes Georgina had identified when I heard that annoying screech and looked out to see someone attaching a lock to one of the practice shacks up near the west side of the Institution: one of the sheds that have a walk-in kiln used to fire pottery. This is quite unusual. Most people don't lock up these little cabins; as a matter of fact, I had never seen that before. I didn't pay that much attention at the time. After everything that happened, I told the sheriff about it."

"Yes. The Jamestown sheriff was able to obtain a warrant and get into the shack," said the Sheriff. "We found a bunch of incendiary materials as well as a number of 'trophies,' including the Princess's tags and Brynn's necklace. Chester admitted that he had planned to burn Brynn's body in that kiln."

"Serial murderers like to keep trophies around," explained Angelique. "They can use them to re-experience the thrill of the kill."

"We also found a bottle of GHBs," the sheriff said. "That's probably what Chester dropped in the drink that Mason carried to Elise so that she would be unconscious and unable to save herself when he set fire to the guest house."

"Horrible," shuddered Ursula, remembering her own ordeal.

"I, for one, am exhausted, and I'm sure you are as well.," Teresa said, ushering everyone out of the room. "It's time for us all to go to bed. Tomorrow we will come together as a community to begin to restore Chautauqua to its safe leisurely pace."

Epilogue

It was almost eleven A.M. when Elise emerged from the bedroom. Georgina was sitting in the garden with a carafe of coffee reading the Chautauqua Daily. Anxious not to overwhelm her daughter with the relief she was feeling, she waited quietly as Elise poured herself a cup of coffee and inspected the assortment of scones Georgina had purchased at the St. Elmo bakery. Finally choosing a blueberry pastry, Elise settled onto a green and cream striped chaise lounge and sighed contentedly.

"Are you feeling rested this morning?" Georgina asked, fighting to suppress the frisson of terror that surged through her body as she thought of what might have happened last night.

"Amazingly, yes. As heavy-hearted as I am about the loss of Brynn and Princess and all the others, I am glad it's over and that that monster is in custody."

"We can all breathe a sigh of relief."

"And I'm grateful I wasn't paralyzed with terror last night in the fire. I was paralyzed by some drug, but not so much with fear. In my 12-Step program, I am working with fear-based behavior; as I was frozen in my chair, I kept repeating to myself that all would be well. Fear is simply false evidence appearing real."

There was nothing false about the evidence last night, thought Georgina.

"I'm glad you proved to yourself that you're a woman of courage. If you're sure that you are feeling alright, there are some things I would like to talk to you about."

"If you are going to talk to me about dad, don't bother. I already know all that I need to know."

"What do you mean?"

"When I was interning at dad's business, the women there filled me in on what a serial seducer he was. I've known for some time."

"Well, I'm sorry. I believe that girls do better when they have a solid relationship with their fathers. I didn't want you to know."

"Mom, you couldn't keep me from finding out."

"But what I wasn't going to talk about is your father; that's between you and him. I want to talk to you about my history of depression. I let you down; I'm so sorry. I realize that many times when you needed a mother, I wasn't there for you. So many times, I just wanted to go to my bedroom and hide, and I did that a lot. Too much."

"Mom, I now understand that you were reacting to your situation."

"I didn't realize at the time that it was up to me to make a different choice. I was a victim, and now I'm committed to being not just a survivor but a thriver. Back then, I thought it would be better to stay in the marriage, but now I see I was wrong. When you were captured by addiction, and your health and life were threatened, I felt that you were suffering because of the choices I made or didn't make. I can't tell you how much I regret what happened. I promise to do whatever I can to make it up to you."

"Woulda. Coulda. Shoulda. Mom, I don't blame you. I'm sure you were convinced it was the best decision for everyone at the time. As they say, hindsight is twenty-twenty. And it's not just family background that sets the stage for addiction."

Georgina took Elise into her arms and hugged her. "Pain is inevitable, but suffering is optional. One day I woke up and realized that my life was what it was; the only thing that I had the power to change was myself. And I thank Goddess that I was born with intelligence and in a part of the world where women are free to pursue their own goals. I know that I can achieve whatever I set my mind to. That is everything."

"Mom, there's something I want to do. Wait here," said Elise, pulling back from her mother's arms. She went back into the house, returning in a few moments with the journal she had written in treatment. Silently, the two of them walked over to the spirit pouch that Yan had given Georgina and placed the pages inside, giving them up to the Goddess.

"Is anyone home?" a voice called as the garden gate creaked open. "I've come to check on Elise," called Eric. Georgina smiled as she watched a delicate flush color Elise's cheek. It was good to see her happy.

"I was just on my way to the farmer's market, so I'll catch you two later," said Georgina.

"I wanted to see how you are doing today. I was concerned that you might not be able to sleep after your ordeal," said Eric, his voice gentle and his eyes brimmed with concern.

"Actually, I slept like a baby. I just got up a little while ago."

"I'm glad. I wish I could say the same. Unfortunately, I seem to wake up every couple of hours."

Eric paused for what seemed like an eternity, his head down, grappling with some intense interior experience.

"The firemen said two more minutes, and it would have been all over. "

Elise moved to him and put her arms around him, patting his back soothingly. "Shh. Shh. I'm alright. I'm safe."

Eric lifted his head and returned Elise's embrace. "I don't think I could bear to lose you."

The two remained twined together in a tight embrace, eventually loosening their hold on one another and coming to sit side-by-side on the rocker.

"My father was killed along with my sister in an automobile accident. My mother couldn't live with the deaths, and so she jumped into a bottle and numbed all her feelings."

"Terrible loss."

"I lost everything I loved. It was all taken in an instant. I didn't want to love you. I swore I would never love someone who had a history of addiction because of what happened to my family. But I know I want to be with you."

"I can only imagine how hard this is for you. You have suffered so much because of alcohol. You know that abstinence is one day at a time. I can only promise today. But I can tell you that I am willing to go to any lengths, to do whatever it takes to remain clean and sober."

"I guess that's all a person can ask," said Eric, cradling Elise's face in his hands and leaning in for a deep and tender kiss. "MMM. You always smell like L'Air du Temps," he sighed, inhaling deeply.

***

Carrying a gaily-colored bouquet of gladioli, Georgina hastened past the plaza and down the incline toward the lake. She looked forward to the task of arranging the flowers in their cut glass vase; she was always able to center with this simple, mindful activity. It was such a relief to have danger behind her and to look forward to the comforting scaffold of schedule. Coming around her hedges, she stopped short.

Owen was awaiting her on the front steps. Feeling a flood of dread seeps through her torso, she waited until the adrenaline surge had moved through and out, and only then did she determinedly pull up a pleasant mask and walk through the front garden and up onto the porch.

"Owen," she nodded.

"Georgina. We need to talk."

"What do you have in mind?"

"I know you're upset with me."

"I have been. Often."

"I told Kim that I will be responsible for the child, that I will provide financially, but I can't be with her, and I have told her that most definitely. There are just too many differences between us, and besides, it's you that I love." He held up his hand to forestall Georgina's attempt at the interruption. "I know how deeply I have hurt you; I know that you have been publicly humiliated and that knowledge gives me more anguish than I could ever say. But we belong together. We're partners."

Georgina smiled ruefully. "To be totally candid, Owen, I am no longer concerned about what you think. In the past, my heart was full of hope. I wanted what you told me to be true so much that I believed my ears rather than my eyes. But now, it's too hard for me to trust. As recently as yesterday, you misled me. That doesn't bode well for intimacy. A relationship is like a fire; when lovers are throwing logs on the fire and vigilantly fanning the flame, it continues to burn bright and keep them warm throughout the days and nights of a lifetime partnership. But when one of them dowses the fire, the flames go out. You never know at what moment the embers are beyond reigniting, but that is where I am now. I have neither the will nor the desire to try to reignite the fire of our relationship."

"But this isn't like you. This isn't the Georgy I've loved all these years."

"This is the new me. This is the way I was as a child, even through adolescence and young adulthood. You probably forgot, but when you met me, I was fearless and curious. Since then, my path has been derailed: I have been shunted to the side-rail of wifedom and motherhood. I was content to do it, but that phase of my life was over. It may be that this new shift was provoked by your betrayal of me, but I know in my heart that this is where I truly belong."

"Sounds like you've found yourself another relationship and one with a younger man, Rafael!" Owen's hands were clenched at his side.

"This is not about my having a relationship with another man; this is about my relationship with myself." Georgina shook her head. "You couldn't possibly understand the caldera inside of me, an empty crater where the person who I was intended to become should have grown. My path now is one of individuation and self-actualization. Society had not prepared me for the next phase, and so I intend to break new ground. I can't commit to you or to anyone. I don't yet know who I am or who I will become."

"But Georgy, I promise I'll do better. I understand that you don't have any reason to trust me. I promise that I will seek treatment for my sex addiction! Just give me one more chance to make things right," cried Owen.

"I hope for your sake that you do seek treatment, but for your own sake, not for me or for some fantasy that we will get back together. Our values never aligned. You know it's hard for me to understand what drew us together in the first place. What was I thinking? I must have been 'love-drunk' on a dopamine high, as our daughter would say. I can't imagine that we will be friends; we have so little in common, but I'm sure we will be meeting in the future, we may have a wedding to plan, perhaps the births of grandchildren to celebrate. But beyond that, I can't imagine what we would have to discuss." Georgina became absorbed in putting the finishing touches on the flower arrangement. She turned her back on her former husband, went into her house, and firmly closed the door behind her.

"I'll just leave her alone for a while to cool off," Owen said to himself, staring at the door that was now closed to him. "She'll come around; she always does."

***

Down at Bell Tower Point, it was time to call in the darkness and close the Circle. One by one, the Goddesses filed by, each robed in her sacred color, chanting softly, absorbed in their own internal process. Candles lit in remembrance of loved ones outlined the curvatures of the labyrinth. The Inukshuk constructed by Yan at the beginning of the Circle had now been dismantled and laid out in the center; each of the Goddesses would select a stone to be carried with her to the next gathering.

As a lead celebrant of the Chautauqua Circle, Angelique was garbed in Bronze, an olive branch in her hand as an homage to her ruling Goddess, Athena. She invited each of the Goddesses to say something about what the Chautauqua Circle had meant for them. She offered the first comment. "You are all owed a debt of gratitude for the part that you all played in the rapid resolution of the deaths here at Chautauqua. I'm sure that everyone here at the Institution is breathing a sigh of relief with the murders being solved so quickly and with the killer in custody. For me personally, it gave closure to another case: the Harbridge case. Finally, we know what happened. Chester has confessed and so will be charged with that assault along with being charged for the murders here."

"Amen to that," responded the group.

Ursula was next to speak, wearing the white garments sacred to Artemis and flourishing a golden bow. "As you are all aware, my passion has been to pursue a connection with the energies of women across space and time. This Circle has been especially powerful for me because of the contact that was made with the spirits of the powerful Seneca Clan Mothers. These women were the forerunners of the Suffragette movement. They, together with the Clan Mothers of the other five nations of the Iroquois Federation, established the traditions and laws of their peoples; and decided when to move from peace, which they clearly advocated, to war if necessary. They decided when to order the young warriors into battle if their efforts for peaceful resolution of issues were not successful. It has been a privilege to be in their presence."

Alex, dramatic in purple, spoke. "I just want to extend my deepest thanks to you all. It has been a great pleasure to be among you; my own energy sources were depleted prior to my arrival; they feel quite restored by our Circle. But my antenna is all aquiver with anticipation: I am full of curiosity about what the beautiful Catharine has to report to us tonight."

The Goddesses turned as one now to look at Catharine, stunning in flowing pale blue, who was standing at the outside edges of the circle.

"I couldn't expect to keep anything secret from Alex. Her intuition is too powerful. It is true. I am pregnant; my body is already in the process of preparation. I can sense it."

"But when? Who?" asked Ursula.

"It must have happened the night that Jonah was killed. I remember that I entered an altered state of consciousness, not like the Goddess realm; more like a drugged state. I'm certain that someone else entered the room and entered my bed. At first, I hoped it was Jonah, but it turns out that that was impossible."

"Beltane!" Yan murmured.

"What is that?" asked Georgina.

"An ancient fertility rite. The timing may be a little off, but the scenario is the same: a priestess prepared for a sexual encounter, she enters a trance, and an anonymous male arrives to partner with her in creating the next great leader. It all fits."

"You are all invited to attend the birth; it should be next March," drawled Ursula. "The baby should be almost due to be introduced to the world in the midst of a great Texas tradition, the South by Southwest music festival in Austin. This baby is indeed destined for great things."

"I also have an announcement to make," proclaimed Yan. "As you know, I have been complaining that I no longer had the psychic energy you all deserve to have in your leader."

There was a general murmuring of dissent.

"For some time now, I have felt a need to pass along the many things I have been honored to learn in the past many years; that need has become more urgent. There is someone here who has made unimaginable strides during this present circle, someone who has earned my deepest trust. Georgina will practice under the auspices of the Goddess Demeter and has accepted my invitation to become my acolyte. With this in mind, I am gifting her my Goddessence satchel that contains materials for the mindful skill that we use in our meetings."

Yan approached Georgina, embraced her, and draped the verdant-green woven satchel over her shoulder. Georgina nodded to each of the Goddesses as they turned to look at her.

"We can't know whether she is destined to be your next leader, but she and I will be working together from now on to ensure that she possesses all the knowledge I have to offer."

"The leadership of the Circle will unfold as the Great Goddess desires, I am sure," the voice of Alex broke the ensuing silence.

Ursula concluded. "This Circle has been particularly meaningful for me because I had the opportunity to lecture here at the Institution and to talk about the work of developing the power of the female across the globe. I received a great deal of feedback about this work, there seems to be a lot of enthusiasm about forming new groups throughout North America to broaden this effort, and I have hope that a great deal will come of this experience. Stay well until we meet again in the Goddess Circle."

"But no more murders," pleaded Georgina.